SKATEBOY

SKATEBOY

a novel by

KEVIN KLIX

<u>Also by KEVIN KLIX:</u>

Biflocka: A Novel
A Lion In Your Number: A Novel
Elevator Music: A Novel

SKATEBOY. Copyright © 2015 by Kevin Klix. All rights reserved. Printed in the United States of America. No part of this publication may be reproduced, distributed, or transmitted in any form or by any means, or stored in a database or retrieval system, without the prior written permission from the author. For information about permission to reproduce sections from this book, email to Permissions, Kevin Klix, at kevinklix@yahoo.com.

FIRST EDITION

Designed by Kevin Klix

Edited by Madeline Reiss

Library of Congress Cataloguing-in-Publication Date is available upon request.

ISBN: 978-0-9965410-7-7
eISBN: 978-0-9965410-8-4

To anyone who remembers . . .

Read This First!

(Author's Note)

The skateboarding industry is made up of millions. This surprises most people that aren't involved in the skate world, and that's okay—most of what we skaters call "non-skaters" don't understand the concept of trying trick after trick for hours on end just to get maybe three seconds of footage for a video that may or may not happen. That's the point of the skate industry: You skate, try tricks, and if they are good you gain a sense of *status*. Then people in the industry "know you." YouTube is huge for the skate community because you can find skaters doing the most insane things and getting recognition. That's how people get noticed and sponsored. The skate industry is poppin'! You'll feel accomplished!

Now, I've never wrote an introduction to my own book before because I think it's egotistical, but I wrote this to tell you first-hand I wanted to make a novel that showcased the world of skateboarding in a new light. There isn't a single book that shows what it is really like to be a skateboarder. It's hell! You have to prove to people that you don't like that you're worthy of this *status*. It's a mess, and I have to say, it's sad. I see that now, but that's what skateboarding is all about. You chase the status because you are chasing recognition. In many ways, that's how skateboarders get so hung up on skateboarding and landing the best tricks, because it's simply an artist at their craft, looking for an audience for which to showcase their work. That's what it's all about. And that's why skateboarders make skate videos and work so hard on them. It's an art form.

I guess you could say I fell into skateboarding because I'm very much an attention-seeker. This idea is sort of ingrained in our heads as skateboarders. It's honestly a joke to want to care so much about what people think of your skateboarding. That *status* and that insatiable need for attention on my own art, has transcended into my adulthood and caused me great sorrow in the process. You can apply that hunt for attention into every aspect of our lives. This is the new millennium of people trying to "make it big," and skateboarding is no exception. I have no idea what it is, but showcasing artwork as been so heavy in my psyche that it makes me nauseous.

In most cases, this novel also shows the *lifestyle* of the skateboarding industry. Most skaters are scumbags because we find humor in the idea of being a scumbag. That's just the way skateboarding is. We trash-talk, we treat people like crap, and we are genuinely awful. That was a part of growing up, being a kid, and being influenced by skateboarders that are total scum. Everyone does it, and when you see something often enough, you tend to get desensitized by the scumminess, and then you become it. That's what the main character in this novel goes through.

Carl Klitz is the main character and is happily my alter ego. This is a semi-autobiographical novel, but is loosely based on real events. I can still say it's fiction because this is a span of a decade into a person's life, so it's rightfully impossible to showcase every little detail of said life. Regardless, I still say that this life Carl leads is not the least bit interesting.

I know what you're thinking: *"This author-guy is stating that this is a semi-autobiographical novel about skateboarding and he says it's not interesting?"* Yes, I'll say that over and over! This book consists of nothing but pure, petty bullcrap. That's just what it is. That is the point of the book. There are so many characters in this book, so many different outlooks and sayings and actions that they all seem to blur together. That's another point of the book. I'm also showcasing *life*.

In life, whether you're a skateboarder, lawyer, YouTuber, cop, mom or dad, you have the things you care about. The problem with Carl is that his cares in life are all over the place, and he just happens to fall into skateboarding rather than truly *wanting* to. Everything Carl does is influenced by others for the simple purpose of "fitting in." For me, this novel is a complete exploration of my sense of self. I wanted to make a roadmap for myself and to see where my thoughts came from, why I reacted the way I did, and what I can come up with in the present moment.

With this all in mind, it's hard to say I had any opinion in these scenes during the times when I was living them. I was a child, a teenager, and I was just *living*. I had no real opinion, and for this, there is barely any commentary or opinion on subject—only rarely. The book can read monotonous if you are a "non-skater," but if you have known what it's like to be a skateboarder, been in high school, have had relationships, or have problems, then skateboarding isn't the main plot in the story—it's just a conduit for something larger.

There is no set plot when it comes to real life, in my opinion. The events in these upcoming pages lead into each other from prior events, questioning the ideologies of Determinism through Carl's life. This is, by proxy, how Carl becomes so frustrated and out of control. He felt ultimately nothing because he is just *living* in the monotonous lifestyle, wondering if he was truly in control. That is the point of reading the book.

This novel is basically not just for publication reasons or for personal financial gain, because I do not anticipate it being a best seller (upon writing this). It's a dark book with many different backdrops, and for me this is a novel that is for the people that are characters based in the story, and for me to understand more about *who I am*. That's also another reason I wrote this garbage.

I feel bad if you consider reading this, because you probably will not like Carl in the slightest: he's self-inflicted, crass, angry, sad, annoying, silly, funny, depressing, and he can really frustrate you sometimes. This is actually how I am in real life, but obviously I've grown since these phases. There are moments when Carl is a very heartfelt creature, but it's all ties into the realism of the book, so if Carl offends you, I wholeheartedly apologize—I'm just trying to showcase something *real*. He very much contradicts himself in each chapter, and it's very hard to understand what he's thinking and feeling. That's also your mission to figure out if you plan to read this cover-to-cover. I am giving you fair warning, and that's my reasoning for this introduction.

I also want to say that, while the characters in this book are based on real people, all of their names have been changed—their looks, actions, and everything else—to protect said people from any embarrassment or praise caused in this book. I care a lot about the individuals in this book, and I harbor absolutely no feelings of hatred toward them. On the contrary, if they find themselves in this book, they are actually *important* to Carl and his growth as a fictional character.

This was no easy book to write . . . I must say. I actually cried upon its completion because a lot of this book shows darker meanings behind my own sorrows, and it is clear that Carl is a very troubled individual dealing with loads of baggage and mental issues. Like I said, this book is a journey and road map into my discovery of my sense of self and who I am. It's a book that I can look back on and know, without a fraction of a doubt, that I lived a life. It was good, it was bad, and I feel as though anyone who reads my previous works should pick this up if they would like to know more about me and my thought processes.

That said, if you haven't read a book of mine, I suggest putting this book down because this is not a great book to start with. I would like to say my previous novels have done well for me, but that's because I have worked on plot and character development on each of them. This book you are considering is based on fact, and uses a straightforward tone to narrate the events, so it may not be enjoyable for you to read—both for my regular readers and my new readers. This would have to, in some way, shape, or form, be a *collector* copy of my work, if you could level with me on the idea.

If you are not involved in this novel—and aren't close with me, and have no idea what it's like living in Florida or being a skateboarder—it may be very, *very* difficult for you to understand the jokes, concepts, and everything else highlighted in this novel. For that, I apologize. If you decide that you do not, in fact, want to purchase this book. You are forewarned in advanced so you cannot say I didn't tell you so.

But pay no mind to me! I *love* this book! I personally think it's my best and I favorite it more than my prior books. So take what I say with a grain of salt. I hope you enjoy!

— Kevin Klix, 2015

SKATEBOY

mid-2001

A child's toy consumed my life.

It started the day a friend of mine, Cody, told me that YMCA's ramps were big. He dragged me along on his little "find-out" mission when I was, at the time, nine years old, going to Palm Springs Elementary School. It was there that I met my said friend, Cody. It was Cody's birthday. He was turning ten years old. Cody was into skateboarding, just a little. He dabbled but wasn't very good. He wanted to celebrate his birthday, just him and I, at the skatepark. So I guess that was the thing to do.

The day was very sunny, I remember. It was like the Florida sun was shining down pure rays of positivity—or a stifling, overabundance of heat if you look at it pessimistically. I remember there was a kid there; he had to've been only about four-five. I wasn't much taller, but still, Cody was five-foot and I was hella shorter than he was. The shortness of the kid, well, it had an edge. He had style, like he owned the place, and that I could respect in a kid, even at the time.

At first he was riding down those ramps like a damn monkey. Ooo-Oo-e*Eee-AH!* That sort of monkey. He wore this crazy black & white striped shirt and some Walmart shorts. I was sitting on a bench under a pavilion with Cody, my mother on the phone off somewhere in the background.

"Cody," I said. "That kid!"

"Yeah, I see him. Wanna move up closer?"

"Heck yes!" And I did. Cody followed.

I had my face up to the chain-link face, my fingers curling around the wire.

"Dude! That *kid* . . . Holy *crap!*" My eyes were huge, looking back and forth while this kid was just charging at the ramps.

Then, get this: the kid went up this kicker—which, if you are not a skateboarder, is an incline or decline you go up or down—launched in the air (the board staying under him), and landed on top of a four-foot tall railing just ahead of the kicker, glided along it, then finally dropped off and landed down on the cement. Perfectly.

It was love at first sight.

I whirled around and yelled at my mother.

"Mom! I want to be a skateboarder!"

Lo and behold, I became one.

Cody and I lost touch. What a pity.

● ● ●

Next day I went through every nook and cranny of my closet. "No, not here," I was saying to myself. "Nope. Not there, either." And then I found it. "YES!" I found a Walmart board, bought five years prior when I was probably four years of age. It had cobwebs on it. The wheels didn't move much. They were plastic, not polyurethane.

So I went outside the front of my house (which was a trailer home, yeah—but pretty nice actually) and set the board down on the asphalt. Scary. I didn't really have many friends, much luck with being cool, or much confidence in sports because I was so damn short. So standing on this piece of wood with a turning mechanism and four wheels . . .

Well, it was scary, I'll tell you that much.

My mother came outside to tan, but to also look after her little geeky boy about to go stepping onto a little, geeky, Walmart board, "the most dangerous of dangers," she said.

I fell immediately when I stood on top of it. I put one foot on, then the other. WHOOPS! It slid right from under me.

"MY BABY!" my mother yelled. "OH, *NO!* MY BABY!"

She started running toward the street. Then she picked me up by one arm from the ground.

"Are you okay, honey? I saw that fall!" She didn't think I was brave enough to be able to do a sport.

I just smiled. "That was awesome," I said.

Then, a second try: I set the board back down on the cement, took a deep breath, and stood on top of the board.

That second time I didn't fall.

•   •   •

My mother brought me lessons at the YMCA. She wanted me to be taught "professionally," which I now know is not *really* taught by professionals, but just some high school kids who worked at The Y. They were just out to make a quick buck from the parents, YMCA sponsored and all.

The first thing this tall, geeky-looking, nerd-boarder told me about was a kickflip.

"Okay, Carl. So here's the deal. You got a kick-flip, here." He stood on his board, directly in front of me. "Here, I'll show you a thing or— Wait. Stand back, bro."

So I did. Geeky was regular footed, so he had his right foot on the tail of the board, and his left foot was toward the middle, both wobbling to crap. Then he snapped the tail with his right foot, slid his left foot up at an angle, and knocked the board over in a barrel roll of one spin, then landed.

"See, Carl? See? That's a kickflip."

"Cool," I said. "I can't wait to do that."

•   •   •

A few days later, some time after school, I was at The Y with the geek-trainer. He was showing me a few things. We were not inside the park, per se, but just at the basketball court, behind the pavilion looking out toward the park. It was like being dick-teased, except I was nine so I didn't really know the feeling just yet.

There was a lone ramp right-centered on the court. Geeky was teaching me about just plain old riding down the thing.

"Okay, Carl, now listen. You listenin'?"

I nodded. "Yup."

"Okay. So. You gotta stand up on top of this ramp." He was tall, so he picked me up and placed me on top of the ramp, then put my Walmart board under me. "There . . . we . . . ah, *go*. Okay, now then. Stand up straight. That's right, that's right. Okay. Now what you got to do is pump."

"Pump?" I said.

"Yes. *Pump*. You have to lean down onto the ramp, not just stand up straight and ride down it. . . . PUMP!"

So I laughed, and tried to "pump."

The first try went like this: I push a little bit passed the start of the ramp's incline, then jumped back and my board flew down the ramp, and I was left standing there where I started. I felt really shameful at the fact that I may, or may not, get this down right.

"You can't be scared, Carl," Geeky said. "Listen. This is not something easy, but trust me you have to get over fear."

Get over fear. That was something I'd never done. "Okay," I said. "But it looks so scary!"

"It is, Carl. Try again."

"Okay."

So I tried again.

The second try went like this: I took one look down the ramp, took a deep breath, relaxed, tried to embrace the idea, and then took a small, slow push. The back two wheels passed the start of the incline. I skidded and wobbled and fell on my ass, sliding down the small four-foot ramp. I felt better about that try, like I could really actually land it.

"That's good," Geeky said. "Try again?"

Normally, I would have cried but this time I didn't. I said to Geeky, "Yes," and nodded.

The third try went like this: I rolled down the ramp, got two-feet on flat, skidded, fell.

"Better," Geeky said. And then he gave me a high-five. "Much, much better, bro."

I learned that if you tried long enough, you'd make the trick.

The next time I saw Geeky at The Y, I finally rolled down that ramp, in style. I cheered. My mother saw, and she cheered. We bought ice cream after. I never attended another lesson after that.

•   •   •

The trailer I lived in was small, but outside was a completely foreign to me because I was so young and outside was like the equivalent of doing something the "big kids" did. I would skittishly walk out front, board in hand, and try to do pushes on the flat asphalt a few times. Nothing was like it. The wind in my face; the feeling of gliding; the feeling of flying. But the craziest part was that I spent so much time out front of my house, I eventually I got sick of looking at the same old pebbles on the asphalt. I needed OUT. I needed to FLY.

So I went a few feet down, a few feet more, closer, closer closer. Until finally I was on the main roadway, six houses down from mine. The roadway was always empty. On that corner, though, was a little Mexican boy. His name was Ray.

I was back to being that elementary school type of bashful, as lame as that sounds. Ray was there, but we never spoke. He was only three houses down from the corner of the main road, just skateboarding, doing the very thing I was doing. I had to introduce myself. So I rolled on over to him.

"Hey," I said him.

"Hey!"

"Wanna play S.K.A.T.E.?"

"Huh?"

"SKATE!"

"Oh yeah. Sure," he said.

We were kidding ourselves. I had seen him skate before. He could barely ollie. So what we did was basically just ride into the grass and get a certain distance. If you got passed the person, you got a letter. We may have gotten about eight or nine feet at the most. I forget who won.

"What's your name?" the kid asked me.

"Carl. What's yours?"

"Ray."

This was how I met my first skater buddy.

•   •   •

Everyday Ray was at my house. He was an annoying little nerd-boarder, but was so passionate about his skateboarding, like how I was. He told me he had another friend the next street over that was his buddy that skateboarded too.

"Cool," I said with fake indifference.

"Wanna meet him?" Ray asked.

"Yes."

It was a Saturday. Why not?

•   •   •

The kid's house was just like mine, only dirty as hell. He was a red-haired, lanky, twelve years old, and flea-infested from head to toe. Literally, one second he's talking and the next second you got a flea on your arm. He was a good kid though. He was sweet and wouldn't hurt anybody. He liked snakes too. A snake fanatic in fact.

Ray knocked on the kid's door. The kid swung the door open, stared at us both, then walked back inside his dark house.

"Come on," Ray said, looking over at me.

I was sketched out. Ray and I walked in. The first thing I smelled was something like wood chips and poop, and the ground was sticky and black. Food was on tables. Dishes weren't done. A pigsty. "Come check out this new game I got, bro!" this dirty kid said to Ray from his couch in the living room.

"Oh shit, it's the new *Tony Hawk Pro Skater*. Is that number three?"

"Yeah, bro . . ."

"What's Tony Hawk?" I said.

The two of them looked at me, looked at themselves, then rolled their heads back and howled with laughter.

"What's so funny?" I asked them.

"Nothing," Ray said, still sort of laughing. "It's just . . . well, um . . . in skateboarding he's like the most famous dude."

"So . . . ?"

"And that's it."

"I think it's better if you just play it, man," the dirty-kid said. "What's your name, by the way?"

Back in those days, introductions didn't matter until it was time to actually *have to* introduce. We were kids, you see. Little pricks.

"Carl," I said. "Yours?"

He said that his name was Stephen, and then handed me the controller. I played that thing for the next three hours, hogging the thing. Ray and Stephen got pissed that they couldn't get a turn. They skated outside, finally, after admitting defeat.

•   •   •

The next day Stephen and Ray knocked on my house's sliding-glass door, eager and waiting. I was just waking up and putting my shoes on. I kind of didn't want to see either of them, but I guess it's always nice to see people even if you don't really want to. The only reason why I didn't is because I thought they were immature and annoying. All skateboys are immature and annoying, including me.

I went up to that sliding glass door, picked up the wooden blocker from its latch, slid the door over and asked them: "What?"

"Carl!" said Ray, immediately coming in, Stephen followed suit, "there's something crazy happening!"

"What?"

Stephen butted in: "The Y, they are having a contest. It's the Etnies contest."

"Cool," I said. "What do you do there?"

"Watch," Ray said.

"Do they have food?"

"Do you really care about food, man?"

I shrugged.

"Lets just go," Ray said. "My mother is outside, man. Come on!"

"Oh, all right," I said and got a move on.

•   •   •

I didn't bring my board to The Y since Ray and Stephen told me we were "just watching." It was weird because there was a huge crowd there. I guess I never heard of a "contest" until now.

This projector was playing under the pavilion while we waited for the show to start. It played some very old, very crappy skate video, but I didn't judge it like that at the time. I remember some guy did a manual—that's where a guy balances on just the back wheels—and he did it on one wheel. I thought that was insane. The crowd screamed wildly.

For a second I was confused and I didn't know why. It was probably because I didn't understand the concept of tricks. So, after the video was done I got up and then, for the first time, went out into the park, where all the pros in the video I saw were congregated.

There were so many of them—all doing flips and tricks in every direction. One moment, they were launching five-feet in the air and landing on a plastic barrier, and the next, they were doing twists on the hip ramp. I was in the love with the idea; I always was creative, so therefore, I wanted to experiment and create new, exciting tricks, just like those pros did. My friends were next to me viewing this in awe; they hadn't realized what had sparked inside me, this explosion to make and create this fine, beautiful work of art.

•   •   •

If I wasn't at school, I was skating the front of my house. I didn't play many video games anymore on the Nintendo 64. All I wanted to do was skate. Even when Ray and Stephen would come over to skate, they would get tired of it by eight o'clock and go home; meanwhile I stayed out. My mother noticed the obsession. I would skip out on dinner sometimes. My mother liked the idea that I was getting interested in something, but she didn't like the idea that it was consuming me. She also didn't like the fact that she was spending so much money buying me shoes which only lasted for about three weeks and then, *poof!* they would become shredded and unusable. I had no clue. I didn't know what money was. Boy, what an odd thing now, looking back. Not knowing what money was.

• • •

My father was supposed to pick me up this one Saturday. He drove a Ford F-150. The guy did screen enclosures and his company was called "The Screen Guy." That's it. There was vinyl on the side of his truck, showing this. My father had many employees, but not enough work. The guy smoked four packs of cigarettes and drank one case of beer a day. Sometimes scotch when he had the money. Mostly Budweiser though. I hated that he drank so much, and I didn't want to be around it, but, by proxy, he was my dad and I was his son and so in order to see him I had to suck it up and deal with it.

He called my mother when I got up, which was nine a.m. He told her that he would be there at two o'clock to pick me up. He told me that he wanted to take me to the water park near his house in Stuart, Florida, which was one hour north.

"Carl has started a new hobby, Stephen," my mother said. His name was Stephen, just like Ray's friend.

"Oh. Is that right?" I imagined him saying. I never heard the other end of the line, ever. I'm glad I didn't.

"Please be here at two, Stephen," my mother said. "I mean it. And please, for the love of—"

Then she stopped. I heard growling and yelling from the microphone of our house phone, and shortly after my mother would hang up. Then she came up to me in the living room as I was eating a bowl of cereal she made for me.

"Your father is going to be coming down at two o'clock, Carl."

"Is he?"

"I hope so."

"I hope so, too."

"But for the love of God, just go skate with your friends until then. Come back and two, son."

"Yeah, Mom."

"Love you."

"You always say that."

"What?"

"Nothing," I said.

(My father never asked what my hobby was.)

I was skating with Ray and Stephen outside Stephen's house when two o'clock came.

"Guys," I said. "Watch this!"

I pushed, pushed, pushed as hard as I could—then KICKED my board toward a trash can. *Slam!*

Stephen goes, "*Shit* man! What the heck! That was my cousin's house! My fuckin' *uncle's* house!"

"I didn't know," I said. "Is he going to notice?"

"Most likely," he laughed passively. "I mean, look at the dent on that hoe."

He wasn't kidding. The dent was gnar-kill. A steel trash can. "Oh," I said, "well, um, I gotta go anyway guys."

"Okay, kid . . ." Stephen said, "but if my uncle asks, I'm saying *you* did it. I don't want that guy on my ass. Forget that shit."

Ray laughed.

"I gotta go," I said. I wanted to get out of there as soon as possible because the thought of getting into trouble was too much for me. So I left, heading home.

•   •   •

It was 2:30 p.m. when I finally got home. My mother didn't even get mad at me, mostly because (a) My father wasn't there, and (b) She was tanning. She was always tanning. That, or doing lawn work. We had the best lawn, I remember that clearly.

I was playing video games with my legs crossed on the carpet when I heard my mother obviously on the phone with my father.

"Stephen, I swear to God. . . . He's your *son*. . . . Where are you?! This is messed up, Stephen. . . . I do NOT want to hear it from you . . . For God's sake, he's your *son!* . . . You know what . . . No! Forget it. Bye," and she hung up.

Then she came into the living room from the dining room and told me the gist of it.

"Dad isn't coming, honey."

"Why?" I asked.

"He's . . ."—she didn't want to say it—"working."

If I was the version of myself today, I would have said: "Typical," and continued on with my life, but I was only nine so I said, "Okay, Mom. It's okay."

I could tell my mother was about to cry.

•   •   •

I left the house once I knew my father wasn't coming. It was that way. My father was a drunk, and he was probably drinking and forgot to pick me up. He was a relaxed son of a bitch, but oh well, what was I to do about that? I left, that's what.

I went back to Ray and Stephen, in front of Stephen's house. They were still there but they weren't skating. They were in front of some house close by, talking to some older guy.

I rolled up on my board and stood there listening to them talking.

"Yeah, man, the news is pretty crazy nowadays," the old guy was saying.

"Really? Pops says those guys are loaded," Stephen said.

Ray was just standing there.

"Absolutely," the old guy answered, "it's nothing but a bunch of rich morons lookin' to scare you. I don't watch it no more, except for the hurricanes obviously." He sucked in his nose, hawked up something in his throat, and spat on the asphalt. Then he looked at me: "Who's this kid?"

"Oh," said Ray, "that's just Carl."

"Is he the kid that hit my trashcan?"

"Ah . . ." Stephen hesitated. "I don't kn—"

"Don't pull a fast one on me, Stephen. He has trouble written all over him. Look at him. Looks like a damn thug."

The old guy left after saying that, and went back under his archway, closing the gate behind him. To the left and right eight-foot tall, perfectly cut, bushes circled his entire house. His lawn was a lot better than my mother's, which was hard to top.

"Is he mad at me?" I asked Ray and Stephen.

They shrugged.

•   •   •

Next weekend my father flaked out again. It was a recurring thing. First, Mom would give a time. Second, Mom would call, call, call, and get a run-around. It was like going insane. So, in the kitchen, finally, I laid it down for her real sweet as she was chopping some vegetables.

"Mom, he's not coming. Can I skate with my friends?"

"Honey, it's getting dark."

"It's only six."

"I know, but—"

"PLEASE!" I shouted.

My mother was startled. "Carl, don't you EVER do that again, you hear me?"

I nodded.

My mother continued, "You can go. But be back around dinnertime. Your father isn't coming, but I want you to be here for the food I cook. Okay? Please don't be late, and please, please, *please* be safe."

I nodded. Then I left the room, went into the dining room, grabbing my board. I came back into the kitchen.

"Mom?"

She turned around over her shoulder. "Yes?"

"Do I look like a thug?" I asked her.

"No, son. No. You don't. You look like an angel."

"Oh," I said, then left my house.

•   •   •

For the longest time I've had the fondest memories of Donald. He was probably one of my best friends. He was taller, muscular, slimmer, thirteen years old, had black straight hair that draped perfectly over his forehead and ears, and he was always talking about chicks. Chicks were always the thing, I remember. It was all we talked about. He was also the son to the guy whose trashcan I damaged.

I was skating down my street cutting the corner left, skating about another block down, cutting a corner left again, and then seeing Stephen and some kid—no, it was Ray.

I was sort of tiptoeing my pushes down the street. "Who is that?" I said to myself.

As I got up to the two of them, "and this chick was grinding on my lap," was said by this kid, Donald. "She just kept going."

"Really?" said Stephen. He was laughing. "Man, what's her name?"

"Kat. It's really 'Katherine,' but I call her Kat. Everyone does."

"Hey guys," I little kid'd, my voice all high-pitched. "What's going on?"

"Who's this?" Donald asked Stephen.

"He's this kid that skates with Ray."

"Ah. Cool. Hey, kid. What's your name?"

I said, "Carl."

"Cool, man. Ever heard of the cop joke?"

I shook my head.

And Donald said: "Really? Never?" He looked at Stephen who was laughing. "Okay, so it starts like this: This guy is driving his car down the highway. Going *fast* man. I'm the guy. Then I see these cops right in my rearview. So I pull over. I wasn't scared or nothin'—yeah. Anyway, I pull over, look in my rearview, and this girl cop is walking from her car."

"You forgot the other guy," Stephen corrected.

"Oh yeah. Thanks. So anyway, it's this guy, Stephen, and another guy next to him. That's you, Carl. It's all three of us in the car. So the girl cop comes up to me and I roll down my window. The girl cop goes, 'License and Registration.' So I hand her it, she looks. Then she says, 'You guys were going fast, but I'll make a deal with you.' So of course we all nod or whatever. The girl cop goes, 'Show me your cocks. If you are passed two-inches you don't get a ticket, Mr. Donald.' We all shrug and we start pulling our cocks out. The girl cop goes to me: nine inches. She goes to Stephen: eh . . . six inches. Then she goes to you, Carl: one and a half inches!"

Stephen was laughing like crazy.

Then Donald says, "The girl cop says, 'Close enough,' and walks away. We drive off. And then, get this: you say, 'Good thing I popped a boner.'"

I never saw two guys laugh as hard as they did in my life. They we leaning over touching their knees and shit.

Then I ask them: "What's a boner?"

Donald and Stephen stop laughing and Donald asks me, "You really don't know what a boner is?"

"No."

Then they really started laughing even more.

•   •   •

Later, Donald brought over what he called *The Shreder Sheder Video*. We watched it. I saw Bradley Kromer, Toaster, Sam Burgeon, Mark Turner, Charles Leslee, and a bunch of other dudes in there. They all killed it! I was so inspired! The intro to the video played a song call "Brand New Colony," by The Postal Service. To this day I still listen to that song and smile.

late-2001

I hadn't seen my dad in close to four weeks. I was missing him. I always missed him, even though we never did anything whenever I *did* see him. I'm not sure why. He was always so nice to me. He was a good dad, in that way. My mother was really trying to get him to show up that weekend, which was another Saturday.

It was six o'clock and I found my way to front of Stephen's house, which was three trailers down from Donald's house. Donald and Stephen were there; and Ray was there too. They were all just skating out front Donald's house. I rode up.

"Hey, dudes!" I said.

Nobody looked up. So I skated up to them; they were skating flat-ground (meaning that there wasn't a decline or incline, just flatness), doing flip tricks. Donald was good. He was doing kickflips; and he did them with style, better than Geeky at The Y.

Donald landed a kickflip and rode right into me. "Woah! Hey, Carl. What's up, lil' man," he said.

"What's up?"

"I heard you were the one that fucked my trash can up."

I didn't say anything.

"Nice shirt," Donald said.

"My mother bought it," I told him. "My dad is coming and she wanted me to look nice. I can't skate as hard or fall because it will make the shirt dirty."

"*Oooooohl!*" Donald said with his eyes big. "I see! Well! How about we do this!" and he grabbed me by the shoulders—it was almost as if that was queue for Ray and Stephen to help him, because then they came over and grabbed each of my feet. I started to scream.

"NO! NO! STOP!"

They were picking me up and walking we over to the trashcan that was at the end of Donald's driveway.

"My dad beat my ass for you bending this shit," Donald was saying. "He had to buy a new one, kid. I gotta teach you a lesson." He was saying this calmly, as if it wasn't a big deal. "We have arrived."

I looked over my shoulder, toward the ground. What came into my visuals: the asphalt's shells blurring diagonally, then the open container of the trashcan. I could see little flies circling around in there.

"STOP! I DIDN'T MEAN TO DO IT! STOP!" My voice was cracking.

"Too late, Carl," Donald said. Then all three of them dropped me inside the trashcan, where I felt something mush under my shoes. It stunk immediately.

I started crying.

"WHY?! NO FAIR! WHY! WHY DID YOU GUYS DO THAT?! I DIDN'T MEAN TO MESS UP YOUR TRASHCAN! NOW MY DAD'S GOING TO *KILL* ME! I STINK!"

Ray, Stephen, and Donald were all laughing. Donald said, "Maybe next time you'll know better, won't you?"

I wiggled and the can toppled over with me still inside it. The can dropped. Stinky water was pouring out of it and lapping out onto the ground, like guts. I squirmed out of the trashcan, stood up, and grabbed my board. I heard Ray, Stephen and Donald laughing as I sped home, crying.

•   •   •

My mother immediately noticed the smell.

"Carl! You're filthy!"

"I'm sorry, Mom." I truly was. "My friends dropped me into a trashcan."

"That's awful! I'm going to have a talk with their parents, you just wait and see!"

"NO, MOM! DON'T!"

"Why would they do that?!"

"I dented their trashcan."

She gasped.

"Young man!"

I frowned with my head down.

"Sorry, Mom."

•　　•　　•

About thirty-four minutes later my father showed up, drunk. He rolled up in his truck and had his flood-lights on. We immediately knew he was home because our house was made of this really crappy aluminum and was sort of see through, so the lights would brighten the house a bit. Not to mention his truck was messed up and made lots of noise.

My mother and I walked out front. It was dark outside but I remember seeing my father climb out of his car, beer cans flooding out, and him closing the door. He walked up to us and reeked of beer and stale cigarette. His belly was popping out of his shirt. He looked, smelled, and acted like hell.

"Sorry I'm late," he laughed.

"Can always count on you, Stephen."

He laughed again, and then kneeled down to me. "Hey, buddy. You ready?"

I nodded.

"You're not taking him like that," my mother said. "Hell no."

He looked up. "You don't tell me what to do with my boy!"

"You're drunk, Stephen."

"No I'm not. I'm buzzed. It's not a big deal. I can drive."

"You're NOT taking your son like this!"

"Watch me," he said. Then he grabbed hold of my arm and started tugging me. "Come on, son. Come."

I was getting scared but I hadn't seen my dad so I wanted to hang with him, it was such a long time since I had done that.

"NO, Stephen!" my mother was saying. She was pulling his shirt. "STOP! KIDNAPPER!"

He shrugged her off. "Get off of me."

I remember my father opened his truck's door and threw me in. He told me, "Hop over to the passenger side, will ya, buddy?"

So I did.

He got in, and I saw my mother tugging some more at his shirt. He shut the door. I was hearing, "MY BABY! MY BABY!" from my mother outside the car. The windows were up so I couldn't hear it too well.

My father put the car in reverse, put his head behind my seat's headrest, looked back, and reversed out of my mother's driveway. She was screaming and screaming and screaming.

"I'M CALLING THE POLICE, STEPHEN! I SWEAR!"

He grinned. By that time, we were already out on the street. He rolled down his window. "He'll be back tomorrow." He blew a kiss. "Bye, Kay!"

"YOU ASSHOLE, STEPHEN!"

We sped off.

•   •   •

It was raining and it was dark inside my dad's truck. The rain was so heavy that all you saw was the glass and the beads of water smacking down. My father didn't have the radio on for some odd reason. I think he liked the rain or something.

"Dad?"

"Yeah, buddy. What?"

"How can you see in this?"

He pointed his index with his hand still gripping the steering wheel. He said, "The lines. The headlights light up the lines on the streets. That's what you look at."

"But, Dad, how can you see cars in front of you or to the side of you?"

He laughed. "You don't. You just hope they aren't there."

I looked out the window and notice my shirt smelled horrible. My father never commented on it.

• • •

After getting to his house though, he crashed out. It was only eleven o'clock. He was on the sofa and passed out to *Wheel of Fortune* on the TV. Before that he was watching the Sci-Fi channel. What was playing was this weird space odyssey. He was always either watching that or soft-core porn. There was always a beer in his hand. His eyes never left the TV. If he wasn't doing that, he was playing *Starcraft* on the computer. His leg always shook whenever he played the game. He never answered to his name. You had to repeat "Stephen!" about twenty times before he would snap out of his gamer trance and look at you. That night when he was sleeping, someone knocked on the door. There were flashlights moving side to side and up and down through the window. I answered it. It was two police officers dressed in blue.

"Hi, sonny," one of them said. "Excuse me. Grab him, Jon."

Jon took hold of my arm. I saw the other cop walk through the house and into the living room where my dad was asleep on the sofa. He poked him with the flashlight. "Stephen Klitz," he told him. "You're under arrest."

He was snoring away.

I'm not sure what happened after that because there were two cars and I went inside one with Jon and was drove home, back to my mother's house. He asked why I smelled bad and if my mother neglects me too.

Two weeks later at Boy Scouts, my mother met a guy named Chaz. They started dating and I became good friends with his sons, CJ and Shawn. Eventually I was just going to Chaz's house with my mother after school. CJ was the cool one, Shawn was the youngin'. I was a year older than CJ. Shawn was three or so years younger.

Kingdom Hearts, a video game by Square Enix and Disney, came out and was the highest-selling game on the market. Mainly because it was a platform game with a mixture of all the famous Disney characters and their worlds, plus all the excitement and style of the *Final Fantasy* franchise. My mother bought it three months after the release because she didn't have the money when I asked for it. That's why I was over CJ and Shawn's house. My mother didn't mind because she was having sex with the dad, I guess. But I don't want to be crude so . . . "making love."

•   •   •

Report cards for the quarter came, which was shitty for me because my mother grabbed the mail from her P.O. box before we drove to Chaz's one day.

"Oh look, Carl. Reee*port* card!"

I buried my face in my hands.

•   •   •

We got to Chaz's house and there he was: Chaz, sitting on his porch and smoking a cigarette in one hand and sipping beer in the other. He stood up when my mother and me walked up.

"Hey, my fine piece of ass!"

"Hey, Chaz." My mother blushed.

They embraced, kissed, all that. Afterward, my mother asked, "Did Shawn and Chaz" (meaning CJ) "get their report cards?"

"Oh yeah!" Chaz said. "They did. Shawn's actually in his room right now. He got all *C*'s and a *D*."

"What'd CJ get?" my mother asked.

"All *A*'s."

"Of course."

"What'd Carl get?" Chaz said like I wasn't there.

"Don't know. Haven't looked," my mother said.

Then Chaz sort of looked over her shoulder and said, "*OoooOooooo* troubleeeeee!"

That's when I knew I hated him.

•   •   •

In the kitchen, Chaz had finished making steaks. He was always making steak and potatoes, which was odd because he was obviously an Italian man. Fat. Big gut. Beer-drinker. Ass-hat.

"Kids! CJ! Shawn! Dinner's ready!" Chaz shouted. Then, to my mother, "You want a big steak or a little one?"

"No thanks. I'm fine." She set the report card down on the table. "Should we open up Carl's grades or something? I don't know."

"Sure," Chaz said. "I'll do it." He walked over the table, picked up the envelope, put his index finger under the flap, and tore the thing open.

After skimming, his eyes got big.

"You fucking coward . . ." he said.

"What?" my mother goes. Then she took the letter. "ALL FAILURES! OH MY GOD, CARL! ALL *F'S!*"

I go, "Probably two *D's* and an *A* in Art."

That didn't help.

"You don't get any steak," Chaz mentioned. "Only good kids get steak. You can have *this!*" and he got a box of cereal from the top of his fridge and set it on the table. "That's what failures get you."

My mother was like, "Chaz. Come on. He *can* eat a steak, if he wants one."

He looked at her. "Not in this house."

We left early because they fought about it long and hard for one hour. I briefly played *Kingdom Hearts* with CJ before we left. He asked me why I got so many *F's*. I told him, "Because it's just not worth my time."

• • •

Grounded. This was always the case. My mother made ultimatums with me to do my schoolwork. Like if I got a *C* she would give me one hundred bucks. I told her that a *C* was impossible. I also asked her why she cared so much.

"Because."

"Because why, Mom?"

"Because I have to do work, and you have to do school, and that's just the way it is."

"Huh?"

"Carl, there are things in life that you HAVE TO do, not because you WANT TO but you HAVE TO. Do you get that, Carl?!"

Boy, was she right on that one.

• • •

CJ's house was always the place to be, despite the fact that I hated Chaz. The boys and I played video games, we played pool, we had pool parties, we had BBQ's with his family, and it was all around the best. We played this video game called *MapleStory* and we were so into it. We would sneak to the computer room at night and play it when we weren't supposed to. It was magical.

All I can admit is that CJ was smart, Shawn was dumb, and I was just sort of . . . there. I was the oldest, always the most fun, and it was clear that I had more balls than the others to speak up about stuff.

CJ's father came into the room, probably drunk. I don't remember.

"Boys. Get your ass to the kitchen."

"Why?" I said. "Can't you see we're *busy?*"

"I don't care, Carl. You guys need to eat. That's final."

My comment sparked more balls in the room.

"We're not hungry," said Shawn.

"I DON'T GIVE A GOOD GODDAMN! GET YOUR ASS IN THE KITCHEN! NOW!!"

I started laughing.

"YOU THINK THIS IS FUNNY, CARL?!"

I was still laughing.

"WE'LL SEE WHO'S GOT THE LAST LAUGH, YOU PIECE OF SHIT!"

He went toward me, and before I could do anything (though I wasn't strong enough in reality), my mother grabbed his arm.

"WHAT THE FUCK IS A MATTER WITH YOU, CHAZ!"

He stopped, looked at me, and then just grunted, "All of you, get in the kitchen. Now."

So we all did.

•   •   •

Eating there at the table was mostly silent. Then Chaz spoke up and said something positive.

"Hey, family. We got big news."

"And what's that, Chaz?" my mother asked. She looked like she was bored and over it. I always felt that she was most of the time for things.

"Laren"—his brother—"and my mother are planning a Disney trip in a couple months," Chaz smiled.

"Ah, *again?*" Shawn asked. "We just went there *last year.*"

Chaz's head slingshotted toward him. "Boy. Don't back talk. They go every year. What's the problem?"

"Nothing . . ." Shawn said.

"We're going, and that's final."

My mother goes, "Whelp, I guess we're going, Carl."

"Yippie," I said, bored out of my mind, though I didn't have a true reason for being bored—I was just a punk kid who didn't want to be involved with a family event that I didn't want to be apart of in the first place.

•   •   •

A month passed and pretty soon my mother and I had to get in the car, drive to Chaz's, and hop on the gravy train to Disney. I went to Disney *too* long ago, so I was excited, but it's not always great to go on a vacation with people you don't like, meaning almost the entire family I went with I hated, even if I contradict myself on the matter. It becomes tragic.

Walking up Chaz's lawn, my mother was generally concerned that something bad was going to happen.

"Carl, make sure you behave yourself."

"Mhm."

"Carl?"

"Yes?"

"I love you. Make sure you behave yourself."

"You just said that, Mom."

"Twice is a charm!" she said. Then she knocked at the door, went on in, and before we knew it, four hours later, we got to Disney world.

Wow. Disney. What can I say? I had been there before, but I was much younger and I was with my father. That's when my mother and him were still married. Happy. Those were the good times. Sadly, I don't really remember them much anymore. It sucks.

"CJ! Shawn! Chaz!" this old lady, who I hadn't met, said just outside the Disney's ticket stands. "How you guys been?!"

"Grandma!" Shawn said.

"HEY KIDS!" She ran up and gave all of them a big hug. Then she looked at my mother and I. "Hello, Sharon," she said, and hugged her. Then she looked down at me and asked my mother, "This must be Carl, correct?"

"Mhm."

"He's got such messy hair. What shampoo do you let him use?"

"I'm not sure."

"I'll get the good stuff for you here. They have some."

"Okay," my mother said with a sigh. I'm assuming the grandmother was very into material items, but nobody liked to say things like that. People are always scared of other people.

We all paraded around the park like aimless ghosts. CJ, Shawn, and I, we all were fighting the entire time. We kept trying to poke each other and punch each other in the face—you know, kid stuff. But Chaz wasn't having it.

"SETTLE *DOWN!* I swear to *God,* if I see you guys messin' with one another *one more time,* I swear I'll have a fucking heart attack!"

We all stopped . . . temporarily.

Then we got up to Space Mountain. I really didn't want to ride any rides, but Chaz was insisting that I try it—not in a nice way, more like taunting.

"Look, Carl! Even Shawn is doing it."

Shawn was two or three years younger than I was, so that was meant to be an insult.

My mother was like, "Stop it, Chaz. If he doesn't want to ride it, he doesn't have to."

"You baby him way too much. Come on, Carl!" He grabbed my arm and led me in the fast line—the grandma was rich and had passes that could make you slip on by in a jiffy (material items).

Coming up to the front of the line, I was pulling back on Chaz's grip. "No!" I was saying. "I'm scared!"

"PUSSY! STOP IT AND RIDE!"

We came up to the carts, passing everyone after waiting almost nothing. I was looking around. My mother wasn't there. CJ and Shawn were next to Chaz and I. We finally got onto the carts, sat. I said, "How fast does this go?"

Chaz grinned beside me.

"You'll find out shortly." And he pulled the latch down on us.

Then we were moving. I remember the *click click click* noise and going up, up, up. I was gripping the lever, hard. I remember clinching my teeth and eyes, I was so afraid. Rides are always so frightening when you first go on them. I think that's how skateboarding is, honestly: You try a trick and don't know if you can do it, but you go for it anyway.

We got to the top and Chaz and I were in the very front seat, which was probably planned in advance. I was looking down this huge drop. And you could see the entire park. You could see the looptie-loops, the rides, the spins, the . . .

And it *dropped!*

I was whirling and spinning and my stomach was tickly from the G forces. I felt like I either had to poop or vomit—one of those two. The drop was so quick that, before I knew it, it was already over. Then we did the loop. That was quick, too. I was only upside-down for a second, and it was over. I actually, you know, had fun surprisingly.

●　　●　　●

After the coaster-riding, my mother went up to me, grabbed my wrist, and told Chaz that that was completely uncalled for, and that she won't be seeing him ever, ever again. But then she sort of took it back when she realized that Disney was about a four-hour drive, and that he and his family were the ones with a car.

They all were trying my mother and me the entire ride back that night. She broke up with him when we got to his place. I sometimes wonder whatever happened to Chaz. I heard he had a heart attack and died, or is in incredibly terrible health. I hope he's okay, even though he was a drunk, miserable, ass.

●　　●　　●

In my fourth grade art class, my teacher, Mrs. Brown, was leaning over my shoulder and telling me that what I was drawing was "splendid." She always said I was "a genius." She always talked in a soft-spoken tone and I would have a major case of Autonomous Sensory Meridian Response (ASMR) where my ears would have this "tickling" feeling, and I felt "comfortable," and "happy" inside my chest and head—a sensation that I still try to recreate to this day.

I really liked Mrs. Brown. She was a cool lady. She liked walking her dog or something—always talked about it. Very passionate. I remember she had helped me with an oil pastel art piece that was a replica of a Rembrandt portrait. It looked great for a nine-year-old. But I liked her mostly because after school, during our downtime, she would "help out" by drawing on the Rembrandt with her professional pastels. Just sort of doing her thing with my artwork. She entered it into ArtiGras, in the adult division, and I won second-place. I was very proud but I always felt ashamed because I had so much help.

•   •   •

Fifth grade was even crazier because I still had Mrs. Brown as my teacher and we were building a "portfolio," which, at the time, I hadn't known what that was. "It's a collection of art pieces by you, Carl," Mrs. Brown said.

I spent all year after school with her building that damn portfolio. I didn't know what it was for. "It's for your *audition*," Mrs. Brown told me.

I didn't know what was going on but apparently I was very gifted in all my art classes during my Elementary School years, and Mrs. Brown and my mother decided that it would be great for me to attend art school. I was building a portfolio for that. "Bok Middle School of the Arts" is what the school was called.

•   •   •

I nailed the audition for the art school. What can I say? Piece of cake. Like gravy, baby!

late-2003

School was starting and it felt like I wasn't ready because I had just turned eleven. I nailed the audition and had been excited all summer to start middle school, regardless of my nerves. My mother always drove to school during my Elementary School years, and I was worried because now in middle school I had to take a school bus. The night before the first day she made Macaroni and Cheese and began to tell me, "Carl, tomorrow the bus is going to pick you up and it's going to be only you and a bunch of other kids, okay? You're going to go onto bus number 214 and sit down. I got your clothes ready on your bed and I want to you get up at five a.m. with me because I have work, too. So, Carl, I want you to make sure you get ready because the bus gets to your stop at 5:30 a.m." And what my mother was explaining was explained to me over and over again before.

•   •   •

The next day I woke up twenty minutes late and my mother was rushing me to put on my clothes. I didn't eat breakfast, but I wasn't hungry because I was more concerned with my headache from my mother complaining for me to wake up. I grabbed my backpack before walking out the door and she was already inside the car and had already started it.

I ran out the door holding my backpack straps. I hopped into the passenger-side and waited. My mother drove quickly down the street, cutting a left turn, going one block down to our neighborhood's back gate.

"Bye, honey! Make some friends! Good luck, good luck, good luck!" my mother said.

I got out of the car, slammed the door, and still held my backpack straps tight. I walked out the back gate's opening to the bus stop that was supposedly right there.

I waited and waited, until finally, some Spanish kid walked out the back gates, like me, and held his straps tight with his head down. We didn't speak much. He probably didn't have good English. He was my first "acquaintance." We talked at the bus stops throughout the year. I can't even remember his name, unfortunately.

The bus showed up and I got on.

•   •   •

When I showed up one hour and sixteen minutes later at school, the bell rang and kids were swarming in all different directions. I got lost four times and had to ask two different teachers where to go. They were nice and pointed this way and that. I went into the wrong class once, and, when I finally found the *real* class, the teacher was a total ass to me because I was late. Even in art class the teacher was mega-serious and wasn't into all this nonsense with "ice breakers," which, I found out later on, was what other middle schools were doing. I experienced depression for the first time that day.

•   •   •

When I got home later that first day I went straight over to Stephen's house to skate. Donald was already there, and had apparently just learned back big spins and had them on lock. A back big spin is when the board flips front ways in a 360-degree turn while your body spins with it 180 degrees, then you land it.

•   •   •

Some kids were obviously better looking than me in my classes. Most of them were rich and stuck-up. I didn't know it at the time, but I envied them immensely. Most of them talked about clothes and friends and cars and parties. Some of them talked about cigarettes and what flavors were better than others. I thought those kids were *so* "cool."

I was in art class when all of a sudden some kid name Brian came up to me while I was drawing. He asked me, "Why do you wear shorts, kid?"

"Uh, I'm not sure," I said.

"And why is your hair so short?"

"I guess that's just the way I am."

"Well, here in this school it's long-hair only. If you don't have long hair, you're not cool. And you want to be cool, right?"

I nodded.

Brian said, "How tall are you?"

"Four-nine."

"Jesus Christ. How big is your dick?"

"Three and a half inches."

"Fuck!" he laughed.

"Soft," I reiterated.

"We got a lot of work to do, kid."

•   •   •

I was in the Cafeteria one day and I sat next to Brian. He was with some of his friends, talking. I was just listening.

"You guys ever heard of KR3W pants?" Brain was asking the table.

"No."

"What's that?"

"Yeah, what's that?" I asked.

Brain grinned. "It's *these* pants. They're tight. Check 'em *out*." He stood up and put one of his legs on the stool, showing off his pants.

"Wow!" one kid said.

"I'm not impressed," another said eating his Mexican pizza. "I just get Maddox."

"The fuck is *Maddox*?" Brain asked the kid. "*Fuck* Maddox!"

"Where do you get these 'KR3W pants' at? The *mall?*" The kid laughed.

"Shreder Sheder," answered Brain.

The kid got silent. I don't know why. I think it was because that was a well-known shop and was prestigious.

• • •

I got home that day and asked my mother, "Mom, I want you to buy me KR3W pants."

"Where do you get them, sweetie?"

"Shreder Sheder."

"Where's that?"

"No clue," I said.

She Google searched it.

She bought two pairs a week later. They were sixty dollars each plus tax. I don't know if she could afford it. Probably should could because she, in fact, got them, and I don't recall her complaining about it. I still actually felt bad though. Adults work hard for their kid's happiness.

• • •

Everyday it seemed like a new kid was skating in our neighborhood. One minute it was just Stephen, Donald, Ray and I, and now you got John Shmoe from God-knows-where in the neighborhood horning in on our little skate sesh. I always hated when random skateboarders would try to "fit in" in our crew—but I guess that's the name of the game.

We mostly skated in and around the neighborhood, but occasionally when I was feeling like a rebel, I would skate outside my neighborhood and cross over to Publix Food Market with the fellas. We would skate there for hours. I think my mother knew about it because she never seemed to ask me where I was all day. She just let me go. I loved it.

Another thing: Donald was better than all of us combined. He would learn so quickly and he had the coolest shoes (éS shoes) and the coolest style of any kid I ever saw. His kick-flips were flawless. He would visit his dad's house (again, the guy who I destroyed his trashcan) only on weekends, so that's when we would all actually skate Publix. There were banks behind there. Donald often told us about how him and some of his "other friends" would film there and get a bunch of tricks done. He called the team Structure or something.

•   •   •

Simultaneously while I was getting into *Kingdom Hearts*, I was playing a new card game called *Yu-Gi-Oh*. Before school inside the cafeteria, kids would play tournaments of these cards and they were totally serious with it. I stood over their shoulders because it was fascinating to me.

"Watch it, kid!" one of them said. "You're freaking me out!"

I went to the next shoulder.

"There!" a kid said to the kid across from him. "All your Life Points are gone! Give me your Alakazam!"

"It's a 'Dark Magician,' you dumb-tard—and plus, if you can't say the *name* right, you don't get the card. So *ha!*"

"I'll see you after class, Pete."

"Bring it, you fat dumb-tard *Pokemon* wannabe!"

They really did fight after school that day. I saw it off in the distance when I walked through the bus doors, near the school's back gate. I thought they were so immature and were fighting for no real reason at all. That's just how all kids were, including me.

early-2004

It was a couple weeks before spring break and I didn't have a plan for what I wanted to do during my week off.

"What are you going to do for spring Break, Carl?" some kid I vaguely knew in my English class asked me on the bus.

"I don't know." I shrugged my shoulders.

"Rosie and me are going to Disney."

"Who's Rosie?"

"*Oh!* She's a friend of mine. *Look.*" He pointed behind his seat.

I looked at her. Wow. She was the most beautiful girl I ever did see . . . well, as a twelve-year-old. She was Hispanic with silky black hair, almond skin, brown eyes, and a smile that could light up a room. She would also laugh and it made me feel warm inside, but also a little intimated. Girls in middle school were always scary to me because it was so foreign and new—I didn't want to mess up. So I came up with a backup plan for success.

"Could you tell her I said hi?" I asked this kid next to me. I was counting on other guys to ask so I wouldn't have to feel embarrassed or afraid for trying. That's just how it was.

"Sure," the kid said.

•   •   •

The next after school bus ride, Rosie sat at the seat beside mine.

"Hey," she said.

I touched the top of my head. "Hey," I said. She made me nervous as hell.

"Ralph told me you said 'Hi' to me."

"I did," I said.

"My name's Rosie." She lifted her hand for a high-five. I smacked it. She smiled. "What class are you in?" she asked me.

"I major in art. What's your major?"

"Dance."

"A lil' boogie-woogie, ay?" I laughed. I was being stupid. Girls I like always made me stupid.

"You're weird," she said smiling. "What are you doing for spring break?"

"Nothing, probably. I'm grounded."

"Shit. Well . . . I'll see you around, Mr. Kid-Who-Doesn't-Say-Who-He-Is."

Before I could say my name, she got up and walked down the bus to the back where all the cool kids sat. I thought she was a bitch.

•   •   •

In Science class my teacher was drawing some kind of diagram for us. He had to draw a circle. It was a perfect circle, for free-handing it. We all commented on it. I laughed. One time the guy said that he goes to The Y, but on the weekends at night. That was not when I would go, anyway. I hadn't been to The Y in months, sadly. The Y at night only consisted of adult dudes.

I noticed Rosie was in my Science class, which was odd because I should have noticed her all semester. Back in those days I often slept in all my classes; that's how I maintained my straight *F*'s.

I went up to Rosie—making a rather crooked smile—while we were partnering up for some sort of "board game" project (don't ask), and asked her, "Will you be my partner?"

"Aw! You're sweet! But no, I have Susie here as my partner."

Rosie pointed to the girl sitting beside her.

"Susie, this is . . ."—she turned to me—"Carl, right?"

I nodded. I didn't know how she knew my name. I hadn't told her. Probably just heard it in passing on the role call, or something.

Rosie said, "Yes. Carl."

Susie said, "I've seen ya around." She was hot.

"Uh, uh . . . UH!" That's how I imagined I was speaking to them. I totally just lost for words. "Can we all three partner up?" I asked them.

"I don't think Mr. [Whatever-The-Hell's-Name-He-Was] would like us to do that," Susie said. "And plus, we want to have girl talk. So run along, kid."

"Is that an iPod?!" I was looking down by her hand. It was an iPod Mini—just released. It was pink. Those things were super expensive, so I assumed Susie's parents were loaded, the freakin' beezy. (A "beezy" is "bitch" by the standards of rapper Mac Dre.)

"Yes it is," Susie answered me. "Can you beat it, please?"

I liked Susie because she was so mean.

•   •   •

I won't go into too much detail, but honestly, two days later I decided I really, really liked Susie. I don't understand why. I think it was because she was shorter than me, and hard to get. Girls play hard to get a lot, but she had flare. She was simply the type of girl who would be nice to you but then flake out altogether. I found that this became a trend with the women I liked . . .

So I got on the after-school bus. Susie was on it, with Rosie. They actually sat together. I did the most craziest thing: I moved from the front of the bus to the back of the bus. I sort of had to move slowly and quietly, without the kid's knowing. The ride was an hour long, so I had to scoot as more kids got off the bus. It's weird. I felt like one of the neighborhood kids trying to horn in on I and my friend's skate sesh: trying to "fit it." The kids that sat in the back were always the first ones to get off the bus. It's like: "Hey, let me waste my time by walking an extra few feet to get to my house." So dumb.

Finally, I made it to the back

There weren't many kids left. Just Rosie, Susie, a couple hispanic ghetto-like kids, the kid who introduced me to Rosie, and me. Rosie and Susie were talking some sort of nonsense or something, I remember.

"I went with Jake to see that movie. You know the one?"

"YES!"

"Yeah. And guess what, he totally kissed me in the middle of it."

"AW!"

"I KNOW!"

"What else happened?—Jake's so sweet!"

"I know he is! We just held hands. I want to kiss him."

"And do what else, huh?"

"Oh stop, Rosie. He's gotta *earn* my blow jobs."

"SHHHH! There are people here."

"Oh. Right."

I always was curious as to what a "blow job" was, at that point in time. I sort of didn't know at all but I didn't want to ask because I liked Susie and she liked that Jake fellow so I didn't want to make her feel weird by asking it if it had to do with someone she liked.

So I sat there, alone in my seat, bored. I was trying to summon the courage to ask Susie out. But she had a boyfriend, obviously, since I just overheard her saying something about this guy she went on a real date with. I was one friggin' seat in front of them, just listening. They often talked about boys and who was the "cutest." They never once talked about me. I always wondered why. Maybe it's because they knew I was listening.

•   •   •

"Mom, I like this girl name Susie."

My mother grinned, ear to ear. "What's she like?—*Aw!* My little baby boy has a *crush!*"

"What do I do?"

"Tell her how you *feel!*"

I left the house and went to Stephen's.

· · ·

I hadn't seen all the skaters in awhile. Stephen was outside his house, just skating alone. "Stephen!" I shouted, speeding toward him on my board. "Stephen!"

He looked up. "YO! WHAT'S GOOD, CARL, MY BOY!"

"Nothing much, man!"

I got up to him, gave him dap, which is a "skater" handshake between two people: they hold out their fists and bump them from top to bottom.

"Where you been lately?" Stephen asked me.

"School."

"For months?"

"Yeah. Sorry."

"It's cool. You know Ray moved, right?"

"No way?"

"Yes way."

"What about Donald?"

"He's still around. But he skates with other people. Something about 'Structure,' or something."

Then I finally came to him for my real reason: "I got a problem. I need advice."

Stephen went, "Okay," before laughing. "Sup?"

"Some chick at my school," I started, "is super mean, but um, uh . . ."

"You like her, don't you?" Stephen started laughing. "That's usually how it sort of goes, man. The chick you like is always the one that doesn't like you."

"I sure hope she does. What do I do, I mean, can I just ask her out? How do you do it?"

"Dude, I'm not the guy to ask this shit to," Stephen admitted. "You should talk to someone else about this."

I skated home. Stephen wasn't much help. I just wanted a friend that could level with me, is all.

· · ·

So I got onto the bus brave and a bit scared, a weird mixture, and noticed Rosie and Susie weren't there, which was odd because they always took the bus. I got off the bus and went about my usual boring day, walking passed the phone booth that was on the wall. I knew didn't work and wondered why it was there. Then I went into my English class, where Mr. Whatever taught us about verb usage and comma usage and I got bored and fell asleep. Much later, after I woke up to the second bell, which was the late bell to get to class, I got a tardy slip and had to go to detention the next day (which I didn't go to, or, rather, for*got* to go to) and I was pissed. Art class was killer because I got to draw pictures of spheres on the tables and nudge the lights secretly to the left to mess everyone's drawings up. They all got pissed, especially the teacher, who told me that my shenanigans "ruin everything for the entire classes' artwork."

When the final bell rang while I was sitting there in my History class, I got up and ran, got briefly yelled at by Mrs. Von, an old teacher of about seventy years old, to slowed my roll, and went to the bus loop. I saw Rosie, who wore a red dress that was super sexy, and Susie, plainer than plain Jane, both walking up the bus steps and sitting in their usual seats in the back, with all the other "cool kids." The entire ride was madness because I was thinking about asking one of them out. Remember, I didn't have a father, a reliable male figure in my life, or anyone to really give me usable advice, so I had to go about this in the blind. I figured, Hey, why don't I go the honest, *direct* route and just ask Susie out straight forward; maybe that's sexy and noble, I thought.

The whole ride was loud and I asked Susie if I could borrow her iPod Mini, since she wasn't using it. She told me sure, that's fine, and gave it to me. That thing was so slick. I was listening to "Fall Out Boy," even though I didn't really like them. That's the thing. You can tell a lot about a person just from the music they listen to. Susie was a punker. I wasn't too into that, but hey, not complaining.

It was getting to be that time. Susie's stop was just ahead. It was about one more stop to go along Jog Road. Her stop was just one before mine. Rosie told Susie that she was going to the front of the bus to say, "Hi," to her friend from Science class. Susie just nodded and they both hugged each other and said, "Bye."

Just before she stood up, got her bag, and started to walk down the aisle, she stopped and turned around and walked back. She came to my seat.

"Carl, I need my iPod." She held her hand out. "Now, please."

This should have been my shot to ask her out, but as I took the ear buds out, and wrapped them around the iPod, I chickened out. I handed the iPod to her, shaking.

"You're weird," she said, and got off the bus.

I felt so stupid. I knew I should have asked her out but I thought, "Oh well," I guess I had to pick the alternative.

So I got up and went to the front of the bus.

I saw Rosie and thought, Eureka! I could ask *Rosie* out! By God, I was happy. Rosie was hotter than Susie. I liked them both, I realized. So I was sitting in the seat beside her and her friend, across the aisle. They were talking about something in their Science class that they learned for the day. Something about space and the moon and how the ocean's current is directly related to it. It was literally only a couple cars until my bus stop.

Finally, the door opened—I could see them—so I stood up, leaned over Rosie's friend, and tried to get Rosie's attention.

"Hey, Rosie."

She looked up with her big brown eyes.

"Yes, Carl?"

"Will you go out with me?"

The moment I said the words, I immediately regretted it. I felt so stupid and started to shake. I could feel my face getting hot and my brain starting to jerk.

Rosie let out a soft, hidden *pfft* noise, like she was giggling under her breath. She had her hand up to her face. Even her friend was sort of wide-eyed and looking down at her lap.

"I have a boyfriend, Carl," Rosie said.

So I said "Oh" and got of the bus.

I crossed the street.

When I got home, I got my board and skated on over to Stephen's house. He was with these two tall kids with black hair. They were skating out front.

"Hey, Stephen," I said. "I asked Rosie out."

He started to laugh. "Really, huh?—What did she say? *Yes?*"

"No. She said she had a boyfriend."

"That's how it usually is, bro," Stephen said.

We skated until nine p.m. I still felt accomplished to say the least.

•   •   •

There were these two tall boys that started to hang around Stephen a lot more. They wouldn't skate out front Stephen's house though, so a majority of the time I had to skate around the neighborhood and the main roads to find them. They usually were around Stephen's friend Wendian's house. Her place was on the main road and was a doublewide trailer, one of the nicer ones, like how mine was.

I skated up to them. They were drinking Cokes and Sprites and talking about Paramore, the band.

They were all standing in a circle in front of Wendian's house. Wendian had braces, a gut, was short, and had a bad attitude. Stephen was still lanky as hell, obviously, wearing his brother's hand-me-downs and holding an old squared-out skateboard that needed to be trashed. The two tall, black-haired kids were twins, I found out.

So I stood next to them, not saying anything.

"Who's this kid?" Wendian said. "He's weird."

"Oh, this is Carl," Stephen introduced me. "Carl, meet Wendian, Tom, and John-Luc."

"Sup?" said Tom.

"How's it goin'," said John-Luc.

"He's still weird . . ." said Wendian. "Where the hell is Robin?!"

"She's coming," John-Luc said. "She usually is slow as heck whenever Star's home." Star was their older sister, by about six years or so.

"Carl, these guys are twins," Stephen said.

"Actually," Tom was looking at me, "we're triplets. Robin is the third."

"Woah!" My eyes got big. "How?! You guys don't even *look* the same."

"Well, we're fraternal triplets," John-Luc explained.

"Oh," I said. Then I sort of got this random idea in my head. I started smiling, for a weird reason. "Hey, John-Luc," I said.

"Yeah?" he said. "You okay? Why are you smiling?"

Tom was laughing, I remember that.

"Well, John-Luc . . ." I said, "I want to be just . . . like . . . *you.*"

"What?" he said.

"I want to be just . . . like . . . YOU!"

We all started laughing.

"Why?" John-Luc asked me.

"Because. Look. The eyes, the black 'stache . . . I want be just like YOU!"

"You're weird, man."

This went on for fifteen minutes, me just making fun a stranger. I always like to be goofy around people; that was sort of my thing. I liked to keep people on their toes and to say the most random things just to get them to smile and to like me. That's just how I was/am.

•   •   •

In skateboarding you have special "spots" you go to frequently and you give them names. There was this one place we named Church Three. It was a rinky-dink, three-stair—about one and a half feet in height. I was hanging out with Tom and John-Luc more than Stephen because they always wanted to hang out after school. It was great and we often skated out front of Tom's house, which was right next to The Park: a run-down crappy basketball court/pool-house. As we were doing flat-ground tricks and playing each other in S.K.A.T.E., I asked them something.

"Tom."

"Yes?"

"Want to go to Church Three?"

"Where's that at?"

"About seven blocks down Jog Road."

"Far," Tom said.

"I know."

"What do you think, John-Luc?"

"I couldn't care less."

So we went. I ollied a bunch of times along the way, and John-Luc acid-dropped (which is where you run and jump in the air and throw the board under your feet to finally land and ride away) over the small handrails. Tom skated flat and didn't want to try the three-stair. He was sort of just starting to skate, so it was no big deal. Tom's my best bud.

•   •   •

It was that time of the day at school, and the bell had finally finished ringing fifteen minutes before I woke up. I knew I had missed my bus. I was in deep doo-doo. My teacher was sitting at the desk, just writing.

"Hey!" I said. "Why didn't ya tell me to wake up! Now I'm late for the bus!"

"Not my problem, young man," he said. I always hated when teachers had to prove a point to their students just so they could feel empowered or something in the idea that the were right and you were wrong. "Looks like you better call your parents to come and get you," he continued. "Maybe next time you'll learn to not sleep in my class."

That was true. I slept in all my classes. But still . . .

"Dickhead," I said, as I got my bag on and ran toward the door.

Before I closed it behind me, I heard a "what did you s—?"

I ended up not being late, just by a hair. Thank God.

•   •   •

Another day I came home after school. It was super dead out—nobody was around. I went to Tom and John-Luc's house and they weren't home. I went to Wendian's, and they weren't there, either. I went to Stephen's and he wasn't there. It was odd. Nobody was home. I was just outside Stephen's house, skating slowly down the street when finally I was in front of Donald's house. I heard voices.

"Dude, fuck! I want to get that damn trick."

"Yeah, man." That was Donald's voice. "You almost fuckin' had it, but yeah—spot's retarded."

"Yeah, the bank is really curved weird, dude."

I stopped in my tracks and looked over. They finally walked all the way down the driveway and into the street where I was.

"Who's this kid?" a really, really tall muscular kid said to Donald.

"That's Carl. He's the kid in the neighborhood."

"Yeah? Hey, Carl. Wanna play S.K.A.T.E.?"

I hesitated. "Uh, yeah, sure. I guess."

"You got 'S.'"

"Already?!"

Donald and the kid started laughing.

"What's so funny, guys?"

"Do a kick-flip," the tall kid said.

I stood on my board, gave a good push, and flicked my board and did a kick-flip. Bolts (which meant my feet were on the bolts of the board upon landing). It was my first one!

"Woah," the tall kid said. "Holy shit. Do an ollie."

So I did. Nailed it.

"Yo, come with us," the tall kid said. "My name is Braydon. We're going to Church Three."

"Oh yeah?!" I was excited. "I *love* that place!"

"Slow your roll, big cat," Braydon said. "And you better keep up."

•   •   •

We spent thirty minutes skating all the way down Jog Road. Seven gigantic blocks! It was a damn monster!

Church Three, like usual, was empty. It was a Wednesday, I think, and no cars were around.

"You like Jesus?" Braydon asked me as we were walking up to the three-stair. "Huh, Carl?"

"Huh?"

"Do you like Jesus?"

"I don't know," I said. I wasn't paying much attention. "Should I?"

"Are you Jewish?" he asked.

"No."

"Good," he said. "That shit ain't real, big cat."

We got up to the stair when he said that.

"Okay, Brandy," Donald said, "you going to shuv-it" (which is when you pop the board and it spins 180 degrees under you and you finally land on it) "this, or what?"

"Nah, man, I want to see what Carl's made of. Hey, Carl!"

I was standing near them, I didn't know why he was yelling. "Yes?" I said.

"I got a proposal for you."

"What?"

"Me and Donald have a skate team."

"You do?"

"Yeah."

"That's awesome. What's it called?"

"Structure Skate Team."

"Cool!"

"Can you say the word 'Fuck'?"

"Ah, no. Uh, yes? I'm not supposed to."

He laughed. "Anyways, Carl. I have a proposal. See that three-stair over there? If you kick-flip it, and land, we'll put you on the team."

"Really?!"

Donald goes, "Yeah, Carl. The fuck you think we are, liars?"

They high-fived and started laughing.

"Okay," I said. "I'll do it."

"Good," Braydon said. "Get up there."

So I did. After fifty-six tries of hard labor, spin upon spin upon spin, and flips and landing on the underside of the board, and screaming and yelling and getting the worst headache ever, trying my very hardest, getting the most raw hands from cement sliding across the soft belly of my forearms and elbows and hard pebbles grating downward, making me bleed—I landed. *Finally*. I landed and it was the greatest thing in the whole friggin' world, to me. I landed. I LANDED!

"YES!" Braydon was shouting, "FUCK YES! YES! YOU FUCKING LANDED THAT *BOLTS!* YES! YOU'RE ON THE TEAM!"

"Fuck yes!" I said, then I cupped my mouth.

"Ah, shit, man," Donald said. "That's the first time I ever heard him curse."

"That's what I'm talkin' about," Braydon said. "He's going get along with me *real* well. What's your name?"

"Donald told you, Braydon. It's Carl," I said.

"No, no, no. You're *full* name. What is it?"

"Carl Klitz."

He stopped in his tracks, looked at Donald, and whaled the heaviest laugh I ever did see.

"HAHAHAHAHHAHAAHAHHA! HAH-*GAGAHAHAHA!* Holy shit, man! That's great! We're calling you 'Klitz' from now on. That's fucking priceless. Like a clit, bro. Like a *clit!* YES! You're on the team!"

That was the start of a brand new me, and that was the start of my preteens. I was a late bloomer.

early/mid-2004

Basically Braydon, Donald and me, about two days after my landed kick-flip, were plotting at Donald's house on how to break the news about the team to my mother.

"Okay, Klitz," Braydon said, "you're on the team now, and in a damn good time. We're planning a trip to Fort Lauderdale. We're filming for a skate video. The idea is to go down there and get as much footage as we can for our video parts."

"Where's that?"

"It's about fifty minutes from us."

"Oh yeah? Why? Why can't we skate around here?"

Braydon looked at Donald.

"Because, Klitz."

"Dude, why?"

"Klitz, there's more spots there!"

"Ohhh! Cool!"

"Yeah, and me, Donald, and Teddy—another kid on the team—are going to take the train there."

"The train?"

"Jesus Christ, Klitz. You never heard of a fucking *train?*"

"Nah."

"Okay, basically we have to talk to your mom, A.S.A.P."

"Why?"

"Klitz, there's no way we're not going to need permission."

We skated to my house. I didn't really understand the point of a trip when we had spots around the neighborhood, but I was excited nonetheless to be apart of something larger.

•   •   •

"Mom!" I said as we entered my house. "Come, look! New friends!"

From the living room, my mother shouted, "Okay, Carl! Lets meet 'em!"

Donald and Braydon started laughing as we were walking down the hallway to the living room.

We got there, and my mother was filing her toenails. It smelled like rubbing alcohol in the air.

She looked up.

"Hey! You guys are big kids." Donald and Braydon were 16 and 17—something like that.

Braydon went, "Yes, Mrs. Klitz, we are. You're son here is an amazing skateboarder."

"Is he, now?"

"Yeah. And, ah, we sort of have a question to ask you."

"Yeah?"

Braydon and Donald looked at each other. Braydon sighed.

"Okay. So. Basically your son is on our skate team. We have a trip planned. I realize your son is only thirteen and—"

"Twelve," my mother corrected, "he's *twelve* years old."

"Yeah. Twelve. And anyway, we have a friend that has family in Fort Lauderdale. We want to plan a trip for this weekend coming up. We were going to go anyways. It jus' so happens your son came into the picture last minute."

"Okay, and what's your name?"

"Oh!—My bad! Braydon. Braydon's my name. Sorry."

My mother smiled.

"It's okay, Braydon. Okay. Where is this place again?"

"Fort Lauderdale."

"Yeah, but where?"

"Teddy's family's house."

"How are you getting there? And how old is he?"

"Tri-rail. And 18."

"Oh gosh. Okay. This is pretty big, Carl."

I looked at her.

"Yes, Mom?"

"If you're going to go with these boys you need to promise me you'll call me everyday you're there. Promise?"

"Yes, Mom."

"And Braydon?"

"Yes, Mrs. Klitz?"

"You have to promise me you'll have him do that, understand?"

"Yes, ma'am."

"Because if you don't, it's your ass. Got it?"

"Yes, ma'am."

"And I'm not bailin' you guys out of jail if you do anything illegal. I'm not savin' your asses. No rides from me."

Braydon laughed.

"Okay, Mrs. Klitz."

"Call me Sharon."

"Okay, Sharon."

"Now give me both your phone numbers."

They did.

●　　●　　●

Basically I had no clue my mother would go for it. The morning of the trip, I got picked up by a big, run-down tan car. Braydon, Donald, and some kid were in there. They pulled up. Braydon's mom was driving. I said, "Bye," to my mother, and ran outside. They opened the door for me. I hopped in.

"Klitz," Braydon said, "this is Teddy."

"Sup, bro," Teddy said.

"Sup," I said.

"Klitz," Braydon said, "now that you've met Teddy, we gotta tell you about Jimmy. He's also new on the team."

"Okay."

"Yeah. He's at Donald's house right now."

"Cool."

We drove off.

* * *

We got there and Jimmy was outside, doing flat-ground tricks on the cracked, withered asphalt. He still killed it despite the roughness. That was always his thing. He always killed it despite whatever got in the way. I admired that. The only probably was he was so scummy it wasn't even funny: dirt under his nails, hair always greasy, elbows thrashed, teeth never brushed, mouth always had some weird dirt or food on it, and he always wore the same clothes. He was 13 and he was well-respected in the skate community for his skills. That was how it was. People would overlook faults for talent.

"Jimmy!" Braydon shouted once we all four, Braydon, Donald, Teddy and I got out of the tan car. Then Braydon says to his mother, "See ya." The most casual parting words I had ever heard.

"Braydon, my board is cracked like fuck," Jimmy said, riding up. "Who's *this* kid?"

"Oh, this is Klitz. And bro, I just gave you my old board."

"Those shits never last."

Teddy was laughing. "Lets get this show on the road!" he said. Teddy was always a joker.

About twenty minutes later a car pulled up as we were skating flat-ground.

"Here she is," Teddy said.

" 'Bout fuckin' *time*, Teddy," Braydon said.

"Fuck off. She's sick."

"I'll stick my foot in her ass, sick."

"Bro, my shoe is scuffed."

"We just bought these! Fuck! Mine too!"

"Pussies," Jimmy muttered.

"FUCK YOU!" Braydon howled. "We all ain't sponsored!"

Jimmy just laughed. We all got into the car. We drove off. The driver was Teddy's mom and she smelled sort of weird. It was the smell of her, the smell of Teddy's bad breath, or just the inside of the car entirely. I still don't know. They all were scummy, including me.

•   •   •

We got dropped of at the train station. The air was a soft shit smell, and immediately I saw a bum lying in the middle of the huge path leading toward the station.

"Look at this joker," Teddy said to Braydon.

"Ollie him."

So we all got on our boards and charged toward the bum! Pop, skip, and a jump, we all flew passed him. He woke up.

"YOU FUCKING KIDS! I'M TRYNA *SLEEP!*"

"FUCK OFF, ASS-FUCK!" Braydon shouted. Then he laughed. "Man, this is going to be one sweet-ass trip, yo."

•   •   •

After getting our tickets, we got on the train. A few minutes passed. The train guy came up to us.

"Passes."

"What?" I asked.

"You deaf, kid? Passes!"

"Chill, bro," Donald said. "Here." He handed the train guy all our passes.

"Looks to be tip-top," he said. "Have a fine trip, gentlemen."

The second he walked away, Braydon goes, "What a fuckin' dick."

"I know, man," Teddy said. "Klitz is not even ten and the guy insults him."

"I'm *twelve,*" I corrected.

"Oh. Like it's any different."

I just sighed.

"Klitz," Braydon said.

"Yeah?"

"You ever gotten any pussy?"

"Uh . . ." I looked at all the guys. "No."

They all started laughing.

"What? So what if I haven't!?"

"Chill, bro," Jimmy said, "The lil' virgin boy is gettin' heated."
I actually felt like I hated them all.

•   •   •

An hour later, the train came to a final stop.
"Finally," Braydon sighed. "Teddy. You fuck. I thought you said it was a thirty-minute ride."
"It *was*, bro."
"Fuck no, it wasn't! I was on for damn near an hour!"
"Nah."
"Yes, an hour," Donald said. "I timed it, too."
"You guys are dicks," Teddy said.
We got off the train. I thought they were all so weird, cool, and whiny, all at the same time. I wanted to be just like them.

•   •   •

"Where to now?" Braydon asked Teddy.
"It's just up the street."
"Where?"
"Cyprus."
"Teddy, you asshole. Where?!"
"About twenty blocks up."
Braydon paused.
"What the fuck did you say, Teddy?"
"TWENTY *FUCKING* BLOCKS!" Donald said. "Holy fuck, Ted!"
"Sorry, guys. That's just the distance. You guys can ride back."
Braydon shook his head. "Teddy, I fucking hate your ugly-ass," he said.
"Love you too, asshole."
Jimmy said, "You two need a room to fuck in."
They all laughed.

•   •   •

We skated close to an hour and ten minutes up all those blocks. I got so tired, and I always wanted to cry. My legs were dying on me, but I still kept up with them four. Finally, though, we made it! Yippie! I was so excited. I was finally going to get some footage and skate with the big kids. I felt important.

"We're here," Teddy said, as we came up to a trailer park's entrance.

"Jesus fuckin' fuck, Teddy," Braydon said. "That was the worst fucking skate, ever. Wish you would have *told* us it'll take *all* fucking after*noon!*"

"It's two o'clock."

"So!"

"So . . . that's whatever, bro."

"I need to eat," Jimmy randomly said.

"Me too," Donald said.

"Me three," I said.

"You're buyin', Teddy," Braydon said, "you fucktard."

"I'ma beat that ass, Braydon!"

They wrestled to the ground and finally laughed it off. We went over to a Burger King. We all paid for our own meals except Jimmy. He just ate ketchup packets, water and sugar. That's it.

• • • •

As we just got done skating back to the trailer park . . .

"Hey guys!" Jimmy said. "Watch this!"

We all stopped, turned around and stood on our boards, watching him.

"This 'oughta be classic," Donald said.

"I know what he's gonna do . . ." Teddy said.

Jimmy looked up at us.

"WATCH!"

He held up his hand, the index pointed, and then opened his mouth. He placed his index on his tongue and then pushed back into his throat.

"Ugh, guys I, uh, AH, UGH! Watch this, *ah!*"

He was deep back in his throat. Finally his hand shoots back out of his mouth, and what followed was red, like blood.

"HAHAHAHAH!" Jimmy died laughing. "FUCK YEAH!"

"Is this your ketchup?" Donald asked.

Braydon is bawling.

"OHHH! OH-WOAH! FUCK, JIMMY! That was, oooohh, a fuckin' *good* one, bro! Goddammit!"

"That was fucking disgusting," Teddy said. "How do you do it on command? I want to try."

Jimmy got pissed.

"SHUT UP, ASSHOLE!"

I thought they were all the coolest kids ever. I had never seen people so hyped on such randomness. It made me laugh. It was like the most disgusting, vile things could actually have some humor that I could never imagine before. It was the humor of a skateboarder.

•   •   •

Before we knew it, after skating flat-ground for what seemed like forever at some parking lot, it was nighttime.

"Bro, what are we doing?" Jimmy said to all of us. "We fuckin' suck! This shit is retarded."

"I know, fuck, Teddy!" Braydon said.

"Dude, fuck this, I take you guys along, and you guys are bitchin'. Lets go back to the trailer, then!"

So we did. We skated more, and more, and more. But we were on a different path than the original one from the train station. So we had to hop this weird fence that was behind the trailer park, closest to the parking lot we skated.

"How do you hop it?" I asked them all.

They all laughed.

"Figure it out," Donald said.

So I see Little Jimmy (Jimmy's nickname, sometimes) run and jump and catch his foot on the base-bar, then LIFT himself to the top of the fence, sit astride, and then jump down to other side.

I thought it looked easy enough. So I threw my board over the fence, and what do you know it, it hits Little Jimmy square in the forehead. He was bleeding everywhere. Holding his head and screaming is full head off.

"FUCK, KLITZ! FUCK!!!"

"Fuck," I said, "I'm so sorry, Jimmy, I'm so *sorry!*"

"FUCKIN' PIECE OF SHIT, FAGGOT!"

As I was climbing the fence, trying to do it the same way Jimmy did, I was hearing, "FUCKIN' FAGGOT, KLITZ! FUCKING FUCKER! FUCK!!!!"

I jumped down. I saw Teddy and Braydon and Donald already over. They were laughing their sweet asses off.

"Fuck, Klitz, you're crazy," Braydon said. "Take it easy, Jimmy. You're okay."

"Nigga, I'm *bleeding*, you dick!"

We walked toward Teddy's cousin's house. Jimmy bitched the whole way there. Because it's Jimmy, and that's the way he is. Always blowing things out of proportion. Even though he was hurt pretty bad.

We were almost at Teddy's cousin's trailer, when we stopped at this guy's house. We stopped because his living room window was wide the hell open, blinds out. You could see everything in there. Braydon stopped.

"Guys, look."

So we all stop, naturally.

"What's going on?" I said.

Braydon started laughing. Then he whispered.

"He's watching porn! Oh shit."

So we all watched the screen, bright as hell, and it was showing a chick with huge, *huge* double-Ds getting plowed by a black guy's cock. The pervert was in the living room, masturbating.

"Dude, that's fuckin' gross," Donald said.

Then Jimmy stepped up and cupped his mouth, making a organic megaphone: "HEY, ASSHOLE!! YOU GOT A SMALL-ASS DICK!!!!"

The guy turned around, fell out of his chair. We all were laughing our asses off. The dude in the living room stood up and shouted out the window. Dick was out and everything, I swear.

"YOU FUCKING KIDS! GET THE FUCK OUTTA HERE!! I'M CALLING THE MOTHERFUCKING COPS!!!"

We all booked it out of there. I couldn't believe the insanity of what I was getting myself into. I was just watching and not really thinking— that's how I was back then.

•   •   •

Teddy's cousin was sort of a dick.

"Teddy, I don't have a place for you guys to sleep," he said.

"Why?"

"I'm fucking poor, bitch. Get on somewhere."

"You suck."

Braydon and all of us could hear what they were saying from behind Teddy.

"Teddy, you can sleep out back, in a tent . . . or something."

So we go to the back of the trailer, where said tent was given to us by Teddy's cousin, and began to set it up.

"This is bullshit, you fuck," Braydon said.

"Whatever," Teddy said.

Pissed. We all were.

•   •   •

Then we got done with the tents in the backyard.

"Lets go somewhere," said Braydon. "I don't want to spend this trip in this shit-hole."

"Ditto," said Donald.

"Where do we gonna go?" I asked Braydon.

"Not here. That's for sure."

"I know a place," Teddy said.

"Oh, Jesus, you again? *Please.*"

"Braydon, shut up! We can go to this farm close by."

"What?"

"Cow-tipping!" Jimmy said.

"Right, exactly," Teddy said. "Cow-tipping. I know where it is."

"Lets do it, I guess," Braydon said.

•   •   •

By the time all five of us got to the field, Braydon and Teddy were the only ones brave enough to do it. Jimmy, Donald, and I decided it was retarded because the fields were miles out, it was pitch black, and we couldn't even see cows at all.

"Pussies," Braydon said. He was always saying we were all pussies for some reason.

"Lets do it," Teddy said to Braydon.

"Fuck yeah."

So Donald, Jimmy, and I waited for these two ass-clowns to get done with this little charade. We ended up waiting for an hour by the fence.

"Are they really this stupid?" I asked Donald and Jimmy.

"Yes," they both said simultaneously.

Then Braydon and Teddy finally came back, around the corner.

"Holy fuck!" Teddy said. They both were completely dirty and soaked full of water up to their waists.

Donald was laughing. "What happened?" he said.

Braydon looked at Teddy, Teddy looked at Braydon. Then Braydon looked at us, sighed, and explained: "Okay. We hopped the fence, and fuckin'—we're just walking around this open field and— Okay, dude. Fuck. Basically we were walking and not able to see shit. It's dark as fuck out there. So we're just walking and walking and finally we see this thing in front of us. It turns around and goes, *"Huufff."* It was a fuckin' *horse,* bro. A gnarly, pissed-off, scared horse!"

"No way!" Jimmy said.

"Yeah, bro. So me and Teddy know this fucker is about to charge us because he's all smashing his huffs down and shit. So we run our asses off to the nearest fence, and bro, there was a lake—or a *puddle,* or *some* kind of shit. We hop the fence and got all this fucking water on us. I'm fuckin' pissed, bro. This sucks a fuckin' dick!"

"We just bought these shoes," Teddy said. "Goddammit."

"I know, bro. This totally blows dick."

"I'm hungry," I said.

"Of course you are, Klitz," Braydon laughed.

•   •   •

We skated down the road, away from that field, and we ended up at this gas station. We skated at that parking lot for awhile. We didn't have cash, no coupons, nothing to even eat. We were completely unprepared. All we had was enough money for tickets back, that's about it. And that was a necessity if you wanted to get back home.

"I'm starved," I said, holding my stomach. "Fuck."

"Klitzy," Braydon said, "just shut up. There ain't shit we can do about it."

We're all skating flat-ground, pissed off, hungry, Braydon and Teddy soaked, Jimmy and I bitching about food, and Donald just chillin' on a curb. We were all NOT happy.

Then this big ass truck drove on up. He parked right up against the curb. It read KRISPY CREAM DONUTS on the side of it. "What I wouldn't give . . ." Jimmy said. "Damn, I want something sweet."

The truck guy went up to the gas station's door, right there on the side of the place, and walked in. Five minutes later, he came out with boxes and boxes of donuts. The guy stopped, looked at us skateboarders, and said, "You guys hungry?"

We all look at each other and grinned.

"HECK YEAH WE ARE!" Jimmy said.

The truck driver just laughed. "Well boys . . ." he said, "I got here some donuts that we're about to throw away. You can have them if y'all want."

"Fuck yeah, man!" Braydon said. "Thanks!"

"Mhm," the truck driver nodded.

He just kept giving us all these boxes of donuts from the place. We filled an entire garbage bag full of them. We ate like kings. We actually said that if we ever came back to Fort Lauderdale, we'd have to stop by that gas station, at that hour (three a.m.) and get some donuts. We never went back there, though.

•   •   •

The trip just ended. Jimmy got five clips, I got one, Braydon got none, Teddy got two, Donald got three. We just wanted to skate and film ourselves and go to spots that were interesting. We hadn't done that but it was close enough. Not to mention the skate back and the train ride home were faster than the first, but mostly uncomfortable for our own particular reasons. No sleep. No success. Just skaters on a train. That's how it always was. And you know what, I fell in love and would do it again and again and again in a heartbeat. Oh yeah, and Braydon and Teddy stole a skateboard. It was Teddy's cousin's. A "Toy Machine" brand of board. Frickin' buttery.

•   •   •

Friday at school I was in the cafeteria, bragging about the trip.

"We got laid, we drank beer, we ollied a bum!"

I always lied, but not entirely.

"Bull*shit,*" Brain said. "what tricks did you get?"

"I kickflipped a seven."

"You're lying." He said this in front of five other kids at the table. They were staring me dead in the face.

"I did!" I said.

"Prove it! You got the footy?" Brian said.

"Footy?"

"Jesus fuck, Car. You don't even know what 'footy' means?"

All the kids at the table started laughing.

"Dude, Car, it means FOOTAGE! You fuck!"

"Oh, footy . . . footage," I said. "Yeah. I . . . um . . . got it." That was a lie, obviously.

"I want to see it Monday," Brian said. "You better have it or else you're just a little *poser.*"

•　　•　　•

After school I got home and got a call on my house phone from Donald.

"Hello?" I said into the phone.

"Klitz. It's Donald."

"I know," I said.

"How?"

"Caller I.D., genius."

"Don't get wise with me. We're swooping you up."

"Right now?"

"Yes."

"Hell yes!"

"Don't have an orgasm, faggot. We'll be there in ten."

He hung up.

•　　•　　•

They picked me up and talked about going to this college that they wanted to skate. Palm Beach Community College. They said there were awesome spots there and hella staircases. I was so excited. Maybe I really *could* skate a seven-stair and film it for Monday, I thought. That was on my mind up until we got there. As we parked, Braydon's mom said, "I'll be back in two hours." Braydon nodded. She drove off. We all five skated up to this three-stair that circled around this courtyard.

"Holy fuck," I said. "So. Many. Stairs. Holy *shit*."

"A skater's heaven," Braydon said. "Get your tongue off the cement, faggot! WOOO-HOOOOO!"

They all charged for the stairs. Jimmy was kickflipping damn near everything. Donald just had learned switch shuv-its and was doing them on flat-ground and eventually landed it on the three. They pulled out this handi-cam and he got it first try on camera. So sick. Braydon was skating flat and trying to boardslide this handrail that was flat and would extend out passed the three. He got close. Hella close. Never landed it, though. And Teddy would ollie frickin' everything: cones, up the three, down the three, over the three-block, everything. Big ollies. I would always wondered how in the hell he could pop that high. I still don't know. Maybe it's having a new board. Then again, Teddy couldn't afford it at the time, so probably it was natural.

"Lets skate the seven," Jimmy said. "It's over on the other side of the campus."

"Where's the security guard?" Donald asked.

"He doesn't come for another forty minutes. I know his route. It's always thirty-three passed the hour when he comes here, and forty-six passed the hour when he goes by the seven. We just gotta hide during those times. We should be fine."

"Fuck yeah, Jimmy," Braydon said. "Always got shit on lock."

"You know it, nigga."

Then we skated and skated and skated all throughout the campus. We had to take a couple stairs to get to the seven, it was on the second floor I think. We skated, cut corners, and finally we got to the seven-stair. I looked down it, the rest of them were behind.

"Holy shit this is small," I said.

"Move, Klitz!" Jimmy said, charging for the stair.

I moved out of the way in time. Jimmy was going so fast and then, *pop!* He went the air, flipped his board—doing a kick-flip, caught it, and landed bolts. Perfect. I cheered.

"FUCK YES! HOLY SHIT!!"

Then Donald charged. He ollied it. Braydon charged. He tried to ollie, missed. Teddy ollied over the frickin' handrail. Bolts! Big-ass ollie!

"You try, Klitz," Braydon told me from the bottom of the staircase.

He pretty much was saying this eye-level to me.

"Can't," I said.

"What do you mean 'you can't,' Klitz. You *have to*. We didn't bring you down to this set for you to just *look* at it. Ollie the bitch. It's little. It's like the three-stair."

"Okay," I said. "I'll try."

"Good. Go fast, bud."

So I skated all the way back. I was afraid. Adrenaline was rushing through me. From far back on the run-up to the stair, I could see all my friends as short midgets: just their heads and then this big drop-off from the edge of where to pop. That feeling is indescribable.

Then Jimmy stepped up the stair, skated fast and hard toward me, power-slided and stopped right beside me.

"Klitz, it's not that scary. Just go fast and *pop*. Just go for it."

"Okay," I said.

From down on the bottom of the staircase, I saw Braydon, camera in hand. He made a thumbs-up.

"COME ON, BITCH! YOU NEED TO OLLIE IT! I'M PRESSIN' RECORD!!" And I heard a faint *beep* noise from his way.

"Fuck it," I said under my breath.

So I threw my board down, lunged forward with my front foot on the grip-tape, pushed with my other foot as hard as I could, again and again, and saw the edge of the staircase inch forward in seconds. I popped as hard as I could, saw my friends under me, around me, watching me closely, and the stairs moving under my board, and then the ground coming up toward me, upon which I, *bam!* landed perfectly and coasted off.

"FUCK YEAH, KLITZY!" Braydon was saying, coming toward me with the camera, still recording. "FUCK YEAH! Yo, how the fuck does it feel to have your cherry popped again, you lil' clit?!"

I was smiling like crazy. They all rushed toward me. Hugs. Dap. Everything was so inviting. They truly cared that I landed just an ollie down that stair. And that was enough for me. I felt complete, like I was doing something important in my life.

•   •   •

When we were about to leave the spot, I turned to Braydon as he just finished filming Jimmy doing a kick-flip down the seven on his first try.

"Braydon."

"What?"

"Can you give me that tape?"

"Why? We're going to import it soon. We gotta drop you off."

"Can I be honest?"

"Yeah, man. Sup?"

"These kids at my school don't believe I can skate. I told them I kick-flipped a seven, and come Monday they want 'proof' on it. I want the tape so I can show them and they won't make fun of me."

"So you want footage of Jimmy to show to them, but you're going to say it's you?"

"Yes," I said.

Braydon started getting pissed.

"*Fuck* no, Klitz. I would never do that. And fuck what those little assholes think. You do you. Fuck them. You gotta earn that shit. You landed an ollie, and we're fuckin' proud of that, man. Fuck what those little preteens think."

"I'm just nervous, is all."

"Don't be. We're going to celebrate tonight, all of us. You deserve that shit, bro."

"Thanks, Braydon."

"Yeah. And Klitz?"

"Yeah?"

"We need to get you laid. Big-time."

"Why?"

"Because it's the best."

"Dude, I've never jacked off before."

"Jesus, Klitz. Just jack off."

"I'm scared of what it'll feel like."

"Jesus, Klitz. . . ."

We left the college.

•   •   •

Back at Donald's house, Braydon, Jimmy, Teddy, and Donald were walking into the gate. I looked up and saw a previous NO SKATEBOARDING sign hanging above the outside window. Only, the sign's "no" was crossed out and was replaced with "fuck yeah," so the final was FUCK YEAH SKATEBOARDING and I thought that was funny. I asked Donald where they got it.

"We stole it from that one spot in Fort Lauderdale."

"The bank spot," Braydon elaborated.

"Oh," I answered. I realized I didn't actually see them do it.

•   •   •

They walked into Donald's house and Donald's dog, Tigger (pronounced like the stripped "Winnie The Pooh" Tigger), comes up licking the shit out of Donald.

"TIGGER! FUCK *OFF!*"

Donald slapped the shit out of Tigger. She cried and scampered away somewhere. I still don't know her hiding spot.

In the kitchen, we all sat at the counter. It was a small kitchen with the dishes stacked so high that there would be no way to wash them except by putting them on the ground first. The pantries never had plates. Donald only used paper plates. That's it. He opened the fridge, leaned in, and grabbed some chicken wings from Popeyes. He grabbed a paper plate and put all the chicken on it, started eating.

Braydon, Teddy, Jimmy and I, we all looked at him eating and he never, ever offered.

"Where's the party at?" Jimmy asked nobody in particular.

"There's this place near Gun Club that my friend is having," Teddy said. "But it's B.Y.O.B. Which sucks because none of you asshole have any money."

"Bullshit!" Braydon said.

Jimmy started laughing.

"Hey," Teddy said, "they're serious this time, Braydon."

"Dude, we never, ever, EVER pay for that shit."

Teddy started laughing.

We all stopped and looked over at Donald, still eating away.

"Hey, fat-fuck," Braydon said, "how's about you come back to the world."

"Fuck, this shit is *good*," Donald said. "Fuck."

"Wish we knew what that was like," Jimmy said.

"*Pfft!* I paid for this food!"

"Know a party, fat-fuck?" Braydon asked.

"Yup. This place near us actually."

"Where?"

"Greenacres. Those crappy apartments. Pancho is going with his girl."

"Awesome. We're going."

Then Braydon and I go into the living room to this computer with the biggest screen I ever saw.

Braydon sat down.

"Klitz. Check this out."

He pressed a few buttons, searched a few files, and pulled up this video. It was of us!

"Check it, Klitz."

I watched and watched—it was amazing. They were playing some song that was Punk/Screamo. I didn't really like it but it was edited pretty well, I thought at the time. After it was done, I looked at Braydon.

"That was the best."

"I know," he said. "But this is better."

Then he clicked another video on another file. What pulled up was a *Girls Gone Wild* scene with two of these really drunk chicks making out. A guy comes up to them and asks if they would like to party. They of course screamed and said "Fuck yeah!" as loud as they could. Then this crappy cube transition happened and it was another scene, at night. The girls were kissing and touching, all that crap. They looked at the camera and asked, "Wanna join?" Another transition: They were naked and grinding on each other.

"How you liking it?" Braydon asked.

I had a boner, not saying a word.

"Klitz?"

"Yeah?"

"You're fuckin' re*tarded*." He laughed and turned it off.

Later, we skated, played video games, and talked about nonsense until the nighttime.

• • •

The time came to leave for the party.

"Klitz," Braydon said, "get ready."

I was on the computer.

"KLITZ!"

I turned around. "Yeah?"

"GET YOUR ASS UP!"

"We're going to a party," Jimmy put in. "We're almost ready."

"I don't know, guys," I said. "I sort of want to stay here."

"Why?" Braydon said. "Alone? You're a weirdo, bro."

They all were making fun of me all the way out the door. All of them: Braydon, Teddy, Donald, and Jimmy. They always made fun of me whenever I didn't go out with them somewhere. Basically I didn't want to go because I was too scared to be around a party.

When they left, it was dead quiet. So I looked down at the ground and realized that I had the house to myself. Then I looked over at the computer screen. It was giant. I straighten myself in the computer chair, pointed the curser down at the bottom left of the screen where the "Start" button was. I searched "*Girls Gone Wild.*" Dozens and dozens of videos pulled up. I clicked one. This girl with huge tits pulled up. It was a three-minute video of her touching them and pushing them together. She was softly asking the camera if "you would like to touch me, big boy, and fuck me?" I got a boner. More videos had this trend of talking into the camera.

After watching dozens and dozens of these videos, I found this one that was different from the rest. There were two girls and they were in a hotel room. One had really small tits and one had huge tits. They both had great butts. Anyway, the girl with the big tits was on top of the girl with small tits and the big tit girl was holding the bed's backboard. She looked into the camera and said, "Carl, do you want to join?" Apparently the camera guy's name was "Carl." In the video he said, "Yes," then she got off the bed, kneeled down in front of him, and pulled his pants down.

It was so hot. It was a POV scene of her sucking his dick. I had the hardest boner in the world. I pulled my pants down. I didn't touch myself because I was scared to. On the screen, the girl with big tits was saying Carl's name over and over and telling him what a big dick he had and how hard it was. It was hot because I envisioned her as my "girlfriend." I actually thought she was. So I look down at my dick, it was almost twitching. I look up and she was stroking him so fast and strong. She was telling him to cum. I leaned back, looked down, and my dick was straight up, pointing at me. I looked at the screen and the girl kept saying for Carl to come. So I looked down and rubbed the head of my cock. Then I winced and felt my dick feel like a bubble being popped and squeezed, and out came all this gooey grey-white stuff out onto my stomach. It pooled. There was so much of it.

I got scared and stopped the video right when the camera-guy came too. I was leaning backward and making my way into the bathroom near the kitchen. I turned the faucet on and was splashing water on my messy stomach. Then I grabbed toilet paper and was wiping myself off.

I felt really weird. Even hours later when Teddy, Braydon, Donald, and Jimmy came back drunk from the party, I never told them that I sort of jacked-off for the first time.

•   •   •

Monday came and I was stressed out because I had to break the news to the kids at my school that I really didn't kick-flip the seven. I didn't want to say that, though, so I lied about it in the cafeteria.

"Yeah, man. I kick-flipped it, but they lost the footy."

"Oh yeah?" Brian said. "I don't believe you, poser."

The kids at the table started laughing. Then the bell rang to get to class.

I stood up, ran toward my Science class. I was about ten seconds late. The teacher scolded me.

After class, the teacher asked me to stay. So I did. He was sitting at the edge of his desk. He said something really weird.

"Carl, I'm concerned about you."

I didn't say anything.

"Basically . . ." he continued, "I want to see you succeed but I can't. You seem be 'spaced-out' all the time. You don't seem interested in anything I'm saying."

"I'm not," I said. "We can't use any of this."

"Sure you can. This lesson was about environments. In the lesson I was explaining that environments have a lot to do with how we operate in our daily lives."

"Okay," I said.

"My real concern, Mr. Klitz, is that you seem like your environment is putting a hindrance on yourself."

"Why?"

"Because you aren't into your studies, so you sleep, don't listen, and it's because something is bothering you. I'm concerned."

"Nothing is bothering me, sir."

"I sure hope so. I really do."

I still don't know what he meant. But I guess now I can get a picture.

•   •   •

The weekend came, it was cloudy, rainy, and nobody wanted to skate in my neighborhood. So I called Braydon.

"Hey, man. It's Klitz. What you doin' today?"

"Goin' over this girl's house."

"Cool. Can I come?"

"Klitz, I'm trying to fuck her."

"So . . . ?"

"Okay. Come on, then. Can you skate here?"

"You live on Congress."

"Come over and skate."

"Okay," I said, and hung up.

I left my house, skated four miles to Braydon's. It was slightly raining. I knocked on Braydon's door, and he came out five seconds later, board in hand. "Lets roll," he said.

We skated across the street, passed Publix, passed a bank, and into the back fence of this apartment neighborhood. We kept skating through all these different streets and landed somewhere that looked like the front of Donald's apartment.

"What's this girl's name?" I asked Braydon.

"Terra. She's got *huge* tits."

"Oh yeah?"

"Huge! Fucking giants!"

"Okay," I said.

We walked into the gate. There were flowers and a really nice porch. Everything was tip-top clean. Everything. We walked up to the front door. Braydon knocked a couple times.

"Don't embarrass me," he said to me.

"Okay."

Then she came out.

"Hey, Brandy!" she said.

Brandy. I thought that was cute. "Terra!" he said. Then he gave her a big hug. "This is Car— I mean, Klitz."

"Klitz?"

"Yeah. I know."

"That's hilarious! Hi, Klitz!" She smiled at me.

Braydon was right. Her tits *were* huge. Not only that, but she was the same height as me. She was skinny and hot. *Wow!*

We all three walked into Terra's house. "My mom's gone," she said.

"Great," Braydon said. He looked down at me and raised his eyebrows.

There was a staircase. We went up that, around the bend, and into Terra's room. It was really nice. It smelled like peaches or cinnamon. I thought it was cute. She had posters of all her favorite bands hanging up. Like Bright Eyes, Slipknot, and The Misfits. I thought she was so cool.

"Terra, show us your tits," is the first thing Braydon said.

She laughed. "No way! Show me your dick!"

"Okay," he said.

"No, Braydon! Stop," she laughed.

"Whatever, Terra. Yo, you should make-out with Klitz."

"Why?"

"Nah, man," I said. "Chill."

"Klitz, you need to get some pussy. She's right there in front of you, bro."

She just stared at me, blinking.

"Make-out with her, Klitz."

"No," I said.

"Fuckin' *pussy*, Klitz. Just do it, pussy. *Pussy!*"

Braydon reminded me of Chaz at the roller coaster he made me go on a while back when I was younger.

"It's not a big deal," Terra said. "I'll kiss you."

"Lets just chill," I said.

"Fuckin' *pussy!*" Braydon said.

Then Terra stepped toward me.

"Come on," she said. "One kiss."

"And Klitz is a fuckin' *virgin.*"

"Really?" Terra's eyes got big. "*Wow!*"

"Show Klitz's your tits, Terra."

"Okay," she said. Then she lifted up her shirt. She wasn't wearing a bra. They were perfect. One had a mole on the side, but they were perfect. The nipples were small, not the size of dinner plates. I hate boobs like that: when the nipple covers the entire titty. Hers were perfect though.

"Klitz, touch them," Braydon said. "Don't be a pussy."

I stepped forward, looking at them.

"Touch them!" Braydon said.

So I poked the left one.

"Jesus Christ, Klitz. . . ."

"What, bro?"

"I'm trying to get you laid."

"It's really okay, Klitz," Terra said. "Touch them." Then she grabbed my hands and placed them on on her boobs. They were so soft and firm.

"HELL YEAH, KLITZY!" Braydon said. "FUCK YEAH!"

"Cool, huh?" Terra asked me.

I smiled. "Yeah, guys, it's pretty neat."

"Now kiss her," Braydon said.

"Nah, man."

"KISS HER!"

I started to cry.

"I DON'T WANT TO, BRAYDON!!"

Terra pulled her shirt down, turned to Braydon, and said, "What's this kid's deal?"

"Klitz! Stop being a motherfucking *pussy!*" he said.

I was holding my face. I ran out her door, down the stairs, and into her living room. I cried and cried on the couch. I didn't even know why I was crying. I still don't know. I waited and nobody came down. Later, I found out Braydon fingered Terra.

mid/late-2004

In Middle School we all had a Myspace. We always had crazy names. Sometimes I would spend hours building a really great profile design. I would linger into the morning, frickin' decking this thing out. Now I just think it's stupid, considering Facebook (the biggest social media site nowadays) doesn't let you do such things. I would make the best, most-simplest profiles on Myspace that everyone at my school adored. They all would compliment me. I would get loads of comments. I liked the attention. I thought I was going to be a graphic designer; but, obviously, that's just a pipe dream from a Myspacer thinking he was cool. But anyways, I also remember that everyone always had cool display names. I eventually picked one that had no display name. That was pretty cool. But then I eventually landed on "Déif Biflocka," a made up name I made. It meant nothing. Or so I thought. . . .

•　　•　　•

School was over and summer had finally come. I asked my mother for a camera because I wanted to film. She bought me one, surprisingly. The issue was that I couldn't use it right away because I was sick. Dead sick. Every time I would cough a little bit of blood and green-green mucus would seemingly explode out of me. Everything hurt. I was weak. Picture that really chilly-heated *uncomfortable* feeling numbing your body and paralyzing you. That's what it was like. So my mother took me to see a doctor.

"He has mono," he said to her. "Make sure he doesn't do any physical activity."

"But why?"

"Because his spleen could rupture if he hits it. That's why."

"Oh Jesus."

So that's when I knew I couldn't skateboard for a bit.

•   •   •

Life went on. I took it easy. It was tough, and boy, did I want to skate. But I resisted.

Then I got a call from Braydon. I answered.

"Hello?"

"Klitz?"

"*Ugh*, yeah"—*cough cough*—"what's up, buddy?"

"What's wrong with you? You sick?"

"Real sick. I got mono."

"That's fucked, bro. But hey, listen, we're going to Seabring."

"The hell is that?"

"It's this town where Taylor lives." Taylor was Braydon's girlfriend at the time.

"Okay . . ." I said, "what's up?"

"Klitz, it's a trip. I'm inviting you."

"I can't skate."

"Why?"

"I have mono!"

"So . . . ?"

"I could die if something hits my stomach."

"Bull. Just go."

"Okay. Whatever, I'll go. Come over. I got a cammy by the way."

"Cool. Donald has a car. Bye!" He hung up.

•   •   •

It was a Friday afternoon. They showed up later on. Braydon, Donald, and Teddy. Jimmy was doing another trip with other kids (*KinesisFilms* kids, who were more famous than Structure Skate Team). Whatever. So Braydon banged on my door. I answered.

"Knock loud enough, asshole?"

He just laughed; I did too. They all three walked in. My mother was in the kitchen. We got there. As I was about to ask permission, I had the worst croupy cough.

"UGH AHHH UGH FUHH-FUH-*ACKKK!!! UGH!!!*"

"Carl, you're sick," my mother said, "why are your friends here?"

"Ugh! Crap! Okay. I'm ready. Okay. Basically Braydon and them want me to go to Seabring."

"Where?"

Braydon said, "Seabring, Mrs. Klitz. My girlfriend's family is there. We want Carl to go because he has a camera."

"Carl can't skate, Braydon. I'm sorry."

"He doesn't have to. He's not going to bring his board."

"Then what is he going to do?"

"Film us skate."

"Oh. Okay! Make sure he doesn't get hurt. His stomach is a real dangerous thing. It can cause lots of issues. He could die."

"No problem, Mrs. Klitz," Braydon said.

I packed my camera, some clothes, and no board. It sucked. But it also didn't suck at the same time, you know?

•   •   •

Off we went! We traveled hella far. Three hours. The place was flat, small and ghetto. I saw a big-ass sign toppled over from last year's hurricane. I didn't even see that many cops on the road. Nothing was there. It was dead.

We finally got to Taylor's house. We parked, did all that, unpacked, knocked.

"Braydon!" she screamed when the door opened. "HELL YEAH! MY BABY!!"

We all laughed at him. He felt her titty. "Good to see you," he said. Then we all went inside.

The house was a pigsty. I couldn't even believe it. I saw so many cans and clothes and Polaroid pictures on the ground it wasn't even funny. I noticed, but the rest of them didn't care. You didn't care if you were a skateboarder. You had better things to worry about.

"Lets smoke weed!" Taylor said to Braydon.

"Hell yes. . . . Boys? Lets get toasty!"

Taylor rolled a blunt, Braydon lit it, and they all were in a circle, passing it around like a hot potato. Finally, it got to me.

"Klitz, smoke," Braydon said.

"Nah man, I'm good."

"Don't be a pussy, bro."

"I don't want to. I'm not going to. I'm sick."

"Whatever, bro," he laughed. "Lets skate after this."

•   •   •

We skated Seabring the whole day. We found this spot in front of a police station that had a long tan ledge that extended out about fifteen feet. Braydon, trying it forever, boardslided the ledge. I filmed it decently. I didn't have fisheye lens so it didn't look too good. Then we left there, skated another place that was a five-stair. The rail was square. Nobody landed anything.

•   •   •

Nighttime came and we all went back to Taylor's. Her mom was there. She was old and didn't do much. She stayed in her room most of the time. I think she was sick, too, like me. Regardless, this enabled us—if someone were to call it that—to do whatever we wanted.

"Lets go down the street and get some brewskis," Teddy said.

"Babe," Braydon said to Taylor.

"Yeah?"

"Know a place?"

"No. They all never give me it. My fake I.D. doesn't even work."

Braydon laughed.

"SHUT UP!" Taylor laughed too. "You're such a dick!" She flirt-punched his shoulder.

"Babe, I think I could get it."

"We don't have to."

"Yeah?"

"I got a case of Bud Light."

"FUCK YEAH! I LOVE YOU!"

Taylor smiled. She busted out the case. There was about thirty of those bad-boys. Teddy and Donald were drinking a lot, but Braydon drank about ten of those beers. They were on the couch, and I was on the loveseat, alone. Braydon saw me.

"Klitz. . . ."

"Mm?"

"Get a beer, fag."

"I'm sick."

"It's a beer, Klitz, not a virus."

"Is it gonna hurt me?"

Everyone laughed when I said that.

"What? I'm just curious," I said.

"No, faggot," Braydon said. "Take a drink. Do it."

"Okay," I said.

So I stood up, walked over to Taylor, where the case was, and grabbed myself two cans of beer.

"WOAH!" Braydon said when he saw, "WHAT A *BADASS!*"

I laughed, then walk back to the loveseat, sat down, and cracked one can open. I drank. I drank like hell. Before I knew it, both cans were gone. I loved it. I thought it tasted warm and nice. Everything made sense with it. The taste was so damn good. So I stood up, went back to the case, grabbed two more.

"Damn, Klitz," Braydon said. "Chill. Slow your roll. We only got about four left."

"You tell me to drink, then get bitchy when I *do* drink?"

Everyone laughed at Braydon.

"Okay, you made a point, Klitz," he said. "Drink up."

So I did. I pretty much chugged those two beers. Once I got to the last drop, I felt this warm feeling in my stomach. "Woah, I feel weird," I said.

Braydon looked at me and smiled.

I was walking over next to Braydon. "Woah, I feel fuckin' *weird*." I sat down next to him, scooting his girlfriend over. She didn't mind. She was laughing. "Braydon," I said.

Laughing, he said, "Yeah, Klitz?"

"I fuckin' *love* you, man."

"Yeah?"

"I fuckin' fuckin', uh, *love* you, man!"

"We get it, bro!"

"I FUCKING LOVE YOU, BRAYDON!"

Everyone laughed. For no reason, it seemed. Everything was just . . . fun. That's the only way I can describe it. Fun. I hate no thoughts, I just was having a grand time.

•   •   •

In the morning, I woke up with a monstrous headache. "Fuhhhhhh-*ck*, bro," I said, rising from the couch. I looked around. On the floor, all of them slept. I got up. I went into the kitchen. There was a fly on the counter so I swatted it. I hated flies. Then I saw a box of cereal, went into the fridge, got out the milk, and made a bowl. I ate. Then Teddy came into the kitchen. "What are you doing, Klitz?" he said.

"Nothing."

"Dude, hahaha, you're funny."

"Why?"

"You just are, bro."

"Okay."

"Yeah, Klitz. Okay. Can I have some?"

"It isn't my cereal."

"Goddammit, Klitz. Hand it over."

So I did. He poured himself a bowl.

•   •   •

Much later, around the afternoon time, which is the time most people wake up, everyone was still asleep. It was just Teddy and I. Talking.

"Klitz, ever wondered about the Universe?"

"Sometimes."

"Do you believe in God?"

"I'm not sure . . . I think so."

"Yeah, well, I think you should drop it."

"Huh?"

"He's not real, Klitz."

"Okay," I said.

It went on like this for a while. We spoke a lot about a variety of different topics. I know now that most of them are pointless. Most people who are Atheist tend to make me anxious, but I don't think that that was the case at that point in time; I was perfectly fine because I was a kid and didn't think about that silly sort of stuff like I do now.

•   •   •

Everyone woke up. Everyone. They were all hanging out on the couch. Taylor went into the kitchen, and we all were in the living room, watching some random skate video Taylor just so happened to have.

"Who ate my cereal?" she said from the kitchen. "Teddy!"

"WHAT!" he shouted.

"WHAT HAPPENED TO THE CEREAL!!"

"ME AN' FUCKIN' KLITZ ATE IT!"

Us boys started laughing. Then Taylor stormed into the living room. She looked at Braydon.

"Fix this!"

"Huh?" Braydon said. He was high.

"FIX IT, BRAYDON!"

"OKAY!!!" Braydon looked at Teddy. "Dude, can you *please* go to the store. Get some cereal."

"Fuck, man," Teddy said. "Goddamit."

Taylor looked pleased.

"Only if Klitz goes . . ." Teddy said to Braydon. "He had some too."

Braydon laughed. "Yeah, whatever."

•   •   •

It was just Teddy and I. We literally put our clothes on and started walking. I didn't have a board, so it was pointless for Teddy to have one. He wouldn't even be able to go fast or anything.

"Dude," Teddy said. "What time is it?"

"Twelve-thirty."

"Fuck. We gotta leave around two."

"This trip was so fast," I said.

Then Teddy looked at me. "Bro, you won't believe it. This one time I fought this kid—his name was *something* or other, I can't remember—and I hit him so hard his face looked like it caved in."

I laughed. "What the hell does that have anything to do with anything?"

"Everything," he said. "That was another trip we made here. That's what happened. Now *that* trip was fast."

"Whatever," I said.

Just then, from out of nowhere: *HONK! HONK!* There were these Mexican guys in this weird-ass Chevy passing us.

"HEY FOOKERS! YOU WHITE BOYS ARE FAGGOTS!!"

Teddy goes, "FUCK YOU, NIGGERS!" And he flicked them off. "Assholes," he said under his breath. "I swear, I hate that bullshit when they do that, Klitz."

"Why would they randomly do that?"

"Because they are Mexicans, Klitz. That's why."

"Oh."

"Trust me, if a Mexican ever howlers something at you, just do what I do and—"

What cut him off was the Chevy parked in front of us. It came out of nowhere. Right there. Over a curb and everything. A guy came out. Actually, four guys did. The driver was mean-muggin' Teddy.

"HEY FOOKER! FUCK ME, HUH?! FUCK *YOU!*"

Teddy held up his hands. "Come on, fuck-boy," he said.

Next thing I knew, they all charged him. He got the living shit kicked out of him in five seconds. One of them looked at me.

"GET THAT STUPID FAGGOT KID!"

I held my stomach. I was nervous because if I got kicked in the stomach, my spleen would rupture and I would die. So I ran the opposite way, as fast as I could. Nobody chased me. I ran two blocks.

•   •   •

I stormed into Taylor's house. "BRAYDON! BRAYDON!" I shouted. "TEDDY'S GETTING *BEAT UP!*"

Braydon got up from the couch, out the front door, and I saw him book it down the street through the window. Donald slowly stood up. He looked lazy as hell with a beer in his hand.

"What happened, Klitz?" he said.

"I don't know. I ran!"

"You didn't help him?"

"Dude, I can't fight! Plus, I'm sick! If I get kicked the stomach, I'll die!"

"Oh," he said.

•　　•　　•

Teddy had bruises by the time Braydon got there. The Mexicans left and everything. In fact, Teddy was walking back bleeding when he saw Braydon. He wasn't mad at me for running. He understood. There's not much to say. We just left Seabring after that. No point. Three gorgeous hours it took to get back home. Teddy slept the whole way back. I think karma got to him from beating up a kid on his last Seabring trip.

•　　•　　•

Some weeks later, little did I know that that karma reverted back in Teddy's favor. So get this: Braydon, Donald, Teddy, Little Jimmy, and I were skating around Greenacres park, minding our own, when Teddy gets this weird phone call. Basically Teddy was yelling and screaming on the phone to some kid or something. His was pacing back and forth, about to punch a wall or something. I didn't understand. Braydon was laughing, so I thought it was a joke. Then Teddy hung up and came up to us. "I gotta whoop a kid's ass," he said. "I have to. Fuck!"

"What was *that* all about, Ted?" Braydon said, putting an arm around him. "You got some lil' boys around you?" Braydon gave Teddy a knuckle sandwich.

"Screw you, bro!" Teddy was laughing. "Fo' real, though. This kid was talking so much shit . . ." and I can't remember for the life of me what the "shit talking" was about. Remember, back then shit talking was always this or that. We never got a break from it. Either someone else was shit talking or you were shit talking them, or pretending to shit talk . . . or visa-versa.

•   •   •

Donald had a car. So yeah, we drove all the way across town, just for Teddy's stupid ass. Donald was pissed. He made Teddy and Braydon pay for gas. I remember the kid and Teddy were texting back and forth, talking hella shit. Teddy and Braydon were all hootin' and hollerin' and it was really weird for me because I have no clue what the hell was going on.

•   •   •

We got to the place Teddy's enemy told him to go. Now, Teddy was all fired up. So was Braydon. Donald was all, "I'm not going. I'm parking and you two can do whatever the hell you want." Jimmy basically said the same. I did too. I couldn't fight. Still can't. It's whatever.

Braydon and Teddy got out of the car and they said, "We'll be back." And I swear to you, after they left it was hella silent in the car. I mean, don't get me wrong, music was playing—Smashing Pumpkins mostly— but it was down low. It was damn near silent in the car. Nobody talked.

Minutes turned into dozens of minutes, not hours, thankfully. "Where are these ass-tards?" Jimmy asked.

"I don't know," Donald kept saying back. We all waited for them. Then, from far out, we saw them.

"Look! *There's* the faggots!" Jimmy said, nose pressed against the car window.

"Why is Teddy carrying two boards?" I asked. "He only left with one."

"Oh jeez," Donald said. Then he started up his car.

Braydon and Teddy hopped in, faster than I ever seen anything get done. "DRIVE! NOW!" Braydon shouted. Outside the car, I could see hella kids in a group charging for the car. Donald reversed fast as hell out of the parking spot he was at. "DRIVE! DRIVE!!!" Braydon was shouting. Donald drove hella fast down the back of a supermarket. Publix, I think. "HOLD UP!" Braydon said, and while the car was moving, he jumped out. Donald stopped driving, stood still.

Braydon ran all the way back down. I turned my head and was looking out the back window. I could see him and the kid. They were almost like small dots. There was a girl and a scrawny kid. The girl was super ghetto, getting in Braydon's face. Braydon appeared to be laughing.

Then he grabbed the scrawny kid by the collar, picked him up, and threw him on the ground. Braydon had his knee on his chest and Braydon slingshot his fist back and then rammed it into the kid's cheek. Inside the car, I could hear the hard packing noise, *POW!*

So I saw Braydon come running back. His hand was beat-red. He was cheesin' like crazy. I couldn't believe none of that group of kids even took a lick at Braydon. It made me think that kids are all talk, no action.

Braydon got back in Donald's car, put on his seatbelt, and calmly said, "Drive." Donald floored it. I looked out the back window and could see the group looking down at the bleeding kid. Then I heard Braydon say to Teddy, "Fuck yeah! You stole that motherfucker's board, too! Fuck yeah! I stuck the *shit* out of him!"

•   •   •

Much later, cops called Teddy's cellphone, demanding he return the skateboard he stole. "Now, sir," all that mess was said. And Teddy told them, "What skateboard?" then hung up.

2005 & 2006

My grades were plummeting faster than I could put my head down to sleep in class, which was pretty F-ing fast. I slept so much in class I had straight *F*'s. Not the fake kind where kids just bragged about almost failing, I mean the real kind. All *F*'s. However, I did have one A. It was in Art class. My academic teachers actually took the liberty of going into my Art class to see if I was awake. They were pissed to find out that I was wide-awake. I guess I was depressed. I really was. I remember I told my mother, on the phone, that at age nineteen, when I go off to college, I was going to kill myself. That was my very first suicidal wish at twelve or thirteen years old. My mother cried on the phone. I hung up on her and played *Kingdom Hearts*.

●   ●   ●

I was brought into the principal's office. I was "summoned."

"Have a seat, Carl," he said when I entered. So I sat. "Y'okay?" he said. "I brought you into here to say a few things."

"Yeah?"

"How's life a home?"

"Fine."

"Good. You treated right?"

"What's your point, bro?"

"I want to know your family life, Carl."

"It's not any of your business."

"Okay," he said. Then he got up, went to his coffee table, and poured a glass of water. He drank it, walked back, sat at his desk, and continued, "I've been getting a lot of emails about you. It's all anyone seems to be talking about."

"That depends on your definition of 'everyone,' " I said.

"My staff."

"So . . . ?"

"They keep saying you're sleeping in class. I checked your grades."

I kept silent.

"What do you think of that, Carl?"

I shrugged.

"Carl?"

"Yeah?"

"You're failing."

"Why in the hell am I in here, bro?" I said. "Seriously. Are you trying to make me feel guilty? I'm tired. I don't like school. I hate it. I hate everyone here."

"We're going to have a meeting with all your teachers and your mother," this principal, wearing a gold watch, a swanky blue suit, clean-edged shave, great black and silky hair, said.

•   •   •

A couple days later, it happened. Literally. All my teachers, my mother—everyone was gathered together in this long room. Little did I know, it was the biggest gang-up of my life. Again, you had the principal, my science teach, my English teach, my history teach and her college assistant, both drinking Starbucks, all the other teaches, and then my mother and me. My mother sat at the other head of the table, the principal on the adjacent head. He had his elbows up, staring. He looked bored. He said, "How should we start this off?" The first person to speak was my science teach. She was a total bitch.

"Firstly, Ms. Klitz, I have never, in all my years of teaching, seen a student so uncaring, so bad, so disrespectful in all my life! It's a disgrace."

"What?" my mother said. "How do you mean? He doesn't even do anything bad. He doesn't even do drugs."

My science teach laughed. "Wouldn't surprise me," she said. "Always disrupting the class."

"How?" I asked.

"Adults are talking, Mr. Klitz."

"You don't have an answer," I said.

"Just be quiet, Car," my mother said. "Now, guys, you have to tell me what he does."

"HE *SLEEPS!*" my Science teach said. "THAT'S ALL HE EVER DOES!"

"Does he disrupt the other students with his sleeping?"

"YES, MS. KLITZ!"

"I find that hard to believe. . . ."

Then my history teach spoke.

"Ms. Klitz, he's simply not doing anything in all his classes."

"—minus art," my science teach butt in. "KIDS LIKE HIM END UP IN *JAIL!*" Then my science teach started whimpering. "All my . . . ye-year-. . . ." She couldn't get her words out.

"It upsets us, Ms. Klitz," my history teach said. "He's no good, he has no ambition in life, and he doesn't amount to anything."

Then Mr. Principal decided to speak.

"I brought him into my office the other day and he just didn't seem to care about this meeting, Ms. Klitz. Not at all, it seemed. I'm concerned."

"*No,*" I said, "what you *did* was ask me questions to see if I would tell you if my mother was the bad guy."

My mother looked at me, looked at him. "You two did this?" she asked.

"Your son is a liar, Ms. Klitz," he said.

"Yeah, okay," I said.

"SEE!" The science teach started to butt in, yet again. "HE'S A BAD KID!!"

"Stop yelling," the principal said.

"Might I say something?" the college student chick said, raising her finger in the air. "I have a few things to say." She stood. "Firstly, I am new—that I know—but I gotta say, Mrs. Klitz, you're son is by far the worst student I've come across. He doesn't listen, he doesn't act right, he's completely disrespecting my boss here to my right, and he doesn't care at all about anyone or anything's feelings." Then she sat and started slurping away at her Starbucks.

I cried and ran outside the meeting, upon which I ran into this black kid, Ty, and his weird pinky fingers that couldn't straighten all the way—but that's beside the point—and I told him what happened. Strangely, he hugged me and told me that everything was okay. Little did I know, everything was definitely NOT okay. I found that out quickly.

•   •   •

A few days later, something big happened in my life. Basically my mother and I sat down along with her new boyfriend, Ronald, and his one-year old boy, Baxter. Basically my mother was saying how concerned she was about my schooling and how these teachers aren't exactly right to say those things, but she was still disappointed with me. She told me that I have to go to boot camp (The Eagle Academy). She told me that it was best for me. Then, after not saying anything the whole time, Ronald stood up and told my mother that that is NOT a good idea. I thought it was weird because Ronald and I wrestled one time and we took it too far and I ended up calling him a "dirty faggot." Which was odd, but I'm an emotional brat. Anyways, they didn't let me go to this boot camp, but my mother still wanted *something* to go down. She wanted me in some kind of program that was *like* boot camp. So, she found one. Lowridge. My mother explained it as a place you go to when you are a problem child, but not so much so to the point where you're unbearable. And also, you live there on weekdays. And weekends you go home. Swell! (Not.)

•   •   •

It was Monday, at eight p.m. Dark as hell. "Dark" dark, for some reason. Just my mother and I. Her car's headlights pointed toward the ground from the dashboard. Then a circle here and circle there, and my mother parked. I turned to my right and saw a dimly lit front office. My mother told me to unbuckle my seatbelt. I did, obviously. Then her and I walked up to the doors, she opened them for me and I walked in.

Kids were lined up through this glass door in the main room. There was a main office, which was where we were, then you turn left and there was this main room. Kids were all inside that main room with their parents. My mother signed in, took my hand, and walked me through the doors.

I walked in and saw a table full of donuts, hotdogs, and water. I thought that was odd. I ate two hotdogs because for some reason I was starving. I turn my head, my mother and everyone looked over by the wall to hear a guy talk. The speaker was a black man who called himself Mr. Potts.

"Parents, kids, I want all of you to listen up," he was saying. "Kids, what we are going to do is have you follow me; and parents, you guys have to head on home. Everything'll be fine. You have five minutes to say, 'Goodbye,' to your kids. Everything'll be fine. Also kids, we need you to take along your bags your parents left."

I looked over at my mother.

"Bags . . . ?"

"Yes," she said. And she pulled up a duffle bag full of clothes. "You're staying here."

I don't want to explain all the crying and bitching I did, but basically I went with a dozen other kids, in a single-file line, and we followed Mr. Potts down this big cement-walled hallway.

•   •   •

We all walked down this corner passed this red door that said MR. POTTS on it, and Mr, Potts walked inside. Before closing the door, a man with screwed-up teeth walked out.

"Hi. The names Skip, everyone. Follow me, I'll point to where your dorm-rooms are."

So, in a line, we all walked with Skip. He kept stopping at each door, saying, "This is you . . ." and then your name.

We got to the last door and it was some small black kid and me bunking together. He was more nervous than me. Skip turned to us both and said, "This is us."

"Us?" I asked.

"Yes. I'm your counselor. Go in here. You'll be fine."

So the small black kid and me walked inside. What I saw was a group of black kids and one big-ass white boy. They all had flip-flops on and smelled like fresh deodorant. Some old guy was in there, watching them. The black kids all looked up at the little black boy and me. Skip said, "Meet Carl and Floyd." I watched Floyd's eyes get wide. Mine probably did too.

All of those kids started smiling and nodding. Evil. They just looked like rats that just saw a piece of cheese when they hadn't eaten in weeks.

"Floyd," Skip said, "you go in that room *there*," and he pointed to a corner dorm, "and Carl, you over *there*," and he pointed to another corner dorm.

I had all my belongings with me and I walked passed these animals in a circle, talking, snickering, and looking at me. As I walked passed them, what I heard behind me was, "EVERYONE GET TO BED!" Skip could scream louder than anyone I had ever heard. And just like that, it all set in and I knew I was in trouble.

When I arrived at my doorless dorm room, I saw how small the bed was. There were two beds. Both black. To the side of them was an old filing cabinet that acted as a makeshift nightstand. Another filing cabinet that was bigger, maybe for books. I guess that was where I was to put my clothes. There were two desks on either side of the room. The room was encapsulated by bleak, tan-colored, cinder-block walls.

The only white boy in the place came walking in. He approached his bed, pat it, and sat down. He stared at me while I was unzipping my bag, about to begin putting things away. The kid said, "What'd you do?"

I turn to him. "Nothing."

"Why you wearin' tight pants?"

I was a skateboarder. Those KR3W pants that were hugging my ass were not helping me out at this point in time. I said, "I'm a skateboarder."

Then the kid stood up and, without seeming to hear my comment, said, "This here ain't no free ride. I'm here for some bad shit. I cut a dude once, and now I'm here." I think he lied.

I started walking backward, away from him coming closer to me. I couldn't be sure at the time if he was lying or not.

"Carl. Is that your name?" this kid asked.

I nodded. I was pretty damn afraid.

He grinned. "You're just in for a big treat, now, aren't'cha?" And he grabbed me by the collar and lifted me up and put me against the wall. I was terrified and thought I was about to die.

Then Mr. Potts came around the corner.

"Carl, I want you to know—HOLY SHIT! TREY! THE HELL ARE YOU DOIN', MAN!!"

Trey let go of me, and then dusted me off.

"Nothin', Potts, I was just showing this kid a trick."

"You better not be doin' what I think you're doin'. CHAIR TIME! NOW!!!"

"Fuck, Potts, why right now? I'm tired."

"CHAIR TIME! NOW!! AND NO PROFANITY!!!"

Trey grinned and said, "Whatever, Potts." And he walked out and went back into the living room and pulled out a chair and sat in it in the corner. He looked straight ahead and didn't say anything. Everything had no doors so you could see exactly what everyone was doing.

Mr. Potts turned to me.

"Carl, don't mind him. He's just a bully. The kid likes to mess with the new people."

"This isn't jail, is it?" I asked.

Everyone in the whole dorm started to laugh from their rooms. I realized that everything I said in this place could be easily heard by everyone.

"No, Carl, it's not," Mr. Potts said. "This is Lowridge Community Center. And we're here to help you."

He smiled.

•   •   •

I woke up at six a.m. to bright lights and the sounds of a big Chinese gong being hit repeatedly over the grim sounds of hardcore rap played on 95.5 radio station and the sounds of kids saying "Fuck!" as this all was happening.

I just remember my eyes could only see blurs, and they were sticky as hell. I couldn't even open them. I was so tired and hadn't slept well.

I missed my mother.

Mr. Potts came storming in and told me, "Get up, Carl! Get dressed for school!"

"Uh, what? School? *How?* I got kicked out of my school."

"Carl, we have a campus here. GET UP!!"

So I got up and put a shirt on. I had slept in my pants. I slipped on my shoes without socks and walked out into the living room. Everyone was in a single-file line. Mr. Potts was snapping his fingers at me.

"Get to it, Carl! Get in line!"

So I got in line. Then we all walked out into the hallway and lazily marched to wherever we were going. I was so dazed and confused.

•　　•　　•

My first class was insanely boring. It was history class, and our teacher looked like he was severely hung-over. He told us that he was putting on a movie and it was about *The Titanic* and how it sunk when at sea. A bunch of kids were talking about Leonardo DiCaprio and laughing about him. I didn't really care too much.

Then I looked around and saw no girls in the room. And I thought that was odd. I felt very bored and I just didn't really want to talk to anyone because I felt that we wouldn't have anything in common. They were these ghetto-fabs and I was just a skateboarder. I didn't want to be here.

So I went to sleep, like how I did at Bok, and dozed off for about five minutes. Then Mr. Potts, who apparently just walked into the room, awakened me.

"Carl, wake up!" he said.

My eyes felt heavy and I was zoning out. Apparently I was blankly staring up toward nothing in particular at the front of the room. I was told that I was actually sleeping with my eyes open, and that I was entirely unresponsive for about twenty minutes. They didn't even want to shake me awake because they were scared. After that, none of the black kids messed with me. They were probably scared, too.

•　　•　　•

Lots of things happened the entire week, but it came to Friday (the day for parents to pick up their kids at the end of the week) and Mr. Potts and Skip pulled my mother aside and talked to her. I know now that they were talking about something medically wrong with me. They told her that I slept with my eyes open and that they wanted her to have me see someone about it. They said they could help once they know what was going on, and my mother agreed.

•   •   •

That whole weekend as a special emergency situation, my mother took me to see a sleep specialist. We walked into the place on Saturday night. They pretty much put probes all over my head and face, and told me to go to sleep in their bed that was insanely comfy. My mother slept next to me. I was woken up about every twenty minutes the whole time and it sucked so bad. It all sort of blurred together, I guess.

•   •   •

After having the worst sleepless weekend possible, it was back to the old grind at Lowridge. You know . . . I should have felt bad about being a "bad" student—and I don't mean to sound whiny—but I guess I just didn't really have a clue what was going on. The punishment of Lowridge was totally left field in my life, so honestly, I was just going through the motions and was on automatic, in a devoid of my feelings toward the situation. I slept because I saw no point to school. That Monday morning, I got up at six a.m., got to the food hall, ate the best food I had ever eaten (and I really mean that, because Lowridge had more funding for "better food"), and then got off to school, where I slept most of the day, and would receive chair-times as punishment.

The thing about chair-times is that it's just them punishing you annoyingly without having to hit you in the face or something. I still did it because I would sleep sitting up. I often overstayed my chair-time and they would get frustrated with me because I liked chair-time. I know, I know . . . I was a shit-head, but what can I say? During that time sleep was the only form of escape I had!

"Carl, these are the rules," Mr. Potts said, point at a long piece of paper with said rules on the wall, "and you have to follow them."

I looked up. The rules were standard but extensive. They mapped out every single frickin' thing that you could do that was mischievous. Like leaving places, or profanity, or slang, or not cleaning, or whatever. You got a chair-time for whatever.

As the school day was up, we went back to our dorms. Mostly they would have us get dressed to go outside. They wanted us to play football. I thought it was lame because I was a skateboarder/artist. I pretty much just wanted to be left alone. I didn't need to deal with anyone there. So I stayed in my room and drew.

I drew cartoons of things, but mostly aliens in spaceships. I made this one-eyed alien with a long neck and big belly. He had three fingers, and a belly button that was way too over-sized for him. I never made scenes but I always wondered what it would have been like to make a comic book or movie of these creatures. I always had big dreams for myself, even back in those days.

Then Mr. Potts came into my room. "Carl, why aren't you outside?" he said. "We all were wondering where you were. Come and play some football!"

"I can't, sir."

"Why?"

"I'm too depressed to play," I said.

Then he got silent, nodded his head, and walk away from my doorway.

I knew I was in trouble now.

•   •   •

That night we had this meeting. It was a group meeting between all these kids and a therapist. The therapist's name was Sam. Just Sam— nothing more, as far as I was told. He had this very low voice and talked very clearly and over-annunciated everything.

"Hi, everyone. Today we're going to talk about guilt, and feelings of guilt."

"Oh, here we go again . . ." said some other big white kid whose name I can't remember.

"Excuse me, but I'm speaking. There'll be no commentary. Understood?"

The kid didn't say anything.

"Right," Sam continued. "Back to what I was saying. Guilt. We all have felt it. What does it mean to you young men, though? Is it always around you? Do you ever feed into it? Does it eat you up? Show of hands for anyone who feels guilty. . . ."

I raised my hand. I was the only one to raise my hand.

"Ah, Carl, new guy. Glad you took initiative. What makes you feel guilty? Tell us."

"I really don't want to," I said.

"Carl, it's not a bad thing to discuss this. It's entirely confidential. Right, guys?"

Of course they nodded and said, "Yes."

"Might as well . . ." I said. "Okay, basically I'm just guilty for being here. I guess I feel bad for not doing what I was supposed to do."

"Why, Carl?" Sam asked.

"I don't know. I think I just feel bad because I made my mother disappointed. But the weird thing is that it feels more comfortable to make her feel disappointed in me than it does to make her feel proud of me . . . is that strange? I'm really weird about that sort of thing. I feel weird. I feel more comfortable around bad people than I do around successful people; and I think it's because the successful people leave me feeling anxious, uneasy, and small, while the bad people I feel I connect better with."

Nobody said anything.

So I continued, "Um, okay, I guess I'll just keep talking, then. Basically I just feel like I couldn't avoid what I was doing in my school. I did poorly but it's whatever to me because I couldn't avoid it. The whole sleeping in class was just an urge. I didn't want to be there. Shit, I don't want to be anywhere."

"No profanity, please, Mr. Klitz," said Sam.

"Right. Sorry. And yeah, like I said, I just feel guilty because I'm in this body. I just feel guilty for not being able to be a 'somebody,' and do as I'm told."

"Wait, what?" the white kid said. "You don't like to be in your own body? The fuck is that?"

"No swearing!" Sam said. "Guys, *please*, keep it PG13."

"My bad," the kid said. "I just feel like that's a weird thing to feel."

"I just feel stupid," I said, "for not being able to deliver what's expected of me. I feel dumb for trying, so I just sleep. I sleep because I don't want to be here in this life."

"Do you ever dream?" Sam asked me.

"Sometimes. Mostly I dream about my father."

"Why? Did he abuse you?"

I laughed and said, "Lil' direct there, Sammy. *Ha!* Uh . . . basically I have weird dreams of him all the time."

"What was the most recent one?"

"Last night."

"What happened?"

"I dreamed he got beaten up by a bunch of kids in my neighborhood. I just watched. I felt like I was flying around and I couldn't get caught. I was just watching my dad get the shit beat out of him."

"CARL! CHAIR-TIME!" said Sam.

Everyone laughed at him, this guy who actually was probably not good at his job, considering he didn't really care enough to talk more into what I was explaining at that time. I was the only kid speaking up. The guy was just doing his job, that's it, I feel like. I don't know. I always hated how therapists only would ask questions just to get you to say something of an "epiphany" that could "cure" you, which is probably what Sam strived for.

That was the last time I talked about my father to him.

•   •   •

All my friends didn't like the fact that I was going to Lowridge on the weekdays, because I guess I was just never around five days of the week, obviously. They liked the idea of having someone to skate with after school. They had each *other*—I'm not saying they didn't—but I was the best one out of the bunch. I was really talented on a skateboard, and skaters always like to watch other, more better skaters to have some sort of "progression," I guess . . . and because it's fun as heck! They didn't have that anymore. I missed them. Basically all I was seeing day in and day out was a bunch of black kids and white kids who didn't want to be in the same place as one another, and me missing my friends. I needed my friends in my life. During that time, I would have given anything to just hug my friends. Thank God I had those weekends.

•   •   •

About a month and a half later something sparked inside me and I started doing very well. I think it was because the idea of missing friends, my mother not being around, and the fact that I had no skateboarding pretty much and basically I was surrounded by some of the worst, most annoying kids possible. That shaped me up. I wanted to do better. They had weekly meetings at Lowridge with the entire school where they basically would give praise and announce things that are going on within the dorms. Oak House (my dorm) was doing exceptionally well. We got gym privileges and could lift weights whenever we wanted. That was nice, frankly, considering I stayed inside most days. I only wanted to get out because being inside all the time was some of the worst form of depression, and my confidence was building hardcore at that point.

What was crazy about this particular meeting was that they were talking about me. They leveled me up, which was awesome. The school had privilege levels one through four, and I was leveling up almost every week. They were giving me level three this week, which meant I got to be first in line at lunch and I could pick food I wanted before it ran out.

It was nice to have the praise but I felt odd about it; it was like I didn't deserve it. All I was doing was the stuff I was supposed to do, like my mother once said before, but I felt that I wasn't doing anything special. I was doing "okay" in class, I was displaying better sleeping habits, and I was contributing. These were all crazy things to me, especially since I never was that way. I guess my level three was deserved, I think. I just wanted to be a better citizen and help people out as best I could. Most kids I would help out—like by telling them to contribute, to not be influenced by peer pressure, and to always tell the truth to gain a sense of "freedom," if you will—but mostly the kids came and went. Not a whole lot of kids completed the program. They were just sort of there, lollygagging. It was sad but I understood it all. These were kids you couldn't save. They were just here to mess around. I didn't want to play that game anymore. I just wanted to feel good, whatever way possible. It was like looking into my reflection and seeing my past Self fighting with my now Self. But my past Self wouldn't listen to my now Self. The kids were obviously in the past Self mode, so to speak.

● ● ● ●

I don't want to talk about Lowridge anymore because it got super strange. It's odd: The idea of getting better felt like it was phony, and wasn't who I was. The people around me felt like monsters in a broken kingdom. I became a level four, and I was around the privileged kids I always saw, sitting at their own table. They had a movie night every Friday, and I went there. It was me, a chick, and one other kid. They were totally fake. The girl would always talk about having sex with other guys, and the kid did hella drugs when he left the place. I felt dumb for being there, because, though it probably isn't *believable*, I felt that I was "better" and "cured" and able to conquer the world and be a better individual to society. I wasn't the one being "fake" with my treatment because I genuinely wanted to do better.

(Random thought: At one point, back then, they didn't allow soda, but, when being a level four, I was allowed it. The only issue is they didn't let anyone drink caffeine. So all the soda was either Sprite or a strange ginger ale called Schweppes. I picked the Schweppes because it seemed cooler, and newer, than Sprite. I loved it! Now, whenever I go to the grocery store, I always pick it up and think about being a level four till this day. I don't know why I'm mentioning this, but it seems awesome to say.)

So I decided to be a level four but have the privileges of the level ones because I didn't want to be around people who worked their way up with no real accomplishment except beating the system by not doing what they were suppose to outside of the program. That was *not* what I wanted to be around. I wanted to be around my Oak boys because at least they weren't fake with what they did. They did everything honestly, and felt strongly about what they did. They respected that about me, even as I explained it to Sam and all of them in one of our weekly routine meetings about this. They thought it was strange. Oh well . . .

Days flew by those last few weeks. Mr. Potts and Skip were acting pretty emotional with me. They knew how badly I wanted to be a good sport, but they knew I had a bleak outlook on life and crazy depression. It's like I saw the opposite of life from all different directions: the "good" kids did bad, and lied to get their way, and the "bad" kids did bad, but did it so badly that they always got caught in the process—nobody did good, they just all were fighting for happiness. I told Mr. Potts and Skip all the things I wished that could be around. I wanted to be around "real" people. They understood that, I think. I always bonded with them in that way.

• • •

The last week I was there, Skip brought me into his office. He actually was upset that I was leaving.

"Carl, in all my years here, I haven't met a kid that I so deeply cared about. You have inspired so many kids to do better, and you have inspired I and Mr. Potts to be better individuals. That's just something so great, and I want you to know I will miss you when you leave here."

I started to cry. "Thanks, Skippy," I said. "You've been a huge help." And I really thought that. I always tried to help out when I could because I felt that I was around people who actually gave a crap about other people. Sometimes it wasn't true but sometimes it was. I don't know— and I can't ever really explain it.

"No problem," Skip said. "If you ever want to stop by and just visit, you can at any point in time. You're very welcome here."

"Thanks so much."

He gave me a hug.

"Carl, just remember, when you leave here, all the good habits you formed here can stay with you. You're your own human being. I know you're going to be successful. Just keep at it and never give up."

"I won't. I'll do my best," I said. And that was it. I didn't really have much of a chance for growth as an individual. Life just sort of gave me little spurts of confidence here and there, and then often it would crap on me and that would be it. The only good things in life come at you in small waves.

• • •

I left a week later. There was a huge party and it was actually really awesome. We watched movies my last day. It was actually a huge event for Oak House. Not one kid there got a party for leaving, but I did (and I really didn't know why, to be quite honest) . . . but it makes me upset sometimes looking back because I was just doing things I was supposed to do, that's it. Lowridge got shut down years later. They couldn't find state funding for the place to keep it open. Too expensive. What a shame, I always think. And I have no clue what Skip, Mr. Potts, or Sam are doing now. They probably are just living their lives. I sometimes wonder that if they would remember me if I saw them. Probably not.

That would be pretty weird, regardless how much they supposedly like me. I just don't think seeing past people is cool sometimes. And oh yeah, and side note: I decided I wanted to make a full-length skate video with my Structure Skate Team boys. But I had to get all the rest of the footage for it though.

<h1 style="text-align:center">2007 & **early**-2008</h1>

About a month before starting my first day of high school, I had just turned thirteen, and my mother married Ronald and had moved into his house while I was at Lowridge, and didn't bother to tell me. . . . Some would say lots of big life changes were happening.

"I'm not sure what school to go to," I was telling Tom, the brother to the mustache kid I randomly said "I want to be just like YOU" to back when. Tom and I were in front of his house sitting on our skateboards. "Shit worries me," I said.

"Just go to PBC." PBC stands for Palm Beach Central, a school at the sat at beginning of Wellington, when you cross the Okeeheelee bridge.

"Nah man," I said, "Woodhill."

"Fuck that."

"Why?"

"I hear it's straight hood kids."

"True . . ." I sighed. "Most of the Lowridge kids go there."

"See, bro." Tom patted my back. "Go to Central."

"It's out of my district, though."

"Oh yeah, that's right," Tom said. I had moved completely out PBC's school district, upon moving in with Ronald. I was in a pickle.

"But, bro, Terra goes to Woodhill," I said.

"Terra?"

"Mhm."

"You mean the chick who Braydon made you feel up?"

"Yeah," I said.

Tom laughed.

"What's funny about me feeling her tits?" I said.

"Dude, don't go to a school just for a girl."

"I like her."

"Trust me, just go to Central."

"Okay," I said. Then I stood up, got on my board, and did a perfect tre-flip. It was baller-status.

•　　•　　•

A few days before the first day of school, I got a call from Donald and Braydon about skating this grass gap called Vista Gap. It was semi-large and had been in multiple, local, skate videos I had seen. Donald said he was going to pick me up. I got ready, got my backpack on, waited twenty minutes out front and skated flat-ground until they finally showed up.

Driving way down Jog Road, we got to Okeechobee Road and saw that it was a construction site. They were building a plaza there, I could tell. Donald turned into there.

We came up to these gates that were orange-painted and surprisingly complete, like they had just been built. They were open so Donald just drove on in. There were skateboarders already there skating the gap. Vista Gap, I remember, was pretty famous at the time because *KinesisFilms* (a popular skate-site) recently filmed there and got lots of tricks for their montages.

"This gap is small," Donald said to Braydon as he was parking.

"I know. I probably got a shuv-it on it."

"I could probably back-heel it."

"*Pfft!* Bull."

"Watch."

They both got out of the car.

We skated up to the gap. There was a black girl, a Mexican kid, a white kid, and an Asian boy with bright-red DC shoes. I talk about race a lot, because I guess living in Florida race is a big thing to me. I can't explain (but it's not a bad thing). The Asian boy was heel-flipping the gap —or trying to—and he looked so cool doing it. All while facing forward, he would pop high and slam down—you could tell he was hungry to the land the trick.

I dropped my backpack and got out my camera. The kids noticed as I walked up to the gap, got down to the bottom on one knee, and look down into the viewfinder with my fisheye lens (that I had happily just bought at the time) and it looked absolutely amazing.

The Asian kid from back down the runway said, "You ready?"

I yelled, "YEAH!"

He charged it, rolled fast as hell, popped his heel-flip, and landed bolts. Everyone cheered. I put my hand in front of the camera lens while it was still recording after he rolled away to signal that it was a land when I go to import the footage later.

Then we all went to Chipotle. Had laughs and screwed around. Whatever. Just kid stuff.

•   •   •

We decided to skate Conniston three-block. A "block" is just a bigger-size stair step. It was this three-block the size of a long six-stair. I had never been before, but everyone was saying it was perfect so we all drove there and parked at some gas station. While getting out of the car, Braydon said, "Klitz, we gotta hop a fence to get into the school where the three-block is." The place was a middle school, apparently.

"Huh?" I said.

"Klitz, get your camera—stop dickin' around. We gotta hop the fence. Sometimes there's security."

"Okay."

"Get your shit."

All seven of us skated across the street and straight into the fence, threw our boards in the air, rainbowing them the hell over the other side. It was crazy.

"The name's Chewie," the Asian kid said, passing me. He jumped, got to the base-bar, and threw his body over.

"Woah," I said. Then I tried to do the same.

I fell. Nobody cared. Everyone was already over. I gripped my backpack as we ran toward some hallway. They all stopped. Braydon and everyone were against a wall. Around the corner, Braydon looked both ways. When the coast was clear, he turned around to us and said, "Keep going. It's good." So we went.

Finally, we skated all through the hallways at high speeds. We cut hella turns and went this way and that. We ended up at some big courtyard. Beyond that, we went through this huge threshold. There was a big balcony behind the most perfect thing I ever saw: Conniston three-block . . . It just sort of came at me. I don't know what it was, but I'll tell you this: when you see a skate video that you love, one that is super enjoyable and keeps your attention the whole way through, and you see a spot, a famous spot, that you just wish you could ollie or kick-flip or do *something* on, and then you finally see it in front of you . . . there's nothing like it. I know I saw Vista Gap, but this place was just stellar! It's like looking at a legend. That's what made skateboarding so mesmerizing. I can't explain. You'd have to just see it.

So we approached to the three-block. Chewie ran up the steps, and I immediately got my camera out. I put it on auto (as opposed to the "manual" setting for better colors) because I really didn't care about the colors or how they looked, I just wanted to film right away. Auto was quicker. I always just learned cameras as I went.

Chewie, from all the way at the beginning of the run-up, said to me, "Ready?"

I leaned down and pressed the record button, heard a *beep*, and said, "Yep."

Chewie charged it. First try he did a back 180 and it was epic. Bolts. Everything about it was "butter," which is a term used to call something as perfect as possible to be, you know, buttery as all hell. I can't really explain. It all means perfection.

"TEXTBOOK!" Chewie yelled, rolling away.

Later I found out from Chewie that "textbook" means the same as "buttery"—except they have a different vision/feel of the two. I don't know how to explain. It's a skater-thing.

Next thing I knew I heard, "YOU MOTHERFUCKERS!!! I SWEAR TO FUCKING *GOD* WHEN I FUCKING *CATCH* YOU ASSHOLES, IT'LL BE THE END OF YOU!!!"

We all turned around and, sure enough, on the balcony was a big fat security guard waving a nightstick.

"YOU ANIMALS!" he screamed. "YOU BETTER STOP RIGHT THERE!!!"

So of course I saw Chewie, Donald, Braydon, the white kid, black girl, and Mexican kid all start to run.

I ran too while fumbling to put my camera in the bag. I'm not sure to this day how in the heck I got the camera in my backpack so quickly and zipped it up so fast. I guess when adrenaline hits, you just sort of say, "Screw it."

So I was running with them, twisting through all different parts of the hallways. We scattered because we saw the security guard chasing us on a golf cart (serious business)—I had no idea how fast he got to us, but he did.

I ran with Chewie and he was laughing his ass off. We eventually hit grass so we couldn't skate away. Instead we both picked up our boards and started running. I looked ahead and saw three fences.

Those fences seemed impossibly high, but we didn't care. Chewie and I just jumped all three of them in a row like crazy-ass monkeys. *Ooo-Oo-eEee-AH!* That sort of monkey.

After jumping the third one, Chewie turned to me and said, "Klitz, we gotta go around. Oh shit! OH WOW! HAHAHA! This is crazy, bro!"

I was laughing my ass off. I knew we got away.

So we ran around some bushes, crossed some street, and went to Donald's car. Mexican kid, black girl, and white kid all were there, laughing. We looked over, and wouldn't you know it, Braydon is tug-o'-warring with the security guard for dibs on his skateboard. We could hear from across the street what the two of them were saying.

"GIVE ME MY BOARD, RENT-A-COP!"

"YOU FUCKING FUCK!"

"NOW!!"

"YOU'RE GOING TO JAIL! HAHAHA! YOU'LL NEVER SEE YOUR *PRECIOUS* SKATEBOARD!!!"

Then finally, Braydon yanked so hard and pried his board free. He ran his ass off and threw the board over the fence. The security guard was chasing him, but—too late—Braydon was already over.

Behind the fence, the guard was screaming.

"YOU RATS! YOU FUCKING RATS!!! I'LL TELL YOUR PARENTS, YOU RATS!!!"

We all got in our cars and left. Later, I got Chewie's phone number. I'd say we had a good day of skating.

•   •   •

I accepted the fact that I couldn't get Terra to like me. That wasn't too bad, considering I really just wanted to be with my friend, Tom. He was my everything, and still is. So I applied to the Engineering academy at PBC, and I got in! I was super excited! Not because of the program but because I could go to PBC with all my friends. I never liked school, just the *idea* of friends. They accepted everyone into the program though.

•   •   •

I woke up bright and early the first day of school. It was blue outside, but still pretty dark out. I got dressed quickly and ran all the way to the PalmTran bus stop near my house. It sucked because I had to pay, and I realized I would have to pay $.75 every time I would go. (Later, the school arranged for me to ride for free, because it was my only way to get to school.)

The first day I was dressed in tight fitting, maroon, spandex corduroys, a white tall-tee, and all-black DCs. I was looking retarded as hell, I realize now. But back then, forget it, I didn't understand the concept of "fashion-sense."

I got out of the bus, walked across the street, and thought, Hey, I'm a damn high-schooler now! I thought this was rather crazy. The movies I saw about high school always showed bullies and kids always talking about sex and drugs and parties. Little did I know, all those things were somewhat true. But at the time I thought it was probably just movies being far-fetched.

I walked around everywhere looking for Tom. He was somewhere at the front of the school talking to his friends. That's the thing about high school: you had your "high school friends" and you had your "real ones." When I finally found him, we gave dap, he told me how "ridiculous" I looked, and then the bell rang to get to first period.

The excitement faded quickly because everything turned to panic! Everyone was running in all different directions. I had no idea where to go. I ran around and around and I couldn't find anything on my schedule.

Then I saw Donald.

"Hey, Donald! YO!"

He turned around.

"Oh shit, Klitz, what's up, bro! Nice threads. You look gay as fuhhh."

"Thanks." I shook my head. "Anyways, how do I get here?" I showed him my schedule.

"Fuck if I know," he said.

"Thanks," I said, and then walked off, where I found a teacher who directed me to the right classroom.

•　　•　　•

All day long it was nothing but teachers putting up a front and telling us kids that they are the bosses and they won't tolerate us freshmen being late or back talking.

I soon found out it was mostly bullshit, because the teachers themselves were just like the kids and looking to seek their supposed happiness on the daily grind, and quickly I didn't give a crap about school after that first day. I came home, got on my iTouch, and jacked off to iPinkVisual, the only porn site for iTouches at the time, with two black guys with ten-inch throbbing penises screwing the crap out of some white chick, deeply, and her screaming, "More! Deeper!" and coming.

I came so hard, too.

•　　•　　•

During my Engineering class my teacher, Mr. Knauff, was explaining the idea that energy always depreciates whenever you put energy toward something. Upon which I asked him, what if you put magnets in a circle and spin it on a turbine to create perpetual motion? Everyone of those frickin' nerds laughed and Mr. Knauff said, "It's impossible, Carl," and he rolled his eyes and shook his head.

"But if we had perpetual motion," I said, "there wouldn't be anymore jobs in the world. We could just have machines work for us. We wouldn't need people anymore."

"Yes, but it's impossible. Nobody has ever discovered perpetual motion. It's impossible."

"Just know that'll be the end of the world when it does get discovered."

Then everyone shut up after I said that, and Mr. Knauff, again, rolled his eyes and continued ranting on about some bullcrap generator that, he claimed, we would have to build eventually, and everyone in the class blowing their load over the idea to do "hands-on" training, engineering-wise.

A kid turned turned to me and said, "Yo, what's your name?"

I looked at him. He had blonde straight hair, tall, and my age. He was a good-lookin' kid, the kind that women would pride themselves on if they were to date him. "Carl," I said.

"Cool. You skate around Jog, right?"

"Yeah. How'd you know?"

"I see you around. You shred. The name's John."

"Sup, John."

"We should hang at lunch."

"Okay," I said.

Then I looked down at my seat and felt something weird brush against my arm. I looked down and saw nothing. I lifted my arm and there was a little pea-sized bump in the middle of the elbow and armpit, but I thought nothing of it.

• • •

At lunch one day, John and I were walking and talking about skating this spot called Liberty Ledges and discussing how Bradley Kromer, the best local skateboarder ever (who now is a professional skateboarder), did a nose-blunt on it. Which was especially impressive considering there's no runway and there's a pole in front of you before you pop the board. John said it's some freak thing.

As we walked, I saw this pale, tall white kid walking with two chicks. He had his arm around them and everyone was pouring out the classes. A kid came up behind this white kid and pulled down his gym shorts, revealing that he was "going commando." From where John and I stood, we saw his ass. Apparently, from the front-side view he had a nine-incher because he lifted his gym shorts up slowly, even as everyone saw this happen and laughed. But he had the last laugh, I guess.

Just as John and I walked up to this table for lunch, I saw this short kid who I noticed was in my Engineering class. His name was Margo. He and a few other skate-nerds were all sitting at this table. John introduced me.

"This is Klitz."

Everyone stared at me. A kid said, "*The* Carl Klitz?"

"Yup," I said, thinking they were messing with me.

"Dude! You know Jimmy White!"

"Yeah . . ." I was unsure what he was getting at. "Your point?"

"He's on *KinesisFilms*. You're famous by association."

I laughed and said, "It's not that crazy, bro."

John and I scooted into a seat. They, for the remainder of the hour lunch period, talked about chicks that were hot, that sat from afar and walked by. They were all "pussies," I thought, even though they were all the same skateboarders that did the same skateboard shenanigans.

•   •   •

I got home one day after school and went up into my mother's room and said, "Mom, there's something I want to show you."

She stood up. "What is it, son?" She paused the television. "You okay?"

"I'm not too sure," I said, "but I gotta show you something."

"Okay." My mother stood up and came up to me. She said, "What's going on?"

I lifted my arm and showed her something that I found to be odd. I said, "Look." The tiny bump on my arm from Engineering class had enlarged to a golf-ball size lump in the middle and to the right of my left tricep. It was bulging. I said, "I don't really know what this is, but it doesn't look too good, Mom."

She gasped. "Holy fuck." My mother never cursed, really. Only on "special occasions," if that makes any sense. "We gotta go to my office tomorrow. You're taking off school."

"Sweet!"

"Carl, this is serious. This isn't just a day off. That's not good at all . . . not good at all."

That's when I knew to take things more seriously.

•   •   •

The next day, my mother just brought me into her office, without an appointment.

"Excuse me, excuse me," my mother said to another nurse, dragging me into the place. "Where's Dr. Khamberlain?"

"Where's his appointment?"

"This is an emergency."

"The doctor is in her office—but you do know she's going to be pissed, Sharon. You need an appointment. You know this. Seriously."

"I'll take my chances."

My mother pulled me along to the doctor's office. She didn't knock. We just went on in.

"Dr. Khamberlain!" my mother blurted, "look at *this!*" My mother held up my arm and showed her boss my lump.

"Holy smokes," she said. "Woah. You need to take him to the ER. That looks like something out of my realm. Go to the ER."

"Can I take off?"

"Yep. Just let me know what happens."

"Thanks, boss."

"Oh yeah, and Sharon?"

"Yes?"

"Next time he really should make an appointment."

My mother and I left the office.

•   •   •

Hospital time. Great. Grand. Wonderful. My mother and I were pretty much tripping-out at this point. My mother signed me in, we waited in the waiting room for a while, and I was eventually seen some hours later. Hospitals are like that I guess.

So I was there in the room, still waiting with my mother. She was just trippin' out on me.

"My baby, aww. My baby!"

"Mom, stop."

"I'm so nervous!"

"It'll be *okay*, Mom."

"My baby is sick . . . It's not okay!"

"Mom, stop babying me. I'm in high school."

She didn't say anything.

At long last, a Mexican doctor came in with a clipboard in hand.

" 'Ello!" He shut the door behind himself. He pulled a chair out, sat, and said, "What seems to be the problem?"

"My son is, is . . ." my mother was stuttering. "Just . . . *look!*" She grabbed my arm and showed the doctor my lump.

"Woah," he said.

"I know!"

"That's pretty big. *Wow!* Let me take a look." He got closer to me, said a bunch of "hmms" and "I-sees" and stuff. Then he said, "He has to stay here for a full evaluation. I'm not too sure what this thing is. It looks very odd."

My mother started to cry.

"Please, doctor, please help my son!"

"I will."

I face-palmed myself. My mother is embarrassing.

•   •   •

After two MRI scans, being transferred to four hospitals, having blood taken from me every four hours of the day, including in the middle of the night when I was sleeping, they came to the conclusion that I had brain cancer, on account of the fact that they found "masses" in my entire body. They told me that they'll take good care of me, but everyone didn't want to keep me long for the "liability" reasons of the matter. Hard to believe it, but it's true! People with cancer are not easy to keep around, especially if you're not equipped to treat them. I wasn't that sad about it; I was just sort of expecting it to occur. For some reason, I always thought I wouldn't live very long. I can't explain. After they saw I was going to stay there a while (since I was hospitalized for two weeks straight) the nurses decided to let me eat whatever I wanted. And what does a fourteen-year-old crave the most? I must've asked for ice cream all day every day. Eventually I cleared out their fridge. I began to get fat. My mother actually came into my room one day, holding back tears, to tell me that she wanted me to walk around the hospital halls with her. I wanted to as well, but I was very weak. I was lying in bed for two weeks and my feet were leaned forward the entire time. They felt stiff and weak and I couldn't get them to work properly. I was walking very slowly. My mother had to guide me around the hallways. The nurses looked very sad to see me like that. I just wanted to get better; I wanted to walk, to breathe, to live (even though at the same time I didn't want to). Then I ended the day with looking into the mirror to find out that I had clearly gained about ten pounds. It's amazing how fast you can let yourself go, if you let yourself do it.

•　　•　　•

Watching TV in my room, I heard a soft, quiet, *calm* knock at my door. I grabbed the remote, paused the movie that was playing, and said, "Come in."

The guy that came in was a priest. He actually was dressed in the whole black get-up with the white-collar thing on his neck and the perfectly pressed pants, loafers, all that.

"Hello," he said. "You're Carl, right?"

"Yep."

"Great. May I have a seat?"

"Yep."

He sat down at the end of my bed.

"So, Mr. Klitz, I'm hearing about your, uh, health problems and what that means for you. Sounds extremely, uh, unnerving, is that right?"

I said, "Yep," bored out of my mind.

"I see . . . well, how are you feeling about all of this?"

"I'm not feeling. I'm just trying to get out of here."

"Why are you trying to get out of here?"

"Because I want to skate. I'm bored."

"I see . . . well, do you really like skateboarding?"

I wanted to smack him, he was asking stupid questions. "Yep," I said.

"Hm, well, Mr. Klitz, I wanted to ask you what you think of God when it comes to this matter of your illness."

"Why?"

"Because I just wanted your thoughts."

"I don't know. I haven't really even thought much on it, I guess."

"Oh," he said, and scratched his head. "Er . . . this is difficult for me to explain, but you do know your illness is . . . life threatening. Right?"

"Yep."

"So what do you think of dying?"

I kept silent. I didn't know what to tell him.

"It's okay," he finally said, breaking the silence, "I understand. It's a heavy thing to face. But I wanted to let you know that if God lets you go, it's going to be your time. He has a plan for you."

"That's cool," I said.

"Are you sad about it?"

"Nope. Just dandy."

"Am I upsetting you."

"Yep."

"Do you want me to leave?"

"Yep."

"Okay, Mr. Klitz, I'll leave. But I just wanted you to know that God has a plan for you and that you're okay."

He stood up, flatted his shirt, and walked out. And, get this: At the same time he was walking out of the door, my mother came inside. She started crying. I guess it was because a priest was in my hospital room talking to me about death. Was I scared? Not really. I just wanted to die soon, so I could get on with my life.

•　　•　　•

The very next day, by the time I decided to want to die, and to prepare for it, I was told by one of the head doctors that my lab results came back and they found that actually the root of my issue was actually viral, and they were sorry for concluding I had brain cancer, which they really thought was so. I had cat-scratch fever. False alarm. Crazy. So they told me to take some antibiotics. My mother cried tears of joy, and I was sent home and off into a continued life that I accepted to leave just a day before. It's crazy how life works. I really don't understand any of it sometimes.

•   •   •

In Photography class, my only class with Tom, I was being asked, in front of everyone, by my teacher of what the hell happened in the two weeks I was gone.

"I had cancer," I lied.

The whole class gasped.

"But I'm fine, now. It's cool," I assured them. "Honest."

My teacher was saying how insane it is, and that she was glad I was alive. Tom was really, really concerned, and so were a bunch of other people. But within twenty-four hours everyone soon forgot about it and treated me normal.

It's crazy how when you appear to be dead, people are quick to give their regards.

•   •   •

During lunch, as I was sitting with the nerd-boarders and John, Tom brought me aside. I thought he was going to indulge more into my hospital stay, but he didn't. Sympathy is always great when you have grounds to do it.

"Klitz," Tom said, "yo. I gotta tell you something."

I stood up from my seat, got off the bench, and said, "Yeah?"

"Okay, Klitz, a friend of mine says that you—uh, basically a friend of mine says that some girl likes you."

"Really?"

"Yeah."

"What's her name?"

"Tenna."

"That's a weird name, bro."

"I know. She's really skittish. She likes you a shit-ton. Thinks you're hella cute."

"How does she like me when I've been in the hospital?"

"That's the thing, she's been liking you—the whole year, bro."

"She hot?"

"She's my girlfriend's friend. She's cute."
"Cute or hot?"
"Cute."
"I gotta see her, Tom-burger."
He laughed.

•   •   •

Couple days later, I saw Chewie.
"Chewie!" I said.
He was walking with swagger, listening to his iPod and mean-muggin' everyone who passed him. I ran up to him.
"Chewie!" I said, tapping him.
He pulled out his right earphone. "Yeah?" he said.
"Bro! It's Klitz!"
"Oh shit, man, what's up, my nigga?"
"Nothin' much. What you doin' after school?"
"I don't know. Might skate."
"Where?"
"This one place near my house I found."
"Can I come?"
"Uh, if you want. You got your camera?"
"No, but we could skate tomorrow, or go to my place and skate around local."
"Nah, just come over. You got your board?"
"Yeah."
"Okay. We'll skate."
"Sweet!" I said.
Then we parted ways because the late bell was about to ring. You never had time to talk with that damn late bell looming up on you.

•   •   •

After school, I waited by the PalmTran bus stop, where everyone mostly waited, and saw Chewie crossing the street. He was still walking with over-the-top swagger, and he just looked like a crazy-ass kid. I remember that clearly. Like he was a gangster. An Asian gangster. I ran up to him.
"Yo, Chewie!" I yelled.

He looked at me, grinned, and started sprinting across the street away from me.

I ran after him and into a semi-rich neighborhood called Olympia. As I was chasing after him, crossing through the bushes and into this neighborhood, I saw him start walking again. I ran up next to him, winded.

"Shit, *bro!* Why you runnin'?"

"Klitztopher, what up, man?"

Chewie was always bazaar. You could never tell what his actions meant. He just ran because it was exciting for him to mess with me I guess.

"Nothing, man," I said. We were walking and talking. Then this girl started walking up behind us. She bumped into me. Chewie looked her over and said, "Tenna. What's up! You got the homework for English 1?"

"Yeah, I'll get it to you later," she said. Then she looked at me and said, "Hey, Carl." She smiled.

"Hey," I said. Tenna was lanky, had braces, and she had a bit of a slouch. She wasn't bad looking. What was crazy is that I knew she liked me, so I was pretty weirded-out by that notion. But then it hit me. I looked at Chewie and said, "—Wait a sec . . . you're in English 1, Doo?"

"For some reason I didn't pass it," he said.

"Aren't you a senior?"

"Yes, Klitz."

Tenna look at both of us. "I'll see you guys later," she said. "Bye, Klitz." And that's when I knew she just found out my nickname.

"Come inside my crib," Chewie said.

•   •   •

When we got inside, Chewie's house smelled oriental. I knew it would because he was Asian, but this was a true Asian smell. It had this brothy, sort of spicy *new* smell that was completely euphoric. I still say to this day that he and his family always made me feel calm—the whole Zen fashion. The house made me feel like it was my sanctuary in an odd way. The singing bowls with dragons looping around themselves; the sounds of Asian music humming and chanting; the way a totally American house could be transformed into an organized, clean dojo. Maybe these were the reasons I attached to Chewie so greatly. I think I'll always have his back until the day either one of us dies.

I saw this small white-colored yorkie, Pucci, run up and start barking at me. "PUCCI!" Chewie said, "STOP MESSIN' AROUND!" She was going ape-shit. I guess she didn't like strangers.

"Is she going to bite?" I asked.

"No—and take your *shoes* off."

He took his off, and I took mine off.

We got to the kitchen and the pots and pans were hanging by hooks. Everything was always in place. If you looked in his drawers, there were literal chop sticks and soup spoons. I loved it.

"Yo, Klitz, want to try some good food?"

"Hm?"

"Okay. Ever had beef jerky?"

"Yeah."

"Okay. I want to show you some shit you will never have in your life." Chewie pulled open the pantry and brought out a Ziploc bag with this weird-looking, black crap inside it.

"What the hell is *that?*" I asked him.

"It's Octopus Beef Jerky. Try it." He reached inside, nibbled on one, and then reached inside again to hand me one.

I grabbed it, looked it over, examined it, heard Chewie say to "just try it, pussy," and put it into my mouth. Mmmmm. I remember it. It was actually really flavorful, but sort of gooey. It tasted like regular beef jerky, but it had a gummy sort of bite. Very chewy.

"What'd you think?" Chewie asked me.

"Shit's good."

"Fuck yeah. Yo, you want to skate the school?"

"Which one?"

"It's this Wellington elementary school. It's fun."

"Awesome." I didn't say anything more.

Then Chewie sort of looked blank-faced and randomly said, "Yo, you want to see some of my old footage?"

I thought it was odd, but I said, "Sure."

We went upstairs to his room. It was actually like a college dorm: a bed, bookshelf, no TV, a messy desk, and a MacBook Pro. Chewie opened up the Macbook Pro.

"Come check *this* out," he said.

I leaned forward, watched him. The cursor moved around a bit, then he opened a file. It had a bunch of clips together. He looked very young. He did lip-slides, back-heels over sets, 50-50s, nollie heel-flip noseslides, and a shit-ton of other stuff I don't even remember.

"Wow," I said. "Can I have this?"

"Why?"

"For this video I'm making."

"What video?"

"Donald, Braydon, Jimmy, Tom, they're all in it. I want your footage to be in it too. It's called *The No Way Video*."

"Okay," he said.

Then he put it all on a CD and I left for home.

•   •   •

I remember clearly that there was this girl named Pat and she had the best ass that anyone at our school had ever seen. Literally. Her ass was so big and so round and so heart-shaped that when she walked it actually was pushing OUT and WAGGING back and forth. That ass. I couldn't believe it. God took his time with that ass. Anyways, I would actually wait a little bit after the bell rang—mostly because the PalmTran would take twenty-five minutes to get to my bus stop. I would wait near the actual bus-loop, where all those yellow buses were. I would wait, alone, without my friends, just to watch this majestic ass walk by. And there it would be, beautiful and big and proud, and I would stare. I think everyone stared— I wouldn't know because I was staring too. That ass. Jesus. It was a sign that God did really exist. And she was stuck-up. I always found that beautiful women, at least in Florida, were always, always stuck-up. I think she had a boyfriend, who was probably a jock. I just don't get why women that are hot decide to pick men that have high replication value, or some crap. I just don't know. Whatever. Then I would go to my bus-loop, go home, skate, eat dinner, don't do homework, stay up all night, maybe jack it to porn, and then have a dreamless sleep . . . repeat.

•   •   •

I never really saw my father much, but I was supposed to see him on weekends. He mostly was busy with work or getting trashed with friends. My visits with him are all a blur, honestly. My parents (Ronald and my mother) called my father to come in when he dropped me off from his weekend with me.

(This was the last time I saw my father, because this was the same time that he got into trouble with a class-action, multi-lawsuit sort of thing. He stole from hundreds of people. He would take the material money from his screen-enclosure business and his customer's jobs to buy Cocaine, or houses, or whatever else he wanted. So yeah, he was robbing Paul to pay Peter for a while. Never saw him after this. Also, I have no idea what is the truth of the matter: if he really was stealing or anything—this is all just speculation but I think there's part truth to it.)

He came in, tired. He looked stressed. He always looked tired and stressed. It was probably because he was coming down off drugs or alcohol. He sat at our dining-room table. Ronald spoke first.

"Stephen, I got some things to explain. First, Carl has been doing very poorly in school. He doesn't do his homework, he always skates, he sleeps in class, he always has us talking to him about these issues, and he continues to do them. We thought you should know. . . ."

I had my hands to the sides of my head, my elbows on the table.

Ronald said, "Get your arms off the table."

I put my arms to my sides.

After a sigh, looking over at my mother, then at Ronald, then at me, my father said, "Well . . . Carl . . . um . . . er . . . Well, *I* never did well in school. I mean *hell* I probably *never* went to class! HAHAHAHHA! I just hung out with friends, mostly"—and later on in life, I learned to never, ever followed in his footsteps for anything, ever—"if you know what I mean, Carl. HAHAHAHA!!"

And my Dad sat back in his seat. That's all he had to say.

Ronald looked pissed. He was biting his lip, then stood up.

"Okay, Stephen. I just thought I'd let you know. You can leave."

Ronald guided my father out the door and they spoke a bit outside, no yelling though. Then Ronald came back inside. He looked pissed. He had the kind of look that said: "Who the hell tells his son the wrong things he is doing are okay." Ronald never said it, though. He just went to the living room and watched TV. My mother sat in the dining room for a while. I went to my room to edit my skate videos. It was all I had to help keep my mind busy from life's trials.

•   •   •

I skated after school with Chewie almost everyday, and even weekends as well. I skated all around my neighborhood with him, and I skated all around his neighborhood with him. Sometimes we would even go downtown and just kick it at Starbucks. Even Tom would tag along. All my friends loved Chewie. He was our little Asian golden-boy. He knew what he was doing on a skateboard. He would ollie this, and ollie that. Ollie, ollie, ollie. He loved Anthony Pappalardo, a professional skateboarder, and so in turn I did too because Chewie was pretty much a father to me. Even though he was incredibly odd in more ways than one. He once skated with me down to the Starbucks about five blocks away from his house in Wellington, which was about five miles from my house—I always had to take the PalmTran to go see him, one way or another. Anyways, we skated to Starbucks—or were going to, I thought— and then, looking back at me and skating ahead down the sidewalk, he grinned, picked up his board, and ran off somewhere. At which point I didn't follow him back home and just went back to his house, where his mother fed me steak. He came home an hour later, pissed off because I left him in the dust. I just laughed. I thought it was hilarious in a weird way, because of obvious reasons: it backfired, I got steak, and he was lost in his own neighborhood probably looking for Yours Truly. It was rather funny, I think.

Besides his antics, Chewie and I always got footage. He got more footage than everyone combined in *The No Way Video*, in a matter of two months, Even more than Little Jimmy, who was the best one in the group. Chewie would do smith-grinds, 50-50s, nose-slides, heel-flips, back-heels, nose-manuals to other stuff, and a ton of tricks that I hadn't seen before. Basically he would look at spots in a totally new way that I couldn't envision. This heavily influenced me, and it stuck with me during my skating career. I just wanted to be the best, but he wanted to be the best, humble, and the most original. So yeah, that's the thing about skateboarding: Everyone wants to be the best, but they are not willing go the extra mile when it comes to being original. That changed quickly when new videos came out with this same idea.

Fully Flared, this skate video that every skater and their mother had anticipated (including Chewie, heavily so), had come out and was sold at Shreder Sheder. Chewie and I went in and bought it, went back to my place, and basically became mesmerized by the film. It changed the way I would film, edit, skate—everything. It was a revolution to skateboarding. Shortly after that *SkateFL 2*, this skate video that featured Bradley Kromer, Jo-jo Ragalo, and a bunch of other Shreder Sheder heads, released and was premiering in Miami. Chewie, Tom, and I skated down to Shreder Sheder because we didn't have a car to see this video in Miami. We were bummed, but Shreder Sheder was dead so it wasn't that big of a deal to us. We just wanted to hang out, enjoy the shop, look at a few things, maybe even watch some skate videos, preferably local.

We saw this guy in there with this crazy hair. I forget his name. He worked at Shreder Sheder. Anyways, he told us that he had *SkateFL 2* on his computer (he was told that he wasn't allow to show anyone), and he told us that he'll show us it because he thought we were "cool" kids. We actually were homies with him. So we watched this skate video and basically I was even more mesmerized by the skateboarding than *Fully Flared*, only because of Bradley Kromer, my favorite local skateboarder that I had watched since I was in middle school. His new part was truly amazing. He had the best songs, he did tricks that I didn't even *think* were possible, and his did everything with amazing style and precision. Till this day *SkateFL 2* is one of my top favorite skateboarding videos.

Those two videos came out, and they basically changed my life—or my skateboarding life, to be exact. I had been skating with Chewie almost every day, I had seen brand-new footage of the top local skateboarders in West Palm Beach, and I saw *Fully Flared*, the top skate video that to this day, is famous for being revolutionary. I'd say freshmen year was pretty great, minus actually being at school.

•　　•　　•

Chewie was always influenced by things he was into at the time, like most people in their lives, and he showed me rapper Mac Dre. He loved Mac Dre; everything about Chewie's eyes showed that he could actually be friends with the guy and fully level with him. He showed me the gift of California's king of hip-hop. I still will always listen to Mac Dre's work and smile at the good times I had listening to him in Chewie's white Honda Civic and riding down those open streets in City Place at the crack of noon.

•   •   •

Braydon called me about a party at Allie's house. Allie was Braydon's friend. Frankly, I didn't want to go because I hadn't ever been to a huge party before. It was in October so obviously it was a halloween party, and you had to dress up as your favorite characters and creatures. Donald, Braydon, and Jimmy, they all dressed as skateboarders . . . figures. I did too.

Basically Donald drove up in his car and I was all like, "I'm not so sure about this, guys," and they said, "Pussy." "Pussy" was always the word I would hear when I was scared.

Donald parked, they all got out, and I stayed. From outside I saw Braydon turn back around, see me, turn back to Donald, ask him something, take his keys, and walk back over to the car, upon which he unlocked it. "Dude," he said to me, "what in Hell's name are you doing?"

"I don't know, dude. I think I'm going to stay here."

He shook his head. That was it. There was nothing for him to say other than that. So he locked the door and walked away.

I stayed in that car the entire night, watching ghouls and goblins roam about drunkenly, puking and reeking havoc on everything around me. They looked so happy and free. They looked like they were living life. And I was stuck looking out that glass window, wondering where I went wrong with deciding to join them.

The next morning, I found out that Donald was peed on by Jimmy, that Braydon had sexual intercourse with four girls at the same time, that Teddy smoked so much weed he "saw God," and that I was, indeed, rather "pussy"-like.

We skated downtown City Place, and got no clips. What a pity.

Summer came, and freshmen year was obviously a blur, only because I had been (somewhat) partying so much with all my friends. I don't want to say all their names in this account because, frankly, it would be too extensive a project to accomplish. I had many, many friends, and that's all anyone should have to know.

I had been grounded virtually my entire freshmen career, and I ended up getting a 0.8 GPA in all my classes. The school threatened me several times to get my grades better since I was in the Engineering academy: a magnet program that apparently was highly requested but had a high acceptance rating. The academy was actually a great thing, because it provided students with the tools to succeed in said major, but the issue was that I hated Engineering. However, I maintained a 3.0 GPA in that class only. Odd, right? I think I was *trying* to. I can't remember.

•   •   •

Chewie, Tom, and I were skating a lot more. We would skate almost everyday if we could during that freshmen year summer of mine. Tom had to work at Little Caesars, and Chewie worked at CVS. If they had to work, we didn't skate. It was that simple. I actually told them to quit their respective jobs. They just looked at each other, grinned, laughed maybe, and told me that that wasn't that simple, and that they need money . . . I didn't get it back then.

It was a Saturday and all three of us actually found a day where we all were "free"—meaning *they* were free, I was always free. We decided to skate this new skatepark that just opened up: Wellington Skate Park. We get there and, basically, it was packed to the brim. Everyone and their grandma was there.

"This is a packed rat," Tom said.

"Even fruit-booters are here," I said. Fruit-booters are really roller-bladers. I was mocking them, *duh!*

"We can't skate here," Chewie said to Tom and I.

"So," I said. "We gotta try."

Needless to say, we tried . . . and failed.

We must've skated there for about fifteen minutes before we were about to leave. Just before we were getting out of the gates, a big Mexican kid came up to us. He tapped Tom on the shoulder.

"Tommy-boy!" he said. "You skate?"

"Hell yes! Dude! José! You skate, too?!"

"Yup. And is this Klitz?"

"Yeah, man."

"*The* Carl Klitz?"

"Just Klitz," I said.

"Yeah, I'm a huge fan. What's up? Where you bros skating?"

"We don't know," Tom said, "we're thinkin' Boyton."

"Oh, hell yeah! That's what's up! Could I come?"

Tom nodded, gestured with his board to follow us, and that was how I met the kid.

•   •   •

José was sixteen. Six feet zero inches tall, Mexican, sarcastic, decent at skating, hella funny kid, went to PBC with Tom, Chewie and I. He knew Tom because I guess they took classes together. Science, I think. And I think Chewie was in there too, because Chewie wasn't opposed to him joining us—which he usually was weird about that sort of thing, on account of his paranoia. And as we were coming up to Boyton Skatepark, José asked the car, "You guys wanna smoke?"

"Fuck yeah," Chewie said.

Tom, Chewie, and José, all smoked together in the car. They asked me to smoke and I said "No." I always said, "No." I think it was because I was scared of it because my mother always told me it was bad for anyone. My big brother, Stephen Jr., went to jail many, many times for weed and breaking-and-entering. My father, Stephen Sr., was just a piece of crap. They both smoked. Together, sometimes. So I associated weed with "failure." It was a weird thing to think, I guess.

"Pussy," José, a stranger to me, said.

We got out of the car, headed over to Boyton. Nobody was there, mainly because everyone was skating at Wellington. Wellington was shittier than Boyton, but who's to judge?

Chewie went into the gates, threw his board down, and charged for whatever ramp. I was walking with José and Tom, just behind Chewie, about to get into the gate.

"I hate this place," Tom said.

"It's, eh, I don't know, it's okay," José said. "I'd rather skate street."

"That's what me and Klitz always say."

"Dead as fuck, I swear."

"Ditto," I said.

Then we got into the gate, dropped our boards, and started skating.

I kick-flip 5-Oed the ledge that was just in front of the quarter-pipe. I looked up and saw Chewie as he heel-flipped the small-ish six-stair. He landed bolts. I cheered.

"YEEEEEE!!!"

He went up the kicker and ollied over this bench that was right after it. He always sped whenever he skated. Luckily, no kids were there, so in a way it was worse, his speeding.

I looked over and Tom was back-180ing the hip ramp before this quarter-pipe. He didn't land, but he tried a few more times and got it.

I glanced briefly to the six-stair, for some odd reason, and noticed José charging toward the thing. He popped the biggest front-side flip I had ever *seen!* He caught it, and it was like slow-motion. Then he turned the rest of the way and landed. Perfect. The *clap* sound of when he landed was so clean. I was impressed. He rolled away, hands to his sides.

"HOLY *SHIT!*" I heard Chewie shout. Then, shouting higher-pitched, "TEXTBOOK!!!"

Tom charged toward José, saying, "GODDAMN, JOSÉ!!" José grinned, Tom and him gave dap.

I skated up to them. "Guys," I said, "we should skate that big two-block down the street."

José said, "You mean 'Warehouse'?"

"Yup."

"I front-side flipped that shit."

"I got a cammy."

"Wanna film?"

"Is Chewie Asian?" I said.

José and Tom started laughing.

"Then I guess lets go," I said. Then I shouted toward Chewie, who was skating the hip ramp or something, "YO! LETS SKATE WAREHOUSE!"

He nodded. And we all left.

•   •   •

All of my friends were skaters during this time. That means they usually liked the idea that if you landed a trick everyone in the world would see it. The way they all would see it was by footage.

We drove all the way from Boyton Skatepark and went basically two miles. This place was trash. It was an abandoned lot; totally closed off and fenced around. I think the hurricanes destroyed it. It was a big concrete slab with two blocks everywhere, a one-flat-seven, and other little things. It was a loading dock, I should say.

"So which one you skating, José?" I asked.

"I don't give a shit. Whichever."

Then he went to the middle one. I followed, set my camera bag down, and got the cammy out. I pointed downward while standing. The angle made it look huge.

"GO!" I said.

And José charged for it, pushing and pushing. I saw him approach the edge, pop up, flip his board, turn 180 degrees, and then he fell.

"Shit, you were close," I said to José.

"Nah, nigga. Not even there. Fuck this shit." And then he jumped over his board, lying flat beside him, wood up, and slammed his feet into its middle, snapping it in half. "Fuck this board," he said. "I hate Mysterys."

Then I looked up and saw red, blue flashing lights.

"COPS!" I heard Tom say. "RUN, RUN, RUN!!"

I saw him and José gun it with their boards. Chewie was running toward me.

"Klitz. Get your ass *moving!*"

"I have to put my camera away."

Too late. The cop was parked, sirens on for a sec, then off, and then already running toward us. We had no time.

"Go against the wall, now!" the cop said.

Chewie said, "Fuck."

We sat against Warehouse's walls on our boards.

"Where are your friends going?" the cop clearly asked Chewie, the obviously older one.

"Fuck if I know."

"You better know. Call them. I want them here. Now."

"*I'll* call them," I said. Then I got my cellphone out and dialed. I waited and waited. Finally, Tom picked up.

"Klitz! Where you at?"

"Dude, the cop got us. He wants you guys here."

"Fuck that, niggie!"

"Look. Get here. Now."

I hung up.

About five minutes later, the two of them showed up. José sat first, Tom stood. The cop was standing with his arms crossed.

"Need I.D.'s. Now."

We all pulled them out, handed them over. The cop eyed them.

"José, huh?" he said.

José nodded.

"Where's your board?"

"Under there."

"Under where?"

We all start laughing. The cop said "underwear."

"What's so funny?" the cop asked us. "I could put you all in juvey."

Then José started talking in Spanish. The cop was Mexican. They both talked. Then the cop laughed.

All I remember is we got away because José spoke something in Spanish. We all called it a day and went on home. Close call.

•   •   •

Tom and I were skating together around my neck of the woods, at the Publix near my house. We pretty much were skating flat-ground— nothing *too* crazy—and we were having pure fun. I missed Tom and hadn't seen him in a bit during that time. Then it was time to go back home so we skated back to my house on Military Trail and were going very, very fast. I remember looking behind me and seeing Tom fall on the ground. I was laughing like crazy. Then all I remember hearing was a skid and a crack. I fell forward and my back pushed my arm into the ground ahead of me. My arm pretty much was crushed and wrapped around my back. I broke my arm and was yelling, "Fuck! I broke my *arm!* FUCK! I literally have to be in a *cast* for a *month!* FUCK!!" I wasn't even scared really. I was just pissed that I had a wear a cast and that I wouldn't skate for a month. So, Tom and I skated back to my house. Tom looked sort of speechless. I got to my house, woke my mother up, and showed her my arm. She was calm as rain. Tom left. My mother told me I had to take a shower to go to the hospital. I told her that that was silly, but I was yelling it at her. She told me that I had to. So we got into the shower and she had a washcloth over my penis. I was cupping it with one of my hands and she was washing my body with another washcloth. We finally got done. She had to dry me. Which sucked because I couldn't hold my washcloth and have her dry me. So she cupped my penis with a washcloth over it. It wasn't, like, *weird* or anything looking back on it. But it was uncomfortable having to go through it. So then we got into her SUV and went to the hospital. I remember when I was lying down in the hospital room there was a man wearing a Hawaiian shirt. My mother knew him from college. She said he was a "great doctor." He said, "We gonna give him the *good* stuff." He came up to me and put a needle in my arm, and he said, "Bye, bye." All I remember is nothing. Just dreaming. I remember being gone and I couldn't see much. I thought the doctor was skating on the ceiling. Then I woke up. He was gone. I was yelling, "I'm so high!" to my mother. She was laughing and telling me to shut up. I was laughing too. "I'm so HIGH!" I was saying. I looked over and my arm was wrapped up and casted. "I'M SO HIGH!" I bellowed. "DAMN!!" And we stayed until the morning. I had to handle a cast for a month.

•   •   •

I went to this place that was on Jog Road. It was a neighborhood, and it had a perfect ledge to skate. All the skaters went there. I remember there were neighborhood kids that skated there every single day, and they were pretty damn good because they actually had a "spot" to skate. That was great for them. I remember I went there with Tom. There were multiple black kids there who skated. One of them was really cocky, one of them was really tall, one of them was super nice, and one of them was so nice it was sickening. The sick-nice one ended up becoming one of my best friends.

He said, "Hey, man! You skate?"

I had my board in my hand. I said, "Yep."

"The name's Gee."

"Hey, bud."

We shook hands.

Gee said, "Want to play S.K.A.T.E.?"

I said, "Hell yes."

So we played skate. He was damn good—better than most. His style was great too. He had the pop of a god, and literally would pop as high as my waist with every trick he did. And he would *tweak* it like crazy! I was impressed. I won S.K.A.T.E., though. I had more tricks on him, but the tricks he did have were so much higher than mine it wasn't even funny.

I said, "Good game."

Gee said, "Hell yeah, man! You killed it. What's your name? I didn't catch it."

"My bad. My name is Carl. I'm bad with giving out my name, sorry, bud."

"It's okay. Want my number?"

"What?"

"I know it's crazy, but do you want my number?"

"Why?"

"To skate, man! You're Carl Klitz. You're making a video, right? I mean, that one video with all your friends and stuff, right? I've seen the promos."

"Holy, wow. Yeah, man. What's your number?"

He gave me it and I texted him mine. He said, "Cool, I got yours now. We gotta skate soon, lil' man."

"Pronto."

We skated the entire day at that ledge spot.

•　　•　　•

Gee and I skated very often, mostly because he was one-block away from my house. I found that out quickly. We skated everywhere around our neck of the woods because the spots were obscure and nobody knew about them. Gee was the only one that could skate them because they were too high for any regular skateboarder to clear.

I remember he came over one day after I built a box out of wood. I put angle iron on it and everything. Gee killed it. We actually filmed there and he put it into a part. He really wanted to be in the video, so I let him have it.

We skated downtown City Place all the time as well. He always wanted to go from spot to spot. Sometimes he didn't even want to film, but I knew I had to push him if he was to have a part. Everything I told him to do involved him popping his life away. He had the highest kick-flips I ever saw. He actually kick-flipped up White Tops, which is this four-feet tall by five-feet in length gap. He went *up* it. Insane.

Chewie and I invited him to skate. They quickly became friends. Braydon, Donald, and everyone else in the video really didn't like him too much. I think it was because he was so nice. He was a good kid and wouldn't harm a fly. He was always so hyped on life. He also dressed sort of gothy for a black kid. They didn't seem to like that either.

When we were in this parking garage one night, we skated down the garage bank. Gee actually popped over a pole and into the bank. He rode down that son-of-a-gun the entire way. Chewie was screaming his head off! He was super hyped on Gee and I was too. We filmed like crazy.

Often Gee would want to go into his friend's neighborhoods and he would want to skate these weird, obscure spots. Once we skated this pool that was near my old trailer park that had a drop gap and a flat-ground gap. Gee did everything on it. He tre-flipped the drop, which is pretty insane for not having run-up. Chewie hard-flipped the flat-ground gap, later on . . . butter. Both butter.

And pretty soon Gee's part was finished in the video. It was actually surprising to me considering we filmed it basically in a matter of two, three months. Even Chewie couldn't film a part that quickly, and he's an O.G. on a skateboard.

•   •   •

Gee called me to come over to his house, which again was one block away from mine. So I skated from my house to his. I had never been to his place, mostly because he wouldn't allow me to come in. I remember when I knocked on his door, he stepped out almost immediately. I found out after stepping inside that his room was right beside the front door, enabling him to reach it in a hurry.

I walked into his bedroom and I remember seeing the TV playing some *Resident Evil*. That was so epic to me. Nobody had been playing that for *years*, at least that I knew of. He was actually really great at the game, and would point his character toward the direction even when scary things popped out. I jumped, he didn't. I was always jumpy to those sorts of things—still am to this day.

Then Gee said to me, "Want some food?"

"Sure."

He stood up and said, "You can play," and walked out.

I actually handled it pretty well. I took the controller and was walking around this dark forest with a knife. I remember it was dead quiet—not even background "scary" music was playing—and I was looking around the place. The objective was to find a key. So I was looking around and around, and I remember I eventually was led to a gas station. From there I actually remember I found the key, but then these bats starting swarming me and I actually jumped up and screamed. I laughed, shortly after, but then noticed that Gee wasn't in the room.

I stepped out of his bedroom to see where he went. I could see and hear him and this woman arguing. The woman was a lot bigger than him weight-wise. I assumed it was his mother. She seemed to be belittling him, telling him about his "skateboarding nonsense," as she put it, and "Why can't you do something 'regular' like basketball?" She also said, "You got some white folk in your room in there screaming to God-knows-what, and I'm stuck here paying the bills while you eat up *my* food and *my* money on *your* friends!"

I remember looking at Gee and seeing this anger in his eye that I never seen before. The optimism that I saw in him everyday almost seemed like a front in a way. He had problems, too, and his own sufferings. I quickly went back into his bedroom and played more of the video game. The scariness lost its luster, and I was no longer frightened of anything. Life seemed to be more frightening than zombies arbitrarily coming after you.

Gee came into the room and said, "Sorry, Klitz. But you have to leave."

"Why?"

"My mother doesn't want us to hangout."

"That's bull."

"And I can't skate. She broke my board."

"That's . . . messed up."

"Yeah. It's life, man. I also have to find a job."

"Wow."

"I'll see you."

"See you, man. Take it easy."

He nodded and led me out of his house. I never saw him after that, really. He just never really seemed to call or text me. I think he works as a mechanic now, which is a shame because he was an excellent skateboarder with real talent, in my opinion.

When I got home, Ronald told me that I "forgot to clean the dishes," which he had continually asked me to do apparently, but I didn't listen. So he grounded me. I did the dishes, went into the bedroom and slept. I had problems, too. I thought life was a drag.

mid/**late**-2008

Before I knew it, the summer after my second freshmen year (I failed, obviously) was in front of me. I had finished *The No Way Video* skating with friends—which I can't remember finishing for the life of me, considering that it was so long ago—getting footage, making Day in the Life videos, promo videos, and posting them to YouTube. Those were all great things I was doing, but what actually concerned me the most was the fact that my grades were so bad that PBC kicked me out of their school for performance reasons. Literally. Kicked me out. Gone. I was pretty devastated, only because it was better than the alternative. But I tried to look at it like this: My friends from my first freshmen year were my best friends, and they were mostly seniors—minus Tom, who moved and changed school districts (but who I still saw the whole time). So in essence, the only people I saw that whole second freshmen year were my "high school" friends. In high school, you had your "high school" friends, and you had your "real" friends. I didn't have many real friends in school. I just saw them outside of it. So that's how it went: I would see my real friends outside of school and would hate every minute of being inside school. I was looking at everyone in my classes—my "basic"-like classes—and seeing them fool around and not care. The teachers didn't either. They just sort of gave work and told everyone to "just do it." That was the mentality, I think. I guess I can't talk because I didn't care either.

So I was kicked-out and I had *The No Way Video* all done on my computer. I made about twenty-five copies of it with crappy Memorex DVDs. That's all I made. I told Chewie, Tom, Braydon, Donald, and Jimmy to come over. They all did. They sat down on the ground in my living room and just waited patiently for me to bring a copy out. I got one, pressed the "Eject" button, put in a copy, and pushed the tray back in and pressed "Play." God, the menu was silly. It was of everyone in the car goofing-off and making fun of each other while I edited some cartoons coming out over the footage. My friends all laughed at that. Then I pressed "play."

The intro, Chewie's part, Friend's part (which "Friends" means random people spliced together in a part of everyone we knew), Braydon & Donald's part, everything about the video was magical. I knew what it was that made everyone think of it as special: this was our youth in front of us. We spent two years trying to pull this together. The sweat, the anger, the boards broken, the gas burned, the endless amounts of editing. It was a trip. We didn't have any worries, no troubles, no nothing. We just skated and that was it, and that was enough.

Then the video ended. I remember everyone actually clapped after a moment of silence. I almost cried. I felt so proud. I knew everyone else felt the same way, too. Chewie even had a smirk, which didn't happen too much outside of skating. I looked at everyone and said, "Whatcha think?"

They all pretty much said, "Hell yes, Klitz. You killed it."

I remember that day like it was yesterday. My friends and I were proud as heck. I remember feeling like a god for a split-second.

And then it all ended. We said our goodbyes, they all left, I picked up all the plates of microwavable pizza that I made for everyone, picked the trash up, threw it all away, and like hellish magic Ronald came home. I was outside. He looked pissed.

"Hey . . ." I sighed.

"Come inside, Carl. I gotta talk to you."

Then, like more hellish magic, my mother came home.

Ronald and I went inside the house and sat at the dining room table. We literally sat at the table, waiting for my mother to get out of her car and come in.

"Hey guys," she said, opening the door. "Gosh, my day sucked."

"Sit, Sharon," Ronald said. "We gotta talk to your son."

" 'Kay." She probably didn't want to deal with this.

She went to the kitchen, dropped her purse, and came back and sat down. The first to speak was Ronald.

"Carl, we have to talk about your schooling."

"Yeah?"

"You did shit."

"I know, I want to go to G-star," I said. G-star was a film school up the street. All my friends went there.

Ronald looked at my mother, my mother looked at Ronald.

She said out loud, sighing, "Jesus."

"Carl!" Ronald said. "You really don't *get it!* You're not going to go to *any* school of your choice—that didn't work out apparently considering you did shitty in *all* your classes this year passing."

"So . . . ?"

"Oh my God I'm gonna *kill* him, Sharon."

"Carl, listen to Ronald: he's telling you what's final. You're going to Woodhill High School."

"Woodhill?"

"Yes."

"You guys . . . *uggggggghh!*"

"That's final, Carl," Ronald said.

I got up and went to my room after nodding my head a bunch of times to them bitching at me about my crappy grades. That's all I ever did with my parents. I was non-confrontational. I never cursed, never fought, and never bickered. I just nodded my head until they were done. It usually ended with Ronald saying, "Yeah, you always say, 'Yes,' but you never make a change—so you're grounded, bucko." Then I would go to my bedroom. I hated the fact that I couldn't have things work out.

•　　•　　•

I remember Ronald and my mother would go to the dog park often and they would bring all their dogs. My mother would just watch them. The

story goes that some guy was bringing this golden-brown Chiwawa–
Terrier dog by the name of "Bella" to the dog park, and he felt bad for
the dog because she was left home all day. The guy's daughter who
owned Bella was never home to take care of her. So he actually went to
the dog park just to make sure she could run around, at least. That was
Bella's freedom. So one day, the man actually saw Ronald and my
mother and how well they took care of their dogs, and the man said to
them, "Hey, want another dog?" He actually handed them Bella when
they were about to leave the dog park. My mother said, "Sure!" She
loved Bella from the start. She was a good pup. I love Bella very much,
even to this day. She is my freedom, my best friend. She is the best dog
ever and that's all there is to it.

·   ·   ·

Yes, I was grounded most of the summer, but it was okay. I went out
sometimes because my mother felt bad and let me while Ronald was at
work. I basically skated a lot with Tom and Chewie, didn't see Donald or
Jimmy or Braydon or Teddy, because Teddy moved, Donald worked
three jobs or something, Braydon did his own thing, and Jimmy I think
went to jail (but later came out).

That summer was crappy, but I guess that was what it was. I skated all
of my first years in high school, finished a skate video, and felt good. I put
ten copies of the video into Shreder Sheder, the skate shop (which, to my
surprise, moved to Dixie Highway), and the owner, John, told me that I
would keep all the proceeds from whatever sold.

By the end of summer I only sold two copies of the video at Shreder
Sheder, and I went in with my mother to get the eight left. I asked John
where my twenty bucks was, and he told me that he gets it—lying about
the deal. I told him what the deal *actu*ally was and he snickered, giving
me twenty dollars from the register. He was pissed. I took my twenty and
my eight copies of my "crappy," non-best-selling local skate video, and
went home with my mother.

I asked her if what I did was wrong. She told me she was proud of me
for standing my ground. John never, ever talked to me the same ever
again after that day. Pity.

late-2008

Summer was over. I had to start sophomore year of high school. I already had the open house stuff done, my supplies, everything. I just had to get on the eastbound (not westbound, like I would to PBC) PalmTran, and get movin'. I waited and no other kids were there. The good news: I could sleep-in an extra hour because the county was doing this case study on Woodhill students to see if our test scores would improve from getting extra sleep. They didn't. Regardless, I thought it was neat.

It was two weeks into school, so when I got on the PalmTran it was quiet. Nothing was going on. I felt odd, I guess. I was starting a new school. It sucked because it wasn't one I wanted to go to, but hey, I guess beggars can't be choosers, right? But I suppose now that I think about it, I really didn't show any remorse to the idea of this new school move; I just thought my parents were punishing me. . . . Then I finally got off the bus.

I walked down the sidewalk, holding my backpack straps tight, and I remember everyone was in the driving lane, holding everything up. I felt bad for those suckers as I walked through the gates with all the other students. It was strange when I looked around and all I saw were Spanish kids. No white kids. Maybe one or two, but that was it. Lots of black kids as well.

I walked inside the gate into the courtyard, and it was a madhouse. I just headed toward my first period English 2 class. The way was far, and I knew I would be late but I didn't care. I couldn't get into trouble. Everyone ran late. Who cares?

I got into my class, looked at the teacher, and she said to me, "You're late."

"So?"

"Have a seat."

"Yes . . ." So I sat.

We had to take a test. I remember it was always FCAT prep. FCAT is the standardized testing of Florida. They do it strictly for funding. I always wondered why it was so powerful. School made it to where you couldn't graduate if you didn't pass. I usually didn't pass much because I didn't care.

As I was doing this test, I heard something over the intercom.

"Mrs. Pratt?"

"Yes?"

"We have a student running toward your class—"

And just then this black girl came barging in.

"I HEARD YOU WERE RAPPIN', BRO!!!"

All I remember is she was looking at this tiny black girl, and all the students around her moved their desks. This barging-in, black girl just came right toward the tiny black girl and was choking her and beating the living crap out of her. Then more black girls came in, yelling. I remember they beat the crap out of her some more. She had to go to the hospital, I think.

I looked over at this lispy gay kid in my class and I said to him, "What the fuck is this?"

"Don't ask me." *Do'n Asth meh.*

And that was all the remembered. Cops came and broke it up. Apparently it took them forever because the black girls bolted the doors shut so nobody could get in the hallways. Clever girls. They wanted to kill, I think. That was all I remember about my first day at The Hill. That and this kid I met the first day, who I called "Mr. Potter" (because that was his last name), was showing me off to everyone and saying, "Fresh meat!" That was funny.

•   •   •

One day Chewie and I went into Shreder Sheder, out of the blue, just to "marinate" as Chewie called it. Really it was just chilling, but whatever. We were there and it was all after *The No Way Video*, we were proud mothers, and Chewie said to me as we were watching *Fully Flared* on the couch, "Klitz, I just got an idea."

"Oh god. What?"

"I got a video name. Our next video."

"Dude, I want a break."

"No breaks. Lets do it. It's a dope idea. Wanna hear it?"

"Yes . . . ?"

"Okay, okay. It's called *Elevator Music*. What do you think?"

I paused. I was floored. I said, "Holy shit, that sounds so *rad*."

"I know!" Chewie said. "The idea is to film kids 'having fun,' instead of just getting really crazy clips together. The idea is for us to just have fun, enjoy our time, and when people see it, I want them to get that same feeling too. Maybe they will see it years later and reminisce. Lets start filming for it."

"Okay. Deal," I said. Chewie was weird, but I almost always love his ideas.

•   •   •

We filmed for a little bit on *Elevator Music*, but then life comes and gets in the way, taking away your hopes and dreams. Things just sort of . . . changed. I think the whole reason Chewie picked *Elevator Music* was because the sound just had a ring to it—I don't know. It just felt like it was inspiring, or had some value to it. Something friendly. Which was what his vision was.

•   •   •

I went into my Art 1 class one day. The teacher told us to draw a picture of flowers on the table. I did it while nobody else knew what they were doing and it looked amazing. I showed the teacher. Her eyes went big and she said, "What the hell? You made this?"

I said, "I used to be in Bok Middle School of the Arts. Then I quit Art for a couple years and came here."

"Wow. You need to be in a better class. This is going to be unhealthy competition for the other students. I want you to meet Ms. Merchee."

"Who?"

"Ms. Merchee. She's the Advance-Placement 2-D Art Design teacher there. *Woo!* Kind of a tongue-twister."

I laughed and said, "Cool. I'll try it."

"Go now," my Art 1 teacher said.

•   •   •

I went down the other side of school to meet with Ms. Merchee. She was a really sexy black lady. Immediately when I came in, she said, "Who are you?"

"Carl Klitz. Um . . . my Art teacher told me I was 'too good,' so she told me to see you to see if I could go to your class."

"Too good, huh? Okay. Lets see. Where's you portfolio?"

"At home."

"I see, well . . . I can't determine if you're 'good' without a portfolio. Some of the students in my class have worked their way up and built up portfolios the whole four years of schooling here. If you don't have a portfolio you won't be able to pass the Art exam."

I handed her the drawing I did of the flowers.

"What's this?" Ms. Merchee asked. "Did you just take that from one of the cubbies over there?"

"No," I said, "this is the one drawing I did in Art 1 that made my art teacher want me to come here."

Ms. Merchee picked it up, held it up to the light. "Holy crap . . . *Wow,*" she said. "This is phenomenal, Mr. . . ."

"Klitz. Carl Klitz is my name."

"Sounds famous," Ms. Merchee said. "Okay, you can transfer here. But, tomorrow you must bring—I swear, you have to remember this, Carl—must, must, *must* bring your portfolio. Got it?"

"Yes, ma'am."

"Okay. Stay in here and draw the flowers we have setup."

"Can I draw something else, Ms. Merchee? You know, considering I already finished this assignment."

"I see . . . sure. Draw something. Mingle. Do whatever."

I sat behind the kids and watched them draw . . . they all sucked, no offense to them. I just hated people who would ever try hard. I think it was because I would try hard and fail, they would try hard and fail. I just would laugh at them and tend to shy away from my own faults. But I was good at making art—don't get it twisted.

•   •   •

Chewie and I knew this kid named Gordon Fox. He was an employee at Shreder Sheder. I knew him briefly in middle school when I was skating with Teddy, Braydon, and Donald because he had a camera and was sort of a photographer.

Chewie, Gordon, and I went to A1A inlet and skated. We filmed a bunch of goofy footage of ourselves. We were humping the air in the car, we were acting like fools, and we didn't really care. I remember Chewie dropped Gordon and I off and we skated some place near my house. I fell and bunch of times. Gordon was filming me fall and laughing his ass off as I was getting pissed.

Gordon and I went to my house and called Chewie. We were filming Gordon talk to Chewie in a weird way. Gordon was sort of being retarded. Then Chewie was about to hang up. I remember Gordon asked him, "Say something funny before you hang up."

I was filming the whole thing.

"Kookamonga," is what Chewie said before he hung up.

Gordon and I looked at each other and died laughing.

"Fucking Kookamonga . . ." Gordon said. "Jesus, Chewie."

When Gordon left, I imported the footage and made and little video entitle *Kookamonga*. It got three hundred views in a day.

I never was cool with Gordon after that. He always hated me for some reason. Maybe Shreder Sheder was the influence on him.

•   •   •

I started hanging out with John more. John was the kid in my Engineering class back at PBC. John was neighbors and best friends with this guy Phillip, and they both went to PBC. I liked those kids. They were incredibly funny.

Phillip was more of a nice guy, and John was cool. They both skated and I skated too, so naturally we all were friends. I went over their houses to skate close by, near Jog Road. It was John's birthday.

They were already skating out front and it was almost dark. I remember I sort of gave them dap and then we went inside John's place.

John's mother was a great person. She knew my mother, I remember. I had known John when I was really little, and John's mom used to baby-sit us together. I just didn't remember until this time.

John's mom said, "Carl! You hungry?!"

"No, ma'am. I'm not. Thanks, though."

"Just let me know if you are. 'Kay?"

"Okay."

Then John, Phillip, and I went to John's room. It was messy, but that wasn't unusual for a skater.

"Yo, Klitz," John said, "Stevie's coming over."

"Who's Stevie?"

"That one kid that Nito filmed, remember?"

"Oh, from *GotItOnFilm*?"

"Yea . . . he did that big taildrop."

"Holy shit!"

"He's coming, man," Phillip said.

"Okay, cool," I said.

Then we played Playstation 2 for a bit. Phillip was on his iPhone. It was the very first one and kids were going nuts over it, I remember. Nobody had ever seen a phone that had touch-screen capabilities.

Then, twenty minutes later, we all heard loud knocks.

"JOHN! TELL YOUR FRIENDS TO STOP KNOCKING LIKE THAT!" is what I heard from outside John's room or something.

"OKAY, MOM!" John screamed. Then he turned to Phillip and I and said, "Come on."

So we got up, went out his room, and went to the front door. John opened it and said, "STEVIE-BABY!"

"What up?"

"Chillin'. Klitz is here."

"Hell yeah! *The No Way Video*."

"You seen it?" I asked. "I thought nobody saw it."

"John showed me." Then Stevie stepped in. "Dang, I'm hungry. MOM!" Everyone called John's mom "Mom."

"Yes, Stevie?"

"What you makin'?"

"Mac and cheese. Steak. Bunch o' stuff."

"Can I have some?"

"Sure!"

Then we went outside and grabbed our boards that were out in the front yard, left there.

John's place was cool because John's dad built a lot of stuff for John to skate. Like ramps, rails, ledges, everything. So it was all setup out front his house. We skated it like crazy. We did every trick imaginable. Stevie was killin' it, more so than me I felt. My friends always thought I kept up with them, and I think I may have. That day, however, was great because it was after *The No Way Video* and I hadn't skated with friends in awhile. New friends. I thought things were looking up.

Then it got really dark and we were using flashlights to light up the street. Eventually, it got so dark that if you skated away from the lights and hit a rock, you would brake-check and fall. We did that a lot because John's street was fucked up. Eventually we all went inside when John's mom called us for dinner.

We ate the best meal ever! I remember steak, potatoes, sweet potato skins, jalapeño poppers—you name it. We ate like kings!

Afterward, John said, "Mom, we're going to my room."

"Okay, son."

We all went.

I remember John put on *How the Grinch Stole Christmas* with Jim Carrey. John's birthday was in November, so that's why he put it on. It was a funny movie and he could get hyped for Christmas. That movie always brings back memories.

John and his other friends that came were dropping like flies. All of them one by one started to fall asleep. Phillip was the first.

"Guys, lets silly him," John said to us.

"What's 'silly him' mean?" I asked.

And John pulled up silly string.

"Oh," I said, laughing. "Cool."

So we all got a bottle of silly string. I got my camera out on my phone. It was a crappy camera. I said, "One, two . . . THREE!" and John and them all silly-stringed the crap out of Phillip's face. He woke up.

He said, "WHAT THE HELL, MAN!!"

We all laughed. It was simple—always so simple.

Then we all crashed, and I thought: "today was a pretty good day."

●　　　●　　　●

In Ms. Merchee's class she told us to draw self-portraits. I said "hell no" to that, went to the back of the class, and got out my phone. I looked for landscape photos in Google. I found one in particular that stood out to me. I set up an easel, got some paint and brushes, and started doing my thing. I held my phone up with the photo to the easel's frame. Simple enough. I started drawing. I drew and drew and finally, I got the paint out. I painted like crazy. Hell, I think I skipped lunch just to continue to paint. I loved it. I was into it! After everyone came back from lunch, including Ms. Merchee, they all seemingly hovered around my workspace to look.

"Holy, wow, Carl!" Ms. Merchee said for everyone, who stood silent on the backside of me. "This is magical." She really, truly said the word "magical" about my art. "Jesus, Carl. I swear. One day you will have your fifteen minutes of fame."

"I hope that day comes, Ms. Merchee," I said.

I finished the landscape and hung it to dry.

Later on, Ms Merchee, because I didn't do the *actual* assignment, gave me a C-minus on the Landscape piece. And I was like, "Whatever." (About four months later, it would sell for $800.00 at a private art show in City Place.)

●　　　●　　　●

John and Phillip were coming over my house a lot more. They were little skate rats that wanted to street skate. Coming to my house wasn't the best place for street skating, but I was me and they were them, and you'd just have to be there to know what that meant.

They both came over one day and I told them an idea I had.

"Dudes, I want a VX1000."

They gasped, literally.

"Yeah," I said, "I want to go legit."

"Those things will cost ya," Phillip said.

A Sony VX1000 was *the camera* to have for skateboarding. The fisheye was the widest, and it was convenient to film with. The handle was perfect, the colors were great, and the import was smooth. Everything about it was great. And what's crazy is that it was made in the '90s. Only about 100,000 were made. Pretty crazy.

"I want to get it," I said.

"Use Craigslist," Phillip said.

"Not eBay," John said.

"What's Craigslist?" I asked them.

They looked at each other and laughed.

"What?" I said.

"Just go on it!" they both said.

So I got on my computer and made a post:

> WANTED: SONY VX1000,
> WILLING TO PAY TOP DOLLAR
> ($800.00) THANK YOU!!!
> cell: five61-five44-five777
> email: carlKLITZ@gmail.com

The "thank you" part was cute, I thought. Then the emails and text messages started rolling in as I was sitting in front of my computer. "Holy crap," I said, "woah."

"Told ya," Phillip said.

Later on, when John and Phillip left, I got a call from a nameless guy to sell me a VX for $700.00, which was lower than what I was asking for. I was too young to know that this was a scam, but I told him to come over the next day to sell the camera to me.

•   •   •

Basically this guy came out, late. I eventually went to the front of my house and waited for him until nighttime with Phillip. We were hyped but pretty retarded to wait that long.

The guy finally came, and he was very, very shady. He came out of the car. "Hey," he said.

"Hey."

"You the guy?"

"Yes."

"Okay, lets get down to business."

He pulled a VX1000 with a battery and charger from the backseat of his car. He put the battery in, slowly.

"Okay, so here it is," and he looked through the viewfinder, then said, "The colors. Look." He handed me the camera. I looked through it. Wow. It was dark out, so all I saw were grain specks. That could have been my first clue that this guy was a scam. Selling a camera at night so I couldn't test it.

"The colors are great!" I mindlessly said. "How much?"

"$800.00," he said. That's when I really should have known he was a scam.

"You said $700.00," I said "Here." And I pulled out seven Benjamin's.

"Well . . . okay," he said. He took the cash, passing me the camera with the battery inside it and the charger. "Pleasure doin' business."

He got in his car and left.

I looked over at Phillip, Phillip looked over at me. "Woah," he said, "you have a VX now."

"Yeah . . ."

We went inside my house.

When I looked through the viewfinder in the light, I noticed how foggy everything looked from the camera. "Jesus," I said, "this shit looks foggy as hell. Look, Phillip."

I passed him it, and he did.

"Jesus. Looks like crap," he said. "Maybe the lens needs cleaning."

So we got a dishtowel, cleaned the camera lens. I looked through. Still foggy. "Fuck me," I said.

Then I dialed the guy who just sold me the camera: "The number you have dialed is no longer in service."

"I've been had," I said to Phillip.

"Chill. Maybe it's easy to fix."

"Maybe."

"Look through it again."

"Shit. Now the viewfinder doesn't work."

"Yup. You've been had."

"Yup."

"Call Nito."

"Who?"

"*GotItOnFilm* filmer."

"What's his number?"

"Here."

Phillip gave me Nito's number.

• • •

I called Nito a couple days later, around the end of 2008, and he told me he wanted to skate with me and look at my VX1000. He said he was going to skate with Stevie, John, Little Larry, and me. ("Little Larry" was the little kid that did 50-50 on the railing from the kicker when I was nine years old at the YMCA with Cody. Crazy, huh? Small world! He was a kid who had trouble with his height, but really was quite old.)

It was nighttime and I thought that that was bad because where could we skate? We didn't have lights. Most places you had to travel pretty far to get to the well-lit places. So I thought it was odd. I called Nito. He answered.

"Yeah?"

"Where you at?"

"Down your street. We'll be there."

He hung up.

In front of my house I saw headlights. "Woah," I thought, they had a car. I was sixteen and most of my friends didn't have cars. I went out front with my board and VX1000. I hopped in the back of their car.

"Put your board in the trunk, Klitz," Nito said from the front seat.

I got out, put my board in the back, and got back in, still with my VX1000. We drove. Little Larry was the driver, I noticed. I think he was 19 years old.

"So, Klitz," Nito said, "let me see your camera."

"Okay. Here."

I handed him it.

He turned it on, looked through it, and said, "Woah, fog."

"I know."

"This is, like, *really* foggy. I think this camera actually has damage. Like real damage. This is actually *inside* the camera, if that makes sense."

"Really?"

"Yup. You're fucked, bro. You can't do much. You'll have to replace the entire lens."

"Well . . . shit," I groaned.

We skated these ledges, Stevie, John, and Lil Larry sat down the entire time. It was just Nito and I filming a line. ("A line" is a series of tricks filmed together and landed many times in a row, or "line.") We had two plastic benches that were a couple feet away from each other. I was trying a nollie 180 tail-slide to fakie, then switch back 180 on flat-ground, then a front board-slide 270 shuv-it out. It took forever but I finally got it. When I landed it was so buttery-looking. Nito showed me the footage. He actually took the tape out of his VX1000.

"Why are you taking the tape out?" I asked him.

"Because. These VXs are old. You can't playback footage on them or else it damages the heads. You have to use a cap-cam to view it."

A cap-cam stands for "capture-camera." It's basically like you're buying a crappy one hundred dollar camera just so it can playback your VX footage. It was surprising the same exact camera that I used to film *The No Way Video*, which made me feel retarded.

He showed me the footage and I was like, "Wow." Holy crap, I thought. This looks amazing. I really thought it did. It looked golden, in a way. The sound was perfect. And Nito even setup stage lights for each of the benches, with a camera-light on top of the VX. It looked so professional. I was hooked.

•   •   •

A couple days later, I went on Craigslist and listed the broken VX1000 but without mentioning that it was broken. Some guy from the YMCA called me. He was an old dude. He said he was a nurse and he was saving for a couple months for a VX1000. I felt bad, but that's how you learn I guess. So I told him to meet me at The Y. He got there. Nice dude. Clean. I showed him the same things of a camera that are good: colors great, spiced it up with extra MiniDVs (which are the small tapes used for recording), gave him the camera to hold. He bought it. $800.00. I actually came up 100 bucks. Wow, I thought I could make a killing doing Craiglist deals. But then I felt bad. I never went back to The Y much after that, for fear of seeing the man. He never called or texted me, and probably thought the camera wasn't broken. Who knows . . . ?

•   •   •

I decided to ask my mother if I could buy an iMac. I figured, Hey, if I can't film, I'll be an editor, which is my real passion in skateboarding videography. I liked putting the clips together with songs, editing the colors, and basically making it all come together. That was my thing. I remember I sold lots of art pieces during that time. I didn't have a job, so I just basically got money from here and there. Actually, I don't really even know how I made my money. It's still a mystery to me. I was the kind of guy to just made things happen. I do remember that my mother gave me $300.00 for the iMac because I was short on it a bit. So yeah, I ordered a 2009 iMac.

I waited a week and it was torture. Finally, I remember I heard from the front of my house, "MR. KLITZ! MR. KLITZ!" It was a Mexican lady. "YOU HAB A PACKAGE! MR. KLITZ!!"

I went out front, signed off on the box, and smiled at her. She looked at me like I was a frickin' retard. It was sort of weird, I guess. I took the box and went inside.

I hooked it up and by golly it worked! Everything was perfect. I always wanted a Mac and now I had one! "Good ole Steve Jobs," I was thinking.

2009

2008 turned into 2009. Around January–Febuary-ish, Chewie left Florida completely and moved to San Antonio, Texas. Tom was working a whole lot. Braydon and Donald were doing their own things with their girlfriends. Probably getting laid. All my friends were pretty much gone —at least, all *The No Way Video* friends. So I got this idea: I had a good time skating with Nito, filming that line. Why don't I give him a call? It was worth a shot, so I did. I dialed his number. He answered.

"Yeah?"

"Nito!"

"What?"

"Can I come by?"

"Uhhhhh . . . *sure* . . . You know where I'm at?"

"You're over by John I., right?"

"Yeah, I'll just text you my address."

"Okay. Cool. I'll just skate over."

"It's far."

"Whatever. Two miles."

"Okay. I'm not really doing much, though."

"Whatever," I said, hanging up.

He texted me the address and I skated on over.

•   •   •

I knocked on Nito's door. He came out in blue gym shorts and a Nike T-shirt and socks. I said, "Sup?" He said, "Yeah . . ." and he stepped aside. I walked in. Wow, I thought it was a nice little place. He had a big screen TV and the kitchen was right there with a table too. It was perfect. Nito lead me to his room. Just ahead, down the hall. His door was open. He went back on his computer. He was playing *StarCraft*.

"Holy shit!" I said, "you fucking play *StarCraft*?!"

"Pawnin'."

"Damn that's dope. I would have never known."

"Yeah . . . You know, I actually hate skaters."

"Really?"

"Yup. Hate them. All they do is use me for my VX, they come in here demanding to see footage, and in turn wanting me to give their footage to them. It's annoying."

That's vaguely what I was doing. "Oh," I said.

"So you know what?—fuck it. I think I'm going to sell my VX, not get phone calls anymore from these goons, and just chill."

"But Nito, you're good at filming."

"I'm good with other stuff, man. I make beats. I'm a photographer. I do other things, but all those guys want to do is use me for my camera, get footage, and pretend like it means something. Showing off your skateboarding doesn't get you anywhere, and the moment they find that out is the moment they quit skating."

"Jesus."

"I know."

"Well listen, man. I'm here because I thought you were cool. Instead of just filming skating, we should film other shit. Did you see that YouTube video I made called *Kookamonga*?"

"What?"

"*Kookamonga*. You basically splice random shots of everyone into a video and post it. It gets lots of views, man."

"Oh yeah, I remember now. I guess so . . . But I don't really know what to do."

"Well, it's already sort of dark out. Why don't we go to SkateUSA or something? Just check out what we could film."

"Okay," Nito said. "Let me get ready."

•   •   •

Nito bought his camera but we didn't film much—just me making fun of clothes. He talked to the owner about Lloyd, the owner's golden, skater child. Lloyd was sponsored by Baker, DVS—all that. Nito filmed Lloyd and the owner hooked him up. I didn't like Lloyd at the time. (But as I got to know Lloyd, he was a pretty cool, nice kid. But when you're young and a skater, you tend to hate anyone who is in the limelight above you.) We left to head back to Nito's house.

•   •   •

Nito had his camera and we were in his hallway. He setup his lights. I remember he was wearing a yellow shirt and he said, "Now what?"

"Dude, just do whatever."

I remember he had a bunch of doors. So we would go into one door and out the other and act stupid. Then cut it and you would be going into another door. It was classic movie magic. I remember one door I came out of I actually started humping the air. I was really ramming it. Then we would just keep doing that.

"Want to come over tomorrow?" Nito asked me afterward.

"Sure."

•   •   •

The next day I went over to Nito's house, and we decided to skate this railing next door. I was trying a 50-50 pop out on it, riding into grass. It took forever, but I did it. Then I said, "Lets do it in a line." So I switch 180ed up the sidewalk, and then 50-50 pop out the railing. It looked perfect. Then I did a 50-50, 180 out, on it as a single clip. I landed perfectly and Nito filmed it perfectly.

I remember that as we were walking we came across a duck. I was chasing the duck and pretending to be like it while Nito filmed. He was laughing his ass off. That was always funny. We imported and Nito gave me the files on a CD, I felt like he was starting to open up to me.

•   •   •

I added this kid on Myspace named Bret Overcuffler. He was a tall, lanky, *smart* kid—but a total badass. I added him because he had a picture of him and his VX1000. I guess you could say it "enticed" me.

I told him, "Nice camera," he said thanks. We basically ended up exchanging numbers. I told him that we should skate sometime. He said, "All right."

Basically I remember we met at downtown City Place and decided to skate this pier that was way downtown, near Tamron. The place was real nice, and the ledges were perfect. I remember that clearly. I remember Bret and I were kind of weirded-out by each other, as most people who first meet are at first. He was in a van, a white one, and I thought it was a "creeper van."

"Free candy!" I told him.

He laughed.

We filmed a couple tricks there, and got everything we needed and then went back to my house.

"Want to import?" I asked him.

"Sure."

"What you doin' tonight?"

"It's Friday, and I don't work—fuck it."

Bret was nineteen.

"Wanna stay over?" I asked him.

"Sure . . ."

And he did.

I remember that basically we imported footage on my iMac, and he was mesmerized by my computer setup. Shit, I still was too.

"We should film something," Bret said.

"Like what?"

"I don't know."

"Hey . . . check *this* out."

I pulled up iTunes and played Mac Dre. I was getting hyphy (a Mac Dre term for "hyped" or "excited," mostly in the form of dancing), and Bret was laughing his tail off. I played "Jealousy," by I.M.P and I was rapping and carrying on with my shirt off. Pretending to be a gangster. Bret was dying.

"DUDE! LETS FILM THIS!!"

"Okay!" I said.

He got his camera out and filmed me singing this song. He filmed and filmed. We finally got done, looked at the footage (into his viewfinder, not a cap-cam), and imported. We edited it pretty fast, put it onto Youtube, and I thought, Wow! We did it! We made a video. The next day, when we woke up, the video had eight hundred views.

• • •

Nighttime. I was at Nito's house with Bret. Nito brought over this girl and her name was Erica. She was kind of chubby, but she was cute. She was a girl that would knock your socks off, tell you off, and be like one of "the guys." She and two other friends: a tall blond one, and a short fat one. I can't remember their names for the life of me.

We were in Nito's backyard. No grass, just bricks on the ground laid out like a patio, and he had a basketball hoop. Bret was killin' it because he was six-feet tall and that was that. We had fun though.

Bret was on top of the roof of Nito's dad's mancave that looked straight onto the court. Bret was filming Nito and I playing basketball, and I was acting retarded. Nito just threw the ball at me and hit me on the head and Bret caught it all on camera. It was hilarious. *Bleh!*

Then we started to fuck around with the girls there. Erica was the first, I remember I went up to her and asked her about sex or something—I was immature in a way.

"Oh, yeah, Klitz, yeah," she said.

I looked down—both Erica and I actually—and saw a snail, just sort of slithering away down a path.

Erica said, "Oh *yes!*"

Then another snail came by . . .

"Erica said, "Hell yes!"

She grabbed both of them and started rubbing them together. I grabbed Bret's camera and filmed her.

On camera Erica was moaning: "OH YES! AHHH!! OH YES!! SNAIL PORN! FUCK YES! AHHH! OH!"

I thought she was weird. But I also thought she was cool to actually participate in a *Kookamonga* video, which is why we were filming in the first place.

Then we filmed the fat girl. She was talking about how she has sexual intercourse with black guys. She also was saying how she sat on a remote of some kind and she couldn't find it now. She also sat on her hamster once. Nito and I started bawling. We laughed so frickin' hard. Bret filmed the whole thing.

That night, when Bret and I went into Bret's white creeper van, Nito told us goodnight.

"See ya, man," I said.

And Bret and I drove off to my house.

In my room, Bret and I imported all the footage from the night. That was always a good feeling, I remember. To see the footage you created and to see it as it was: a memory, a piece of you. You were then a character, like an actor in a movie, and you were alive. You were "a somebody." That was always the best feeling.

When I got all the footage, Bret had to go. I said my goodbyes, and he drove home. That night I stayed up until 5:00 a.m. editing *Kookamonga 5*, and it came out great. I posted it in the early morning. I had footage saved from all different times I skated with friends so I just mashed them together.

That next day/afternoon when I woke up, *Kookamonga 5* had two-thousand or more views.

●　　●　　●

On Myspace, I got a friend-request from this girl. Her name was Sam. She was Spanish, had black hair, and she was cute and a shorty. I remember that clearly. I remember her and I basically started talking, and discovered the both of us were artists. She added me because she stumbled onto my art through a friend. She admired me, and had also seen my *Kookamonga* videos.

I asked her if we could chill, and she said okay. I proposed we meet at the A1A inlet to take drawings of the beach and stuff. She told me that that would be great. She picked me up in her dad's SUV. She was waiting out front of my house when I came outside, got in her car, and said, "What's up."

"What's up," she said back.

We drove to A1A.

It was six a.m when we got to the beach, and I remember we wanted to see the sunrise. What a beautiful thing, that sunrise. We drew pictures of it in our sketchbooks. We didn't speak much. We were actually very awkward.

"Want to leave?" I asked her.

"Sure."

We went back to her place. She lived with her parents, naturally, in Boyton, near A1A. She lived in an apartment. We walked up the stairs, she put her key in the door, and we went inside. Nice digs! The hall to the right had a HUGE painting that was of drippings and such. I asked her about it and said, "Cool," after her explanation—I don't remember it.

We went inside her room and the first thing I noticed was a black tree with an owl painted on the wall behind her bed. It was all black, like silhouetted, and I thought it was cool. Her room was pretty basic though. It just had a bed, a dresser, an easel, and a desk with a computer on it. She wasn't your typical girl, obviously. . . .

"So . . . uh, where do you go to school?" I asked her.

"I don't."

"Huh? What do you mean?"

"I'm home-schooled."

"WHAT! HOW?!"

"F.L.V.S., silly. Look, I'll show you." And she sat at her computer, pulling up the website. "See," she said, "look." She was showing me all her classes. I couldn't believe it.

"Wow," I said.

"Yup. I hate my homeschool, so I do everything here. Also, I get done faster, so most of the time I'm just hanging out and doing things I *want* to do—like painting."

"Damn, you're lucky."

"Eh, kind of."

"So what do you do for fun?"

"Painting, and *oh!* skateboarding too."

It was a sign from God.

"Holy . . . fuckin' . . . shit!" I said, jaw gapped. "Are you joking?"

"Nope. Dead serious."

"I skate."

"I know. I've seen your *Kookamonga* videos."

"Really?!"

"Uh-huh."

I smiled.

"Sam, lets make some breakfast."

"Okay." She smiled too. And we made breakfast in the kitchen.

After eating, we went back into her room. I asked her, "So . . . Sam. Um . . . I was wondering . . ." I was scratching the back of my neck. "Uh, do you have a boyfriend?"

"Yes. Will's his name."

"Shit."

"Yup. Three years."

"Jesus . . ."

"Why?"

"Just wondering, I guess."

"You're silly," Sam said.

We chilled the remainder of the day. We just spoke about whatever. Her dad came home, and I remember he was nice. They dropped me off at the front of my house.

I liked Sam, a lot. A *whole* lot.

•   •   •

In the lunchroom one day, I got my food. I was looking around for a place to sit. I went down this aisle, that aisle, and then, get this: This kid literally yelled, "KLITZ!" and I turn around to face him. I walked up to him.

"Yeah?" I said.

"You're Carl Klitz, man."

"Yeah . . .? What's up?"

"I'm George. I know who you are. You're that *Kookamonga* kid."

"Oh, cool!"

"Yeah, man, I watch those videos like crazy—actually, me and my friends all do. I skate at Phibbs Skatepark a lot."

"Oh awesome. You skate. Sweet."

I sat down beside him.

"Yeah," George said, "you should come down to Phibbs one of these days. Lots of people would be hyped."

"I will," I said.

We ate lunch and talked about Bradley Kromer.

•   •   •

That weekend my mother and I got into her SUV. I was to start driving because I had just gotten my permit. My mother was very proud. We drove down our street, and everything was fine. Then, we got to this median not that far from the end of our street, and we go to do the U-turn. I just went because I couldn't see anybody, but the moment that I turned a guy in a motorcycle whizzed on passed us. He turned around and flicked us off. I felt so stupid. *Gosh!* I felt stupid. I fell silent. My mother knew this.

"Want me to drive?" she asked.

I nodded.

We pulled over into this close Taco Bell parking lot. We switched.

She drove me to Phibbs. When I got there, everyone was cheering and saying that they loved *Kookamonga*. I was feeling so awesome. I literally felt like a million bucks. Nothing can ever break that feeling of importance. I hated always being an attention-seeker, though.

I met this kid named Fletcher—he was George's buddy. I was telling him about our idea for *Elevator Music*. He was damn hyped on it. We exchanged numbers. He was really, really good, too, at skating. Really *urban!*

•   •   •

In Art class my teacher told us to paint this weird project on Picasso. I said, "No," and went to the back of the class. I setup my easel and started to make this triangle piece with three triangles. Two of them smiled and laughed, and one sat sad. I thought I was the sad one, looking over at the laughing and smiling ones. I put an aura around him to try and make him happy . . . He still was sad.

early-2010

Before I knew it, 2009 turned into 2010. Little did I know, this was to appear be the most memorable, most fun, most tragic, year of my life. I wished I would have known, so I could have been more prepared.

My brother, Lance, who was twenty-four, had just broken up with his girlfriend. He was in some financial troubles because he needed a roommate, but those sorts of things are tough for anyone in Florida. He asked my mother if he could stay at home with Ronald and her. She said, "Yes," of course, because everybody—when they are going through a rough time—should be helped. Also, I was very excited to have him over.

One day, a Friday, it was just him and I at the house. Ronald and Mom were at work. Lance turned to me and asked, "Want to get Dunkin' Donuts?"

"Sure!"

So we went.

I got an iced coffee; he did too.

We drove back home.

After that we just sat at home on our computers doing nothing. It was literally two hours of nothing.

"Want to make a smoothie?" I asked Lance.

"Hell yes."

We got out the blender and started to get out the bananas, strawberries, milk, ice, etcetera. We blended all of it together. When it was done we drank them. We drank and we drank. Then Lance looked at me and started laughing.

"What?" I said. "What's so funny?"

"Dude. Wow. It's boring here. What the fuck? Literally that was the highlight of my day, making smoothies. You literally do this all day, just sit at home?"

"Yeah. Pretty much, until a homie calls to skate."

"Sounds boring. I would go crazy."

"Sometimes I do," I said.

We slept the remainder of the day.

*   *   *

At night, Lance got a call from his friend Lars. Lars was a tall dude. He was always nice. Lance and Lars and a bunch of his friends from the trailer park used to come over. Lance used to torment me a lot. His friends would be off in the background giggling. Lance would act like a fool making fun of me. It actually tore into me kind of. I have bad self-esteem because of it I think.

(This one time when I was five years old, Lance and my other older brother, Stephen Jr., got this life-size replica of Jason, the serial killer, and put it beside my bed while I was asleep. They tickled my feet. I woke up and started to panic and scream. Stephen and Lance giggled but my mother didn't. She had to get out of bed for this in the middle of the night, and hoot and holler at them for being such asses.) I still love Lance, though.

So anyways, he was on the phone talking to Lars.

"Yeah. . . . Julia is crazy, man. . . . Nah, she literally just snapped. She would go off on me for no reason. . . . Bro, I literally had to drink just to deal with her. I had Jack & Coke, I had everything I could drink just so I could drown her out. . . . Yeah. . . . Yeah, I know. . . . What can a guy do? . . . What? . . . Are you serious?"

Then Lance turned to me.

"Carl, you want to go bowling?"

"Hell yes."

Lance said into the phone, "We'll be there."

He hung up.

•   •   •

We went bowling with Lars and a lot of Lance's friends. Lance bought a couple pitchers of some brew. We all drank. We all got drunk and bowled. We sucked—or at least I did—and it didn't really matter. We just had fun, and I thought, "Gosh, Lance's awesome."

We went back home and slept: Lance on the top bunk, me on the bottom. Yes, I had a bunk bed. Baxter was Ronald's son. He was usually the top bunk, but he wasn't there—only on weekends, I think. Or, he may have temporarily slept on the couch while Lance was staying. I don't really remember.

•   •   •

It was a couple weeks later and Lance and I were watching TV. I remember him and I were just watching *Family Guy* and enjoying ourselves, laughing at nonsense, when all of a sudden Ronald came home late. It was around nine p.m. Ronald came inside, dropped off his stuff, and came into the living room. It was real tense.

First thing he said while standing in front of me blocking the TV, and looking directly at me, "Why aren't the dishes done?"

"Oh man I'm sorry, Ronald. I wasn't thinking. Lance and I were—"

"I DON'T WANT TO *HEAR* IT!"

The room went silent. I remember Lance and I were just sitting there, looking at him.

My mother came from her bedroom and into the living room.

"What's going on?" she said.

"Oh, nothing," Ronald said, "except that your son FORGOT to do the DISHES! Listen, Carl, I've had enough of you *not doing the dishes.*" He got up in my face, while I was still sitting on the couch. "Listen up, 'cause I'm only gonna tell you this once: you better get your damn act together. We didn't PUT you into no counseling for you to go and fuck it up. I don't want another Stephen in this house" (Stephen being my father) "so you better shape up, or get out."

"Whatever man," I said. "You're crazy."

He got silent. I think I actually saw his eyes dilate.

Lance said, "Guys, what is the matter—?"

And just then, Ronald grabbed hold of my shirt.

"WHATEVER!? WHATEVER!! I'LL SHOW YOU WHAT WHAT-FUCKIN'-*EVER* MEANS!"

My mother shouted, "RONALDO! STOP!!"

Ronald had me by the shirt, and pulled me up off the couch. He had one arm on my shoulder—whipping me around and around. He threw me into the kitchen, and next thing I knew I was on the floor with him standing over me.

"BOY! I SWEAR TO GOD, I AIN'T GONNA TOLERATE NO KID DISRESPECTIN' *ME* AND *MY* OWN HOUSE! I AIN'T GONNA HAVE NO PASTY, PUNK KNOW-IT-ALL IN *MY* FUCKIN' HOUSE! YOU GOT THAT!?"

"Fuck you," I said.

The room got silent.

Ronald, in a low voice, said, "What?"

"I said, 'Fuck you, bitch.' "

That really set him off.

"Fuck you!? FUCK YOU!? COME HERE!!!"

He grabbed me but the shoulders and dragged me up. He actually picked me up. Everything went sort of blurry for a second—like it wasn't really happening.

My mother was shouting, "RONALDO! STOP!! DON'T HURT HIM! STOPPPP!!! RONALDO!" She was actually crying. She didn't know what to do.

He was guiding me into his bedroom. Both my shoulders ached. He threw me on the floor.

"BOY! I AIN'T DONE WITH YOU!"

I lost it. I shouted, "PUSSY-ASS BITCH CAN'T EVEN PICK ON MOTHERFUCKERS HIS OWN *SIZE!* PUSSY!!! PUSSYYY!!!"

He didn't say anything—his actions spoke louder. He grabbed my stomach, picked me up, and threw me on top of the bed.

I shouted, "FUCKING PUSSY! PUSSYYY!!!" I felt like Braydon and Chaz, when they both said it to me.

Ronald started choking me. I remember he was choking me hard, and my mother, off in the background beside him, was shouting, "RONADO, STOP IT! STOP IT, RONALDO!! STOP!!!!!" She was crying so loudly.

I was feeling everything go silent. I was feeling the world around me fading. Then I came back. I came back to reality, and adrenaline went away. I started laughing in his face.

"P-pah-pussy . . ." I said through my crushed throat. "Nothing but a b-bah-baby-b-*bah*-back bitch."

He face was red, he was squeezing as hard as he could.

I go, "Fuckin' cocks-sah-sucking p-pah-*pussy!*"

He looked at me and said, "You think those crazy eyes are gonna do anything, boy?"

Then I got mad. I started pushing the shit out of him. Kicking. Kicking balls. Kicking everywhere. My mother was pounding on his back, telling him, "GET OFF MY SON! GET THE FUCK OFF MY SON! NOW!!! YOU'RE CHOKING HIM!!!!"

He got off me and walked out the room. My mother followed. I remember I sat on my mother and Ronald's bed for a moment. Ronald saying that this was *his* house, and that nobody, not any of us, had to live there. Lance was telling him to calm down. I remember Ronald was saying that Lance, *for sure*, didn't have to be there. That he was there because he was pretty much a "need case." He was telling my mother that even she didn't, or couldn't, be there. That this was his house and only his fucking house, and we—almost strangers to him now—didn't *have to* be there. He bought the mortgage, he saved the money for the house, and he lived in it for years before all of us came along. Before meeting my mother.

He said, "That son of yours has gotta *go!*"

My mother said, "He's only seventeen!"

"I DON'T GIVE A SHIT! GET!! HIM!! OUT!!!"

My mother was crying.

"I guess I'm going with him . . ."

"YOU BABY HIM, SHARON!"

My brother wasn't saying anything. I assumed he was probably standing in the background or something.

Ronald shouted, at the top of his lungs, "GET HIM OUT OF MY HOUSSSSEEEEEEE!!!!!" He stomped out the kitchen. I remember the front door slammed, and then silence.

My mother came into the bedroom where I was still laying.

"Carl," she said, "you gotta stay somewhere for the night. Do you know anyone you could stay with?"

"Tom . . . ?"

"That's fine. You just have to stay there. Not a good time."

"Okay, Mom."

I got up, went to my bedroom, and got on the phone with Tom. He said he couldn't have anyone over, but he'd take me wherever I needed. I told him what happened. He understood. He called Ronald an asshole.

Then I did the silliest thing ever: I called Sam. She was still up. She said, "Yeah, come over. Stay over—do whatever. I want you to be safe."

I called Tom back and told him to take me to Boyton. He said, "Sure."

As I got my backpack, my board, and my clothes ready, I stood up and smiled. I remember I just wanted to get out of that shit-house. I remember I passed my mother in the kitchen. My brother just nodded at me. I passed them both. I remember I looked up at the clock and it read 9:16 p.m., and I thought, "Gee, a lot can happen in fifteen minutes. There's my fifteen minutes of fame, Ms. Merchee!" I actually laughed to myself about that.

Out the window of my house I saw Ronald there, crying. He was crying in his shed: The Man Cave. I thought that was odd.

Tom got there and I was off to Sam's house.

·   ·   ·

When I woke up the next day, Sam was still sleeping. I got out of bed, and went to her bathroom. I looked in the mirror. "Holy shit," I said. "Wow. Fucker got me good." I had bruises all over my neck. It sucked. So I shrugged, pissed in the toilet, flushed, and walked back to Sam's room. She was awake. She was in the windowsill smoking a cigarette. She looked so . . . cool. I couldn't describe it.

"Hey," I said.

She turned around. "Morning, Carl. Y'okay?"

"Yeah. Just stressed. Look at what that asshole did to me." I walked up to her, pulled my collar down, and showed her my neck.

"Ow," she said. "That must have hurt like *hell.*"

"Not really. Fuck him."

"What's on your mind?"

I waited a second, looking at the ground. Then I looked back up and said, "You know, I thought about something. If the earth exploded, and there was no more life forms left, there would still be the sun and the planets—seemingly lifeless objects. So that means the Universe is unlimited. We are literally living in an unlimited space. Isn't that crazy? We are in an eternity-style place, but not really, you know? Our lives are temporary. Isn't that crazy?"

Sam just looked at me and said, "You're weird," and she laughed. "You think too much. But that's why I love you. You're very creative."

"Yeah," I said. "I guess so . . ."

"So, Carl, what do you want to do today?"

"Can you drop me off at Phibbs?"

"Yeah, sure. Want breakfast?"

"Sure."

"Lemme finish my smoke. Feels good right now. It's nice outside, too. Gotta love it."

"Okay," I said.

•　　•　　•

Later, Sam and I ate breakfast, talked more, and enjoyed our time together while I packed my stuff. Sam drove me—with her dad's SUV—to Phibbs Skate Park, hours later. She skated a little bit, but then sort of left me there. I was worried because I had to find a place to stay quickly or else I was going to have to sleep on benches at parks or something like a dang hobo.

After a few minutes of skating around the park, George came by. He said, "Hey, Klitz, what's crackin'?"

"DUDE! Literally I'm *so* happy to see you, buddy. I got kicked out my house."

"That sucks. Holy crap. *That sucks!*"

"I'm aware." He wasn't very sensitive, or smart, for that matter. "George," I said, "could I stay at your place for awhile?"

"No can do. My mother wouldn't let me. Shit, she won't even let Fletcher over. But yeah, my birthday is coming up soon. I'm having people over. You could stay, then, if you'd wanted to."

"Yeah, sure," I said. It was better than nothing, sitting on a bench or something.

George and I skated around the park. We played S.K.A.T.E. I always won, for some reason. I could beat everyone, not just George. I skated flat-ground excessively—it was my thing, I guess. I don't know. I was sort of bummed during that time because I didn't want to stay downtown on a bench. Then I got a call from my mother.

I said into the phone when I answered, "Yeah?"

"Baby. You okay?"

"I'm fine. How's Lance?"

"Good. Good. I'm fine too. Did you find a place to stay?"

"No, not really."

"Oh, I am so sorry, honey. I'm talking to Ronald. I'm thinking he will let you back. It was rough, that night—I couldn't stop crying."

"I saw him crying, too, out back."

My mother didn't answer to that.

"Carl," she said, "find a place soon. I worry about you. I want you to be safe, baby."

"I will. I'm just at the skatepark. I'm trying to stay with someone. I'm trying to be okay."

"Okay, baby, I, um—"

"Hold on, Mom," I said as soon as I saw this kid that I knew that just had came out into the park. "Uh, I'll call you back."

"Bye, Carl—"

I hung up.

It was Fletcher that came in.

"Fletcher!" I shouted.

He looked over at me, grinned, and said, "Klitz! What's up?!"

"Nothin' much, man!" I said, skating over to him. I picked up my board and gave him dap. "Dude, I'm in deep shit. Seriously," I told him.

"What's up?"

"My mother kicked me out—well, I lied. Actually my *stepdad* kicked me out. I'm sort of homeless, now, man."

"That ain't good, Klitz."

"Yeah . . . Uh, I got a question."

"Yeah?"

"Could I stay over tonight?"

"Yeah, sure. It's cool."

"Just ask your mother."

He laughed and then said, "My mom? Yeah okay. It's cool, bud. My mom won't care."

"Okay . . . ?" I said, confused. "Okay. Cool. I'm just stressin'. I don't wanna stay on a bench somewhere."

"I feel ya. Uh . . . Klitz? Uh, what you doin' about school?"

"Probably won't go."

"It's school tomorrow. You *gotta* go."

"Fuck it."

"My mother probably won't be cool with that. We'll see. Lets just skate until tonight, when I take you to my place."

"Cool," I said.

We played S.K.A.T.E. I won. The afternoon turned into nighttime, and some others joined us. I met some really, really good skate-heads. One was named Chad Finners. He was fourteen and hella good. I was always hyped on him. He said his filmer (Konner Alboo) had footage of him on a VX1000. That was huge for me. I was hoping he would be in *Elevator Music*. We all had fun and a few laughs—life actually made sense.

•　　•　　•

I went with Fletcher back to his house. His place on Dixie Highway was literally across the street from Phibbs, which lead me to believe that all of Fletcher's talent, was caused by him having such easy access to a skate park. I thought this, and started to get upset, but thought, "It could be the reason, but who cares? He's helping me. He's a great skateboarder." But jealousy sometimes clouds our minds anyway.

We walked up to his front lawn and it was strange because there were huge bushes there—the gardening was really great. The lawn was pristine. I said to him, "Woah, your yard looks awesome," and he didn't say anything back. Then we got up to the front door—it was blue, I remember—opened it, and stepped inside.

The house was cozy. I remember it was real surfy-looking. There were bean bag chairs, pictures of family everywhere, and he had three dogs. "LOUIS! WHAT-ARE-YA *DOIN'!*" Fletcher said in a high-pitched, cartoony voice to the one dog. Then he looked at the other. "TIFFY! WHAT-ARE-YA *DOIN'!!*" He leaned down to pet her. The dogs were barking and going crazy, all happy and stuff. Then Fletcher looked at the third dog that was HUGE. "MOOSEY! MOOSE-MOOSE!" The huge dog slobbered with a smile it seemed.

"That's frickin' funny," I said.

"My dogs are the shit," Fletcher said. "You want to eat? Hungry?"

"Hell yes. I'm starved!"

"Hokay."

Fletcher got out some chicken wings. He threw them into the oven. We waited for twenty minutes, talking about skating, and probably Bradley Kromer. The wings finished and Fletcher took them out. They were so excellent, I swear.

I said, "Dude, these are too fucking good."

And Fletcher said, "I know. My mother makes them. They slay."

"Hell yes."

"She'll be home soon."

"Cool."

"Yeah. Her and my stepdad are on a date. Sunday's date night."

"Cool beans."

"Yeah," Fletcher laughed. "Say, you want to check some footy out?"

"Heck yes!" I said.

We went over to his room. The walls were painted all-Royal Blue. It was messy, I remember. He had his bed in one corner, a desk with MiniDVs everywhere, and his Macbook Pro resting on the bed. His backpack for school was on top of his computer chair. He went to Gstar, a film school that doubled as a high school, and they always had to have the students filming with MiniDVs, especially since he was a skateboarder.

He plopped onto his bed and I sat at the edge. He opened his computer and said, "Peep it." I was looking at footage of him and all his friends at Phibbs. It was stellar stuff. I remember it just looked so fun. That was what always stood out to me. Fletcher and all his friends always looked like they had fun skating.

"Shit's awesome," I said. "We should put that in *eMusic*."

"What's that?"

"*Elevator Music*."

"Oh yeah! Fuck yeah! I'll send you over the footage."

"I got my hard-drive. I brought it."

"Okay, lemme see. . . ."

I took out my hard-drive from my backpack and handed it over. Fletcher plugged it in and dragged-and-dropped footage one by one into the main folder. It was awesome. Anytime I saw stuff like that, I felt like *eMusic* was one step into the right direction. Then—

CLICK CLACK! "We're home, Peter!" a voice said.

"Come on," Fletcher said. "My mother's home."

He closed his computer and went out of his room. I followed.

I heard Fletcher's stepdad say, "I hate this door! It friggin' makes too much noise!"

"Who's this, Peter?" Fletcher's mom asked.

"This is Carl, a friend of mine. Uh, he's having some trouble."

"What is it?"

"His parents kicked him out."

"That's no good."

"I know, and he needs a place to stay—can he stay here?"

"Certainly! *All* are welcome!"

"I need a beer," Fletcher's stepdad said. "Tonight was awesome."

"I know!" Fletcher's mom said. "And Peter, honey, did you eat those chicken wings I made?"

"Yes, Mom."

"Were they good? I'll bet they were."

"Carl *loved* them."

"Oh yeah? Carl, you like 'em?"

"Yes, Mrs. Fletcher," I said.

"OH GOODNESS! Call me 'Margaret.' I'm not Mrs. Fletcher, I'm Mrs. Rosenburgh."

"No big deal," Fletcher's stepdad said from the kitchen. "Make yourself welcome, Carl. Eat whatever you want, stay how long you want —but Fletcher, where does he go to school?"

Fletcher said, "Woodhill."

"Oh! that's *my* school."

"Yup."

"Okay, is he goin' tomorrow?—Carl! How you gettin' there?"

"I'm not sure. Maybe walk?"

"Nonsense, I'll drive ya."

I said to Fletcher's dad, "Thanks, bud!"

"No problem."

"Peter," Margaret said from the living room, "can I talk to you for a second?"

"Sure, Mom." He went over. I followed.

"So what's going on with Carl? What happened?"

"Dad's a douche, kicked him out."

"I see. Well, could I have a word with you mother, Carl?"

"Sure . . ." I sighed, not really wanting Margaret to speak with her. "Here." I got out my phone. Margaret took it, dialed. Waited.

Finally, Margaret said, "Hello? . . . Yes, uh, hi. This is Fletcher's mother. . . . Fletcher is a friend of his. . . . Uh-*huh*. . . . Yup. Yes, yup . . . yes, Carl is okay. . . . Yes, but I would like to ask you something. . . . What's going on? . . . What happened exactly?"

Margaret didn't say anything for ten whole minutes. Literally. She just said a bunch of "ohs, wows, sorrys," and "uh-huhs." Fletcher and I waited on the couch. At long last Margaret said, "Okay, Mrs. Oldman. Yes . . . yes, I'll watch him . . . two weeks . . . there we go! . . . It was a real pleasure speaking to you, Mrs. Oldman." And Margaret hung up the phone and gave it back to me.

Margaret said me, "Wow, your mother is a very nice lady."

"I know. It's just my stepdad that's the asshole."

"Yeah, I know, I know. But Carl, you gotta realize something: He's just trying to help you, mold you into a good man. That's what your mother was saying." (I know this now, but I didn't then.)

"Yeah, okay . . ." I sighed. Yeah right, I thought.

"I know it's tough to believe," Margaret said, "but you will when you're older . . . but!—in the mean time—we're gonna take care of you and take you to school until all is well."

"Really?" My eyes lit up.

"Oh yes," Margaret smiled, "I'll make sure you're okay. But you gotta promise me something . . . I do NOT want you to disrespect me or my family, and I do NOT want you to do anything Peter wouldn't do. Understood?"

"Yes, Mrs. Fletcher," I said.

"Margaret, Carl. Call me Margaret. And also, I'm actually Mrs. Rosenburgh."

"Sorry."

"It's settled." She smiled. "You're staying two weeks!"

And that was it. Fletcher and I watched Netflix in his room. It was nice. Little did I know, this was to be the best two weeks of my life.

•   •   •

So we we decided to plan a trip to Miami. Fletcher said that this kid was coming from Jupiter, a town about thirty-five minutes from us. His name was Konner Murph. I could dig it. I was used to meeting new kids. (Later on, I learned I had already met him at Abocoa Skatepark in Jupiter while filming *The No Way Video*.)

It always started with me being the last to get picked up, at least in my eyes. We had two cars full of skaters. We had Fletcher, Konner, Raniel Ariaz, George, Charles, and some other kids that Konner filmed with who I didn't know at that point. This time, I was already with Fletcher, so I wasn't picked up last. I was inside the car with Fletcher, who was driving everyone. I put the board in the back trunk.

We drove an hour to get to Miami, blasting retarded music and carrying on along the way. We finally parked at Bayside. From there, we got our boards out and went to the eight-stair outside a Citi Bank. Raniel wanted to do a line so immediately the camera was rolling. *Bam!* He did it. He 180 switch nose-bunked the bench, rode along and did a fakie tre-flip, then charged toward the eight and popped the nastiest switch-flip. Landed. Bolts. We all cheered. I ran toward Konner, who was filming VX.

"Lemme peep!" I said.

Konner got out his cap-cam.

When Raniel came up, he said, "That was sketch. I want to do it again."

"Fuck no!" I said. "It couldn't get any cleaner!"

"But I heel-dragged on the fakie tre-flip."

"So! Konner was filming in *front* of you—nobody could see it anyways. Look!"

He looked down at the footage on the cap-cam.

"It's okay," he said. "Kind of lame, though, if I heel-dragged. John wouldn't like that."

Raniel was sponsored by Shreder Sheder, so he had to film for *The Shreder Sheder Video 2* and get clips. John was the owner of Shreder Sheder and Raniel was the youngin' so Raniel didn't want to be the new guy and disappoint.

"Fuck John," I said. "Film for *eMusic!*"

"Nah, I'll pass. Thanks."

He probably thought we were lame or something.

Then Raniel said to Konner, "Did Kayler text you back?"

"Nah, he didn't."

"I want a second angle on this stuff."

I skated away from them. We all skated for quite awhile at Citi Bank without getting kicked out—which surprised me, honestly. But then a cop rolled by, and at that point there were almost fifty kids at Citi Bank. The cop put on his lights and we all dipped in all different directions. It was the only thing to do. You couldn't help but laugh and get that adrenaline rush from being a kid and running away from everything. That's the name of the game.

We ended up somewhere down the street. Our group somehow reunited.

Raniel said, "Konner! Text Kayler about Citi Bank bust!"

Konner said, "Dude, he got there when it happened. I told him we're at the four-block down the street."

"Oh."

And Fletcher said, "Dude! Look at that gnarly tail-drop!"

So of course we all followed Fletcher to this huge tail-drop in front of the hotel that looked next to impossible to land. Then Kayler got there.

"Sup, bros!" he said.

"Get your camera out!" Raniel said. "Fletcher is about to do something crazy!"

So Kayler got it out.

Konner and Kayler were filming. The first try Fletcher fell but thankfully it wasn't *too* bad, because he ran down the embankment.

Then the second try, he landed! It looked clean! We all watched the footage on the cap-cam and high-fived Fletcher. Then it was off to the next spot.

We got to this church rail and Raniel was trying to 180 switch 50-50 on it but not getting close because it was *way* too high for him. I pulled Konner aside to ask him some stuff.

"Yo, man," I said. "Where do I know you from?"

"Abacoa. The skatepark. You filmed that little kid who killed it in the bowls."

"Oh yeah."

"Yeah . . ."

"So, what video are you filming for?"

"It's called *Morning Wood.* I want to make it funny as fuck. But it's hard because my lineup is too small."

"Ours is too. But we keep pushin', man."

"Yeah . . . I'm about to just sellout and give all the footage to Shreder Sheder."

"Yeah, fuck that man. We'll figure it out. Just keep it up, man."

"Thanks, Carl."

And we were buds after that.

Raniel never landed the trick. So we all left.

Then it was getting sort of nighttime. We ended up on the other side of Miami just driving around. There were these beach kickers that were perfect. Bradley Kromer skated them in the first Shreder Sheder video, and that was how they got so famous. So obviously we skated there, and boy, they were hard to skate! Fletcher was trying everything under the sun. He finally did a nose-bunk which was insane. I actually did a hard flip, but it was sketchy, so we decided not to film it. Raniel was doing all types of crap. We were filming constantly. He must have gotten ten clips that day.

Then it was fully nighttime, and we ended up at this hotel spot. It had a huge rail. Nobody wanted to skate it because we had no lights and the set was way too big for that. So we went on the roof. We looked at some stars, shrugged, went back down, and skated all around the streets. It was magical. I remember it like it was yesterday. We all were so free, the wind in our faces, and not a care in the world but skateboarding and having a good time.

We got to our cars and it was time to go home. Kayler was telling me that he would give me all the footage he filmed for the lineup in *Elevator Music*. I was hyped on that. He gave me his number.

Fletcher drove the hour back. I remember Konner was in the front seat. Konner turned around to me and said, "Klitz, I think you guys have lots of fun skating. Shit was awesome."

"Thanks man."

"I think I want to give you all the footage I have for *Elevator Music*."

I smiled and said, "Welcome aboard."

It was a fantastic day.

• • •

After a shitty school day at Woodhill, Fletcher picked me up in the parking lot. Woodhill finished an hour late, on account of it starting one hour later than everyone else. Fletcher had this girl with him. She had incredibly highlighter-blonde hair. It was so bright that when I got into the car I said, "Woah."

"What?" the girl said.

"Your hair," I said.

And Fletcher said, "Uh, this is Krystal."

"Hi, Krystal."

"Hi, uh . . ."

"His name's Carl," Fletcher said.

"Oh shit! The *Kookamonga* kid?" Krystal said.

"Yes," Fletcher said.

"DUDE! I WATCH THOSE VIDEOS LIKE CRAZY!"

My eyes lit up. "Really?" I asked.

"Oh yeah!" Krystal said. "Everyone at our school does. I thought you looked familiar dude!"

Fletcher added, "It's true. You're big at our school."

I said, "Sweet!" I scratched my head for a second. "Yo, Fletcher, are we chillin' at your place?"

"Your place? No man, we can't obviously." He thought I was talking about *my* place.

"No, Fletcher, *your* place."

"Ohhhh . . . No. We're gettin' some grub. Taco Bell."

"You mean Taco *Hell*," Krystal said.

"Same difference." And with this, Fletcher got a move on.

•   •   •

After eating at Taco Bell and messing around, the three of us went back to Fletcher's house. Once inside, I noticed that I felt like a real teenager, not just some kid that was just trying to deal with sadness. That was how Fletcher was to me: a happy-go-lucky kid who had everything in the world, and not handed to him either, just born into something "right." But anyway, the three of us were in his room. The way Krystal and Fletcher were talking made me think something.

"Are you guys . . . like, dating?" I asked them.

They looked at each other and laughed.

Fletcher said, "No way. We're just friends."

"Oh," I said, "my bad."

"It's cool, man."

Krystal said, "Guys! George is having a party this weekend! I just got a text from Jessie."

"I already knew that," Fletcher said. "That's my bestie."

"WELL *I* DIDN'T KNOW!"

"Why are you so rowdy, Krystal?" I asked.

"Bitch, because I do what I *want!*"

We all laughed.

•   •   •

In Art class I thought of drawing some band members, so I did just that. I stretched a canvas over some wood, primed it—not caring if it was dry or not, and went to town. The first one played a sax, so I made him yellow. The second one played a banjo, so I gave him a mustache. The third one was playing something super weird I remember, but whatever, it was all good. I made the stage super colorful. Super abstract. When I was done, Ms. Merchee came and told me that it was the best painting she had ever seen any of her students make. I believed her—mostly because it wasn't probably hard to do. Those kids weren't that good, I'm sorry. Maybe I'm just a picky asshole. Anyways, I thought it was neat, but soon I got sick of the painting. I called it "The Three Band Members." Whatever.

*   *   *

I went over Sam's house because she was looking to buy a VX1000. I thought that was crazy of a girl, and this lead me to believe that she was the perfect girl. She was a girl who was down, a girl who couldn't even compare to any other girl—one who I could marry. But enough with that, I went over her house to help her buy this VX1000 because I knew what to look for in the VX, considering I was ripped-off before. So Sam was covered. This filmer, Kris, came over to sell this camera. I had known of him before. He always filmed Lloyd, this big skater that was in SkateUSA. I say "big" as in his skating was big, but he was built small. He was only in his teens. Like early-teens. But anyways, Kris came over, and we all said our "what's ups" and he came in with this camera. It was decent enough. Everything about it was fine except the viewfinder cable, which had to be replaced. That wasn't a big deal. So I gave the okay to Sam and told her about the cable and she decided to purchase. They exchanged the goods and Kris said, "Pleasure doing business." But before he walked out I asked him about Lloyd's footage. I knew that Nito wanted Lloyd to have a cameo part in *Elevator Music*. Kris was shocked in a way. He actually thought I was a chump—probably because I openly asked for footage—but he had his computer and I had my flash-drive so we exchanged. Kris gave me nothing but throwaway footage. It was an insult. He was claiming to be filming for Shreder Sheder, which was retarded because Lloyd was with SkateUSA and *not* Shreder Sheder, so how in the world was his footage be going into it? Whatever. I didn't ask. So he gave me the footage and that was that. (Later on, I showed it to Nito and he shook his head at how Kris ripped me off. The footage of Lloyd was apparently his worst footage. I felt like I was ripped twice in the whole exchanging of VX1000s crap—but I guess *Elevator Music* was just another random Florida skate video. Also, Sam sold the camera two months later because she didn't want the responsibly of the thing—what with replacing everything on it and taking care of it. She sold it for what she paid for. I don't blame her.)

*   *   *

The weekend came before I knew it. I remember being with Fletcher made the time roll by so quickly. In that short amount of time with him, he had purchased a VX1000 and it was freezing on him. The colors were great but it just was fuzzy in the footage sometimes. You'd have to whack it to make it work, which wasn't a big deal. We filmed a lot of stuff in his bedroom when we could get the camera to work. We knew it was going to be for *Kookamonga*.

George's party (that I had mentioned earlier) quickly got huge around the grapevine. Everyone and their mother wanted a piece of it and wanted to go. All the skaters, all the girls—everyone knew. *Everyone*. I remember Fletcher, Krystal, George and I were all at George's trying to get the party ready.

"How much booze we got?" George asked.

"Plenty," Fletcher said. "Charles is bringing hella weed, and some of his band buddies are coming with plenty of booze."

"Bud Light?"

"Bud Light."

"Fuckin' *hate* Bud Light," I said.

"Don't be a baby-back bitch, Carl," Krystal said.

"Yup," George said, laughing.

They all laughed at me. These are my friends, I thought.

Nighttime came and the party was starting around ten. Fletcher and I were in the backyard were talking about filming spots for *Elevator Music*. We talked about how Chad was kickin' ass because I had just recently got footage from his filmer, Konner Alboo. Fletcher and I were stoked. Then people started coming.

"Hey, Fletcher!"

"Sup, Charles."

"Dude, is that Carl Klitz?"

"Yeah. Klitz, this is Charles."

"Big fan," Charles said.

"Hell yeah," I said. "But I think we skated Miami once."

"Oh, yeah! Whatever. Take this beer, Klitz." And he handed it over.

I took it and said, "Hell yeah," again.

That was the start of the worst time I got drunk.

•   •   •

People were literally *piled* into George's backyard. Two-hundred people, easily. George, Fletcher, everyone was fucked-up, but not as much as me. That night all I remember was just trying to drink as much as I could because I had been kicked out, I was around friends, and sometimes that's just the way it rolls. I drank an entire bottle of wine from some kid. He brought it to "share," but I was Carl Klitz and the kid didn't want to be judged, I guess. (Fun fact: He raped a girl we all later found out, and nobody ever fucked with him again—or maybe it was a rumor, who knows?) So I drank an entire bottle of wine and also a half a bottle of vodka. I didn't stop there. I was sipping everyone's beers. I was literally going up to them and just taking their bottles and drinking. Nobody cared. It was all Gstar kids that *adored* me. The power in that was too much. It wasn't good, but, at the time, I thought it was the coolest thing ever to do what I want.

I found myself going up to this girl who Fletcher and I had talked about from time to time at his house. She was rich beyond belief and super frickin' *hot*. The kind of hot that made you want to literally not have sex with her because of how hot she was. That's a bold statement, but I'm totally serious. So I went up to her because, well, when you spot a face like that, you just know who it is.

"Blara Dunez!" I said, coming up to her.

"Carl Klitz." She said it plain. "You're here. That's cool."

"Blara, you're so fucking *hot!*"

"Um . . ."

"Like seriously . . ." And then I noticed she was standing beside George, who was probably mackin' on her. "Blara! You and George should totally *fuck*. Oh my God! You're so fucking PERFECT! Can I suck on those tits?!" I started humping the air. "Oh, Blara!" I said, "gimme that warm, wet pussy!"

George was laughing like crazy. "Klitz, you need to chill," he said.

"He's really drunk, George," Blara said. "Help him up."

I didn't even realize I was sitting on the ground.

"George," Blara said, "put him against the wall."

"Okay."

So he did. They left.

I was talking to myself.

"Oh my God! Blara fucking Dunez *talked* to me! I'm such a fucking baller. Holy shit! Fuck! Where's Bret? Shit, where the fuck is Nito! That *asshole*, I know he knows that this party is goin' down. Holy fuck. Wait. Is that . . . Nito?!"

I looked over and, sure enough, Nito was there with Erica.

I said, "FUCK YEAH!" and got up.

I walked through the crowd with my arms out. All I remember is everyone was looking at me, the drunk kid, and moving out of my way. The sea of people parted and there was Nito at the end, looking at me and laughing. Erica over his shoulder. *Wow!*

"Dude!" I said. "Holy *fuck*, Nito! You're *here!* Nito!"

"KLITZY!"

I put my hands on his shoulders. "Dude!" I shouted. "I WANT TO FUCK BLARA DUNEZ!"

Then I turned around.

I shouted, "YOU HEAR THAT, EVERYONE! I WANT TO STICK MY DICK INSIDE BLARA DUNEZ!!"

I was pulling my pants down.

I shouted, "I WANT TO BEND THAT BITCH OVER AND SUCK THOSE TITS *DRY!*"

My dick was out. I was moving my hips back and forth. My cock was literally flopping, hitting my hips, making some thick smacking noise on my thighs.

I shouted, "OH FUCK!" I remember George and this girl named Jessie, Fletcher, and Nito all dragged me away from the party. My pants were pulled up somehow even as I walked inside the house. I don't remember it really, but I ended up in George's room.

I said, "What the fuck, guys!"

"Klitz!" George was laughing his frickin' ass off, "You crazy motherfucker, you! Chill! Just go to bed, you're literally WAY too drunk."

"Fuck that," I said, trying to stand up. "I got this shit."

And then I looked directly in front of me and I saw this blond chick.

"Who's this?" I said.

"My name is Terra. Sit. I've been taking care of you."

"TAKING CARE OF ME!? I WANT TO FUCK BLARA DUNEZ!"

"I know," Terra said. "I think everyone at the party knows."

I heard laughing.

"Step aside," I said to Terra.

"No."

"If you don't step aside, I'm going to puke on you."

"No you won't. Bet."

"Uh, Terra," George said, "I wouldn't do that . . ."

"Trust me, George, he wouldn't do such a—"

And I puked on her. I literally stepped forward and covered her. It looked like blood because of all the red wine. She didn't know what hit her.

"WHAT THE FUCK, KLITZ?!" she screamed. Then she pushed me. "WHAT A *DICK!*"

I remember when she left the room, George put his arm around me and said, "You have the biggest balls of anyone I ever saw."

"I know," I said. "Where's Blara Dunez?"

"She left, man. With her boyfriend."

"Oh! Then F *her!*"

"Yup!" George laughed. "Kick back and relax, Klitz."

So I laid down on his bed and he left. Nobody was in the room. Nobody. The room was spinning and all I thought was, "Jesus, this is boring." I couldn't get up though. All I could do was look at the ceiling and see the world spinning. The ceiling fan was just going round and round. I was having vertigo.

"Fuck this," I said. Then I got up. It took about eight tries but I finally nailed it. I was up and I tried to walk. I was stumbling like crazy. But I held the doorknob, twisted it, and all I saw were people in the hallways. Women. Talkin' about . . . me! It was funny.

I said, "Move the fuck out of my way, you beezy!"

They didn't say anything.

I found the bathroom. It was just before the outside door that led out the backyard. I went in there, door not closed behind me.

"Carl!" a female voice said. "Holy shit, Carl!"

Still peeing, I turned around. "What?"

"It's Terra. You just called Jessie and I beezies. I don't even know what a damn 'beezy' is. Anyways, are you okay?"

"No. Fuck off or I'll pee on you."

"Let me help you."

So, still peeing, I turned around and pointed my cock at her. I was peeing on her. The stream. She had been puked *and* peed on in the same night, and by the *same guy!* Too funny! But now that I think about it, we all were fucked-up people.

All I remember is people coming in. I heard Nito's voice. They all dragged me back to George's room. I felt stupid. I cried in George's bed and passed out.

I could tell my life was changing.

•   •   •

I woke up with an incredible hangover.

"My head . . . *ugh,*" I groaned.

I stood up and walked out George's room.

I got in the bathroom and immediately puked. I flushed, turned around, and walked on into the living room. Two girls were there. "Hey there . . ." I said.

They looked at me but didn't say a word.

"Uh, where's George?" I asked them.

"Do you not remember us?" one of the girls said. "I'm Terra, this is Jessie. We were trying to help you. You threw-up and peed on me. Thanks."

"Oh shit." I held my head. "I'm so fuckin' sorry. My bad, Terra."

"George and Fletcher are out getting Starbucks."

"Okay," I said, and walked away, back into George's room to lie down. I thought about what an idiot I was last night. I did this for ten minutes before I finally heard George's front door open.

All I heard was, "Where is he, still asleep?"

"No, in there. He came out and saw us."

"Oh." And then a laugh.

Then the door opened.

"BROTHA! YOU GOT WASTED!"

I looked around and it was George's voice. George and Fletcher. By God, it was weird to actually see them there. George kept talking.

"DUDE! YOU FUCK! You showed everyone you're fuckin' *dick,* dude!"

"Did I?" I held my head. "Uh . . . I don't remember."

"I'll bet," Fletcher said. "Come with us before Terra kicks your ass."

"Yeah, you're right."

So I got up and went out into the living room with Fletcher and George. They didn't look at Terra and Jessie because, well, those two girls were probably pissed as hell.

George, Fletcher, and I got into Fletcher's mom's car and drove toward Dixie Highway, where Fletcher lived.

"So . . . what all happened?" I asked the car.

"Dude," Fletcher said, "I got my dick sucked."

"WHAT!" I said. "Really?! That's awesome! By who?"

"Terra."

"The girl in the living room? The one I *peed* on?"

"Oh yeah."

"NO WAY! FUCK YEAH!"

"I know. Problem was when she and I drove back to my place, she had to change clothes 'n' shit, you assfuck."

"Sorry, bud," I laughed, "but you still got some."

"She was good, too."

"My nigga got dome!" George said. "Fuckin' Fletcher, man. Fuckin' Fletcher. . . ."

Fletcher smiled.

We got to his house and didn't do much that day. We all were pretty hungover. . . . Well, at least I was.

●　　　●　　　●

In the days following, Fletcher showed me this band. They were friends of his. Fletcher and I drove to this warehouse they rented to practice. They were this local reggae band called Roots Shakedown and were hella trippy. They had the best melodies. Fletcher and I went in there, drank beer, chilled, and I met everyone. Nice dudes. I asked them if I could use their music in *Elevator Music*. They said, "Totally!" and handed me their EP. "*Shh!* It's secret," they said. Shit, nobody had that except Fletcher and I. Fletcher's sister, Veronica, was dating the Bass Player, Albert. Fletcher had all the coolest stuff. I swear. But yeah, I had new and exciting music for *Elevator Music* so I was stoked! I wanted to use their first song on it: "Respect the Youth." Great tune. Great vibes. Very Florida. I loved it. I listen to it from time to time still for inspiration. I miss those times, even though I was a complete asshole.

•   •   •

I had to go back home because I had reached the end of my two-week stay at Fletcher's. Fletcher and I had gathered so much footage for a new YouTube video, *Kookamonga 6*, and we were thoroughly pleased with ourselves. Even Krystal was in it. Everyone. Jessie too, even though I didn't know her. Jessie was Fletcher's cousin, the girl that was at the party with puked-on Terra. We posted *Kookamonga 6* without many expectations and surprisingly it gained 3,000 views in a day. Everyone at Gstar knew about it, while everyone at my school—Woodhill—had no idea what the hell was happening. I always hated that. It was like I was living a double-life.

When I came home Ronald was outside. We didn't say hi or hellos—or at least *I* didn't. He always hated when I didn't acknowledge him. I always thought, Forget him! I ain't sayin' nothing to him! And that was the way it was. My mother was in the living room, watching *Law & Order*. I came in and she was ecstatic.

"CARL!" she said hugging me. "HOW'RE YA!? Hey, Carl, could you do me a favor?"

I let go. "What?" I said.

"Please say you're sorry to Ronald. It would mean the world to both him and I."

"Nope. He's the one who started it."

"Carl. Please."

"Nope."

My mother started to cry. "I just don't get you Carl!" she said. "He's your stepdad and you gotta respect him!"

"I'll respect him when he respects *me!*"

My mother sat back down and watched more TV. I went into my room and saw Lance, chillin'.

"Sup," he said. "Missed ya."

"Miss ya, too, bud."

"Ronald was *pissed.*"

"I know."

"He's crazy, man. I don't agree with what he did."

"Me neither."

"But I don't like how you reacted either, bro—not cool."

"Whatever," I said. "He's an ass."

I went to my computer and edited some new footage I got from Fletcher during the two weeks we skated. I got it all from my hard-drive. That was the best two weeks ever. So much fun.

I never said sorry to Ronald, but now that I think about it, I should have. I'm a better person now though. I think I just was too prideful and didn't have the balls to say I was sorry back then.

mid-2010

Very few days haunt my mind as much as this one particular day. Not because of the negativity, but because I would never forget it.

Fletcher, George, Charles, and I, were all going to Sunfest, a huge festival in West Palm Beach, Florida. It was finally in town and it was suppose to be the biggest, that year. They had lots of great shows coming. They had everything.

The boys were drinking from flasks and getting as drunk as they could, but I didn't want anything to do with drinking. I just wanted to have fun. That was spoiled as soon as the liquid reached their lips.

I spent all day babysitting those fools. It was an extra-hot day, the Florida sun was beating and blazing down, and I had to take care of them.

They were seeing all their friends around Sunfest. They would say, "Hi," act belligerent, and talk nonsense. I got the feeling that this was what it was like when people saw me in *Kookamonga* or something.

Fletcher saw this girl he wanted to fuck. She was busty, tall, and tan. Her name was Karly Gogert. She was immensely hot. I remember he was following her around like a puppy-dog, and she knew what he wanted.

"Man," I told him, in confidence, "she's fuckin' with you. She doesn't want you. Seriously."

"Klitz, shut up. You don't know anything about girls. You've never even *had* a girlfriend or *had* sex. I got this."

"Whatever you say, chief."

And that was that. She tagged along, this girl I really didn't have much respect for except to look at those tits, that ass, that face, and that waist. That's all she was good for, in my bleak eyes. Hot girls tended to always bring about the worse in me because I wanted them so bad and they wouldn't give it up.

Night finally revealed itself after day got so drunk it went home. We all were on Clematis Street, trying to find some sort of joy. I remember we ended up at some bar. It was a hookah bar. I remember Roots Shakedown was playing inside it. Charles was vibin' out. Charles was always so funny. He was a Spanish kid, but so white, so irie. ("Irie" is a made-up term used to say "awesome," but we said it because we thought a Rastafarian would say something like it. We were stupid.)

"Carl, mon!" Charles said.

"What's up?" I said. "You good?"

"Oh hella good, mon!"

I laughed and said, "Good."

"Yeah mon, Roots! JAH IS THE *TRUTH!*"

"Irie!" I shouted.

"IRIE!" he shouted.

And we watched Roots Shakedown play.

I remember Karly and Fletcher were dancing together, and Fletcher was trying hard to grab her ass. I looked out into the crowd and saw many chicks actually.

I heard from beside me, this girl speaking to this other girl about the lead singer of Roots Shakedown.

"Oh my God! Ted Stacka is so hot!"

"I know. I would ride him *raw.*"

"Did you know he surfs?"

"Duh! He plays reggae, you 'tard."

"Oh, my bad."

They laughed.

I was jealous of this man who sang beautifully. I was jealous that women adored him. I was so jealous in fact, that I forgot all those times at parties I was also told that I was hot. But when jealousy or depression hits you always forget who you are and all the good things you have, and that most people think of you positively.

The show was over. I shook Ted's hand and said, "You killed it, man."

"JAH!" he said, and turned to more people that were probably going to say the same thing. Ted was actually very cool. He was the king, I thought. His music was so original, so true, and so alive. And I loved it.

Fletcher, George, Charles and I—not Karly, who left with Ted, even though he probably wouldn't choose her, considering other chicks there were hotter and better—all went out on Clematis. I was pissed. I literally felt the back of my neck, and it was burned. I was so sunburned it wasn't even funny. And there they were, still drunk, still drinking, still having fun. It wasn't going to stop.

We all stopped by the triangle play fountain. I thought it was going to be spewing out water, but it wasn't because (a) Sunfest, and (b) It was nighttime. I sat at one of the benches there, though. The rest of them were standing.

"Come on, Klitz," Fletcher said, "don't be a big puss."

"I'm tired, man."

"UGH!" He turned around and his eyes lit up. "Holy shit . . . Terra! Jessie!"

Oh God . . . I thought. Puke girl!

"HEY, FLETCHER!" Terra said, running toward him. They hugged. "Hell yeah! You guys are *here!*"

"I know. We just been partyin' all around."

"Oh, hell yeah! Did you see Ted's show?"

"Yeah!"

"I totally missed it. We just got here," Terra sighed.

Then she looked around. "Hey, Charles. Hey, George. Hey . . . uh, Carl . . . ?"

"Hey, Terra," I said. "I hope you're not mad at me."

"Apology accepted."

"Good, because . . . um . . . I really, *really* felt bad about that night. Shit, I didn't even drink today—I've had a shitty day."

"Damn," she said. She sat next to me. "I'm sorry . . ."

"It's okay. I guess it's karma."

"Carl, it's really okay." She scooted closer. "You're sweet. Everything's fine."

"Do you really mean that?"

"Yes." She smiled. "Do you want to take a picture?"

"Sure!" I said.

We both got up.

"Jessie!" Terra beckoned, "come hither! Take our photo!"

Jessie waddled over. "Okay," she said.

Terra handed Jessie her phone. I remember Jessie held it up and said, "You guys ready?" and Terra held my arm, brought me close, and I stood there, legs out, hands in pockets, grinning like a 'tard.

Jessie snapped the photo. "Here," she said, handing over Terra's phone. Then Jessie walked back to Fletcher, George, and Charles.

Terra opened up the photo. I was looking down at it. There I was—sure enough, hands in pockets, legs out, grinning like a 'tard. And I had black pants that were too tight and too dressy for me. And there she was, in a white flowy dress, I thought she looked cute.

"We look good," Terra said. "Don't you think so?"

"Yes," I said. "But you look better."

Terra gave me a flirt punch. "Oh stop!" she said. "You're honestly really, really handsome, Carl. Seriously. I think you could be a damn model!"

I smiled.

I heard, from Fletcher, "Ohhhhh . . . look at *you two!*" And some laughs.

"Oh stop it!" Terra said to all of them.

Then a minute turned into an hour, and an hour turned into three. And that was it. That was what time was like. I remember I thought Terra was going to be a good friend of mine.

"Let's go," she said to everyone, later. "I'll give y'all and ride."

We all said, "Yes."

We walked all the way from Clematis to City Place. We found Terra's parking-garage and we hopped into her car.

The whole ride was a nightmare. Fletcher was talking about Karly, and how he could have fucked her, and how hot she was. Terra was silent the whole time. I was talking with George about skating.

"Karly doesn't want you, Fletcher," Terra said. "She's got you wrapped around her finger."

"You don't know that," he said. "You don't know anything."

"Whatever, Fletcher."

More into the ride Fletcher was talking about an ex of his (I forget her name) and more chicks he had messed with—minus Terra of course, because we all *knew* that.

Finally we got to George's house, dropped him off, and Terra drove on.

"Ain't it a bitch," Fletcher said, "when women treat you like some sort of simp."

"Yeah it is . . ." I said, "but you know what, woman *can*—we *can't*."

"Yeah, because they got the pussy, we got the money."

Everyone kept silent until we got to Fletcher's.

"Bye," he said, and shut Terra's door.

When he was out the car and went on inside his house, Terra said to Jessie and me, "What a cock-suck! I hate Fletcher."

"I know," Jessie said, "he's being so stupid."

"He was drunk, guys," I informed.

We started to drive to my place. It was going to be awhile.

"I just don't get guys," Terra explained, "I just hate them. I hate them. All they want to do is have sex, have this, have that. Us girls, *pshhh!* We only try to look good for *other* girls! Guys are just there to be boy-toys, that's it! Fletcher is wrong. I hate Fletcher, *God* I hate Fletcher!"

She only hated him because she sucked his dick and he was moving on to the next girl on the list to suck his dick.

I said, "Not all guys are like that."

"Explain . . ." Terra said. "What do you mean, Carl?"

"Well, I say this oddly, but if I was to have a girlfriend I would treat her like a princess. I wouldn't just try to sit there and have sex with her. I would actually treat her right and make sure she was safe and all—that's what I'd do." I was only vaguely lying, but partially telling the truth—I actually *did* want a type of relationship like that, but it seemed impossible for me.

"Wait," Terra said, looking over at Jessie, "*if* you had a girlfriend?"

"Yes. If," I said.

"You never had one, Carl?"

I shook my head.

Terra said, "Hm . . . interesting."

"Yup," I said. "So Terra, chin up. A guy will come around."

"Carl?"

"Yes, Terra?"

"Can I see your phone?"

"Sure. Yeah. I guess."

I got out my phone and gave her it.

While she drove, she started typing. I never understood how someone could drive and type. That's like, the most dangerous thing ever.

Terra handed my phone back to me.

"There's my number," she said. "Text me sometime. We should hangout."

"Okay," I said.

Then, before I knew it, there was my house. We were in front of it. "Thanks, Terra," I said. " 'Preciate it."

"No problem. TEXT ME, SILLY!" She gave me an air-kiss.

I grinned. I noticed Jessie was grinning at Terra, and Terra was grinning at Jessie. Then they giggled and drove off.

I had no idea that Terra liked me. I really didn't. I just thought she wanted to be friends with me and that's it.

Boy, was I wrong.

•　　•　　•

There were only about three weeks left of school and Terra, my new-found buddy, was picking me up in her SUV everyday after school. She would drive me to my house and hang out. My brother and her got to talkin' a lot. They laughed and messed around—my brother thought she was cool.

Terra and I would just lay there in my bed and watch movies on my iMac. It was really relaxing, I remember. We just spoke casually. Nothing fancy. I thought she was a good friend.

"I'll see ya tomorrow," she would say.

And I'd say back, "Yup, see you too," and close the gate outside for her. And she would drive off. We did this until summer started.

•   •   •

I was telling Sam about Terra. I was saying that I liked her and that I was nervous because I was seventeen and hadn't kissed a girl yet. Sam was saying that she wanted to help me and asked if I could come over to her house so she could "teach me how to kiss." I was cautious about that and told her that we shouldn't because how would Will, her boyfriend, feel about that? She stopped for a moment and said, "Yeah, you're right." I think she liked me, but I'm not too sure. Maybe it was nothing. It probably was. Sam's an awesome, awesome girl. I think she liked me, and that's okay. She just wanted to help me and make me feel secure in the kissing department, and about myself. I thanked her for that.

•   •   •

I texted Charles one night that I really thought I liked Terra. He said to not be a pussy and to just "go for it." He told me not to worry about it, that I was a nice guy, a great guy, and any chick would be awesome to actually date me or something. It wasn't gay of him or anything; he was just being a good friend. "Thanks," I told him. He said not to mention it, and that Terra would come around.

•   •   •

Terra came over one day to chill with my brother and me. I went to the bathroom for a second, but when I came back, she just looked sadly at me and left. I didn't get it. Odd.

•   •   •

One night, Terra and I were to hangout at Jessie's house. Jessie's house was really fancy—mansion type of shit. She was a rich girl—her mother was a lawyer. Terra and I drove over to the house and I met this lady there. Her name was Karleena. She was a beautiful MILF, and was Fletcher and Jessie's aunt. Pretty wild. She would smoke cigarettes and tell me how sweet I was and everything. I remember Terra got really jealous of her.

"Carl is a very sweet guy!" Karleena said to Terra. "Why aren't you two dating?"

"Oh I don't—"

I interrupted Terra. "Because we're friends."

"Yeah . . . friends," Terra agreed.

"Cudda fooled *me!*" Karleena said. "Would make a cute couple."

"Yeah," Terra said, "but we aren't, so . . ."

And that was it. The night sort of ended. Terra was driving me home. We were silent for some time. Then, she broke it.

"Carl, what the fuck is *wrong* with you?"

"Wha . . . ?"

"You don't know *why* I'm mad?"

"No . . ."

"Carl, I *saw* that text to Charles."

"What?"

"I saw that text to Charles!"

"Oh . . ."

"You *like* me?"

"Well, I thought I do. I'm not sure . . ."

We drove silent until the front of my house. When we got there, Terra stopped the car and hastily turn to me and said, "Listen, Carl. I don't want to play games. Do you like me or don't you? Don't give me a bullshit answer."

"Uh," I sighed. "I really don't know."

"Answer. It's simple."

"Uh, yes?"

"Yes, what?"

"Yes."

"Yes you don't, or yes you do?"

"Yes I do. I like you. I just thought, you know, I could never have you."

"Why, Carl?"

"Because I never had a girlfriend before."

Terra smiled and got silent.

"Well, that's that," she said. "We like each other."

"Wha . . . ?" I said. "Are you serious?"

"Yes, Carl. I like you. You're awesome."

"Holy shit."

"See you tomorrow?"

"See you tomorrow," I said.

I got out and shut the door. Terra blew me a kiss.

Holy shit! What the fuck just happened? I thought.

•   •   •

Next day, Terra came over.

"Hey, Carl!" she said as I opened the gate for her.

"Hey!"

We hugged.

"What movie are we watchin'?" Terra asked.

"I'm not sure," I said. "Probably something Disney. I'm sort of in the mood."

"Awesome. Which one?"

"The Lion King."

"Yes. My favorite!"

And we went inside.

In my room, my brother was lying on my bottom bunk of the bed. He said to Terra, "Hey, loser."

"Hey, butthead," she said.

"You guys want me to go?"

"Yeah . . . if you don't mind," Terra said.

I had already told my brother Lance about what had happened the night before, so he was all about giving us some space.

She went to the bed when he got up. He passed me and whispered in my ear, "Get it, dude," and shut the door behind him.

I rolled my eyes and went to my computer. I looked through my "Movies" folder and started up *The Lion King* and went to my bed to lay down next to her, like we always did.

"I'm comfy," Terra said, snuggling up to me.

"Me too."

And the whole *nants ingonyama bagithi baba* song played in the intro. I start singing it and Terra was laughing so hard. She hugged me.

"You're so funny, Carl."

I smiled.

We were watching the movie and she was hugging me, doing crazy stuff like touching my stomach and rubbing me. I remember she kept looking up and down: at me, then at the movie, then at me, then at the movie. I was thinking, "What's going on with her?"

Finally, after repeating this motion over and over, she looked up at me and said, "UGH! You're helpless," and got on top of me, wrapped those beautiful legs around me, and pressed her big lips against my thin lips. Hard.

I thought, "Holy shit! What the *heck*, man? This girl is *literally* on top of me! She kissed me! SHE KISSED ME! HOLY FUCK!" Then she got off of me and stood up and smiled.

"So . . . How was it?" she asked me.

"Holy . . . shit."

"What?"

"Holy . . . fuckin' . . . *shit.*"

"WHAT!"

"That was awesome, but that is crazy—I can't believe you kissed me."

"More where that's coming from. But listen, I gotta go."

"Okay," I said.

She left, and I saw her out. Another kiss and she drove off.

Later, my brother came in, and I told him about the kiss. He congratulated me. It was cool. Then he got a call from a friend of his to bowl. So Lance asked me, "Wanna go?" and I said, "Sure," and that was it. We went.

•   •   •

At the bowling alley we all were having a grand time, sipping beer, making strikes, and just chillin', when suddenly I got this feeling.

"Guys, I gotta step outside."

"Sure," my brother and his friends said.

And I went outside. I was holding my head. Something was wrong. I was super dizzy—dizzier than anything. Dizzier than spinning for hours, and I wanted to just fall down.

I got out front and called someone: my sister in Texas. Her name is Krissy. She's awesome. She was late twenties, she had two kids, and she was meaner than sin.

The phone was dialing. She finally picked up.

"Car?"

"SISSY!"

"HEY! HOW ARE YA, CAR?!"

"I'm not doing so good." I was huffing and puffing, holding my head, and looking down at the ground. "Oh my God!" I said. "Holy shit, I'm not feeling so good."

"What's wrong?" my sister asked. "What the hell is going on? Where are you? Are you okay?"

"I'm at the bowling alley with Lance."

"And . . . ?"

"I don't know. I'm feeling so weird."

"What happened?"

"I kissed a girl!"

My sister stopped for a second, laughed hysterically, then said to me, "Holy crap, Carl! You're funny!"

"Huh?"

"You're just in shock. It's okay."

"What's shock?"

"It's basically a panic attack. You're just happy, is all. It's something new."

"Holy fuck," I said, still holding my head. "Are you serious?"

"Yeah. You just did something new, is all."

"Okay, Sissy. I'm gonna go home now."

"I love you."

"I love you too."

I hung up.

"Woah," I said.

That was my first panic attack and my first real encounter with anxiety. And it wasn't going to be my last.

•   •   •

Sometimes, mostly right after she would leave my house, Terra would call me.

"Yeah?" I'd say.

"So, what's up?"

"I don't know you just left, babe."

"I know. Just thinkin' about'cha."

"Cool."

My brother would be laughing as I was standing beside him—he knew the drill of women.

"What'cha thinkin' about?" Terra'd ask. "Want to know what *I'm* thinking about?"

"What?"

"Your cock."

I would get excited.

Then she would randomly start crying minutes later.

"I hate school! I hate my damn life! This shit sucks! CARL! HELP!"

"Babe," I'd say, "a moment ago you wanted 'my cock.'"

"No! What I *said* was I was *thinking* about it, not wanting it, you perv!"

"Sorry, but I'm just confused."

"WHATEVER!" and she'd hang up.

About five minutes of talking to my brother on why girls do this, Terra called back.

"Hey, babe. I'm sorry I called you a perv," she'd say.

"It's cool," I'd say out of kindness.

My brother would laugh. Conversations like this happened so frequently with her that it's impossible to map them out entirely. Pretty much I would spend hours with the girl, comforting her, telling her she was awesome, and she would actually make me happy. I think I made her happy, too . . . if she stopped and thought about it.

●　　●　　●

Terra and I drove over to Howley's one morning, her favorite place to eat breakfast. I remember I ordered some pancakes and she just got this big meal of whatever. The waitress came up. Her name was Katie Swoop, according to her nametag, and she was a friend of Terra's.

Katie came up and they shot the shit. She took our order and everything. It was cool. After we got our stuff and got the check, Katie was telling us about some guy that was super rude to her.

When we got out we saw the bartender chasing after some guy who I assumed was a dick to Katie. Terra said, "What a low-life," as we got outside.

The guy sped down Dixie. We didn't think much of it.

Terra and I decided to go downtown, so we drove there and parked. We walked around City Place a bit. I remember we found this balloon stand: "OH *MY!*" Terra said. "LETS GET ONE!"

We bought three: blue, green, and red.

She was happy. So we kept on walking.

We got to the City Place Towers, the apartment across from the old Barnes & Noble (that is now a gym), around twelve o'clock. We saw a bunch of people out front, looking up. A guy was on top of the tower. He was about to jump and kill himself. This girl had a megaphone and was talking him down. I think it was the guy's girlfriend.

"Crazies in this town," Terra said. "Oh shit!" She accidentally let go of her balloons. "My damn balloons!" They flew right in front of the guy on the roof.

We watch all this go down. We watched and watched. It was scary. He finally came down though. The girl that had the megaphone had her arms around the guy. I overheard the guy tell the girl, "Shelby, I need to find my elevator music." I thought it was a frickin' sign. So crazy. This guy ended up on the News!

"Lets go," I said to Terra.

"Okay."

We went to her SUV and drove back to my place, went inside, watched movies, and we made-out.

What a weird day, I thought.

•   •   •

Dinner dates . . . dinner dates . . . dinner dates.

I can't even remember them all.

Time stood still.

•   •   •

I had a friend named Grent Flan Flan. That was his last name: Flan Flan. He was amazing at photography. He could do anything and everything. Behind a camera, he could make a photo look amazing. For a while I would hit him up to shoot some photos and we would drive anywhere to take them. Once, we went to an abandoned school and were just looking around. No cops came, and we just took the best photos and it was honestly the greatest thing ever. I just remember that. I remember all of the photos we took and how they would come out. We actually made a club after school: "The Photography Club." And people went! There was a darkroom, at Woodhill, which was crazy. Grent just wanted to make the club so he could put his chemicals in there and have his own "private darkroom," he said. He could care less about the other students. We all just did this for a while and it took my mind off Terra, for some odd reason. It took my mind off everything. Art always did that for me. I just remember that . . . I just remember that.

•   •   •

My birthday was coming up on July seventh. My friends and I had been skating a lot, I was seeing Terra a lot, and everything was great. My birthday was coming!

The day of, I had invited every friend I knew. Bret came. Fletcher came. George came. Charles came. Terra came. I invited them all to my house for a BBQ. It was going to be awesome, I thought. And it was, mostly.

Everyone came out—it took until eight o'clock for them all to arrive. We all just chilled in the living room and talked. There was a lot of food and music. Everyone was just acting sort of chill. That's it.

Then nine o'clock rolled around and the birthday cake was coming. Everyone was circled around the cake and around me. They all looked at me. It was pretty surreal. They all sang the "Happy Birthday" song.

I was looking down at that cake. Oh, that cake. It looked so good. It was chocolate. The candles were perfect. I blew them out while everyone was singing. My wish was to have sex with Terra.

Afterward, she came up to me, handed me a letter, and I torn it open and read, in my head: "Baby! Gosh! I can't believe you turned eighteen! My awesome man! You're so sexy. I love you very, very much. You are honestly the best, and I wish the best in the world for you. — Terra XOXO." That was it. I closed it up, looked up at everyone, and closed my eyes. I breathed in the awesome-ness. When I opened my eyes, everyone was looking around at each other. It was silent . . . a very awkward silence.

Bret said, "So . . . uh, I better get goin' . . ."

Terra said, "Well, there's something happening at Jessie's house. We all should go there."

Everyone was just sort of going out the front door, which was right beside the table, next to the cake and me.

I didn't even eat a slice of that chocolate cake my mother made.

•   •   •

Then it was off to Jessie's house/mansion. Bret (who was dating Jessie at the time), Terra, Fletcher, and I, we all just sitting on the couch and laughing and talking about crazy stuff. I miss those talks.

"Where's the beer?" I asked Fletcher.

"I'll get it," Jessie said.

She came back with Vodka, beer—everything. The house was stacked! Apparently her mother drank a lot so, *yippie!*

I drank and drank, and it was great. I drank until I was burger: the kind of drinking where your vision is not only pretty much gone, but the world seems to not even matter.

I found myself in the backyard. I noticed Aunt Karleena was out there smoking a cigarette alone. She was sitting on a plastic chair and another empty chair was sitting right beside her. She looked good. Like *real* good. Better than usual, considering I was drunk. Aunt Karleena was slim, had big boobs, a nice ass, a nice body, great face, a total MILF! Straight up!

"Hey, Carlerz," she said.

"Terra calls me that."

"I know. I stole it from her."

"You wear it well."

Then I sat beside her, in the plastic chair.

"So . . ." I said, "Karleena. Karleena-baby. What's up?"

"Nothin' much," she said, looking down at her phone, the blue light shining in her face. "There's this guy . . ."

"Yeah?" I said. "Who?"

"You wouldn't know him. He's at my gym. Basically, get this: he is ripped, looks great, and he's—listen to this—*twenty* years old!"

"Wow."

"Just think! That's only two years older than you, Carlerz."

"Wow," I said, grinning. "That's wild!"

"I know!"

I thought I was going to have sex with her.

"Anywho," I said, "why aren't you inside?"

"I just don't like to intervene with you guys. I'm actually just visiting here. I'm going to school to be a paralegal. I'm just staying here because my sister lets me."

"Jessie's mom?"

"Yes. She lets me crash here. My boyfriend dumped me. It sucks."

I thought, "Oh yes, I'm going to definitely have sex with her."

"That's so sad!" I said. "I'm sorry to hear that."

"You're a good listener, Carlerz."

"Yeah?"

"No wonder Terra likes you so much."

"Yeah?"

"I must say . . . I do have a crush on you, just a little bit, Carlerz."

"REALLY! Because I feel the —"

And I was cut off but the door crashing open. It was Terra.

"Carlerz!" Terra said. "I'm so FUCKING PISSED at Fletcher! He's being such an ass! Jessie and I are going to the store. Come with us."

"Nah," I said. "I'm going to talk with Karleena."

"Why?"

"Just let him, Terra," Karleena said sternly. "I'll take care of him. Get some beer."

"Okay . . . ?" Terra said, unsure. "See ya, Carlerz. Love you."

"I love you too."

And that was the first time I said it to Terra, in a moment of her very own jealousy of Karleena and I.

She left and I continued to talk with Karleena.

"So . . . Karleena?"

"Yes, Carlerz?"

"We pretty much have the same name."

"I know, right?!"

"But, hey, Karleena. Why is Terra pissed at me, you think? I don't really get it."

Karleena told me a lot of things about women. This whole idea wasn't clear to me, on account of my ignorance at the time. She told me all about the envy of women and their little mind-games, competitions, and overall insecurities in life. Karleena put me into perspective. I have no idea if it was bullshit, but maybe it was just Florida women. Karleena said, "Terra's only jealous of you basically because you and I are talking and she wants to take you away from that. It's that simple."

"Oh," I said.

"And Carl?"

"Yeah . . . ?"

"What's your number?"

"Gimme your phone."

Karleena handed me her phone, I entered my cell phone into there. I handed it back and said, "Well . . . do you want to go inside? I'm drunk."

Karleena laughed. "Sure."

She never texted me. Only called once.

•   •   •

All I remember after that is drinking with Karleena, Terra coming back to the house/mansion, Bret laughing really hard at my antics, me saying fucked shit, me sitting behind Terra in the same chair she was sitting in while she talked with Karleena later in the night, me touching Terra under the table in front of us while she was talking to Karleena, me puking in the toilet, me telling Terra and Fletcher to make-out on the couch and Fletcher being sort of *into* the idea but Terra shaking her head no, and me passing out. I'd say it was a pretty good birthday . . .

•   •   •

Until I woke up with my eyes closed, oddly. I was listening and hearing voices. I found myself lying on the couch in the living room. I turned over and reached down into my pocket to get my cell phone: it was 5:03 a.m. I was hungover, badly. I closed my eyes again and listened. It was Fletcher and Terra talking.

"I just don't get him. I really don't."

"What's not to get? He's him."

"Yeah I know . . . but . . . Look, Carl is great and all, and I love him, but he's really lazy. He doesn't do anything."

"He's a skateboarder."

"That's no excuse. So are *you* . . ."

"Yeah, but I'm different. Carl doesn't even go to Gstar—he goes to Woodhill. Fuck that place. Shit, you'd be lazy, too, if you went there. George even goes there. Look at him."

"I know but still, he's just . . . not . . . you know, *you*, Fletcher."

"What do you mean?"

"He's, well, you know. Remember at George's party when I sucked your dick?"

"Yeah . . . ?"

"I miss that Fletcher. Basically when Carl asked if we could make-out jokingly, I, well—I was thinking about *doing* it."

"Why, though?"

"Because. I don't know . . . Because I like you, in a way."

"Well . . . you gotta figure out what you want to do with him."

"He literally doesn't do homework. He doesn't even care about shit. He comes home, sleeps, eats, shits, watches movies, watches skate videos, edits, skateboards, and that's it. He doesn't care about grades, or any of that stuff."

"Terra, honey. It's not what he's into."

"I know, Fletcher, I know. But I just wish he was, you know, *more* . . . You know, when I start school, it'll be a relief having him around."

"Why?"

"Well, because. . . ."

"Because . . . ?"

"Basically I, like, literally think that I'm only dating him to text all day in my classes to get through the school day. When I go back to school this year at Joe Pope" (a Catholic private school she went to full of rich preppy kids) "and having nobody to talk to, I can count on just texting him in class. I can just text him. Just text, text, text. And—"

I lost it. Seriously. I had to stop her there.

I got up and shouted, "OH YEAH! WELL FUCK YOU, BITCH! FUCK YOU! WE'RE BROKEN UP, YOU PUNK BEEZY!"

She took her hand off Fletcher's arm and just looked straight at me, shocked.

"Fuck you, Terra," I said. "We're fucking done."

"Carl . . ."

"No! Fuck off."

"Carl."

"No, don't talk to me in that tone."

"You really want to do this to me, Carl?"

"Yes. Fuck yes. Just text you? What am I, your lackey? Fuck off, bitch. Go suck a dick or something. Care about me? *Pfft!* Bull! You care about nobody but yourself, bitch. So fuck off. Git!"

Terra started to cry. "I can't believe this, Carl!" She had her hands on her face. "I can't fucking believe you!"

"Yeah, well, suck it up buttercup, because I'm not with you no more. Find somebody else that'll care enough to text you while you're in class, bitch."

Terra stood up, held those crying eyes of hers, and ran out the living room, down the hall, and then I heard the door slam shut.

"Dude," Fletcher said, "you did good."

"I know, man," I said. "What a bitch."

"I tried having your back, man."

"I know."

"You could do better. Seriously, man. I know you've never had a girlfriend, but she's not the best bet, man. Seriously. I actually didn't like you guys dating, to begin with."

"I get it. Lets not talk about it. I feel like complete shit."

"What's going on?" a voice said.

Fletcher and I looked over toward the kitchen. It was Karleena's voice.

"I heard screaming," she said. "What's up?"

"Nothin' much," I said, "except that Terra's a bitch. She said I was good-for-nothing, and that she was going to use me as her texting buddy when school finally starts back up because she's lonely. Then she says that Fletcher was the one she *really* wanted to date."

"Not exactly bud," Fletcher intervened. "She said she wanted to *kiss* me, not date—there's a difference."

"Whatever," I said. "That's what happened, Karleena—I broke up with her."

"Oh, poor baby," Karleena said.

I went home as soon as I could, which was around seven a.m.

●   ●   ●

For three days I did nothing but sulk. I waited and waited but never got a text or call from Terra. I was worried. I was depressed. It was the only thing on my mind. I couldn't even skate. I denied all contact with my skate-buddies to get footage for *Elevator Music*.

But then, out of nowhere one night my phone rang. I looked at the screen: it was a weird number. I answered.

"Yo?"

"Carlerz?"

"Is this Terra?"

"No, it's Karleena."

"Oh, hi Karleena."

"Hi, Carlerz . . . Okay. So. Here's what's happening. Please call Terra. She's sick."

"Sick?"

"She's been throwing up the past three days."

"Since we broke up?"

"Mhm."

"So . . . ? Fuck that cunt."

"Carlerz, stop. You know you love her. She's your woman. Please call her and make her feel better. Please. I'm worried sick. She misses you like crazy!"

"Okay, fine! I'll call. But only for you, Karleena."

"Thanks, Carlerz. Call me back afterward. I want deets. Goodbye."

"Goodbye," I said.

Karleena hung up. That was the only time she ever called me.

I looked at my phone and dialed Terra. It buzzed twice before she answered.

"Carlerz?" she said.

"Yo."

"Carl!" Terra said through tears. "BABY! I MISS YOU SO MUCH!!"

I rolled my eyes. "Okay," I said into the phone, "Now lets make something clear. We aren't dating still. But I wanted to call you because I'm worried about you. What's this I hear about you puking?"

"I've been puking and crying all day, every day, for the passed three days."

"So I hear."

"Lets get back together."

"Yeah, yeah, sure, sure."

"I'm serious! Can I just come over?"

"You can tomorrow. It's about almost midnight tonight."

"Okay. Can I in the morning?"

"Sure."

"Okay, Carl. I love you."

"I, um, like you too."

"Okay. Bye."

"Bye," I said, and hung up.

I never called Karleena back about the conversation.

•   •   •

The next day Terra came over in the morning. She walked up with Starbucks. I could see her from the living room window walking up to my front door. *Knock, knock*. I opened it.

"Hey," I said.

"Hey baby," Terra said. "I brought you a Trenta Ice Coffee."

"Hell yes!" I said, waving her inside.

She walked in.

"Can we just lay down?" she asked. "Lets just lay down in your bed."

"Okay," I said. And we did.

I was drinking my drink in one hand, head lying on my pillow, and she was in my arms, resting on my chest. She was talking.

"Carl, I'm just sooo damn sorry. Seriously. I was a jerk. I didn't mean those things I said, I just worry about you. You're so smart and I want you to turn out okay. It's nothing personal."

Even though I was thinking, "Yeah right, you just wanted to have sexy-time with Fletcher," in reality, I said, "Yeah, I know you're sorry—it's okay."

"Is it?" Terra asked. "I just want us to be back together."

"I do too."

"You do?"

"Yes. I love you."

She got on top of me and we made-out. She took my eighteen-year-old hand and put it to her small sixteen-year-old breasts. Then she grinned to herself about my boner through my pants. She giggled and said, "I love you, baby."

"Awesome," I said, feeling really confused about my feelings toward her.

"Say, Carl. I have a question. This weekend Fletcher, Charles, George and everyone are going to the beach. Do you wanna go with me?"

"Yeah, sure."

"I think it'll be fun. BBQ and everything!"

"Okay," I said.

We made-out for a little longer and then watched some movies. To be honest I don't really remember much after that, but she did stay a couple of hours.

•   •   •

Days later at the beach all my buddies were playing football by passing it back and forth to each other endlessly while Terra was talking to Charles across the way in the ocean and I was there sitting by myself making a sandcastle but then I turned it into a turtle and it took forever but it came out great. Upon which, after noticing that I wasn't there because of how much fun I'm assuming she was having, Terra came up and asked me, "What are you doing, babe?" and I said, "Making a turtle," and I continued my merry way. She shrugged and went over to some more of her friends and it was fine. Karleena was there too. She walked up to me and asked me if I was okay. I said, "No, I'm really not . . ." and left it at that. The beach was great, the sounds were awesome, but I felt oddly depressed and I didn't know why.

•   •   •

Terra came over one day and we were in my room talking. Terra was explaining something to me that she thought was serious.

"Carl," she said, "I don't think I know what we are."

"Mhm." I wasn't listening much. I was on Facebook, playing *FarmVille*.

"CARL!" Terra said, getting my attention.

"Yeah?!"

"I'm trying to talk to you."

I turned off the computer and walked over to her, to my bed, where she was laying. "Yeah . . ." I said. "What?"

"Don't say 'what' like that Carl, you big butthead. I'm trying to tell you that I don't know what we are anymore."

"Are we dating?"

"I just don't think so."

"Well, then we'll get through it."

"I think so." She smiled.

I smiled too, and then said, "Do you want to go to the beach?"

"Oh yes!" Terra said. "LETS!"

So we got dressed for the beach, stood up, went outside to her SUV, and drove off to Lake Worth beach. The place was pretty much empty.

"Whole beach to ourselves," she said.

"Yeah," I said, having déjà vu. "Lets go."

Outside, walking up to the beach, my feet hurt. "Ouch!" I said. "My feet fuckin' hurt."

"You should have brought sandals," Terra said, looking down at her pink sandals. "Missin' out!"

I shrugged.

When we got to the shore we looked out on the horizon. Oddly, I had slight feelings of déjà vu swooping over me. Like life was just beginning and that I wasn't real, and that this life was all laid-out for me, and I had no control of it. No free will, no nothing—I was just an aimless creature here and my mind just sort of beeps here and beeps there for when life comes my way, and it's just a chemical reaction. Anxiety washed over me for a brief moment, and then went away when Terra said, "You okay?"

"Yeah, just thinking too much."

"Lets go in the water Carlerz."

"Okay."

And we did. We went out far. So far out that we couldn't see the people lying out on the sand.

It was just the two of us.

I remember I turned to her, lifted her up from the water, and kissed her on the lips. She giggled profusely, but then stopped. I could see in her eyes that something was bothering her, but I didn't know what. It was something hidden, something wrong—very wrong. And then she spoke.

"Carl," she said, "I just don't know what we are anymore."

I didn't say anything.

"Carl, lets go back to shore."

"Okay," I said.

So we did. We shimmied our way separately to shore. Once we got there, we slapped our wet footsteps on the sand and looked at each other but didn't smile. And then this girl came up to us—I don't remember her name, but I did know of her at the time.

"Terra!" she said. "OH MY GOD! WHAT'S UP!?"

And Terra screamed her name and they hugged, then Terra said, "Nothin' much, we're just out here."

"You're with Carl *Klitz?* Wow! What are you guys, boyfriend and girlfriend?"

"Uh . . ." Terra hesitated, "he's, uh, my friend . . ."

"Oh okay, because that would have been a steal, Terra. Carl is funny as hell. You ever see his *Kookamonga* videos?"

"Yes, I'm aware of them."

"Well, anyways, it was nice to see you."

"You too," Terra sighed.

"Yep," I said.

And the girl went on her merry way.

"Lets go," Terra said, irritated.

We walked all the way back to the car and I thought, "Crap, we were only there fifteen minutes." The drive to Lake Worth is fifteen minutes. Inside the car we were silent for a moment. Terra wasn't starting her car. Then she said, "I can't believe I don't know what we are." Then she started the car and we were off.

During the drive from Lake Worth beach to Popeyes, the place she wanted to eat, I thought about how crappy life was—or still is. I just thought how it could be so cruel, so unfair, so aimless, that I had no control. I remember Terra was playing Ke$ha's "Your Love Is My Drug," and even to this day when I hear that song I always think of her. I thought about all of this life stuff until Terra said to me, "What do you want?"

"We're already at the drive-through?"

"Yes."

"I don't want anything."

"What do you want, Carl?"

"Okay, just get me a chicken sandwich."

"Okay."

She turned and ordered our meals. We drove on, paid (on my dime), parked and ate. She told me how good it was. We actually had some laughs. It was nice.

We drove to my house. We got out of the car. I opened the gate, let her in, and we walked inside my house. Ronald was there on the computer, he said, "Hey!" and we said "Hey!" back. We went into my bedroom. She sat down on the bed while I went to the computer, on Facebook, to mindlessly look at bullcrap.

After a few minutes, Ronald opened my bedroom door and said, "I'm gonna be gone for a few. Call me if you need anything. Okay? See ya, guys."

"See ya," we said.

And he closed the door and left.

"Soooooo . . . ?" Terra said, eying me. "Carl?"

I looked away from the computer and at her. "What?"

"Come here, baby."

"Okay," I mindlessly said. I got up and laid down next to her. "Okay, baby," I said.

"I love you."

"I love you too."

Then she got on top of me and we started making out. Then she wrapped her legs around me—I don't know how—and started rubbing my pants. I was thinking, "Oh shit, oh shit, oh shit," considering I had never had a girl do this sort of thing to me before. I was steadily kissing her. Then she took her shirt off, her pants off, and she was just in her panties. I wasn't taking off anything. I just saw her and started to take charge of her. I was on top of her, kissing her like crazy. Then she stopped me and spoke.

"Carl, wait."

"What, babe?"

"Do you want to have sex?"

"Ah, I don't know."

"Just do it. This is what couples do—do it! Please! I want you to fuck me."

"I don't know, man. I don't have a condom. What if I got you pregnant?"

"You care about getting me pregnant?"

"Yes, Terra. Again, what if I got you pregnant?"

It was a valid point. This question lingered for a few seconds. She laid there, smiled, then flipped me over, got on top of me, stared into my eyes, and she said, in this weird sort of "creepy" way, "Why . . . ?"

I was shocked. I said, "Why don't I want to get you pregnant?"

She giggled.

So many thoughts came into my head. Like worry, doubt, dread, the idea of being unprepared, everything unpleasant.

We made out some more, so much that it led into the living room. She got on top of me on the couch and stood up, grinding my pant-covered cock, and said, "We would have the best sex."

I didn't say anything.

Then she said, "I gotta go to the bathroom."

"Okay," I said.

We both went into the bathroom.

"You're gonna watch me pee?" Terra asked.

"No," I said. "I wouldn't disrespect you like that."

"Okay," she said nervously, and I heard her pee in the toilet while I was looking in the mirror, picking zits.

We went back to my room, on my bed where we made-out some more. She got up, realizing that I wasn't going to have sex with her, and said, "Carl, I gotta go. My, uh, dad needs me. Bye."

"Bye," I said.

And she left me without a kiss. She got in her car and left.

I thought, "Well, this is probably not going to be okay."

•   •   •

Terra and Jessie called about a week later and asked me if they could pick me up to go to Lake Worth for "a bit of fun," they said. I said, "Okay." When they picked me up, it was Terra, Jessie, Charles, Fletcher, and George all in the car. We all were drinking. We parked and got to downtown Lake Worth. I remember they were trying to see a concert from a local band that was friends with Fletcher. Terra pulled me inside when we got inside the concert. She said, "We need to talk."

I said, "Okay."

We left the concert and went down to Rita's Ice Cream. We ordered some ice cream, went out front of the place, sat at a table, and talked. Terra spoke first.

"This is hard to say Carl."

"What? I, uh—damn this ice cream is good!"

"Carl, pay attention."

"Well, okay. Shoot."

"I think we should break-up."

"Why? I, uh . . . Why?!"

"Well, I think we lost touch. I realize that we aren't the same anymore."

"You think?"

"Yes."

"When did you think this?"

"About two weeks ago."

"So you decided to break-up with me two weeks ago?"

"Yes, Carl."

"So, tell me: a week ago you came over wanting to have sex. Were you going to break-up with me if we did it?"

"Um, I hadn't really thought of that."

"Okay, Terra."

"Just listen to me—it's okay. We'll be okay . . ." and more blah, blah, blah.

We talked for about twenty minutes of memories and "good times." Jessie, Charles, Fletcher, and George all came walking down the street toward us. Jessie said, "Lets go. We're done."

Terra said, "Okay," and she got up.

I followed all five of them. I was behind Terra. I tapped her shoulder and said, "Hey."

"What Carl?"

"Just one last kiss?"

"Sure."

And we kissed.

We got into the car and drank more. I drank because I was depressed but also happy at the same time. It was odd.

•   •   •

Two days later I called Terra crying my heart out. I waited. The phone was dialing for longer than it usually did. Then she finally picked up.

"Hello?"

"Terra!"

"Yes, Carl?"

"I want you back!"

She sighed. "No, Carl."

"But, Terra! I *w-wish* you were h-*here!* I can't stop *crying!*"

"Why?"

"I MISS YOU!"

"Carl, it's *over* between us."

"But I *love* you!"

The phone was silent, and then Terra finally said, "I really gotta go Carl." And she hung up.

She didn't say "I love you" back, I thought.

•   •   •

Three weeks later Fletcher's grandpa died and all hell broke loose. Everyone was sad. I was invited to the funeral. We all went there— everyone Fletcher and I mutually knew: Terra, Jessie, Fletcher's family, George, Charles, everyone. We all sat there, crying. I remember I wasn't crying because, ironically, I sat behind Terra. We didn't speak. We didn't even say, "Hi," or anything. It was crappy. Then I remember the preacher was talking about letting the man go, Fletcher's grandpa. It was sad. Once the preacher said that everyone nodded and stopped crying and prayed. I just never got the concept of a preacher saying "let him go." It made me think of myself, and if I had died of cancer, and if a preacher would have said that. Then I realized everyone was wearing black and that I really, truly hated how sad it looked. I came up with the idea that I want everyone at my funeral to wear Hawaiian shirts, and if you wore something plain or dark you were to be kicked out. I just was so mad at the idea . . . Then, as all these bad thoughts and depression came rushing in, the preacher told everyone, "I want all of you to shake the hand of someone near you and say you appreciate them." Everyone started to do it. I was looking around and everyone was doing it. Then I felt a tap on the front of my shoulder. It was Terra. She said, "I appreciate you, Carl," and presented her hand. I knew it was a lie but I shook her hand anyways. Before I knew it, the funeral was over and that was it. I was invited to Jessie's house/mansion for a feast. We all drove there. Terra was there for a little while at the table with everyone. I was eating something I don't remember. Everyone was silent because they all knew we broke up. Finally she said, "I gotta go. Nice to see you all." And she hugged everyone, except me—she made that clear. When she left everyone asked, "What the fuck was wrong with you, Carl?" I guess I was the one who was making it "weird." After that, all I remember is getting really drunk and laughing and being an asshole—but we all had fun. That was it. I knew that I wouldn't get over this idea of love, because it was all just crashing. It's crazy how life works: One moment, you're with friends and a girlfriend, having the best time ever of your life, and the next moment it all goes away.

●　　●　　●

Fletcher decided to sell his VX1000 because he was starting to become the designated filmer for *Elevator Music*, and he just did not want that to happen. I don't really blame him because I felt that way for a long time too. I just wanted to skate, so I bought a computer to edit stuff with and that was pretty much how I coped with skateboarding—it's a love–hate relationship. I just wanted to make something of myself another way—like with art—and Fletcher felt like that as well. He wanted to do better things than just filming others for pretty much no reason. All in all skaters don't really care about who's behind the camera, they only care what's in *front* of the camera. I understood Fletcher but it sucked because that was one less filmer for *Elevator Music*. However, he bought a T2i, because he wanted to have a film camera (for his film school, Gstar) but he didn't want a camera that was totally for VX1000 filming. So he had this HD camera and was filming lifestyle shots for *Elevator Music*, which we still needed badly. That was how it was. Also, he wanted to take *real* photos of skating. So I understood. I always did.

* * *

Shortly after Fletcher got his T2i, we released the first promo video of *Elevator Music* and the hype for our project began. It got thousands of views the first day. People were into it, and I was happy about that. But I was still depressed, if you could understand how my mind was working out my inner feeling toward everything that was happening. Even though I seemingly had everything I wanted, I was missing out on everything as well.

* * *

I went to Barnes & Noble and bought a $15, good-quality journal and a $20 pen—which ended up being crappy anyway.

late-2010

The months that followed were the worst form of depression I had ever faced in my life. I literally cut out all my friends, stopped skating as much, and just cried most days with bothersome negative thoughts about school, Terra, my home-life, everything. I was making post after post, day after day, on Facebook, in the darkness of my bedroom, pretty much hinting at Suicidal ideation. Blog posts, status updates, everything. Every social site, actually. I wasn't ever reported on, because I feel that people don't truly be*lieve* the things said on Facebook. But, finally, my mother one night came into my bedroom and was quite sad. Her eyes were heavy, red. It was about three a.m. She had just woken up, obviously.

She said, "Carl, I just got a call from Aunt Connie about you. She said that you were posting some pretty depressing stuff on Facebook, talking about how you wanted to kill yourself, and it concerns me. I hate that you feel this way—you need to get out, Carl. Go somewhere in the morning. Do something. Everything's okay."

I said, "It's not okay, Mom. I'm so sad" (at this point I was crying) "and it hurts! And I didn't even know I had Aunt Connie as a friend."

"Well, you do! And you know what, I don't want you inside as much. You really gotta get your act together. I love you very, very much and I would be very upset if you hurt yourself. I don't want you to be upset. Terra was a bitch. She was nothing to you. She was just a first girlfriend, that's it. That's all she was. You have to move forward from her. She only is going to be a thought now that makes things worse. I want you to actually get out and make something of yourself. Be happy. You're so smart, everyone loves you, and you have lots going for you, Carl. Seriously. The worst thing in the world is everyone thinks so highly of you but you don't even think highly of yourself. Please, Carl. Please get some sleep. Stop staying up with this and dwelling so much."

"I love you, Mom."

"I love you too, Carl. Get some rest."

And she shut my door.

I laid down, pulled my nightstand's drawer, and got out my journal and pen that I hadn't be using. I had this weird idea that I only wanted to start the journal if I graduated high school, to make sure that I started it off "happy." However, I decided this was to be the best time to do it because this was such a crucial part in my life (or so I thought at the time).

I wrote this down:

> *Dear anyone who reads this:*
>
> *If you are a person looking to find out the mind of Carl Klitz, then you can open this. But if I'm alive and well, and you're just some punk, please shut this book. Thank you . . .*

And I laughed, continued on to the next page, and wrote out how I felt about the situation that led me to this place. I felt so much relief in the fact that I could say whatever I wanted, *whenever* I wanted on this piece of paper, and nobody knew or could say anything about it. I thought it was fun. I hadn't the slightest clue that the writing was the fun part.

●　　●　　●

And just like that, weeks later, I was off to work on *Elevator Music* with my friends. I was often meeting tons of people to skate because social media was booming with all our released promos for *Elevator Music*. Everyone was incredibly hyped on those videos. All skaters from the area knew about it and wanted to be apart of it.

I was at Phibbs one day and this kid, Bronson Razzo, came up to me and gave me his number. I told him sure, and a few days later at school, I got a text from him to go downtown. So after school, I headed down that way to meet him at his apartment in The City Place Towers. Crazily, it was the same building the crazy guy almost jumped from when I was with Terra.

I got up the elevator and meet this guy with a really bizarre smile and a pretty weird uniform: all blue. He asked me, "How are you, boss?" And I said, "Fine. Top floor, please." And he was like, "Okay, boss," and pressed the button to go up. *Bing!* it got there. I said, "Goodbye," or whatever, then went down the hall.

I knocked on Bronson's door. He answered.

"Klitzy . . ." he said with his deep voice. "Come on, bro." And I went inside.

As I was led into the living room, another kid was sitting there.

"Hey," the kid said, standing up and coming toward me, "I'm Zack." He shook my hand. "Zack Burns."

"What up?" I said. "Yo, Bronson."

"Yeah?" Bronson said from the kitchen.

"Who is this kid?"

"I don't know, Car. Some poser with a camera."

We both laughed.

Zack actually laughed too; I liked him.

Zack and I both sat down. Bronson was making a sandwich or something.

"So, Carl . . ." Zack said, "I have watched your videos for forever now. I love what I'm seeing. Everything about those things is funny. What do you film with?"

I said, "I don't film with anything."

"But you know what I mean!"

"VX1000."

"Oh, I figured. I'm actually saving for one. Right now I'm just sort of filming with this piece of crap right here," and he held up his piece of crap camera.

"Awesome," I said.

Then Bronson came in with two sandwiches.

"Here you go, bud," he said to me, handing me one. "Enjoy."

"Uh, Bronson?" Zack said. "Where's—uh, *my* sandwich?"

"Under there," I said, taking a bite.

Zack said, "Under where?!"

And then Bronson and I started bawling, proudly eating our sandwiches.

"Nah, fuck this," Zack said, "I'm making one."

Bronson got up. I could hear the two of them bickering and hollering about how to make sandwiches. Who should get the "last piece"—all this crap. I was just sitting there enjoying the show. They finally finished and came back.

I said, "So . . . do you any of you fuckers have anything im*portant* to say?"

Bronson goes, "I wanted to show you something before ass-hat here *had* to have a sandwich."

"SCREW YOU!" Zack said.

I laughed.

Bronson got out his laptop and sat next to me. Zack followed and sat next to him. Bronson said, "Back off. Nobody wants you here."

"SCREW YOU!" Zack repeated.

Bronson powered on his computer, showed me his Facebook. There was a message from four chicks but I couldn't read their names in time. I thought: "Bronson, you *stud*-muffin!" But then he showed me a message from a guy by the name of Brown Liger. The message was about how Bronson was great and all that, and also how Brown Liger owned a company by the name of Krooked Pointer Clothing and wanted to sponsor Bronson.

"The name of the company sounds super hipster," I said.

"I know," Bronson said, "but it's a company that wants me to rep them. I figure I should do it. His school is down the street."

"You mean Dreyfooz?"

"Yeah . . ."

Dreyfooz High School of the Arts was the follow-up to Bok Middle School of the Arts, the middle school I went to.

"Oh," I said. "Cool. Well, lets skate."

The three of us did. They were really awesome kids.

• • •

A couple days later I looked on Facebook to find that Bronson posted a video of himself repping Krooked Pointer Clothing. He was skating around downtown City Place just doing some tricks. Everything was stylish and I was a bit jealous because I wanted to be sponsored too. So from then on I made up a lie to everyone I knew that I was sponsored by Converse to make myself and my skateboarding more important . . . I think I actually believed what I was saying after awhile.

• • •

Brown Liger eventually messaged me on Facebook. He said that he wanted to sponsor *eMusic* and pay for any funds that came with it: MiniDVs, DVD duplication—whatever I needed. I told him that I would accept his offer and that I would need money for Super 8 film to be processed and put on MiniDVs, which cost approximately $200.00 in total. This was all according to the info I was given from South Florida's finest skate head: Grent Yatsura, who was a great guy—but I hated him at the time. Aside from all that, *Elevator Music* was sponsored! This called for a celebration!

• • •

I got trashed at a local party that night. I came home drunk, and passed out on my bunk bed. I was super hung over the next day. This was my life.

• • •

At Woodhill, I was in class thinking about skateboarding and how much I love it, when all of the sudden on the intercom I was summoned.
    "Mr. Klitz must report to the Principal's office, now."
    Click!
    "Okay, Mr. Klitz," my teach said, "you heard the lady."
    "Okay, whatever. Do I take my bag?"
    "I would," the teacher said.

The class laughed; I didn't really know why that was funny.

So I got up, got my bag, and walked about what seemed to be half a mile across campus to the Principal's office.

The air was stale, I remember that clearly. Dr. Roswell was actually a therapist before he became a Principal. *The* Principal—he always made that clear, and the teachers all made that clear also. He had the well-pressed shirts, the tie—the everything. The funny thing was that I heard he was a huge pothead. I never really believed it, but it made for a good story.

"Good morning, Carl," Dr. Roswell said, motioning with his right hand. "Have a seat."

So I did.

"So, Carl, I have some bad news."

"What?"

"Well . . . you see . . . I can't seem to believe why you're still here."

"What do you mean?"

"You're a senior."

"No, Dr. Roswell, I'm a junior. I failed my freshman year at PBC. I was in the Engineering Academy and failed my core classes. Now I'm making things up."

"Yeah, well you're grades are terrible."

"And . . .? So *what!* I passed FCAT!"

"Don't raise your voice at me young man."

I sighed. I thought, "This guy is dumb as a . . ." I don't even know. Just dumb, I thought.

"The fact of the matter is," he said, "is that you're eighteen years old and I can't have kids in my school that old. It's against the law."

"Uh, I see twenty-two-year-olds here. What about them?"

"Where?"

I gave him a name.

"That kid isn't twenty-two, Carl."

"Yeah, he is."

"No, he's not."

"I'm not arguing with you." And I stood up to leave.

"Sit down," Dr. Roswell said. "I won't tell you again."

"Whatever dude." So I did.

"Now Carl, you have to get your grades up by the end of the year, and if you don't you have to drop out."

"I doubt that very much."

"We'll see what your mom thinks."

"Go for it," I said. "We'll see."

And I don't remember much after that.

•   •   •

Nito wanted to pick me up to go to a party. He picked me up along with Erica (his friend) and we all drove over together. The party was off the chain! I remember there was a kid there that I hated. I don't really remember his name but he always talked shit on me—that was the name of the game in the skate-world. So I was drinking and drinking and the more alcohol I swallowed the more courage I gained. I call beer "liquid courage." So I was sitting on this chair outside, near this kid who openly talked shit on me, and I was literally roasting his ass. I remember people were laughing but then I was starting to get belligerent. I remember I started swinging and running around and chasing the kid—eventually people had to drag me away. It was embarrassing. Nito was embarrassed. I remember George was there too. George was drunk out of his mind. Nito said that he wanted to go home but I wanted to chill with George. George's house was actually close to the party, but still not walking-distance. So Nito drove George and I to George's house and all I remember is the two of us crashing on his bed.

•   •   •

I woke up still slightly drunk. I looked over and saw George passed out. I stood up, got dressed, and after about thirty minutes George finally woke up. He said to me, "Klitz, what the fuck happened?"

"I don't know."

"I think you fought a kid."

"Yeah right, dude."

"No, dude—you did."

"Bull."

George started laughing.

"Klitz, you did."

"Fuhhhh."

George laughed again and got dressed. Took him all of five minutes. Then he said, "I'm hungry."

I said, "I am too. Fuckin' need some grub."

"Lets go get some burgers."

"From where?"

"I don't know."

"McDonald's?"

"Sure. Fuck yeah."

"Okay."

So we walked all the way from George's house to McDonald's. Everything was actually fine. Although, when we got inside there and ordered things started feeling a little bit weird. We ordered a bunch of burgers and then sat down at the other end of the restaurant. We looked up at each other and grinned. George was eating his sandwich, I was eating my sandwich, and all seemed okay.

Until George said, "I don't feel right."

And I said, "Me neither. Fuck, I'm hungover."

George then leaned forward, made barfing sounds with his mouth open, and got scared. "Dude!" he said. "I just puked all over the table!"

"What?" I said.

"We gotta go."

"Uh, okay . . . ?"

So we got up and left. We were literally sprinting and we got to the intersection.

"Fuckin' puked, man!" George said. "I'm fucked-up!"

I said, "Dude, you didn't even puke."

"Wha . . . ?"

"I said, you didn't even puke. Nothing came out of you. You only *thought* it did."

"Am I trippin'? I know I did puke."

"Holy fuck." I was holding my head, and then . . . I don't know what happened. "HOLY FUCK!" I said. "I'M TRIPPIN'!!"

"Dude!" George said, "those fucking burgers had something *in* them! We're both trippin' after eating 'em!"

"That's retarded! FUCK! Holy shit I feel *weird!*"

I cannot even begin to describe what was happening. It was like I was inside of a dream world. It was like looking at everything through a glass fishbowl. It was like watching a movie; only it was my actual life I was watching. I thought I was hallucinating. I thought I was dreaming and was about to die.

"What the fuck man?!" I said.

"Klitz, calm down you're scaring me!"

"I CAN'T!! WHAT THE FUCK HAPPENED TO ME?!"

"Dude, please chill."

"I can't!"

"Okay, we gotta wait for the bus."

"OKAY!!!"

Then we started walking. I thought maybe that would help in a way. When we got to the bus stop we remembered it was Sunday.

"SHIT!" I said. "THE BUS DOESN'T RUN ON SUNDAYS!"

"Fuck dude," George said. "We gotta walk all the way back . . ."

"FUCK!" I was literally screaming. "DUDE!! I'M LITERALLY TRIPPIN'!!!"

"Just calm down. I'm right next to you. We're just walking."

After about five minutes of walking straight and being completely silent I said, "Dude, I'm so grateful to be alive. I'm so lucky to have friends and family. I need to be kinder to people. I need to realize that my life is worth living. I'm tried of being depressed all the time. I need to let the past go. I need to feel better. I need to just let go. I love my family, my life, and I love me! FUCK!"

"Dude, you're okay . . ." George said, "You're just trippin'."

"Yeah. I need to call Nito."

So I did. I dialed his number. He answered the phone.

"Yuh, Klitz?"

"Dude, I'm trippin'. You gotta pick me up."

"What? *Now?*"

"YES! I'M HALLUCINATING!"

"Dude, you need to relax. Everything's cool. You're just hungover. And did you know you tried to fight what's-his-name last night. All my friends know I brought you. That was fucked-up."

"Yeah, Nito, I know! But I need you to help me right now! It's an emergency! Pick me up from George's."

"Okay . . ." he sighed.

"Now," I said and hung up.

George and I walked about two more miles after that and got to his house. Nito was already there when we got there. George said, "Dude, I feel like complete ass. I'm gonna just go to sleep."

I said, "Yeah, bud. Me too."

We shook hands and George went inside his house. I went into Nito's SUV and drove off toward my house.

While in the car Nito said, "You need to chill, man. You have a problem with drinking."

I said, "I know."

"Dude, you need to not do that type of shit. People were literally pissed at you. That's a huge thing for me. Did you know that people were saying that you were the *Kookamonga* kid and they were literally mocking you and making fun of you? People were— *Shit!* People were making fun of *me!*"

"I'm sorry, Nito."

"We gotta not go to parties anymore. Not for awhile."

"I know."

After about ten minutes of driving, we got to the front of my house. Nito said, "Here we are, Carl. Get some sleep."

"Thanks, Nito."

"No problem. Get sleep."

"I will."

I got out of the car, pulled the gate shut, and watched Nito drive away. I turned around and sighed to myself, "What the fuck is happening with me?" I went into my room, took my clothes off, and crashed out on top of my bed naked without covers. (My mother never came in.)

That was my first slight bout of depersonalization.

·   ·   ·

My mother and I were called into Dr. Roswell's office. Dr. Roswell said after shaking my mother's hand, "Okay, so lets just jump right in. Carl here has some of the most terrible grades that I have ever seen."

"I know," my mother said.

"We have to change this."

"I tried to tell him that this would creep up on him."

"I'm sure you did, but we don't have time to look back on things. We have to move forward. What are we gonna do?"

"I figured he just would go next year. That's all we can do."

"Well . . ." Dr. Roswell sighed, "you see that's the issue. He can't."

"What do you mean *he can't?*"

"He can't."

"Why?!"

"He's too old."

"What do you mean? He's fucking eigh*teen!*"

"Mrs. Klitz, if you could refrain from profanity—"

"That's Mrs. *Old*man to you, buster! I'm married!"

"Sorry, Mrs. Oldman, I didn't—"

"NO! HELL NO! You're lying to me! You cannot sit there and tell me my son can't go to your school because he's 'too old,' because that's a load of shit. He's not too old and you know it!"

"Well, law states that—"

"He's eigh*teen.* I don't have to hear this made-up law. It's not true."

"It is."

"Look, Dr. Roswell, you cannot do this. End of discussion."

"My hands are tied, Mrs. Oldman."

"How so? Explain this."

"Well you see, we have this thing . . ."

"What thing?"

"It's this thing about funding. Let me show you."

And Dr. Roswell pulled out this sheet. It had red and green font.

"If you look here," he said pointing at the red font, "these are all the kids not able to graduate. And if you look here," pointing at the green font, "these are the kids that *are* graduating."

"Yeah . . . So?"

"This is why he can't stay, Mrs. Oldman."

"So you're telling me that my son—your student—can't stay here not because of a law but because it would be a negative point to your funding? Is that right?"

"Well if you put it that way, Mrs. Oldman, yes. It is. It appears so."

"I really don't care about your funding. This is my son and he *will* be graduating and I don't care when. End of story."

Dr. Roswell just shook his head and said, "Very well." He retracted the sheet. "Carl, you can go. You may have to sign-up for something, though."

"I will," I said.

"What do you mean 'sign up for something'?" my mother asked.

"Virtual School."

"Gladly," my mother said. "Come on Car, let's go."

We got our things and went out of that office without so much as a goodbye. My mother told me that I had to sign up for F.L.V.S., which was Florida Virtual School. I was glad about that. Sam went to that. So I know it was actually worth a fuck.

•　　•　　•

For a while there was not a lot going on. I went to school everyday (because F.L.V.S. hadn't kicked in), did all my chores, and I was basically a robot. I don't know why but I couldn't shake this gripping depression that was hanging over me. Maybe it was because I was unsatisfied with life, or maybe it was because I just didn't want everything to be panning out the way it was. I just was purely sad. I lost a girl I liked, *Elevator Music* was sort of coming off the radar, and I wasn't getting hit up at all. I was lonely. I couldn't talk to any chicks, I just felt like I wasn't important or worthy of happiness. This feeling was to come and go throughout the years, but my first bout of it was during this time. I truly didn't feel happy for almost no particular reason. Summer ended and I was in school again watching everyone do their daily tasks. I just felt stupid being there. I don't know why that was. I felt like I wasn't in place or apart of anything special. Konner Alboo, our main filmer, was in trouble. Fletcher was dealing with chicks all the time. Konner Murph never seemed to want to chill. Bronson was just . . . *bleh.* I felt like a nobody. I felt like nothing. I felt like my father, in a way. And then December rolled around.

•　　•　　•

John Taco hit me up on Facebook. He instant-messaged me and asked me "what's up?" I was friendly with him, but not exactly the best of friends—more in passing than anything in the skate community. He was telling me that he had been watching *Elevator Music*'s promos and was wondering if he could give me footage for it. I told him yes because I was a nice guy helping a skate buddy out. He said cool and then he told me to meet him and his filmer, Marky, at Wellington Skatepark that same day. So I did. I took bus forty-nine all the way down to the Wellington Mall and skated all the way from the Mall to this skatepark. I was jamming to new music, so I didn't mind the distance. The park was empty when I finally arrived. I called Taco and he answered.

"Klitzy . . ." he said. "Yo."

"Where you at bud?"

"We just got here. Look at the pavilion."

So I looked over and saw two kids. I hung up and went on over to them. They were smoking weed. Typical skaters.

I asked them, "So you want to be in *Elevator Music?*"

"Hell yes, Klitz," Taco said. "This is Marky, my filmer."

"Sup," Marky said.

"Hey," I said.

"So yeah," Taco said, "he would be the guy to talk to about my footage."

I asked Marky, "What you filmin' with?"

"VX1000."

"Awesome. How are you importing?"

"I use iMovie. The footage doesn't even work anymore."

"What? You use *iMovie?* Why?!"

"Well, I don't give a fuck—that's why."

Taco and Marky laughed. I actually laughed too. I thought it was cool that they didn't give a crap how the footage was captured.

Marky said, "I'll have to give you the tapes to import."

I said, "Okay. Do that tomorrow. Can we skate the park? It's empty. Lets film."

Taco said, "Sure."

And we skated the whole day and it was amazing.

•　　•　　•

The next day, Marky came over with a huge box of MiniDV tapes. I was like, "Holy crap, dude."

"I know," he said.

"This'll take me for*ever*."

"Good luck, man." He grinned.

I actually grinned too. It's exciting finding footage.

So when he left my house, I was on a mission. Holy crap, dude! *Wow*. Some of the stuff I found was gold. There was everything in there that was usable. Taco was a champ. He had about eight minutes of footage and I was going to put him in *Elevator Music*. I found a friend of theirs that skated also, and he had a crap-ton of footage for the video. I decided he should have a part too even though he didn't skate anymore. I figured "what the heck, right?" There was so much of the friends footage. Everything was there. I spent the entire day capturing and just enjoying the footage.

I called Taco. He answered.

"Hello?"

"Taco! You fuckin' *kill* it!"

"Klitzy!"

"Dude, you literally have the best footage and the best style. Holy shit. This is nothing but enders!" ("Enders" just means the last trick in a video part: it's their best trick.)

"Thanks man!"

"I want you to have a part. Please tell me you want a part!"

"Fuck yeah, Klitz! That's what I was sayin'! I have all this footage and no video to put it in."

"Well, you got one now. You gotta film with me more though. We need new footage of you. Could we go downtown this week with Marky?"

"Yeah, sure. I actually just dropped out of school."

"Oh . . . Uh, okay! Fine! I'll see you down there at three tomorrow."

"Okay."

"And bring Marky."

"Okay, Klitz."

"Okay, Taco."

And I hung up.

Two new people were added to *Elevator Music* with full parts in one day. I'd say that was pretty epic.

early-2011

Taco and Marky were such awesome kids to skate with. Marky would film anything. He was the kind of filmer who actually just liked to watch skating, and not *actually* skating himself. That was great because we got shit done, Taco and me.

We took the bus down to Okeechobee because we wanted to skate this long rail that was there. I wanted to redo a 50-50 pop-over that I filmed with Bret some few months back. So we got to the rail and I was trying and trying and trying, but I could land it on camera. Then security came our way.

"Klitz, land it," Marky said. Then I heard a *beep* from his camera.

I charged the railing, popped, 50-50ed, popped, and my back trucks got caught on the rail and I flipped over frontward—breaking my collarbone. It hurt like a bitch but it wasn't *too* bad.

I could see the security guard laughing.

"Lets go," I said, "We're done."

We skated back to the bus stop on Military and Okeechobee. The bus stops to Wellington and Military were right next to each other, and came at the same time. So we all just chilled out and waited until we would part ways.

"Guys," I told them.

"What?" they said.

"It's 2011 and my collarbone is clearly broken."

They laughed.

"I'm gonna make a promo tonight," I said. "Screw it."

They nodded.

And before I knew it, the bus came and we said our goodbyes.

I got home, went on Facebook (no ice-pack) and saw I had an email from this filmer named Trahm who wanted to just give me footage. I downloaded it hoping it wasn't a virus and opened the files. Wow. This kid was good. Black kid. His name was actually "Black Dave." He had terrible style and the filming was shit, but it was VX1000 so why complain? (I found out later that Trahm was legally deaf.)

Then I got an instant message from another filmer the same night. He filmed friend of mine named DK. DK was black too. The filmer just electronically handed me footage. I was like, "Sweet!" and opened the files. It was all good stuff—good filming, good style.

I thought, "Hey, you know what? Konner gave me footage of Drew Wong, a really good Asian skater, the other day, and it all was good stuff. Really good stuff. I'll combine these three skaters together and make a cameo part for *Elevator Music*." So I did just that. Editing it all with a broken collarbone.

Then I put together a shit-ton of footage and made a makeshift promo with Taco in it. I put the new line-up. I posted it and it racked up thousands of views instantly.

I got a part of the video done, I released a promo for *eMusic*, I broke a bone, and I slept like shit that night. I'd say it was a pretty damn good day.

●　　●　　●

Zack Burns got a VX1000 and it was game on! He was not good at filming at first because he had filmed with a HandiCam up until this point. I had to break him in so I started skating with him a lot more. That meant he was filming me acting stupid in front of the camera more often. Zack and his cousin would egg me on, so of course I played into it.

Zack also filmed at Gstar, his school, because everyone there knew me and was hilarious. So he would film in the lunchrooms, the classrooms, and even in the bathrooms. Zack would film anything and everything, and that's how we were able to make *Kookamonga 8*. Zack gave me all the footage and that was it. It was done. I got home and edited all of it together. The stuff came out great. When I released *Kookamonga 8*, everyone at Gstar flipped out and that made the views on YouTube skyrocket. I was pleased.

•　　•　　•

All I remember when I first decided to smoke weed was that I was entirely "over life."

I don't remember exactly why I wanted to smoke weed or what was upsetting me so much, but I remember I was skating Daytura Banks with Zack and he was filming me trying to kick-flip from the bank's edge and over the tiles on the side—a big gap that I didn't end up landing unfortunately.

So I decided that night to call Nito who was just getting into weed at the time. He told me that he had some really good stuff, very expensive, and he would share it with me for my first time. I told him that that would be awesome because I was very depressed. He told me that that is probably not a good reason to smoke, but he can't force me not to along with *not* forcing me not to, if that makes sense.

So that night Nito picked me up in his SUV and we drove from my house all the way to Wellington to visit my brother who wanted to chill. My brother was having friends over, which meant he was drunk.

Nito and I arrived and knocked on my brother's front door. He answered.

"AYYYYYYY!"

He was drunk.

We walked inside.

There was loud, techno music playing, and my brother's girlfriend, Julia, at the time was on the couch looking pissed off. A couple of Lance's friends were laughing and carrying on. There was beer pong. It looked like a big party but only eight of us were there . . . I love those kinds of parties.

"Beer pong?" my brother asked me.

"Hell yes. But I need beer first."

"My nigga."

So he went to the fridge and grabbed me a Bud Light. He grabbed Nito one too. We clinked our glasses and sipped.

"Carl, come with me," Lance said. He walked out onto the balcony. It was just the two of us. He got out a cigarette and spoke.

"Carl, how you doin' in school?"

"I don't know, man. It's been hard."

"You gotta get on that. Only gets harder."

"I know."

"So what are your plans?"

"To finish *Elevator Music*."

"Yeah?"

"Yeah."

"That's it, huh?"

"That's it."

"Man, you gotta think bigger! I swear man, when I was your age—or *if* I was still your age—I would be fuckin' every girl I could."

"Yeah . . ." I said.

Then Nito came out.

"Yo," he said.

"Nito!" my brother said.

"You guys want to smoke?"

"Uh . . . *yes*," my brother said.

Nito got out his weed and a bowl. He put the weed inside and lit it. He said, "Take it easy on this, Car. This is, like, *really* good shit."

"Okay," I said.

Nito handed me it and said, "I'm not forcing you, man. If you want it take it from my hands."

So I took it.

"Light it man," Nito said, handing me the lighter.

So I grabbed both my tools and lit the bowl. I inhaled, coughed. It wasn't too bad. I wasn't high.

"I'm not high," I said.

"You have to wait for it," Nito said.

So we started talking and Lance was explaining how politics and democrats don't make any sense to the adjacent of the two, or some shit on that matter—I really have no clue, to be frank. He always talked politics when he was drunk or high. That was just how he was. I remember this one time he—

"Oh fuck," I said.

"What?" my brother said stopping his political rant to Nito, who said, "What?" too.

"Guys, I have this app idea. Okay, what if you take the iPhone lock screen but it doesn't turn the screen light on? So you slide to unlock but without the screen lit up. So it's black. If your phone got stolen, people would think the iPhone is broken! Wouldn't that be kickass?!"

"That's the stupidest app idea, Carl," Lance said. "That makes *no* sense."

Nito laughed.

Lance said, "Carl . . . uh, are you high?"

"Uh, uh . . . uh . . ."

Nito said, "Yeah, he is."

I held my head and went inside. I immediately sat on the couch. Nito followed me, sat down. He said, "What's it feel like?"

I grinned and said, "I feel like a teddy bear."

Nito died laughing. He stood up and walked away.

I literally sat there with my thoughts. They just swarmed my mind at a constant rate. Everything was just a stream of enveloping consciousness. My mind was just going all over the place and I was just lost in time. The high was so deep. I was thinking about stuff but I couldn't seem to remember where the thoughts went or where they came from. All I remember was thinking of my father. I thought of him and all the times he smoked and I felt terrible about it. I just felt like him and I didn't want it to be that way. I felt bad about myself as I was just thinking thought after thought. It sucked—bad. I was uncomfortable. So I started crying.

My brother noticed. Everyone did. My brother came running up to the couch and sat next to me.

"Dude, why are you crying? What the fuck is wrong with you?"

"I feel like DAD!"

"What?"

"I FEEL LIKE MY *DAD!* I'M *HIGH!*"

Lance looked over at Nito in the kitchen and scolded him for giving me the weed. But then he shook his head and looked back into my eyes.

"Carl. Look at me. That's it. Now listen. This is just you being high. Nothing is wrong with you, bro. Your dad is a chump. You're not like him. You're you. Don't be smoking anymore, okay? Just enjoy yourself for now, it's a party man! Have fun!"

So he stood up and put on some techno. He was dancing and shit. Then I stood up grinning, and danced along with him. We all danced.

All I remember is being on the couch and thinking too much later in the night and passing out.

•   •   •

This woman I knew named Jane would come over to my house because I knew her daughter, Olive. Olive went to my high school, and she knew that I was an artist. Jane was a really nice woman. She was forty years old. She was very cool. She actually came over one day because I wanted to take an iPhone 3G off of her hands. So she drove to my house to help me out and ended up coming inside. She actually smoked a lot of weed. We would smoke and just chill out. We really didn't have many worries at all. She would take me to this vegan restaurant a lot. She was a nice lady. I feel like she vaguely thought I was cute or something, but I don't know. I've heard before that she was just a really nice lady and very open with Olive and her friends. I believed it. Jane was always very helpful when I would ask her questions about life. She also bought me art supplies a few times in exchange for drawings. I think Jane is a car salesman now. Eventually she stopped coming over because I didn't want to smoke weed anymore. (For a whole month I also smoked weed with Marky, who would come over often, and we would just get high while my parents were gone, much like I did with Jane. I hated it. So I stopped because I was starting to get really super slow with my thinking and thought patterns.)

•   •   •

The second promo was released and it had lots of hits. I was getting emailed and hit up by everyone under the sun for this new skateboarding film to come out. Everyone wanted to be in it. But there was one crew I wanted most: The *Domokun* crew. It had some many big heads in it. So I contacted Cam Boewing, the crew's filmer. The only problem was I hadn't seen a video of theirs in years. The last time I saw anything was when I was in middle school. So I messaged Cam and to my surprise he messaged me back right away. He wanted to be in *Elevator Music*! He actually said that he just got off his job at a pizza place and would stop by my house to drop off the hard-drive. I was insanely hyped by the idea. It was *that* easy. So I waited until he came over, and sure enough he dropped by and gave me the footage. I told him how much I loved his filming and his crew and how much they inspired me. He felt good about that. He was smiling like crazy. I'll bet life got rough for him, so it was nice to make him feel special about his skateboarding a time in his life that was probably his best. So he left and I got the hard-drive and took all the footage off of it. I made a part with it into *eMusic*. It came out great. The next day, Cam stopped by to pick up his hard-drive. I told him it was great stuff. He came inside and watched the part I edited. He loved it. He left. It was a great day.

●   ●   ●

"Okay class, we have a recruit coming in from New Hampshire Institute of Art and her name is Jessie Karson," Ms. Merchee said to my art class. Afterward, she came over to me when everyone was settled and doing their own thing with their portfolio do-dads.

She said, "Carl, Jessie wants to personally meet you."

"Yeah?"

"Yeah, and she wants you to go to her school. I took the liberty of giving her your cell number."

"Oh, cool."

"Yes. She is very excited."

"Cool."

"CLASS!" Ms. Merchee said. "We have the show coming up in a few weeks. I need you all to produce some of your best stuff and put it all matted and everything."

"Put it all matted" is not the correct way to say what she meant, but she said it that way anyhow. I think I'm just making fun of her.

•   •   •

I got a text that night from Jessie Karson saying she would like to pick me up from my house and take me downtown to the Cheesecake Factory. I told her sure, and about an hour later she picked me up in her car. I went with her and all was well. We drove downtown.

We got inside the restaurant and were sat right away, per a reservation that Jessie had already setup. I was hyped because I was about to eat really great food.

We sat down and all I remember was her giving me all this stuff about college and how my art was amazing, what a talent I had, and that I should go to her school. I told her I was thankful and everything. Then we finished up our meals and she covered the bill with money from the college, and we drove back to my place.

When we entered the front door, Jessie shook my mother's hand.

She said to my mother, "Hi! It's quite nice to *meet* you!"

"Oh the pleasure is all mine! You're interested in my son's work?"

"Oh yes, we would love to include him into our school."

"He would do well there."

"Yes, I think so too . . ."

Blah blah blah.

Then I spoke up.

"Guys, I don't think I can go."

"Why, Carl?" Jessie said. "You're work is perfectly adequate."

"Yeah, my *work* is, but my grades *aren't*."

My mother gave me the stink-eye.

"Show me a report card," Jessie said. "They can't be *that* bad."

"Mom," I said. "Show her."

So my mother, in her most pleasant way possible, pulled the drawer in the kitchen where she kept all the paperwork, and she got out a recent report card. She walked back to us and handed Jessie the thing.

Jessie got out her glasses, opened the letter, and read. "Wow," she said. "Oh dear." Her eyes got big. "No. *No!* This is terrible!"

"What?" I said.

"If I would have known you had grades like this I wouldn't have taken you out to dinner."

"Thanks," I said.

"Carl, I'm afraid to tell you that you need at least a 3.0 GPA to be at our school, or else it'll be very slim that you would get it, even with your talents. We have to have students that show effort. These grades can't even pass high school itself."

"Thanks," I said. "So what do I do?"

"By the time you graduate, I'm afraid you have to get at least a 2.8 GPA to even be considered. I could get it passed, but I need *at least* a 2.8 GPA or else I can't fight for you in the slightest. In fact, if you don't get your act together soon, you're going to end up doing a job you hate and have your dream of art never come true. Do you understand?"

"I understand, Jessie."

"Well, I'd better get going." Jessie handed the report card to my mother. "It was a pleasure to meet you both."

"You too," I said. And I guided her out the door.

When I turned back around, my mother said, "You jackass."

Lucky for me, Ronald was asleep the whole time. My ass would have been chewed.

•   •   •

I wanted to get around better and not rely so much on PalmTran. I decided I should buy a scooter bike. They were cheap, no insurance required, and you only needed a permit to drive them. I had a license but hey, the perks of lessor money involved are perks no matter what way you look at them. My mother and Ronald had a buddy of theirs who was rich named Tad. He said that he could sell me a scooter bike essentially brand-new because he used them once on vacation. He said he would sell it to me for a thousand bucks. I told him sure. That weekend I drove on over to Wellington to meet with Tad at his house. He brought out the bike and told me to drive around the neighborhood. It was insanely fun. I was having a blast with that scooter. I felt alive. I felt FREE. Much like when I first started skateboarding. The thing topped at forty miles-per-hour, the gas was so cheap it was dumb *not* to get it. So I drove back to his house and promptly bought it from him for the agreed upon amount. He wrote the title off to me and delivered it to my house from his truck. The next day I went to the title office, got my tags, and drove that thing like crazy. I was able to get around. That was a huge deal for me.

* * *

Taco and Marky invited me to skate downtown, which was no issue now because I had a scooter. We were meeting up to skate, film—all that jazz. I got down there, parked at City Place, skated along Clematis, and found them at Pizza Girls. Taco had about three slices of pepperoni pizza. He was hyped. I think he just loved the idea of being down there skating. I always did too.

I remember that we were skating the fountains and the sets all along Clematis and a security guard came and we were making fun of him. We actually were calling him names and telling him what a fat-ass he was. I remember we always treated security guards with disrespect because they were defending something that wasn't any of ours and we were just kids trying to have a good time and skate spots. That was our mindset I remember. It was simple.

Then we decided to go to SkateFL Tops and skate the benches that were built there. Taco had so much stuff up his sleeve. He was busting out so much crazy shit at that spot it wasn't even funny. I remember just watching him and thinking, "Wow, this is my crew. These people are the greatest humans that I know." I was thankful for that.

Then I got a text from this beautiful girl names Taven Dedrich. She was gorgeous. She was probably the prettiest girl I had ever seen at that point in time. She texted me and asked me what I was doing. I told her that I was skating. Then she asked if I wanted to come over to hang out. So hell yeah I said yes! I told Marky and Taco that I had to go and they said, "All right, bud, take it easy," and that was that.

I drove on my scooter from downtown City Place to downtown Lake Worth. That's far as hell by scooter, but I finally made it to Taven's street. I went to her house, parked, and knocked on her front door. She came out and told me that she couldn't hang out because she got "grounded." I know now that she was probably stringing me along, but whatever, it's the name of the game. I still spoke to her fondly.

So I left and went home. I was feeling depressed, oddly. I always felt depressed about *something* or other. I always looked at the glass half-empty . . . always. I have the problem of doing that because, well . . . I just do. It's in my brain chemistry.

I got a call form this black girl named Truby Dusick. She was not someone I was interested in romantically, but she was a friend of mine nonetheless. She asked if I wanted to stop by her house because a bunch of our mutual friends were heading over. I told her that that would be fine. I asked what time, because it had already been around six p.m. by the time she called. She told me to just head over right then. So I did.

I drove from Foresthill and Military all the way to Boyton. *Way* into Boyton. On a damn scooter. *Woo!* That's intense! But I did it anyway. I just wanted to shake the depression and sadness I had, so I was always chasing things that would make me happy.

When I knocked on Truby's door, this gay kid answered. His name was Nick. He told me that he was fucked up on this new drug that came out. He called it some weird name and said he got it from a friend of his who knew the guy at Woodhill, my high school. I thought that was strange but I went inside anyways.

I got inside and they were cooking stuff on the grill. Truby's parents were rich, black folk, and that was just the way it was. I remember I went up to Truby's room and it was awesome sauce. I remember all the stuff she had inside it. How many clothes she had, and music, and instruments that weren't being played. And I was jealous of her. I remember just looking at these kids and thinking how silly they all were, to be sitting there and being mindless—to be free from troubles.

"Lets go eat," Truby said to us. So we all went down the stairs and into the dining room where her mother had pork-chops, beef, steak, and everything under the sun waiting for us. I remember we all grabbed plates and loaded up on our food. We all sat down and ate and I remember nobody really spoke much. I was sad about all of that, but there wasn't much I could do—my brain just couldn't seem to let me be happy.

Then nighttime came and I had to get going. We were out front of Truby's house and I was showing off my scooter. Everyone wanted it. They all decided that they would buy scooters. (And most of them *did* end up buying themselves scooters.) The gay kid rode that thing up and down the street and I felt like I was important. I felt like I had everything I wanted and that that world was my oyster. But then the night ended and we said our goodbyes and I remember feeling sad again as I had to drive off.

My mind was on other things. I remember going up to the gate and seeing this pole that was hanging horizontally. It was coming at me and hitting me in the face. I crashed my scooter, it fell over, and I didn't say anything about it. I remember I was very scared because I had crashed my scooter and got hit in the face by a pole. I drove home anyways because nobody saw me do it. I found that comforting.

When I got home I called Taven about the accident and she was worried about me. I just wanted to call a girl I liked because I thought it would make me feel better. I remember just calling Taven and being like, "I got hit by a pole on my scooter," and her just being concerned and scared and asking if I was all right. I told her that I was and pretty much that was the end of the conversation.

I went into a dreamless sleep that night.

•   •   •

Bronson Razzo called me to come over. So I drove on over to him and parked my scooter in front of his house. I showed him it, and he was hyped about it. Then we walked inside his house where he had some weed. He told me that he wanted to smoke with me and I agreed. We smoked and smoked, and it was the kind of high where I didn't even know I was really living. I just sort of was a ghost and not doing much of anything. So I just smoked and laughed at everything Bronson was saying in order to find some sort of comfort in myself. Then Bronson finally said to me, "Carl, lets get *wired!*" and I asked him, "What's that?" and he told me, "It's when we drink a shit-ton of Monster and try to get as 'wired' as possible." "Cool," I said. So we got on our boards and skated on over to the corner store, where we bought ten Monsters. We brought them back to Bronson's place and drank them all. We didn't sleep that night, and we didn't care. We were high and nothing could bother us. So that meant we were content.

•   •   •

My school's art show was coming up. I was actually really excited to help set it up. I was putting up everyone's paintings and drawings from all the art classes together. I was hanging everyone's pieces neatly, and missing all my classes that day just so I could make this art show as killer as possible. Ms. Merchee didn't mind. She wrote me many notes for my teachers. She didn't care. She knew that I was happy and that made her happy to do it. She asked me if she could have a specific painting. I told her yes, thinking nothing of it.

Anyway, we basically had the show at this auditorium that the school hadn't used in years. It was perfect because there was a huge entrance, long hallway, and then in the back we could put the A.P. Art kids to showcase the "really good stuff." I think I secretly was the finale because Ms. Merchee wanted me to have the best spot in the house. I think the other students knew it too, but they weren't exactly butt-hurt over it because they knew I earned it.

I was putting up all the paintings of my peers on the walls as carefully as I could, not to scratch, mangle, bend, or do anything that would damage their work because I knew they would never do that with mine.

"How's it going?" Ms. Merchee said, coming up behind me with more pins and more art. "You doin' okay, Carl?"

"Oh yes, very much so," I said, and smiled.

"Good!" She handed me more. "Put these up. You're doing a great job."

I nodded.

Then more of my peers from A.P. Art showed up. They were there to help me with hanging. I remember that I saw Terra. Not the Terra I dated but the Terra that I *wanted* to date, back before I was about to go into high school, around early 2008. She looked . . . bigger than I remembered. Like fatter—but not a "bad" fat. She still had huge breasts, but it wasn't anything crazy. She was the girl old Braydon made me touch those breasts.

"Hey, Carl!" she said when she saw me. "Long time, no talk!"

"Terra," I smiled.

She came up to me and gave a hug. "Where's your work?" she asked me. "I'm excited to see!"

"Oh, right here," I said. And I guided her to my spot.

When we got there she said, "Holy crap, Carl!"

"What?" I said.

"It's amazing." Her eyes were fixated on those pieces like a child would be for candy. It was really great. I felt special in a way to be part of her fun.

"Thanks, Terra," I said.

"Can I get a picture with you?"

"Sure . . . ?"

She got her iPhone out and held it up. Her and I posed and took a selfie. She looked at the photo and said, "You look so handsome, Carl." She showed me. I really did. My hair actually looked really great.

I said, "Thanks, Terra."

The remainder of the day was mostly work. The show was to start around six p.m, so we all ate lunch and hung out. It was sunny, and we had a few laughs here and there. Everyone complimented my work. They told me it would be a hit. I was really happy about that. I remember them all looking up to me as if they looked up to a father figure, art mentor, or a trusted peer, and I envied them immensely, for those were the things I desired most.

Then six p.m. rolled around. Ms. Merchee was saying, "Okay, guys! Listen up! The show is starting really soon! People are *already* lining up with their families! I'm going to open the doors up now! Have fun!" and she opened the doors.

People were piling in and paying five dollars a ticket, and it was worth it because we had the best food ever in that place. They had a snack bar, and people serving food. I remember how beautiful the women looked. I was so proud to be around them. Everyone was dressed so nicely, and I was very, very happy.

More and more people showed up. Everyone was making their way in the hallway, looking over at everyone's Art. They were literally packed inside there. I was so excited for them to go to the A.P. Art side because honestly, we killed it. We all *really* did! And I wanted them to feel as special as I did. I remember every person I saw leaving the A.P. Art side had such magic in their eyes. The visitors were so happy to be looking at our work. It was like they could forget about the problems in their life for just a moment and it was just them and the art. Everyone would come up to me and ask me to take a photo with them because they were convinced that I would be "famous" one day. I was more than happy to do that for them.

Nighttime came and I called Pancho Mango, my rapper buddy. He was over at Donald's house because they were huge friends. I remember asking if him if he could come over to the show and bring his friend Tin. Tin was middle-eastern, tall, in his thirties, and hella funny. Pancho said of course, and pretty soon they arrived. I was incredibly happy. I remember they came up and were like, "Where's your art?" "I'll show you," I said.

So we made our way over to the A.P. Art side. People were crowded around my art and taking so many photos. So many flashes. I showed Pancho and Tin and they were like, "Jesus . . ." I knew they liked my work.

"There's food, also," I told them. Then I guided them down the hall and to the food bar. They served all sorts of Spanish foods. It was all so delicious, and nobody had any complaints.

Then Ms. Merchee announced, "OKAY, EVERYONE! TIME FOR A GROUP PHOTO!" and all the art kids came swarming. Ms. Merchee had us all together. I remember how beautiful it looked: everyone together wearing the best clothes and looking the best they would ever look. We were all so happy and proud of ourselves. In this moment, I knew that I would remember it for a lifetime. So I got my phone out and stood there next to Ms. Merchee and snapped myself a photo. (I put it in my sketchbook later on to further preserve the memory.)

After that, things were dying down. I remember I stood outside the place where all the tables were, and I saw Terra sitting with a friend. The moment I walked up and said, "Hi," Terra's friend left. I have a hunch they were talking about me—call it instinct.

"What's up?" Terra said. "You were a big hit, Carl."

"Yeah, it was pretty cool to be apart of all of this."

"I'm glad my stuff was in here too."

"I'm really proud of all of us."

"Me too." Terra smiled. "Listen, I wanted to ask you something."

"Yes . . . ?" I said.

"Would you sell me your paintings?"

"Yeah, sure. How much?"

"Well . . . what do you think?"

"I don't know . . . five hundred?"

"*Woo!* Steal! I was going to pay a thousand."

"Damn . . ." I sighed. "Oh well."

"Want to go for a ride to the bank?"

"Sure."

So she got up, we held hands, and then went outside in the parking lot to her car. She drove me down the street to her bank. Chase Bank. It was closed. So we went to a check-cashing place and they were all weirded-out by us because she wanted to buy art and they thought she was lying. So they made us take our I.D.'s out and our finger prints pressed. I got the cash and we drove back to Woodhill and went inside the show. It was getting dark. I remember walking inside and we were taking down the paintings. Ms. Merchee said, "Hey, Carl! What are you guys doing?"

Terra said, "I just bought these."

Ms. Merchee asked, "How much?"

I said, "Five hundred."

Ms. Merchee said, "Carl, that was the painting you said I could have . . ."

I said, "Oh," and sighed.

Ms. Merchee shook her head and walked away. I felt bad.

Terra shrugged and got down the paintings. She and I walked and loaded them into her car out front.

"Do you want to do something?" she asked me. "Lets *do* something!"

"Okay."

"What?"

"I don't know. Want to go see a movie?"

"Sure! The new *Nightmare on Elm Street* movie is out. Lets go see that!"

"Okay."

So we went. We drove to downtown City Place. It was nighttime and we parked at the parking-garage. We got out of the car and she held my hand. Two chicks were looking over at us, and Terra said, "Bitch, he's taken!" and they quickly looked away. Then Terra said to me, "I hate when girls look at *my* man." I had no idea what she was talking about.

We went down this escalator, walked more, then up another escalator. We made it to Muvico. There was a girl there named Sarah, who I went out on a date with once in the past. We went to iHop. It was actually really great. We lost touch because she was flirting with a friend of mine, Tom, and I couldn't accept it. She just didn't think it was a big deal. I still talk to her from time to time now. She lives in Tennessee or something. While we were buying tickets I wondered if Sarah was happy still being at Muvico. Terra didn't have the slightest idea because Sarah and I pretended like we didn't even know each other. So Terra and I got our tickets and walked inside.

We watched the movie for an hour and a half.

As we were leaving, Terra remarked, "Eh, it was okay. Not as good as the old ones."

"Yeah . . ." I said.

"Want to go to my house?"

"Sure."

So we walked back to the car in the parking garage. We got inside and drove to her house. It was still in the same place I remembered from years before. It still looked the same. We parked. She and I grabbed the paintings and went inside her house. We went upstairs in her room, and it was like déjà vu, because I remembered when Braydon made me feel her breasts and was going to make me kiss her when I was in middle school. It was a weird time. "Very eerie to be back here," I thought. Here I was, with her, in her room, alone, and she bought all my art. Wow. She sat down on her bed.

"So . . . what's *up?*" she said.

I sat down next to her. I said, "Remember when Braydon made me feel your breasts?"

She said, "Oh yeah! I remember! Gosh, we were, like, friggin' *kids* then, huh?"

"Yeah . . ."

"Braydon is *nuts!*"

"I know."

"So, Mr. Picasso. What are your plans for the future?"

"What do you mean?"

"You know, Carl. College. What are you going to do for college?"

"I don't know. School is not for me. I just want to skate and finish *Elevator Music*. That's all I want right now."

"No shame in that."

"What are you gonna do?"

"Me? . . . Well . . . I want to, um, basically become a doctor. I got accepted into a program in University of Miami."

"Wow, Terra! A doctor! A friggin' doctor!"

"I know, right?! Who *knew?*"

"You'll make it."

"I know you will too," Terra smiled.

Then we sort of looked into each other's eyes for a while. I remember she was looking so sweet. She was so pretty. I loved her breasts—I don't know. There was something about her that just didn't . . . seem right. I think I had so many memories of her, and it was such along time ago, that I felt like I would be going "back in time" by having sex with her. My freshman year was when I liked her. I remember she didn't really give me the time of day, and now she was all about me. It just didn't seem okay.

So I said, "Can you give me a ride back home?"

She said, "What? *Why?*"

"I don't know, Terra. I just want to go home."

"You don't like me?"

"It's not that. It's just I'm— Well, I'm a v-virgin."

"I understand. I lost mine a long time ago. I respect that."

"I just don't think I like you in that way anymore. I used to, but not anymore. I'm sorry to make you feel bad."

"It's okay. You're not. I understand. Lets go." And she got up. "Thanks for the paintings," she said to me. "You're so sweet, Carl. I know you're going to be famous one day."

"We'll see," I said.

She drove me home and we said our goodbyes.

I remember lying in bed and thinking of her breasts and feeling like a total dummy for not having sex with her. So I masturbated and fell asleep.

•   •   •

Our filmer was back in business. Konner Alboo. He was a kid who was into some drugs and bad stuff, but don't misjudge him, he had straight A's. He was a good kid, just made bad choices with weed. He sold weed, smoked it, and he was happy. He truly didn't see anything wrong with what he was doing. I think he was working with this guy that used to be at Woodhill, Edgar, who was big into dealing. I don't really know. Konner came back after all the stuff his mom put him through. I'm not taking sides, I'm just saying that his friends missed him. Rumor has it she put him in Eagle Academy, the place that my own mother was going to put me through instead of Lowridge. That's when we were filming Chad

Finners a lot more for *Elevator Music*. That was huge both for the video and for me. This meant that we would gain a lot more footage for the final clips to be placed into the film.

I would go to Barnes & Noble with Zack Burns quite often. He and I would hangout and I remember I would dare him to hit on chicks. He had a VX1000 with a film camera. He always had it on his person. So I told him to go up with the film camera and say, "I think you should be a model. Can I take your photo?" I was messing around, but Zack said, "Okay," and would do it. I actually filmed him do it once on his VX, and —no bull—he got the girl's number. I never actually got how he managed that. I just didn't get how a woman could give him a number from doing something so retarded and simple. You go up to a girl with a camera and say she's a model, then end up getting her number. Hell, often he would even hit them up and go on dates. I told him he was a god. It was funny because I would boost his ego often. It's crazy how he had this crappy camera, and Bronson Razzo and I would roast him for it. He would just laugh. We all laughed in those days. I miss Zack. He's a good soul. He's somewhere in California taking photos of models ironically. I guess he always had a knack for it. Oh well. What can you do?

Super 8 film is golden. It's an excellent medium artistically speaking. I think it looks great with the grain, the overall old-look, and the colors involved. It's vintage and it's awesome. Nito had a Super 8 camera, so I called him and asked him if I could borrow it for Elevator Music. He told me, sure, no problem. I picked it up from his house, asked him where I could get the film. It was expensive. Twenty bucks for three minutes, and that was just the film itself. The developing was about another twenty bucks per roll of film. I called Brown Liger from Krooked Pointer—our video sponsor. I asked him to pay me four hundred dollars for the Super 8 and for DVD duplication. He told me that that was fine and paid me in cash when I picked it up. So I ordered everything and started filming with the Super 8. It was beautiful. The flicker of the shutter when you pressed the button, the vintage feel, the . . . everything. It was magical. I could understand why people in the '70s loved it so much. So I sent off all the film rolls and got them processed. Took weeks to get it done. They were cool. They put it all on a MiniDV tape and it was fantastic. I captured it all and Elevator Music had an instant intro. Needless to say I was absolutely thrilled.

Fletcher was busy making a skateboarding company. He called it "Citified Skateboards" because he thought it sounded "so urban." I liked it and I hated it, but whatever. I just was jealous, now that I think about it. He actually did well with it. I did all his graphic designs for him. He never paid me, only gave me the product of one design each for free. He actually made lots of money from my designs, I think. I still am fairly pissed over that because my art made money for another human being. But Fletcher's my long-time friend so I'm not too mad at him. He's a good sport. I wish no harm onto him. But yeah, he actually sponsored *Elevator Music*. He didn't give me money for the film but his brand was going to bring in viewers if we had a premier. So I was excited.

Dave Stossle messaged me one day. He was a huge head in South Florida and North Florida. Eventually he was huge all over the United States for his skate video, *Spread The Good*. I always looked up to him because he was the filmer for *KinesisFilms*, which was huge during my middle school years. Anyways, he messaged me on Facebook about giving me footage. I asked him for this a bit before, and he actually complied and gave me all the footage I needed, including any of the people having full parts in the video. This was perfect because I could add this footage to the final product if needed. I thanked him. He was a good guy. I appreciated all that he did. He's in California now, filming skateboarding from actual professionals. You could say he "made it" in skateboarding. Then I asked these other kids that were making another skate video entitled *FloridaDaze*. It also ended up being huge. They made three videos after their first one later on, and will probably make more. They released after *Elevator Music* though. I was glad, because honestly it was better than *Elevator Music*. But yes, they gave a bunch of their friends clips for the video, so I thanked them. Over those past few days I was on a roll. I was asking everyone under the sun to give footage for the Friend's part in *Elevator Music*. Everyone was really happy to do it. I was glad about that. I felt like I was actually making a really valuable project, and making huge progress towards my goal.

mid-2011

I released the third promo for *Elevator Music*. It was actually really fast-paced. I edited it perfectly. The song was by Cass McCombs, which is a band that still to this day I adore, and the song was called "Prima Donna." It was really humdrum, but people really liked it. I had slow-motion "ramped" footage of the tricks, and I would cut them off before the lands. Often some of them weren't even "lands" to begin with, but by God, they *looked* like they could be lands! Everyone was really hyped on the idea of *Elevator Music* coming out. Heck, I was so excited I just decided to put a premier date to it. Nothing exact, but pretty dang close. I decided that I knew the video would be done in July, around my birthday. So I decided to just put "July '11" as the official release. So people obviously asked where it would premier. By people I mean everyone in the video who was having parts. I didn't know for sure where. That was it. I just had the month and no date or place.

Basically I was jumping through my ass with editing the footage I had. I was trying to find the best songs for each part, the best placements, the best tricks, and of course the enders. That's always insane because nobody ever really knows what's their best thing ever because the moment they pull it off, it's no longer the best trick they ever did. It's just another trick. That's what happens with the progression of skateboarding, and these kids were always progressing. So I had to edit this video like crazy. I had to make sure that it fit exactly to my liking and their liking. I had to often re-edit parts to cater to the needs of the skateboarder. If they didn't like the edit it was no deal, no sale. Which is understandable since everyone and their mothers would probably end up seeing it the moment of the premier (or the moment it was leaked online by a shitty skateboarder). That's just the way it was. So there was a lot of pressure on me to make sure the video was done right. I was editing, editing, and editing some more.

Konner Murph was editing the parts of his people, his Friend's part, and his own part while I was trying to wheel and deal with Brown Liger on the DVD duplication process. Konner told me that he had all his ducks in a row and that his parts were turning out beautifully. He also asked for *Elevator Music*'s font that was used for the name titles so I gave that to him. I knew he was going to make it epic, I just *knew* it. He then decided to come over one day and surprise me. He came with a hard-drive full of the raw video parts, edited, spliced and everything. It was all ready to be placed. So I took the files and we watched them. Man, what gold! It looked as if I edited it, which says a lot. I was happy about that. Elevator Music was vastly on its way.

I texted Zack Burns about the DVD menu. I was in Math class and under the table with my phone texting him. I told him to go to downtown City Place, take his camera, and just skate from Barnes & Noble all the way to Clematis and back to Barnes & Noble. I wanted him to just take photos with his camera and put together a stop-motion, frame-by-frame animation of his skate through City Place. He did it gladly. Within thirty minutes he told me it was done and over with and that it came out perfectly. After school, we met up at my place so he could give me the video file and it was golden. I loved it. At the end of the animation, he put the actual text message of him to me that read, "the menu is done for *Elevator Music*." I thought that looked awesome. So many memories, yo.

Konner Murph came over one day to shoot the shit and see the final product of *Elevator Music*, or what was close to the final product. I showed him the DVD menu with the files placed and everything and he thought it looked fantastic. Then he asked me what we were going to do about the covers. I had this idea of making the video appear to be a music album. I didn't want it to be in a DVD case, but instead I wanted jewel cases. Then I was going to put photos and drawings of mine on the covers, so none of them were the same. Konner was all about it, so we got out my photo album from all the art photography I took over the years and we just looked through them. There were photos of Chewie, Nito, and everybody else. Every memory of *Elevator Music* was there, right in those photos, and I was going to put them all on the covers for the sake of the viewers and fans of the video. Konner drew a dick on a few of the covers because he thought it was funny. We drew a lot of random shit on the photos with Sharpies. We thought they were hilarious! So we got all of them cut out and placed and that was that. I ordered the jewel cases and Memorex DVDs on Amazon and they came about two days later. I wanted them to all look "raw" and I got what I wanted. It looked amazing! Only issue was I didn't have the final product in order to print out the DVD disks.

•   •   •

Sunfest was coming our way, and of course were we going to go! I remember being a home and preparing for it because I wanted it to be a really great day. So many exciting things were happening in my life, like the end of high school, making *Elevator Music*, having friends around me for support, and the overall feeling of safety and security and confidence. It was great. I miss that.

Konner gave me a call and told me that he was picking me up and we were going to stop by Chipotle. I told him sure, and he was on his way over. I got ready, got my board, and got into his car when he pulled up.

Logan was there, this kid named John from *Spread The Good* was there, and this other little kid named Zack (not Burns). We went down Military all the way to Okeechobee and parked at the Chipotle. We were laughing and carrying on about something or other that had to do with skateboarding and probably women.

I ordered a huge burrito, Konner always got his big bowl of cheese and sour cream, and everyone else got their plain orders of beef and other do-dads.

We all sat down. Konner said, "Oh my God, this is literally going to be the tits."

Zack said, "I know, right?" as he was chowing down.

John said, "Listen, this ain't that crazy. How 'bout we go skate?"

Konner said, "Chill, man. We'll skate. I have to eat, though. Where do you wanna go?"

John said, "I want to go to SkateFL Tops. I have this line I've been wanting to do."

Konner said, "Cool."

I said, "Yo, I have this idea. Why don't we start making *Kookamonga The Movie*."

John paused before he said, "That's stupid. Nobody watches those things."

Konner said, "You kiddin' me?! *Everyone* watches them!"

John said, "Whatever, man."

Konner said, "Lets do it. Starting now."

We all chowed down and finished our meals. Then we threw out our trash and went outside. We went over to Konner's car and he got out his camera. He hit record and had the camera in my face. He said, "Klitz! *Kookamonga The Movie!*" and I was going buck-wild, dancing like crazy. I was yelling and screaming and going ape-spit.

Little Zack was laughing. He said, "Dude, I've only drank *one* beer!" which obviously he hadn't.

I said, "I know!" and pushed him into the ground.

We filmed some more antics, laughed some more, and then drove off to SkateFL Tops.

For the next three hours John was doing a line—trying and trying and not even getting close. Zack and I eventually just sat down and watched him try this line again and again. I thought he would never land it. I thought he was crazy if he would try something for three hours and not even get anywhere *near* close. He would stick the last trick a few times, but it wasn't consistent overall. Then, by some god above, I saw him land the first trick perfectly, then the next, then the next, and *bam!* he landed the last trick in the line. I was freaking out! That's just the way skateboarding is: you can do a trick for hours and hours but it's all worth it once you accomplish what you were aiming for, and to finally be imprinted into a skateboarding film.

Nighttime came and John left with some friends. It was just Zack, Konner, Logan and I. We all drove to Sunfest. We parked at City Place, which was packed, and then walked all the way down to Clematis. The tickets were about a hundred bucks each. So we decided to go behind some trailers and hop the fence. "We just snuck into Sunfest," I whispered into the camera once we were over. Then Konner and I got out a bowl. Konner packed it up with weed and we just started smoking. It was wonderful, I remember.

Then it was all gravy. We walked out into the open. Everyone was out there. Zack and Logan paid, the lame-Os. Konner and I laughed at them. We walked and filmed and it was funny. We would film behind the backs of women, saying things about their asses. It was hilarious. Once, I actually said, "Ohhhhh, look at *those* tits," as fast as I could when Konner was zooming into the ass of some hottie. It was hilarious.

We finally made our way into this huge crowd. We were shimmying through it and everything seemed super epic. MGMT was playing a concert, that's why we wanted to go to Sunfest so badly. So we found our way into the middle of this huge crowd. Konner and I were high as hell while the other two were sober, and we were yelling our asses off about nothing.

Fletcher actually came up by himself. Then Chad showed up. Then more people from *Elevator Music*. I thought it was a sign! I thought that everyone was there for a reason and that these were my best friends ever and that life would never, ever end . . . and then MGMT started playing. They were using huge lights and fireworks and it was amazing. They played all our favorite songs from their albums, including all the popular ones of that time. "Electric Feel," "Kids," "Time to Pretend." All those. It was magical.

Then Krystal came. She was the blonde that was around when *Kookamonga 6* came to be. She was Fletcher's friend and was dressed in pretty much nothing. She was just screaming and carrying on in some sort of mosh-pit. We filmed the whole thing, but by that time it was too dark and we had to put on this "high shutter mode" on the VX1000 in order to even be able to see, but it motion-blurred everything in the footage. It was still awesome, though.

Then the concert was done and we pretty much had to run through the crowd. We got back to Rosemary Drive and were just walking along. Konner had the camera in my face. He said, "So, what did you think?"

I said, "Dude . . . MGMT *sucks* . . ." I was high out of my mind. I knew we had a lot of footage that was usable.

It was a good day.

•　　•　　•

I released a promo that stated there was a Premier date for *Elevator Music* on July 23rd at Phibbs Skatepark. I already made the arrangement with them and everything was A-okay. Konner also put together a Facebook event that labeled the exact times the video was starting and everything that was happening at the skatepark that day: contests, giveaways, free products, you name it. It was going to be huge! We all were sending the invites to everyone we knew. The video was to sell for ten bucks a copy at first. Konner was also going to a hold a premier at Abocoa Skatepark, close to his hometown. He was going to make profit from that one, and I was going to make profit from the Phibbs one—that was the deal, considering he gave footage to me from his video, *Morning Wood.*

•　　•　　•

I spent the next few days gathering any remainder footage that Konner, Fletcher, Zack Burns, or anyone else had to offer. I placed everything together and pretty much finalized the video to the T. It was magical. I watched the entire thing over and over so many times and I thought it was crazy, seeing it there on-screen finished. I called Truby. She asked me "what's up?" I asked if I could borrow her projector, because I noticed she had one at her house when I went there a few weeks before. She told me sure, and I asked if I could come over to pick it up. She said sure. So I got up and drove on my scooter to her place. I got the projector. I told her I would return it after the video was premiered (which I did), and she told me "no worries" and "good luck." I drove back home and the files were all ready for processing to a burned DVD disk. So I waited and waited. I didn't sleep that night. I actually stayed up on a school night. I finally had a DVD pop out of my computer, and threw it into the projector and watched it. It was so magical. I didn't want it to stop, but unfortunately all movies must end. I thought that was how life was in a weird way. You go for the ride and it just . . . ends. It's weird. So I burned about a hundred disks that night and placed them in our makeshift jewel cases we made for the DVDs. I liked how raw it looked. I liked that each one looked different. Screw it.

•   •   •

I worked at Little Caesars since I dated Terra. I hated the job. The place was too hot, the owner didn't care if you were safe, and the pay was crap on top of the crap hours. It was a terrible job. I always hated coming home from it. I had to work on my birthday, July seventh, in 2011. I remember I got done from such an awful day, but then I checked my Facebook to see I had about two hundred birthday wishes and people telling me how hyped they were on *Elevator Music* finally coming out. I was proud as hell even though I still felt fairly depressed. But then I got a phone call. It was this girl named Binki who was friends with Zack. She was hot, rich, five foot, black hair, Spanish, talkative, awesome, fun to be around, and yeah—I answered the phone.

"Yeah?"

"KLITZ!"

"Yeah . . . ?"

"Dude, it's your *birthday!*"

"Thanks!"

"No man! You gotta have a party!"

"How? My parents aren't getting me anything because my grades are too bad."

"Dude, forget *grades*. I'm talking about a party at *my* house."

"What's that noise in the background?"

"Nick is being a baby-back fag and throwing bottles on the ground. It's actually funny. So anyways, pretty much we're going to have everyone over—well, we already do—and yeah, you gotta *come*. Can you make it?"

"So you're having a party and inviting me, but it's not actually a party *for* me it just so happens it's on my birthday?"

"You coming, or what?"

"Yes."

"Good. I'll text the address."

She hung up.

I scooted all the way to Boyton. I finally found the place fairly fast. It was quiet coming onto that road, but cars were lined against the trail for miles. Cars everywhere. I saw a couple walk passed me. Then this guy was puking in front of her as they were walking to (I assumed) her car. The girl said to the guy, "We're broken up. I hate you." I didn't get it. Oh well.

I got to the front of the house and could hear it was super loud from outside. Then the door opened and it was like a blast of noise. Music was blasting techno and bass. It made sense why it was a party house: you couldn't hear shit coming from inside if you were far enough away.

I walked inside and immediately saw Binki. I walked up to her and said, "Bink!"

She said, "Klitz! You made it! Here, have a beer."

She turned around, got me a Bud Light in a can, and handed it back to me. I cracked it open. Binki cheers-ed me.

"Who's house is this?" I asked her.

"It's my mother's. This is just our vacation home. I live in Palm Beach."

"Oh, no way! Vacation locally?"

"Don't ask. I just use this house to party in. Screw it up any way you like."

"Hell yes!" I said. Then I started dancing toward a big crowded living room. Lights were brightly fixed onto everyone and their sweaty faces.

"KLITZY!" I heard.

So I turned around and wouldn't you know it, George was there.

"Klitz," he said, "Happy Birthday, man!"

Then some kid said, "Wait, this is Carl Klitz? *And* it's his birthday?! Guys! CARL KLITZ IS HERE AND IT'S HIS *BIRTH*DAY!!"

Everyone in the party seemingly yelled "Woo!"

I felt cool.

Then I got really, really drunk with all my friends. We were in the kitchen and I was doing limbo but with no stick. I remember George was talking about a girl he wanted to have sexual intercourse with, but I didn't pay mind to it mainly because he always said that about every girl he was messing around with. That was just the way skaters were. But then he stopped, looked at me, and asked, "Want some nachos?" I grinned, said, "Yes." Then he went to the microwave and pretty much put Doritos and mozzarella cheese on top of them and placed it in the microwave for one minute. It came out. We ate like kings.

But as the night went on I felt sicker and sicker, but I was dancing. We were listening to really, really, *really* hardcore techno—the kind of techno that would booms for miles and miles, and the echo electrifies your body and makes you spaz out into some sort of jungle fever-like dances, like around campfires, real prehistoric-like. That was amazing, and then I didn't feel sick anymore. I was dancing with all the women there, and they already knew who I was and it was absolutely fantastic. I didn't want it to end. I felt so *alive!*

But then the night died down and I was talking to a skater friend of mine. We were on the couch. He was asking me about *Elevator Music*, and I told him that it was going to be great, that it had everyone in it, that it was absolutely magical, that it would knock the socks off of everyone that watched it, especially shit-talkers. He told me he was ready to see it. He wanted the premier date to come faster. I told him, "I do, too." And then I left.

I wasn't as drunk but I rode my scooter all the way down from Boyton and to my house. I thought about life actually being really special. But I was sort of out of it; feeling as though I was in a dream because of how much alcohol I had consumed, or maybe it was depersonalization. Who knows? I had to deal with depersonalization a lot I guess, but I didn't know what it was. I got home and slept it off.

•   •   •

Mark Row was rapping at Donald's house. Konner and I brought him there because I really wanted him to meet Pancho Mango. I thought they would bond well, and I was right! Pancho was going crazy over the fact that Mark could rhyme and freestyle so quickly and easily. I knew this was to be the greatest moment in *Kookamonga The Movie*, which we filmed for right then. We filmed Mark rapping and rapping. It was awesome. Pancho was really drunk that night and biting the air and people for some reason. They were getting pissed but we paid no mind to it because when a person is drunk all hell breaks loose.

•   •   •

Premier day finally came. I was supremely nervous when I woke up. I didn't even make breakfast or eat at all—I just wanted to get down to Phibbs Skatepark. So I got all my things: shirt, pants, skateboard, projector, et cetera, et cetera, and hopped on my scooter and drove on down Foresthill, cut a left onto Dixie Highway, and parked in front of Phibbs.

It already had about forty people there from what I could see, probably due to Konner Murph marketing the crap out of the Facebook post he made. Kids were skating everywhere. I got off my scooter, unlatched the projector and carried it. I got inside Phibbs, and the first people I saw was Zack Burns and his cousin, Travis.

"Hey, Trav," I said, purposely looking away from Zack. I gave Travis dap.

"Oh, nice asshole," Zack said, laughing. "COME HERE!" He tackled me to the ground. I remember laughing and laughing. "SAYING NOTHING, HUH?! ON *YOUR* BIG DAY, HUH?!"

"Hi, Zack," I said.

"That's better. What's up?!"

"Nothing. Just nervous."

"Don't be. This shit is gonna be epic."

"We hope."

I got out into the skatepark. I looked around. Dave Stossle was there with one of his friends from *Spread The Good*, Mark Rogers.

"Dave!" I said.

"Klitzy . . ." He came riding up. "How you doin'? Big day, huh?"

"I'm nervous as hell."

"Don't worry. I was too when *Spread The Good* came out."

"I'm glad you could make it."

"I wouldn't miss it. Love your stuff."

"Thanks Dave." I gave him dap.

Then Mark Rogers came up like, "Klitz! This video *better* be worth it!"

We all laughed. I gave Mark dap, as well. "Enjoy yourselves," I said. I got out my phone and called Konner Murph. He answered.

"Klitz!"

"Konner!"

"I'm on my way."

"Was just about to ask you that."

"Yeah, I know—my dad is actually letting me borrow his sound system for the premier."

"Hell yes! We needed one. All I got is the projector."

"No sweat. I got you."

"Well, get your ass over here, fag."

"Bye, Dad."

Konner hung up. I rolled my eyes. Konner always called me "Dad" because I was always acting like a father-figure to my skateboarders in the video. Some things are harder to look back on than others. I miss those times when they would say that.

I turned around and wouldn't you know it, Bronson Razzo came up to me. He said, "What it do, Klitz?"

"Hi, my nigger."

"Yo! This is about to be poppin', yo!"

"I know, bro-yo!"

We gave dap.

Bronson said, "So . . . listen. I brought *these*," and he held up some boxing gloves. "We should hold a match."

"What, like, you and me?"

"No, bro. No. Like . . . I'll box people for money."

"I mean . . . *sure*. You can, I guess."

"Sweet. I'll round up some victims."

"Have at it."

He walked away.

About an hour later of me skating around the park and sort of just zoning out, I got a call from Chad Finners, a kid who had a very significant part in *Elevator Music*, the first part after the intro. He said from the phone, "Hey, Klitz, can't make it to the premier."

"That hell? Bro! I literally pushed the deadline by *two days* just for you to make it! What in God's name is keeping you from coming to potentially the biggest day of our lives?"

"My girlfriend . . . she . . . uh . . ."

"What?"

"She can't get a ride there."

"So . . . you're literally telling me you're not going because your girlfriend can't go?"

"Yes."

"Chad. Grow balls and get your ass over here."

"No."

"Okay, let me call you back."

So I hung up. I called Konner. He answered.

"Yo."

"Konner, it's Klitz."

"Yeah I know. What's up?"

"Nothing. Chad is being lame as hell."

"What's new?"

"He literally is not coming to the premier because his girlfriend can't come."

"How gay."

"I know! We gotta pick her up."

"I'm not."

"You gotta. You have a car, Konner."

"I don't care."

"Okay."

So I hung up. I called Chad back. He answered.

"Sup?"

"So Chad, Konner's picking your girlfriend up. Get over here."

"Okay."

He hung up.

I looked over and there was a huge crowd outside of the fences. I saw Bronson Razzo and a black kid with boxing gloves on. I heard Bronson yell, "KLITZ! WATCH THIS!" and pretty much there was a lot of screaming, yelling, all that. I saw Bronson slam a mean right hook into the black kid's jaw. The black kid had pretty good swings, but nothing major. Bronson pretty much owned his ass. He was slamming his fist into the kid's face repeatedly. It was crazy! I didn't even know Bronson could fight like that! Then the match was over. The black kid was bleeding from his nose, but he was smiling. Bronson shook his hand. The energy was great. Then more kids started to box like this. It was really great. There were plenty of bloody noses that day.

Konner came walking into the park with his dad. His dad was a buff guy and was carrying all this sound equipment in one hand. Konner immediately saw me and they came walking up. Konner said to me, "Where do you want this?"

"Just put it by the half-pipe."

"Okay."

And they did. I went inside the main office and got an extra table from them to setup the projector.

Konner said, "Klitz, where's the projector?"

"It's inside."

"Go get it."

I did just that and when I came back out the table was already setup with a blanket covering it. I set down the projector. Wow. It was surreal to watch this all finally happen. All I wanted was to make a skate video with my best friends and release it to the public. I had done it before, but this was *foreal*. I had a premier and everything!

I looked around the park. There must have been two hundred kids there. I remember just seeing everyone and thinking how crazy it was that this was happening. I looked at Konner and said, "Look at how many people are here."

"They better be. Say . . . Klitz, I brought a white sheet for the screen."

"Set it up. Make Zack do it."

"Okay."

Konner walked away and went inside the main office. He got ahold of Zack and came back out. When they were walking, Chad Finners came following them. I walked up to Chad and said, "*There* he is!"

"Hey."

"You excited?"

"Where's my girlfriend?"

"Hold your horses—she's coming, she's coming. Try to have some fun."

"I need my girlfriend here, Klitz."

"Whatever."

He skated away.

I walked back up to the half-pipe, where Konner and Zack were putting up the white screen with clothespins on the baseball fence, and I said to them, "I gotta pick up Chad-boy's girlfriend."

Zack said, "Good luck with that."

So I walked over to Chad on the other side of the park. I said, "What's her number?"

He gave me it.

"Thanks," I said, and walked away.

I was walking out of the front office into the street where my scooter was parked. I thought, "forget it, I'll just pick her up myself." So I called her. She answered.

"Hello?"

"Hey, is this Chad's girlfriend?"

"Who's this?"

"Carl Klitz."

"OH! NO WAY!"

"Yeah. I'm picking you up. Where do you live?"

"You know where Foresthill and Jog is?"

"Yes. Is it at the trailer park?"

"No. *Hell* no! It's the apartments across from that."

"Yeah, we skated there a lot. I used to live at the trailer park."

"Damn. That sucks."

"Get ready. I'm picking you up."

"Okay, Klitzy."

I hung up.

I started up my scooter and drove right down Dixie Highway. Traffic was fairly bad that day. I don't know why. It was also getting dark on top of that. I had to make this premier happen and make sure everyone was happy, including Chad Finners. So I finally got to Foresthill and rode all the way down to Jog. I got into the apartment entrance, got out my phone, and called Chad's girlfriend. She answered.

"Hello?"

"I'm here. Where's your house?"

"Cool. Front gate. I'm ready, I'll be out."

"Cool."

I hung up.

I was looking at the only two apartment complexes that were directly near the front gate. I saw this girl walk out. She looked hot as heck. So I rode on toward her asking, "Hey! Are you Chad's girlfriend?"

The girl ignored me. She didn't even look in my direction.

So I did a U-turn and went back to the front gate. I called Chad's girlfriend's number. I could hear the phone dialing, but also a ringtone. I looked behind me. The girl that ignored me was there, and her phone was ringing.

She said, "You could have told me you're on a scooter. I thought you had a *car.*"

"Nope. Scoot-scoot."

"That's why I didn't say, 'Hi.' My mother can't know!"

"Ohhhhh . . . okay. Well, lets go!"

"How do I get on?"

I scooted forward.

"You gotta be kidding me . . ." she said.

"HURRY UP!"

So she hopped on my scooter, behind me. She held my waist. She said, "Tell anyone about this—even Chad—I'll have a cow. I don't want anyone to know about this."

"It's cool. He doesn't even know you're about to be picked up on a scooter."

"Damn."

So I drove off. I was going a little slower because I wanted her to be safe, and the scooter was bogged down by the weight of each of us. It was gnarly, hectic, and everything unpleasant. I finally got down Foresthill and turned left onto Dixie, even after all the stop-lights and traffic.

We finally got to Phibbs Skatepark. I remember when I parked, Chad's girlfriend was sort of stunned. She said, "Jesus, I thought I was going to die."

I said, "We almost did . . . Twice."

"Really?"

"No," I laughed.

She laughed too.

I parked and we started walking up to the skatepark. She went inside the park, looked around, saw Chad, and ran toward him with a hug and kiss. "Aww," I thought. Cute kids. So I went back and everything was all set up with the sound and the projector. I saw Konner and his dad messing with the actual projector. I said to them, "What's going on?"

Konner said, "Uh, Klitz? We can't get this thing to work."

"What do you mean?"

"It just won't work."

So I was messing around with the buttons. They were right. "Crap," I thought while I continued tinkering. Finally, I got it! The light came on and flashed onto the white screen. Kids were sitting along the half-pipe. I heard loud SCREAMS. I was happy about that. Konner said, "Thank God, Klitz. Now where's the video?"

"I thought . . . oh, crap. Hold on."

"Jesus Christ, Klitz. You don't even have the damn *video?*"

I called my mother. She answered.

"Hey, baby!"

"Mom. I need you to go into my room and get the box of the video. I forgot it."

"You're making a premier for a skate video, and you don't even have the *video?*"

"Stop judging!"

"Jesus. Okay. I'll be there in twenty."

"Thanks."

I hung up. I said to Konner, "My mother is coming with the video and the copies."

"Good."

He skated away and went with some friends.

I got my phone and called Pancho Mango. I asked him if he, Tin, and Mark Row could come by the premier to rap. He told me he was already there. I asked him where he was. He said he could see me. I turned around, saw him off against the wall, hung up, and walked toward him. I said, "Dude, you guys keep low-key."

Mark, Pancho, and Tin all said, "We wouldn't miss this for the world."

I laughed and said to Pancho, "You guys should rap."

He said, "We are. We brought a mic."

"Really?!"

"Yes. Can we hook it up to the speakers."

"Come with me."

We all four went back to the half-pipe, where Conner's dad was, sitting down and looking around. I said to him, "Hey, buddy. Can we connect a mic to this speaker?"

"We already brought a mic. It's hooked up."

"Jesus. Where?"

"Here." He stood up and handed me a mic. I said into it, "Yo!" It was loud. Everyone at the park looked over at me. I laughed into the mic. I said to Pancho, "Lets do a concert."

"Hell yes, Klitz."

I handed him the mic and Mark took it from Pancho. Mark said into the mic, "Yo, yo, yo!" He was sixteen. "Listen up, faggots! Who wants to battle the champ?!"

This big skateboarding kid came walking up. He said, "I will."

Mark said into the mic, "Lets *do* it!"

So Pancho got out his iPhone and connected it to the AUX cord connected to the sound system. A beat was playing. It was fast-pace. Everyone started crowding around. Mark started rapping. He was slaying the big skateboarding kid. Then the kid actually started rapping too. He was okay, but clearly Mark was killing it. Then Mark took the mic and started up again. He said the most violent and disgusting crap about the kid. I was laughing. Everyone was. The kid was laughing too. Then the kid got the mic and pretty much tried the living shit out of Mark. He was pissed. So Mark got the mic back and literally ended him, talking about a Brazzers porn site that was passed around to every skateboarder that the kid knew, but everyone stole his password. The kid didn't say anything. It was hilarious because nobody publicly knew who had the Brazzers porn account to begin with, and who gave it to whom with whatever password given. True story.

Pancho took the mic. The crowd was going crazy. Pancho said into the mic, "I'm gonna lay it down real smooth for you guys." Everyone was all ears while Pancho rapped a song I never heard before. It was a song that eventually Mark and him recorded. It was amazing. Everyone was bobbing their heads. Pancho finished the song.

I took the mic and said into it, "Pancho Mango, everyone! He's the shit! He's the greatest raper *alive!*" Pancho didn't like that. He shook his head, then quickly took the mic and started rapping again. Tin said that that was probably not the best thing to say to a crowd because it blows Pancho up too hard and gives him a lot of pressure in front of the crowd. I felt super embarrassed by it. So I didn't mess with the mic after that. I just let Konner handle everything from then on as far as announcements went.

I looked around. I swear there were three hundred people there. Mostly big heads too. I got nervous. I wanted the video to exceed to everyone's expectations. I had hyped it up so hardcore—I just wanted it to be something enjoyable, something new; something fresh. I wanted it to be my greatest work of art yet!

Donald walked up to me. He gave me dap and said, "Great turn-out, kid."

I said, "Nothing like *The No Way Video*."

"Nothing like it. All we did was have a premier of just us at your place."

"I know!" I laughed.

Donald said, "Do you realize, Klitz, that every girl here is staring at you?"

"Huh?"

"Yeah. Literally. You could go up to any one of these girls and take them home with you to fuck."

"Huh?"

"Klitz. All these girls here *want* you. You're a king here, man. You need to take advantage of that."

"I don't know. I don't think I want to."

"Well, shit, Klitz. What's the use of having a video if you can't fuck groupies?"

"I guess no point . . . I just want this to be a good video."

"Yeah—I get it. Well . . . good luck. I'll be watching from the back way."

"Cool."

He walked off.

I was looking around the park. Donald was right. Every girl there *was* staring at me. I would stare back and them and they would look away and smile. It was odd. I never realized how many eyes were on me. I thought it was insanity.

Konner tapped my shoulder. He said, "Where's the video, Klitz? Your mom had better show up, dude. This is big. This is important."

"Yeah, I'm aware."

I looked out through the fence, and I could see my mother's grey SUV driving up in through the parking lot. I ran to the front office, out the door, and to the parking lot. My mother was already walking with a bag of all the DVDs. She said, "Here you go," and she handed me the bag. "Your welcome."

"Took long enough, Mom."

"Don't give me that! *You're* the one who forgot!"

"I love you."

"I love you too, sugar. Mind if I stay?"

"Sure."

"I wouldn't miss this for the world."

I smiled.

We went through the front office and back in through the park. My mother just kept low-key. I don't even think anyone knew she was my mother. So I had the box full of the video, and I walked up to Konner. I gave him a copy. It had a picture of dick on it. Konner said, "How fitting." I laughed. He opened up the jewel case and got out a DVD. He put it into the DVD player, connected to the projector, and pressed the "start" button.

The menu screen came up. It was playing classical music. The menu had Zack Burns's stop-motion footage from City Place. It was great. It came out perfectly. The crowd was CHEERING! I was literally cheesin' so damn hard. And then I saw Konner hold up the mic and say into it, "Okay, everyone. All you faggots better come on down to watch this damn video, *Escalator Music* — Oh, no! Wait! I mean *Elevator Music*."

The crowd started laughing.

Konner continued, "So, people, come on down and watch. After the video, Klitz is selling copies for . . ." He looked at me, had the mic away. He asked me, "How much, dude?"

"Five bucks each."

"That's it?"

"Yup."

"Okay." And he put the mic back to his face and said, "Five bucks each! So go to Klitz and get a copy afterward." (At the Abocoa Skatepark premier, the next day, Konner was to sell copies for *fifteen* bucks each. He made less than me. Pity.)

Brown Liger was there with a shirt booth. People were buying his shirts like crazy. Which was great because he got his money back that he fronted for the DVDs, the super 8 film, and the everything else. He was a good sport.

Everyone was at the half-pipe. I remember Grent Flan Flan was there. He took a photo of everyone sitting and Facebooked it to me. It was magical to see everyone there. And then I did the honors and pressed the "play" button.

Holy crap was it magical. The intro was playing. Everyone was mesmerized. Then Chad's part played. The crowd was going WILD! Then my part came, and almost every other trick they were literally SCREAMING at the screen. They loved it. Then the Friend's Part, then Fletcher's (who he wasn't there to watch), and then everyone else followed. So much SCREAMING, I tell you! Then the last part came. John Taco. *Wow!* At the second part, when his "enders" played, everyone was screaming so loud that the half-pipe was rumbling under me. I was very, very, *very* pleased with how it turned out. Only a few boos were present, but only from people who actually disliked me. It had nothing to do with the quality of the video. The fact they were there watching just proved that it was worth it for them to hate on.

Everyone was coming up to me to congratulate. They said it was a great video. Girls were eying me like you wouldn't *believe*. I went up to everyone in the video and gave them a free copy. Then people started lining up to be with money. I was surrounded. So I had the bag and was just giving out change and passing . . . giving out change and passing . . . I was collecting all the cash here and there. My pockets were insanely full. I sold forty copies. Not bad.

Mark came up to me. He said, "Carl, you coming?"

"Where?"

"The after-party."

"You know it. I didn't know there was one."

"Well baby, there is."

"Sweet. Hold on."

I walked over to Brown Liger's booth. I said to him, "Here, take the DVDs. They're all yours. Sell them online. Whatever you make, you keep."

"Thanks, Klitz."

(He never sold one copy).

So I hopped on my scooter with Mark on the back. There were a lot of cars, many of which were going to this after-party at Binki's, the same place my recent birthday was held. So I rode, with Mark down Dixie,

Foresthill, and then all the way down to Boyton. It was hectic. I had to ride slow. Mark was *all* about it. He was saying how much he wanted to get a scooter. "Whatever," I thought.

So we arrived at this after-party. There weren't that many people there. Maybe twenty. It was all the kids in *Elevator Music* plus a couple chicks. Chad was there with his girlfriend. One of the kids that bought the video at Phibbs put it into the DVD player and played the video again. He was fixated on the screen. He loved it.

I was sitting down and just thinking, "Wow, this is insane." I had mixed feelings. But before I could ruminate any further, this girl came up to me.

"Hi," she said.

"Hi," I said back. "What's up?"

"Can I show you something?"

"Sure."

She took my hand and led me to this piano. We both sat down at it. The girl said, "I can play elevator music, if you'd like."

I said, "Hell yes."

She started playing the piano. It was beautiful. Her hair was so curly, so blonde, and so beautiful. I thought she was an angel. And then I said, "This is really, really lovely. I appreciate any person who can play an instrument like yourself."

"I'm Cathy," she said.

"Pleased to meet you."

"Pleasure is mine. I hear you make art."

"I dabble, yes."

She laughed. "No—don't be modest! Can you make me something?"

"Uh . . . sure?"

"Hang on." Cathy got up from the piano, went to the kitchen, and came back with a pencil and paper. She said, "Draw me something."

I said, "Okay," and I started drawing. I was making this weird, abstract alien cartoon. It had one eye, pants, and it had a VX1000 in its hand. I gave it to the Cathy. She said, "I love it. I'm going to keep it forever. I know one day you'll be famous." (Years later, on Tumblr, she messaged me and told me that she *still* had the drawing, so I know she'll be keeping it. I know if and when I get "famous," she will probably make a lot of money from that work of art.)

The party was over. I didn't even drink. It was actually sort of depressing. Everyone was real tired because they were at the skatepark all day. I just remember wanting to get on home. I just wanted to go home and sleep. So I said to everyone, "I'm going." They nodded. I went outside and got on my scooter and rode away.

Something weird was happening to me as I rode back to my house. I was looking at the streetlights passing me by. Everything seemed to fade in through itself. I thought I was high or something. I thought I was losing my mind. Was I going insane? I thought. I didn't want the video to end. I had worked on it for so many years, only caring about it and myself. I hadn't seen what was around me: my friends, the tricks, the heartache, and the love of skateboarding. I didn't want it to ever stop, and I never thought it would. As I was riding down Foresthill, I knew that skateboarding had ended, for me in some way. I felt an engulfing sadness over my body. I thought I had nothing left in the world, I thought I was nothing, I thought I was just a kid with nothing but pipe dreams left. I wanted nothing more than to have another project again. Something to live and *dream* for, if that makes sense. But those sorts of things don't come to people that often. I never once felt a sense of, "togetherness" when trying to pursue something creative. I was alone. I had nobody left. I was an alien. I was nothing.

Then I got to the front of my house. I absent-mindedly opened the front gate. Nothing seemed real. I was lost in time. I parked my scooter. It all seemed automated. I got out my key, unlocked my front door, opened it, and walked inside. Everything seemed mapped out in my life. It was like I jumped through time. It was like I lost my sense of self and sense of what I was worth.

I went into my room and sat at my desk. I popped open a DVD, my personal DVD of *Elevator Music*, and I watched it again. I was thinking how great it turned out, and to be honest, I was genuinely proud of it. I don't know why I was feeling so lost. I think it was because that video was all I had. And since it ended at the premier, I was sad because it was the only thing that made me who I was. So I thought to call Chewie. He was living in San Antonio, Texas. He was, in fact, the person to come up with the name of "Elevator Music," after all. He answered the phone.

"Klitzy?"

"Doo-mister!"

"How was the premier?"

"Words cannot describe how I'm feeling. It was literally . . . magical . . . surreal. Everyone liked it a lot."

"I knew they would. You follow my vision of it?"

"Oh yes."

"That's my boy. What are you going to do now?"

"I really have no idea. I'm just counting money."

"Really? How much?"

"It's about . . . eh, I'd say one hundred forty-one bucks— Wait! Fuck! I short-changed myself! A kid game me a five and I gave him a twenty back! This sucks!"

Chewie laughed. "Well, you live and learn. It's about loss-prevention in business. You made one-hundred forty-one, didn't you?"

"Yeah. I guess you're right. Still sucks, though."

"I know, bud. How's school?"

"A drag. I need to graduate."

"Focus on one thing at a time. Focus on that. You're going to do great things."

"Thanks, man."

"I wish I could have been there, bro."

"I wish you could have been there, too."

"Send me a copy."

"Text me your address. I'll be sure to ship you out one."

" 'Kay . . . Well, look, I gotta go—I'm at a bar."

"Cool."

"There's the hottest chick here that I'm really wanting to fuck. Dude, she literally has the biggest tits I ever did see."

I laughed. "Get it, man!"

"I'll see ya around."

"See ya."

He hung up.

I watched the video to the end. I was looking around my room and nothing felt like it was real. I needed a beer. I wanted to just die or something. I know that sounds depressing but the finality of the thing made me feel so empty inside. I felt like I had nothing. I wanted it to never end. I put so much pressure on myself and every single one of my friends that I just didn't realize I was already living my dream. I wanted that back. Ever since then I always would chase that "dream." My mother always told me that, one day, I was going to be a millionaire. I hope that day comes. I really do hope so. Maybe one day I can find myself some real happiness and not feel so damn alone.

I went to sleep that night in tears. I don't know why. I started sobbing so hard. I didn't want it to end this way. I didn't want it to be tomorrow; but I knew I couldn't stop time. So I said out loud, "I miss my friends," and I fell into a dreamless sleep. I was in my hellish sorrows.

•   •   •

School was coming to an end for me because I was doing F.L.V.S. online and not really doing much but staying home most of my days. I was actually really tackling my schoolwork and trying my hardest just to finish everything. I had been in school for five years. I just wanted it to finally end. I wanted it to end and be over with so I could move on with my life and start it. My sister, Lela, would come over and help me. She was great. She actually helped on most of my tests. She pretty much did most the work but I didn't mind it—I just wanted to finish. I would also ask teachers for more time on assignments and they were pretty nice about it. I actually finished everything two weeks after the *Elevator Music* premier. That was huge for me. Things were looking up.

•   •   •

Then I released *Kookamonga The Movie* to hype-up my audience on the idea of the *Elevator Music* ending. It was a journey, for sure. It showed every single time we skated: all the heartache, all the nasty falls, all the laughs, and all the worry-free times we spent together. People loved it. I felt like it was a farewell for me. At that moment I felt extremely depressed to have finished *Elevator Music*. That was my whole life. It was all I cared about. That's a hard thing because for the longest time I just wanted to be understood in the skate community and to be liked for my talents. Once I actually got that and had my fifteen minutes, it was over. It was over and it felt like I wasn't happy afterward. I never understood it. I finished the video so why wasn't I happy? For the most part, my idea of it is that happiness is not something to particularly *look* for, it's more of a thing that just happens on it's own when you get rid of the selfish ideas you have about yourself. It's the moment you can feel good about yourself for all the things you accomplished. When you can accept yourself for who you are and never look back . . . It's too bad I didn't feel this way during this time.

late-2011

Donald messaged me on Facebook about how he was at the premier (which I already knew) and was proud of me. I told him, *"Thanks!"* He was saying that all he does now is play *Call of Duty* and how he's one of the top people in the video game world. I laughed because I totally didn't see him as the type, but I guess people change over the years. I know he had to've since *The No Way Video* we released years before, probably half a decade from this day. But then Donald told me that he wanted to start up a YouTube account because he saw people all over there having all the credit of doing stuff that is supposedly "crazy," even though he could do it better. I told him that he should pursue it, and that if he wanted something bad enough to reach out and grab it. He told me thanks, and he said that he wanted to chill soon. I told him sure, that that would be great. I missed Donald, honestly. He was the whole reason I even got involved in the skate world. If I hadn't known him, I wouldn't have met Braydon, and then Teddy, and then everyone else after that. I always think of that sort of stuff. I always felt like I owed people, in a way.

• • •

I bought a T3i online. It was this really great camera on Amazon by Canon. It had a flip-screen, super HD, and it was perfect for filming anything and everything: friends, skating—everything. I wanted to just make vlog videos on YouTube to post about nothing. I found out later that I wasn't any good at just talking in front of a camera. Pity. But I had the camera nonetheless.

• • •

I was going over to Donald's house more frequently and that meant hanging out with Pancho Mango. He was a king on the mic, and I literally wanted, and tried, to make him famous. So I would go over his house and have him put on a beat with a YouTube video he knew, and he'd rap old verses from his composition book. I would film this and for a while and they were actually getting somewhere. This was really lovely. He was very hyped on me because I was hyped on him. We were an excellent team. I also helped Donald out by filming him talk to his fanbase on YouTube, which was quickly growing because of his apparent reputation in the video game world of *Call of Duty*. Life felt good. I felt like I was doing something constructive again.

• • •

I was on Facebook one day and I added this blonde girl who had huge boobs. I always had a thing for boobs—I don't know why. Maybe it's because of watching pornography all these years, but yeah, she was a rascal. So I added her. She accepted and I sent her a message: "Hey, what's up?" And pretty soon—like anyone who goes online for the finer feelings of love and intimacy—we eventually exchanged numbers and I was well on my way to hanging out with her in hopes of feeling her breasts.

I got a text from Sam, the girl that wanted to make-out with me during the time I was talking to puked-on Terra, telling me that her wedding was that same day—on the spot. I guess her and Will decided to tie the knot. She told me that I *had* to be there and I told her that I would most definitely make it to her wedding because I'm her best friend. She told me that she had clothes for me to wear, to just go and be there. It was at this fancy place near City Place. It looked like a regular house with a big yard, but the greenery was beautiful. Sam texted me the address and I said okay.

So in the meantime before the wedding, the big-breasted girl picked me up in her car. She said, "Hey," and I said, "Hey," and it was all very robotic. "What do you want to do today?" she asked. "Nothing . . . I don't know," I said. "What about the pool?" she asked. "I think that would be fun." "Sure," I said. "Or the beach." She said, "Beach first, pool second?" "Deal," I said. And we were off.

The beach was nice—like it always was—and it was especially sunny, for some odd reason. This big-breasted girl was dressed really skimpy. I think she *wanted* me to look at her body more. She was hot. So I walked down that sand with her, watched her, and she began to put a towel down. She was lying down on her back. Her breasts were like two big melons, or mountains, that you could just admire. I love boobs.

I got next to her, sat. I remember looking at the horizon and thinking to myself, "What a damn good beach, huh? Like, it's awesome." So I said, "Isn't this beautiful?"

The big-breasted girl said, "Yeah . . . I guess so," and she turned over and undid her bra. Oh God, I thought. Then she said to me, "Carl, would you be a dear and put on some sunscreen on my back?"

Um . . . *duh!* "Yes," I said. "I would like that very much."

"Good. Here's the sunscreen." She gave me the bottle.

I squirted it and rubbed the stuff on my hands. I was rubbing her back. It was soft and beautiful. I think I popped a boner.

She said, "I think I want to go. This beach is boring."

Boring? Wow—I thought that was odd. A beach is a beach—it doesn't change. But being a horny man, I said, "Okay."

So we left and went to her car, upon which she said, "Pool."

I said, "Okay."

Pretty soon we were at her neighborhood, which wasn't far from mine, and we were at her pool. It was a public pool. No guards, no key, no nothing. Nobody was there. She got her towel out and draped it over one of the lounge chairs. I watched her and thought, "She's spoiled." So I jumped into the pool.

I swam under the water and could see the light crystalizing on the bottom of the pool. It was quiet. I thought this could be my life. I thought that a fish's life is probably better than a human's: they swim around, not really hearing much, not really bothering anyone, having fish sex, making babies, and not knowing what God is. I thought that would be nice. But then I saw the water *pow!* in front of me. I saw millions of bubbles. So I swam to the surface.

Big-breasted girl had jumped in. She swam toward me and said, "Now we're talkin'." She splashed me. "YOU JUMPED IN AND GOT ME ALL WET!"

I said, "Oh."

I swam from one end of the pool to the other end. Big-breasted girl stopped me. "You're weird," she said. "I've seen your art online."

"Yeah?"

"It's cool as hell. You should do a painting for me."

"Only for women I love."

"I see . . . well, maybe one day you will."

"Maybe. We'll see."

She smiled. "Hey, Carl. Do you make any *money* from your art?"

"Loads of money. Why?"

"Just curious." She swam near me. "Tell me about yourself."

So I was blabbing on about my elementary school years, my middle school years, and pretty much everything that led up to that day. My entire life story. I even told her about Sam and her wedding that was later in the day.

Then big-breasted girl said, "Hey. I gotta get going. Can I take you home?"

I said, "Yeah, sure."

So we got out of the pool and kept walking. We got into her car. We were silent the whole time. Did I say something wrong? I thought. Then we finally got to my street. I said, "Bye," to big-breasted girl. She didn't say anything back. When I shut the door, she sped off.

(Fun fact: She one-word texted me for two days later, upon which I never spoke to her again. I looked at her Facebook later on to find out she had a boyfriend. Hmm, I thought. Maybe they were breaking up and she was "testing the waters" to see if there was any "good guys" besides him. There probably isn't. I'm what you call "The Weirdo.")

So I called Sam. She told me that everyone was there already and to come on over. I hung up, looked at her text message of the address, got my T3i, and got on my scooter and went to downtown City Place. There was some traffic, but that wasn't unusual. So I drove into the parking garage that really wasn't close by and I walked two blocks to my destination with my camera.

There were Spanish people walking out with really fancy clothes—that meant that Sam's wedding was up ahead, because she had a Spanish family. I walked on. There was a door so I knocked. Nobody answered. I just opened it and stepped inside.

I saw Sam right away. She turned around and saw me. She said, "Carl!" She came running up to me. She wrapped her arms around me and gave me the biggest hug she could give. She's very adorable. A short girl. I love her, as a friend. I think she's the smartest, nicest soul. Her husband, Will, should feel very lucky to have her. I know I would be if I did.

I said, "You look great, Sam." She really did.

She said, "Thank you! I want you to meet a friend of mine."

I said, "Okay."

I followed Sam. She held my hand and guided me. Her friend was down the hall. Her friend was a redhead. She was *hot*. "Gosh, I love you, Sam," I thought. Thank you for hooking me up! Sam said, "Carl, this is Suzi."

"Hi, Suzi."

"Hi, Carl."

Sam said, "Mingle, you two."

Suzi said, "We can't."

Sam said, "Oh yeah! Carl! You have to wear these clothes I got you. Suzi, lets hook this man up!"

They high-fived each other, grabbed both my hands, and guided me to a bathroom. They were on a mission. I love women . . . So Suzi had my upper body, Sam had my lower. They took my pants and shirt off and I was just in my boxers, camera wrapped around my neck. They didn't say anything. Sam put on my pants, Suzi put on my shirt. They combed my hair, put on these suspenders that Sam bought. I looked "snazzy."

Sam said, "Gosh, you look good."

Suzi blushed.

I said, "Thanks."

Sam said, "Is that the T3i?"

I said, "Yes it is."

Sam said, "Let me see. Take it off."

So I did and handed it to her.

Sam's eyes got big and she said, "OoooOooo!" She opened up the LCD screen and was snapping photos of me. I was smiling like crazy. That was awesome.

I said, "Do I *really* look good?"

Sam said, "Yes, Carl," and smiled.

Suzi looped her arm into mine. The three of us walked out of the bathroom. Suzi and Sam were following me wherever I went. I went over to the living room, away from everyone. I was sort of bad at mingling with people. Suzi was actually very smart. She was this girl that was from up north and was into art. She loved my paintings—most people did. Sam was always bragging to her about me. Suzi and I briefly slow-danced in the living room and we were laughing and carrying on. It was great. Sam's husband, Will, came into the room. I shook his hand and told him what an awesome wife he had. He smiled at that idea and hugged her. He said, "Thanks, Carl," and walked away.

Sam and I sat on the couch for a long time. Suzi went over with Sam's mother to help her setup tables and chairs. Sam was absolutely beautiful. She was in this dress that looked really great. She made it herself. She told me, later on, that she made my shirt and pants too. I kept it for years afterward. I really thought it was a lovely day.

And then Sam's mother came in the room and said, "It's time!"

Sam smiled and said, "Good. Come on, Carl."

So I stood up. It was time for the wedding. I was just going to take endless photos of everything with my camera. I wanted to remember it all. I wanted Sam to remember it all, even though I knew she would anyway. We made our way outside. Seats were lined neatly. There was a garden, it was sunny, and the entire family was there. It was silent for a few minutes. I had my camera ready and I was standing next to Suzi, off in the background. She seemed sort of bored. She said, "I hope this goes well," and I said, "I hope so, too," and then we saw Sam and Will walk out. Everyone was staring at them. This was Sam's time to shine, I thought. I was excited!

I was snapping photos of her as they walked. They looked so happy, so smiley; so perfect. "What a cute couple," I thought. Sam deserves all that life has to give her. They approached the altar and the priest. He said very, *very* basic vows. Sam isn't the type to have a big formal invitation to marriage, I think. The vows were only for about five minutes and then they kissed. Everyone cheered and I snapped a photo. It was absolutely spectacular.

After the wedding everyone was just walking around talking to each other. Suzi and I were dancing. Music was playing, food was served—it was great. The bar was open, but Sam was only eighteen, I was nineteen, and Suzi was eighteen. We couldn't drink, even though that would have been fun to do. So I had my camera and I took tons of photos of everyone. They all posed, stood together, and smiled. I took so many photos of Sam. I just couldn't believe she was married. I couldn't believe her beauty. Man, what a girl.

Suzi and I slow-danced to a really sad song. We had some fun. I wanted to kiss her but was too afraid. She probably could have sensed it. We stopped and then got plates. We ate steak, pork, veggies—everything under the sun. It was all so lovely. A really elegant wedding.

Nighttime came and the party was dying down. I remember talking to Sam about life and about art. We spoke so much about our goals.

"I just wanted to find peace," I told her. She understood. And then it was time to go.

The lady who owned the building came up to me and asked for my business card. "I'm not a photographer," I told her. I'll bet she was confused, considering I had an expensive camera around my neck (which I sold a month later).

I told Sam goodbye and wished her good luck. I haven't seen her since after. That was my last time. I do talk to her from time to time though. She's a good egg.

I walked back to the parking-garage and I got on my scooter. The moment I did it began to pour. "How fitting," I thought. The girl I liked got married and I was stuck in the rain. So I took off my shirt and put it in the compartment of my scooter. I texted my brother, Lance, who lived in Wellington saying I wanted to come over. He said sure and that he was drinking with some friends. I rode pretty much seven miles in the rain. From City Place all the way to Wellington, taking Foresthill.

When I got to Lance's apartment the party was going. It was only about five people or so, but it was good for me. I was drinking and drinking and drinking. I probably was depressed. I was also soaked. My brother commented on that. He told me how crazy I was to have rode in the rain, or the fact that I had a scooter in the first place and not a car. I told him, "Whatever." I drank his beer. I got so drunk that I fainted on his rug.

When I woke up in the morning, vomit was pooling from my face and onto my brother's apartment's rug. He made me clean it up. I did, and I was still depressed as I rode home that evening. Weeks passed of boredom. What can you do?

•   •   •

I got something in the mail from Woodhill stating to come to their school to pick up my diploma. I was both excited and exhausted. I wanted to just get it over with. So I went down there on my scooter and basically rode into the gates and parked. I went into the front office and asked them, "Where's my diploma?"

The Front Office woman said, "Guidance counselor."

"Okay."

So I walked down the hallway, where my guidance counselor was. Ms. Janet. She was a fat lady, but ultra nice. She was the one who signed me up for F.L.V.S. in the first place. So I got up to her office. I knocked. I heard, "Come in!" and I went inside.

"Hey, Ms. Janet," I said.

"Call me Rose," she said, "you're a graduate now, not a student. Sit, sit!"

So I sat.

"Carl . . . Carl Klitz . . . Klitz . . ." Rose was looking through folders. "Ah! Here you are!" She pulled out this paper. Then she got out this plastic sleeve. It was a fold out. Very professional-like. I rolled my eyes. She handed me it and said, "Congratulations."

I can't even lie. When I took it I actually smiled really wide. I was like, "Yes!" and I was smiling and hooraying. I really thought it was special. I looked at Rose and said, "Thank you."

She said, "Good luck in life, Carl. Be safe."

I walked out of that office. I thought about how crazy it was to get that diploma, how kids spent four years trying to get it, and it took me five. Then I thought about Rose's comment: "Good luck in life." Wow, I thought. Eerie. Why would she say that? Then when I got out of the front office, I saw Dr. Roswell in front of the school. Oh God, I thought. This guy . . .

He noticed me. "Hi, Carl!" he said. He came running up to me. "Wait up!"

"Hey, Dr. Roswell."

"Hey! Congratulations, bud! You got your diploma. I was actually expecting you to be here."

"Really?"

"Yeah, man. I always believed in you. I wanted you to succeed. Can I shake your hand?"

What's crazy is in that moment, I thought about how I always fantasized that I would never walk across the stage, that I would never shake the principal's hand, and that I would just pick up my diploma and never look back. But as I saw this man's hand in front of me, waiting to be shaken—*needing* to be shaken—I held my hand out and shook it. Dr. Roswell said, "Thanks bud. Be safe. I hope you do well in life."

"There it was again," I thought . . . That phrase.

(Later, I found out that Dr. Roswell was actually pushing drugs within the school. He was convicted and sent to twenty years in prison. He had been doing it for many years. Many kids actually got terribly sick from it. He was making money, and kids were getting sick, sometimes dying.)

And then he walked passed me. I thought it was so . . . final. I didn't understand how final it was, getting that piece of paper. I just thought it would be more than that. I though maybe I would actually *gain* something of real pleasure. But I didn't seem to feel it, I guess. Oh well. So I walked on and got on my scooter. I rode down Dixie and wanted to see if Zack was at his house. I didn't even call. I just parked in front.

I knocked on his door. Zack came out with his cousin, Travis. Travis was tall, lanky, and awesome. He was a cool kid. Zack said, "Klitzy! What's *up?*"

"I got *this* today." I held up my diploma. "Look."

"Holy crap, man! Congrats!" He took it, held it up. He gave me a hug. He said, "I knew you could do it, Carl."

"Thanks," I said.

"Let me take a photo."

"Sure."

So he gave my diploma back, got out his iPhone, and I held up the diploma and smiled like a freak. He took the photo. I said, "Let me see." He showed me. I looked really odd, but actually sort of, you know, *cool* in a way.

I chilled with them until nighttime. I posted that photo on Facebook. I got about fifty likes on it. So many "congratulations." So many people saying wonderful things, but I couldn't feel anything but dread, for some odd reason. I went home that night and cried.

•   •   •

I made a Craigslist post inquiring about my iMac computer. I wanted to sell it. It actually sold fairly quickly. I had money in the bank already and I wanted to buy a 2010 Macbook Pro for myself. I was done with editing *Elevator Music* so I didn't have a need for a huge desktop computer. I got a text from a Mexican guy. He was pretty cool. He actually came down super fast. He pretty much just came inside my house and turned the computer on, and that was it. I think I sold it for about seven hundred bucks. Not bad. Macs hold their value, to my knowledge. Oh well. That was great for me!

•   •   •

I was feeling severely depressed because I was thinking about *Elevator Music* and how it ended so insanely fast. I thought about life and how fast it was moving and it was scaring me. I always think about that as I witness my life passing by. I want it to move slower so I can enjoy it but it seems like it moves faster and faster. I know scientifically it makes sense because the human brain gets used to the idea of life, year after year, and days, weeks, months, and years seem to go back faster and faster, exponentially. But as I was thinking this, I called Lance.

I said, "Hey man," once I heard a hello.

"What's up, Carl?"

"You at Apple?"

"Yeah."

"Can I give you $1,350? I wanted to buy the Macbook Pro."

"Yeah. Come on down. I gotta go big man. I'll see you soon."

"See ya, bro."

He hung up.

So I scooted all the way down to Wellington. I parked, went inside, and found the Apple store. I went in there and saw Lance at the genius bar where he worked. He was a "genius" a.k.a a lead tech there. He actually saw me walk up and immediately walked toward me. Under his breath he said, "Listen. You listenin'?"

I nodded.

"Good, because this is my job. If they knew that I was getting you a discount on a Macbook Pro for God's sake they would fire my ass."

"Gotcha," I said. "How can I give you the cash?"

"Just give it now, Carl." Lance held his hand out, sneakily. I got out the cash from my back pocket and gave him it. He put it in his pocket. "I'll go order it now," he said. Then he walked away, to the back of the store, where they kept product.

I wait for about thirty minutes. I was on the laptop I was presumably about to buy. It was literally amazing. I couldn't wait. I just remember being so damn excited surfing the web.

Then Lance came back out with the box.

"Here you go," he said. "Go away. I gotta get back to work."

"Thanks, bud," I said.

Lance walked away to go back to his job.

I walked out of there with the Macbook Pro in my hands. I went all the way down stairs to the food court because I wanted to grub down on some pizza or something. I hadn't really eaten. But when I got there, I found myself just looking around at everyone. I saw a couple together eating tacos. I saw them smile and be happy. I actually felt sort of jealous. I made my way around the food court and could smell the food in the air. Everything mingled together and smelled so serene. I remember that. But then I eventually found myself in front of some wishing well thingy. "Well," I thought, "this is nice."

I turned around and set the Macbook box down on the ground. I got out this penny from my back pocket, which was odd because I never carried change. I thought it was a sign from a nonexistent god or something. So I got out the penny, looked at it, and it was brand new.

Made that year. Super shiny. I looked at the water, I looked at the penny, and I closed my eyes and said, "I wish to be big in the art world, with a hot wife, a family, and a daughter named Penelope." Then I reopened my eyes and tossed the penny into the water. I thought, "Well, shit . . ." and then I picked up my Mac, went out into the parking lot, and left on my scooter. Home, sweet home.

•   •   •

I was in my living room watching *Family Guy* one night, around seven p.m., and I was contemplating what I was going to do with my life. I had my diploma, I made *Elevator Music,* I had tons of friends, tons of love from fans, and that was it. I didn't know what else I needed in this world. It made me sad. I guess the idea is that if you don't always have a pursuit you become empty. That's what I was feeling. So I got up, decided to clear my mind by doing some dishes, and I finished. Then I decided to eat some cereal. I was craving something, but I didn't know what. So I got out a bowl, poured some cereal and milk, and made my bowl. I ate in the kitchen, finished, and put it back in the sink, not thinking much of it—I just wanted to find peace. I was severely depressed.

Ronald came home late that night. He was unemployed, but I think he was doing odd jobs that required him to be out almost the entire day to make ends meet. I didn't know this at the time. When you're a kid, especially one who hates an unemployed stepfather, you tend to think he's out doing nothing with his life. Or you *want* to think it. But yeah, he came home, I was still watching *Family Guy* on the couch, and he came into the living room and said, "Hey. What's this?"

I said, "What's what?"

"You know damn well."

"No. I really don't."

"Stand up."

So I stood up. I was waiting for him to speak. He paused a moment and then said, "Look in the sink."

I walked over to the sink, looked down. Just my bowl of cereal in one side of the sink, and on the other side was the clean dishes. I said, "I don't get it."

Ronald said, "Boy, yer 'bout as stupid as you look—you see *that!* The dishes not done! *That's* what I'm talkin' about!"

"Ronald, I did the dishes. I made *one bowl* of cereal."

"You just never learn. I tell you all day long to do what you're told, and you *still* don't listen—I just will never understand. So you know what? I'm raising your rent by one hundred bucks."

I said, "Excuse me?"

"You heard me. One hundred bucks. It's the only way that I'll get through to you, boy."

I was pissed. I stormed off into my bedroom and shut the door. I just couldn't believe him. I couldn't believe an unemployed guy could do such a thing. So I did what any ignorant teenager would do. I went on Facebook and made a status update:

"Facebook, I want you all to know what a selfish bastard my stepfather is. How can a guy, who's unemployed, have the gall to raise MY rent money by ME NOT DOING ONE DISH!! I can't believe this bull. He's an unemployed loser, trying to take MY money, that's what. And you know what else? My MOTHER is the one who makes ALL the money, while he goes around town and does whatever the hell he wants. He's a selfish prick, and I hate him. Go DIE!"

I clicked "post," and that was it. I got about twenty "likes" on it, a couple comments from people taking my side—because obviously they didn't know the whole story, and know that it actually was partly false, considering he did actually work odd jobs and was trying to make ends meet—and I would respond by saying things that I felt. Not the best idea when you're upset, and I know that now. But after a few minutes, I sat there looking at the screen in silence. An eerie feeling came over me. Did I screw up?

A soft knock came at my door. "Carl?" my mother said. "Can I come in?"

"Yes."

So she opened my door and came in. She had this look to her—I can't describe it. It was like a lost, distant look of worry, frustration, guilt, and shame. I still to this day am haunted by that look. She said, "Come out into the living room."

Oh no, I thought. I'm screwed. Many a time when I had to "go to the living room," it was because I did something horribly wrong. Many, many conversations; many, many times. I never listened to them, only because I never understood. I do now. So I went into the living room.

Ronald was on the couch. He had his face buried into his hands. He was leaning forward. He looked extremely upset. I was worried. My mother said, "Do you have anything you'd like to say, Carl?" I looked at my mother's eyes. She looked tired, like she had just been woken up.

I said, "What's going on?"

Ronald lifted his head and looked straight at me. "What's going on? What's . . . going . . . *on?* Hmmmmm. Well, I just went on the computer, there, and your mother's Facebook was logged in. I was about to go onto *my* Facebook and log her out, but what I found was a little *status* update by my stepson about me 'being an unemployed loser' who 'takes my mother and I's money.' Is that right? Or am I just make-believing this shit?"

Oh God, I thought. I'm in real deep crap. I said, "Oh."

"Oh? *Oh?!* 'Oh' is right, oh! You *never* listen, Carl! You *never* do! How many times do I gotta tell you about how you act? This is unbelievable, Carl. You literally have dug yourself in a hole!"

My mother said, "Ronald has been working with his friend to make us money, to put food on the table, to make sure we are safe. I've been working overtime, too. The economy is hard enough. It's hard enough to deal with that . . ."

And Ronald said, ". . . but to come home to a punk kid, that's another thing I can't handle. So you know what? We've decided that enough is enough. Pack your shit. You have thirty days to get out of my house."

I looked at my mother and said, "You're serious?"

"Yes, Carl. We can't fight with you anymore. I've tried everything to make you a better person, but I can't seem to get through to you."

Ronald said, "You're a selfish punk kid. Let you go into the real world. You'll see. *You'll* start to see what it's like to work for your money, to have to come home to a messy house, dirty dishes, to have to pro*vide* for yourself, take care of yourself. You're going to have to find out the hard way because, frankly, I don't give a fuck anymore. You're done. You have thirty days."

I said, "Whatever," and went into my room. I got my scooter's key from my dresser, put on a shirt and some pants, and I walked out of that house. I got on my scooter and drove. I drove down Foresthill and to the Walmart on Jog Road. I parked. I got off my scooter. When I was walking, déjà vu enveloped me. I was looking at my surroundings and nothing felt real—it felt like a dream. I couldn't believe this was really happening. Was it happening?

I got inside Walmart. I didn't know what I wanted to buy. I just wanted something . . . anything. I just wanted comfort. I was going from aisle to aisle and not really looking at anything. I was just aimless. Then I found the luggage section. I thought, "This is what I need. I'll stay with a friend." So I got a bag and rolled it with me to the registers. I paid for it. Thirty–forty bucks, or something like that.

I went back to my scooter outside. I put the luggage bag on the back of my scooter and strapped it down with a wire. I was looking at that Walmart and thinking, "This isn't happening." Panic came over me, but I shook it off. I was having anxiety, but I didn't know it at the time. I thought that life was something I could never do, get over, or ever even control. I thought I was so small.

I rode back down Foresthill and back to Military. I went down my street, turned, and got to the front of my house— Excuse me, "my parent's" house, I thought. Then I opened the gate, parked, and went back inside with my luggage. Ronald was still on the couch. He was watching TV. He looked really sad, mad, or a mixture of every unpleasant emotion under the sun. A man who was pissed with the simple way things were. It was a look that I developed over the years of working at places I hated, with people I hated, and with people I hated to give money to. I knew that look all too well.

I was laying in bed and thinking to myself if I was a good or bad person. I didn't know what I was. I felt I had no sense of identity or Self. I was repressing everything around me, I was just "going with the flow" and not even caring what I thought about situations. All I did was go with the crowd. I didn't know if what the things I were doing were right and wrong, I just did them because I thought it was better to do them than to just sit and do nothing, which is what my personality gravitates toward. I felt bad that I put my parents through this heavy transition—and I'm a thousand times sorry for that. I was just a teenager. That's all. I went into a dreamless sleep that night.

●   ●   ●

I didn't know what the hell else to do when I woke up that morning. So I called Lela, my big sister, and told her I was kicked out. She told me to meet her at downtown City Place, where she lived. I rode my scooter down there on the double and met her at Starbucks. She was already there, waiting, drinking something.

"Hi," I said to her, and sat down.

"So what's going on, Car?"

"I'm not sure."

"What do you mean? What happened?"

"Pretty much Ronald wanted to raise my rent, I thought he was trying to take my money because he was unemployed, but I guess I was wrong about that."

"I see . . . well . . . what are you going to do now, Car?"

"I don't know. That's the thing."

"Well, I have a storage unit."

"Could I stay with you for a bit?"

"No, Carl. I don't have the room. Have you tried Lance?"

"He said, 'Hell no.' " He really did.

"Tough crowd. Well, I have a storage for your stuff in the meantime."

"Okay."

"Do you have friends to stay with?"

"I haven't really asked, but most of them have apartments. They really can't do much."

"I see . . . I think you have to find a place. How much money do you get from your job?"

"It's Little Caesars, Lela—not exactly anything. It's part-time."

"Ask for more hours, Carl."

"*Ugh!* Why is this happening to me?!"

"Car, it was bound to happen sooner or later, the guy's a douche!"

"I know! But what the hell, man! Mom is just *letting* this shit happen."

"You gotta make the best of it. Seriously. This too shall pass."

"Yeah, whatever."

"What about . . . Krissy?"

"Krissy?"

"Yeah."

"In Texas . . . ?"

"Yeah! Maybe she can help."

"I'll call her," I said. Then I got my phone out, found her number, and started dialing. I heard hums. Then a person spoke.

"Carl?"

"Krissy?"

"Hey, Carl! What's up! How are you?"

"Uh . . . not too good, Krissy. I'm in a bad spot."

"Yeah, Mom told me."

"I need a place to stay."

"Did you ask Lela or Lance?"

"Yes. They said no."

"Well . . . ?"

"I was going to see if you could let me stay at your place."

"In Texas?"

"Yes. In Texas."

"Uh . . . are you sure?"

"Yes. I hate this place."

"I mean, there's not much room. You could stay for sure though. I need someone to help me out around the house anyways."

"Yeah. I could *totally* do that."

"Well, do it! Get your ticket and let me know when you fly in. It'll be very easy."

"Really? Holy crap! Thanks, Krissy!"

"No problem."

"Listen. I gotta go. I'll text you when I buy the tickets."

"Okay. Love you."

"I love you too."

I hung up.

"Wow," Lela said, "good deal."

"It's good. I can just get out of Florida. Sounds nice."

"Lets get your stuff in my storage. We'll get you your tickets."

"I'll buy them tonight."

"A one-way is probably only about a hundred bucks."

"I know."

Pretty soon we just left Starbucks and went back to my parent's house. We packed up all my stuff and loaded up Lela's car. We drove to Okeechobee Road, parked her car at her storage facility, and walked on in. We found her storage unit and loaded it up. It took a couple of hours to accomplish it all, the entire moving of my stuff.

She drove me off to my parent's house. I told her "goodbye" and "thank you." She drove away.

•   •   •

I wanted to spend time with my friends all one last time. So I thought it would be best to see them at their school, Gstar. School didn't start too long ago during that time. It was around October. I wanted to ride my scooter over to Gstar. So I did.

I parked at The YMCA parking lot, looked over, and reminisced about a time when I first started skating. It seemed like a millennia ago. I stopped thinking about it and started walking across the street to Gstar.

It was strange to view everything from that angle. I wasn't in school anymore, I already had my diploma, and I was breaking into another high school. But as I thought this, the bell for lunch rang. I saw kids coming from their classes and ending up in the lunchroom. I followed them in.

I looked around and it looked huge. Kids were everywhere, unpacking bags, sitting on the tabletops, doing whatever they wanted. I noticed my friends off at a table in the back. I made my way to them. Vaguely I heard, "Is that Carl Klitz?" coming from all different directions. I was well known there.

I found Fletcher, Konner, Mark Row, and a few others sitting down there. They were like, "Carl . . . ?"

"I'm here!" I said.

Then they all cheered. I remember they were saying that they heard I was kicked out. They also told me how much that sucked.

"I know," I told them.

I looked over and could see Terra, my ex. She went to Gstar. I saw her coming up with her tray and sitting down at the table beside us. So I walked over to her. I put my hands over her eyes and said, "Guess who?" She got all pissed. I undid my hands from her face and sat beside her. I put my hand over her shoulder.

She said, "Carl . . . what the *hell* are *you* doing here?!"

"Nothin' much, just chillin'." Then I got up and went back to my table. I had a good laugh. Terra's a lame-O.

Konner said, "Hey, Klitz, you gotta come to my fourth-period class."

"What?"

"Come to my class, man."

"I don't think I can."

"Um, yeah you can. Who's stopping you?"

"It's illegal for me to be here."

"You're already breaking the law, Klitz. Live a little."

"Yeah . . . you're right."

We all spent the next hour talking about skating, what they will do after high school, what I was planning to do, and if I was depressed or something (that was me bringing it up). It was absolutely hectic. I also overheard Terra saying to her friends at the table, "Why is Carl here? He doesn't even go here. Lets tell a teacher . . ." but I knew she wouldn't because she lies about everything she does.

Then the bell rang and I went with Konner to his class. I was walking with him and looking around. I saw Taven, this girl I liked. I saw Truby. I saw pretty much every person I had ever partied with, ever, at that school. And they were all walking, together, to their classes. I said to Konner, "What class is this?"

"Film Appreciation. It's a freshman class."

"Why are you in a freshman class, bro?"

"Because I don't give a crap, that's why."

"Oh."

And we made our way across campus. I saw Janielle Jacobson. She was a girl that I always had a crush on. I often wondered what it would be like to date her. (Two years later, we made out under the stars on a beach when I visited Florida again. It was magical.) She came up to me and said, "Carl!"

"Janielle!"

We hugged. She kissed my cheek.

She said, "I wish you went here, Carl."

"I wish I did too. I'd see you everyday!"

"Actually, I'm going to Dreyfooz in the next few weeks."

"Yeah, that place sucks. I was gonna go there."

"True . . . but it's totally better than here."

"Yeah, maybe. I'll see you around, lovey."

"You too, Carl."

We hugged each other again.

I followed Konner into his class. He was shit-talking me about Janielle. He told me I was a lover-boy, but whatever, I liked Janielle because she was a nice person and wouldn't hurt a fly. She was also cute as heck.

Everyone looked super young there, but I heard them all say, "Holy crap, it's Carl Klitz!" They were all pointing. Konner was laughing because, by extension, he was famous too (but I know now that I wasn't even that famous or that cool, so it was all an illusion). I followed Konner to his seat. He was sort of at the front, behind some kid, and kind of off to the side. We were talking about how crazy it was that I was doing this, when all of the sudden the teacher walked in.

"Settle down, class, settle down," she said. But nobody was even talking. "I'm kidding, I'm kidding," she said. "Get out your books. Turn to Chapter Six, and— Wait a second. Who are *you?*"

Oh no, I thought. She was looking right at me. I said, "Uh . . . me?"

"Yes, you. Who are you?"

"I'm, uh . . . new."

"New? Where's your pass?"

"I, uh . . . My mother is at the front office. I'm starting school today. The person at the front told me to go to this class. It was on my schedule, so I went here. I hope that's okay."

The teacher paused for a moment, then said, "Oh! Very well! New student, guys! What's your name?"

I said, "William Bethersmith."

What's funny was I used this fake name in *Kookamonga* many, many times before, and I knew all the kids there had seen the *Kookamonga* videos. But nobody laughed. I think they were hoping I wouldn't get caught. How awesome is that?

"Very well, Will," the teacher said, "mind if I call you Will?"

"Sure . . ." I said. "Call me whatever."

I stayed in that class the whole two hours and we basically did nothing. From that day on I wished I went to Gstar. That would have been the best thing in the world. But I left there and said goodbye to everyone. All of my friends. I scooted on home.

•   •   •

Pretty much the entire world of Facebook knew that I was moving to Texas. I made many posts about it, mainly because I wanted to get rid of all my paintings. So I asked all my friends if they would be interested in buying them. They all said, "Yes," pretty much. I was scooting everywhere to my friends' houses, collecting money, exchanging it for artwork. They all were hyped because I was selling everything for next to nothing.

Then I went on Craigslist and decided to sell my scooter. I got a bunch of nips on it. So I decided to go down to FedEx and get some boxes because I knew I had to ship my stuff and I didn't want to not have a vehicle. So I got those boxes and pretty soon a guy wanted to come over my house to buy my ride. I told him, on a Saturday, to come and get it. He came over, tested it, whatever, tried to low-ball me fifty bucks, I said no, and I sold it for eight-hundred and fifty bucks. That was it. I took my tags and that was it.

•   •   •

I called Lela to get my stuff from storage, so she came to my house a couple hours later and gave me all my stuff. I pretty much thought it was pointless to put my stuff in her unit, but whatever, it was what it was. I bought a lot of boxes. I filled all these boxes I bought with my stuff (minus my Macbook Pro, clothes, and a few other things I needed), even some of my unsold artwork. I got huge boxes, little boxes—all kinds of boxes. I taped them all up. Then I went online and bought my ticket. It was about ninety bucks. Not bad. So I called Krissy and told her. She was excited. That was it. Then my mother got home early and I asked her if I could have her drive all my stuff to the post office in her car. It was only three o'clock. So she said, "Yes," and we went. It cost me about five hundred bucks to ship everything. That sucked. My mother and I drove back in silence.

•   •   •

The thirty days were up. I got all of my luggage and everything I had to move with me. My mother was in a pink sweater, I remember that clearly. I remember she came into "my" room, I was all dressed up, and I had to go to Pancho Mango's mom's apartment. They said I could stay there. When I passed by Ronald, I said, "See ya."

He said, "See ya."

It was very anti-climactic. I hated it.

My mother and I got in her SUV and pretty much she was looking as if she was about to cry.

She said, "You know, Carl. I didn't want it to be this way . . ."

I said, "Uh-huh . . ."

"Carl. Seriously—I didn't."

"I know. He's a jerk."

"He loves you. We both do."

"Is that why you're kicking me out, and you're letting him do it?"

"What more can I do, Carl? You *do not* listen. You don't even listen to one word we say. We have tried literally everything with you. We have been to therapist after therapist with you. We have been to every doctor that specializes in mental health. We have been to behavioral therapists, counselors, everything, and you *still* do not cooperate."

"I don't remember that."

"Of course not. We spent lots of money on you to make you a better person, and honestly, I think this is the best thing we can do. We have to let you go. You have to learn the real world, because this just isn't working."

"Thanks . . ."

"Don't have that face. I'm telling you that I love you. I want you to do well in life. Now, where's Pancho's house?"

"Sherwood and Foresthill."

"Okay, not too far. Anyways, I want you to know that I really didn't want it to go down like this. I wanted you to be safe, but Carl, there's only so much a mother can do. I hope you understand that that man has never hurt me, has never treated me badly, and you may not like him, love him, or anything good-feeling-wise toward him, but you *damn well* have to respect him. He is the man I love and I want to spend the rest of my life with. When you finally find someone *you* love, I have to respect them, too, regardless if I like them or not . . . Do you get what I'm saying, Carl?"

"I get what you're saying." Even though I really didn't at the time. Then I said, "The turn is right there."

"Oh okay," my mother said, "he's pretty close. Anyways, here?"

"Yes."

"Is this his apartment complex?"

"Yes."

"Oh wow. Okay. I'll drop you off here then."

"No. Please park in front."

"Okay."

Then she parked out front and I opened her door, grabbed my stuff, and got out. The window rolled down. My mother said, "I love you, sweetheart."

I said, "I love you too, Mom," and watched her drive away.

•   •   •

I was to stay at Pancho's for an entire week, because my flight didn't leave until then. I remember that whole week was just surreal. I was just counting the days. I was pretty much working out, hanging at Pancho's, going to Walmart to buy junk-food, sleeping a lot, and him and I talked a lot about a lot of stuff. I asked him about life, love, his rapping. I asked him if he ever wanted to make something out of his music. He told me that he just wanted to make the most of his music and make it the best he could. I never realized what that meant—now I do, but at the time I didn't. He just meant that he didn't want to just be famous out of vanity; he wanted people to actually enjoy his work, much like how I feel now. That's all any artist ever wants. That whole week was a real eye-opener. Pancho showed me some of his deepest, darkest work yet. He was rapping and showing me stuff that he wouldn't show to anybody. He kept a lot of songs secret—that was just the way he was. I felt honored. I remember I quit my Little Caesars job on the spot too. They were weirded-out by it. I told them that enough was enough. I made it really dramatic. Nobody understood except Tom, who worked with me. He and his brother actually worked there together. His brother, John-Luc, was the manager. They knew. My best friends always knew everything about my life. They didn't stop me. But I don't know, it felt good to leave with a bang.

•   •   •

I didn't sleep. I was too preoccupied by the idea of leaving Florida that I couldn't sleep. All-nighter. It was around five a.m. I remember I got ready, got all my stuff, and woke up Pancho. He gave me dap. Then I walked across the street of his apartment complex and waited. My mother came shortly. I got inside her SUV and we were off to the airport.

"You okay?" she asked.

"Yeah, I'm fine. Just nervous."

"I know, baby. I know. I know how hard it is."

"Yeah . . ."

"I didn't want to let you go."

"I know."

"Maybe one day, you'll come back and things will be different."

"I don't think so, Mom."

"We'll see, baby. You're going to learn so much from living there on your own, you're going to meet new friends, new everything—you'll see!"

"Thanks, Mom."

"What time does your flight leave?"

"Six a.m."

"Oh, okay. Not bad."

We drove another ten minutes, talking about other life events and things she wanted to tell me that I can't remember right now, and then we got to the airport.

My mother said, "Okay, Carl. We're here. You just go in there and type in your ticket number. Then it prints your ticket."

"Okay."

"And you just go into security and then go to the gate that is on your ticket. Okay?"

"Yes."

"Carl?"

"Yes?"

I thought she was going to tell me it was a joke that I was leaving. But she said, "I love you," and that was it. I watched her drive off.

•   •   •

I went through security fairly easily. It wasn't *too*, too bad. They just sort of checked my bags and said, "Fine," and that was it. Then I got out into the actual airport and was looking down at my ticket. It said Gate B. So I walked around, looking up. I saw D, so I walked through that. Then C. So I walked through that. There it was. B. So I got to it, looked down at my ticket, and it said 22. So I found my way to 22. There were a lot of people there. I sat.

I was looking around and I was really trying to grasp it all. I was just thinking about high school, my life, why I did the things I did. And I was thinking, "Is this all real? . . . Is this *really* happening?" Then I shook my head and turned. There was this couple sitting next to me. The woman's face was absolutely mangled, like she had been burned. But you could tell she was once really beautiful. And the guy she was with had really curly hair. He looked good too. Both of them did, I think.

I asked them, "Is this Gate B22?"

The woman said, "Why, yes! It is! Are you going to Vegas?"

"No, I'm going to Dallas ma'am."

"*Ma'am?* I ain't your mother! Call me Sally."

The man nudged her.

And she said, "Oh, and this is Kevin. Kevin Klix."

He said, "Hello."

I said, "Yeah, I'm moving to Texas. I got kicked out of my house by my family."

Kevin said, "We've all been there, man."

Sally said, "Oh yes, many times. Life gets easier, then harder, but it's all the same. Kevin and I are vacationing to Vegas. We just got back from Africa. We decided that we just wanted to come back to the States and explore the world a little bit."

I said, "That's cool."

"I know! And by the way, I didn't catch *your* name."

"Oh. My bad—my name's Carl."

"Carl. Hmmmmm. You know something, Carl. You and Kevin look a lot alike."

Kevin said, "Yeah, it's uncanny."

I said, "We do, don't we?"

Sally said, "Yeah! Anyways, about family. They can suck sometimes but I found they will always love you no matter what."

I said, "Do you still talk to them?"

Sally said, "It's a long story. Honestly, they all think I'm dead."

I said, "That's awful. I'm sure they don't."

Sally said, "No, they really do. I have journal entries to prove it. Trust me. And actually, Kevin here published that journal."

I said, "Really?"

Kevin said, "Yeah, it's a book that *she* made. Just a journal. She told me to publish it under *my* name so that way her family wouldn't see."

I asked Sally, "How did your face get that way?—I'm sorry if that's offensive."

"Oh, you won't offend me—trust me. Basically, um, lets just say . . . psycho boyfriends are lame as F."

I thought of Terra. I said, "Yeah, I know."

Sally said, "So yes, Carl. I just wanted to say that family's family, no matter what. They always'll have your back, Carl. And through all of the bad times—even when I lost my face, even when it devastated me because I lost all my good-looks in the blink of an eye—it was all worth it. Kevin and I are in love. We travelled all over Africa, and you know what? It's a blessing. Crap, I *love* South Florida. Lived here all my life. So has Kevin."

Kevin said, "All I've ever wanted to do was to love a woman so deeply, and I love Sally Fairfax very, *very* much. I want to take care of her, and make new memories with her, and be by her side. That's all I want."

Sally looked at Kevin and smiled. Kevin smiled back. They kissed. I thought, "These people are saps." I said, "Yeah, I don't think I'll ever find love. Love is just not possible, I don't think. There's too many girls that are selfish and that do things for their own selfish gain. They judge, judge, judge and never take into consideration how *I'm* feeling, what *I'm* thinking." I was talking about Terra.

Kevin said, "Have you ever read *The Perks of Being a Wallflower*?"

I said, "I don't read."

Kevin said, "I'm actually an author. But yeah, *Perks of Being a Wallflower* is a book about a teen about five years younger than you, and in the book the character's teacher says, 'We except the love we think we deserve.' I always reference that quote. And I hope you find meaning in it."

I said, "I don't know."

Sally said, "Didn't you write that in your novel, Kevin?"

"What, *Perks*?"

"No. You're writing a novel about a kid in high school who gets into drugs. I remember you showed me it and you wrote about *Perks of Being a Wallflower* being Edgar's book he read."

Kevin said, "Now that you mention it, yeah! Holy crap. That's crazy. Yeah, that's not done yet, though."

Sally said, "You're so smart, Kev."

They kissed again.

Then I heard on an intercom: "Good morning, people! Thank you for flying with Delta Airlines. Flight B22 will be boarding soon. I want Group One to board first, if you please. And I hope you all have a safe flight!"

Sally said, "That's us! We're Group One!"

I looked down at my ticket. I was Group Three.

Sally said to me, "Carl, it was really nice talking to you, and meeting you. I hope we gave you some insight."

"You did. I'm just a little depressed."

"Then comes anxiety. That too shall pass." Sally got up with Kevin and went in line, where eventually they go onboard.

Déjà vu had hit me.

A few minutes later, Group Three was called. I got up and went in line. I watched everyone lazily just inch further and further. As I got up to the ticket lady, she passed my ticket through the scanner and I was led onboard. I went down the hallway and eventually got onto the plane. It was surreal.

I walked down that aisle and looked to the side. I found my seat. I was *way* in the back of the plane. It was a regular-sized plane. I had the aisle seat. There were two more seats next to me. And then these dudes came on. They were to take the two seats. I got out of mine, they went in, then I sat back down.

Before I knew it, the plane took off. I flipped off Florida through my sweater. I hated Florida. I was pretty afraid though. It felt like the ground from under me was no longer there, which was almost true. But you could almost feel the plane being in the air. I felt scared, that I didn't have control. And then they were passing out water. I asked for a cup. I pulled my tray down from the seat in front of me. I drank and drank.

The guys next to me were talking about Vegas, how trashed they were going to get, how many "hoes" they were going to have sexual intercourse with, how many they would see there, and how much they were to gamble. They actually high-fived. I was envious of them. I wished I was that excited for something again. I was not excited for this move; I was miserable.

I tried to sleep, but I couldn't the whole flight.

•   •   •

When I finally got to DFW Airport, I felt like the life had been sucked out of me. I got on the phone and called Krissy, my sister. She told me that she was fifteen minutes away. She told me to meet me at baggage claim. So I hung up, walked on over to baggage, and waited for my bags. They came. I sat down somewhere, and just waited.

They came after twenty minutes, and I remember my sister was in a dress and there was some tallish weird-looking guy next to her. (I found out, later, that he was Krissy's boyfriend that she met online just two weeks prior.) Krissy said, "Carl! This is my boyfriend . . ." She said his name but I don't remember it.

I said, "Hey."

We walked out. We didn't hug. We just went out into the parking lot and everything felt very surreal. I was in a new place, a new life, and I was afraid. Then we found Krissy's Honda and got inside and drove onto the highway.

Krissy put on an Alanis Morissette song. I was singing it completely wrong. Krissy and her boyfriend laughed so hard. They thought I was silly for saying, "And who would have thought it's the Earth," when the song really said, "It's figures."

I was looking around and all I saw were farms, fields, and no buildings once we got out of Dallas. We drove for a long time. *Too* long. It was about an hour, but in Florida nothing took more than a ten-minute drive. I thought how crappy this all was.

•   •   •

Krissy and her boyfriend finally got me settled into Krissy's house. It was in the woods in the middle of nowhere, and it was pretty much a trailer. Krissy had just divorced, so she pretty much had no money and was on unemployment. I got my stuff from her car and went inside. Krissy led me down this hallway and showed me the room where I was staying. It was smaller than the room I had in Florida, which was insane. It was about two times smaller than it. And all my packages were bunched in the corner of the room. My paintings and all. Then I put my stuff in there and Krissy told me that she wanted to take me job-hunting. She told me there was a Little Caesars down the street. So we got in her car and drove from Pottsboro, Texas, for twenty-five minutes to Denison, Texas. We got to the Little Caesars and I remember it looked really slow and peaceful, like they hadn't seen no more than two people in there at one time. There were two guys there: an older guy, and a younger, more "country-looking" guy. They both looked country, honestly. I said, "Hey, are you guys hiring? I've worked for Little Caesars for two years." The more-country guy said, "Yeah, you're Carl." I said, "What?" He said, "Yeah, we're expecting you. You're old boss called us and told us that you were coming in from Florida, looking for a job." I said, "Holy crap." He said, "Yeah, it's nice to meet you," and he held out his hand. I shook it. I also shook the older guy's hand. He was the *owner!* I was hyped. The owner said, "When can you start?" And pretty much they gave me an apron and that was it. I walked out, told Krissy about it, and pretty much I had a new job within an hour of coming to Texas. I thought that was neat. So we drove back to Pottsboro to Krissy's trailer. When we got there, Krissy and her boyfriend said they had to go to Walmart. So they left. I was alone in that house. I was alone and lying on the couch and thinking to myself how crappy this was. I was crying like crazy. I thought that I didn't want to work for the rest of my life, that I wanted to skateboard, that I wanted my friends back, that I wanted to be a famous artist but couldn't at this country-ass place. I thought I made a mistake. So I thought it would be best to kill myself, considering I could never go back to Florida and succeed.

epilogue

In Texas I spent majority of my days sulking in the darkness of bedrooms. I actually hated myself to the extent that I wanted to purchase a gun, put a bullet inside the barrel, and point the muzzle into my mouth. I wanted to pull the trigger and feel what it felt like to die and not be alive anymore, to be just an object. I wanted the world to see me. I wanted the world to know what it did to me. I wanted the blood to splatter on the walls . . . but I didn't want my family to see it all. I often fantasized about placing my body in a thick plexi-glassed box in the middle of the woods, dug deep in a hole, and blowing my brains out that way, just so my family wouldn't see. Maybe I would call cops. Who knows . . . but as I was planning this, looking up ways to buy a gun, I remember I vaguely told my friend Tom, "Goodbye." He felt uneasy about it and assumed otherwise that I was suicidal. So he called police officers on me and they knocked on my house's front door. They knocked hard, and I didn't know they were the police. Then my sister's boyfriend actually got out of bed and answered the door at two a.m. I heard it all. Then he knocked at my door. I answered.

He said, "Carl, two police officers are looking for you."

I faced my consequence. When I was outside, they were nice. Eventually this led me into the hospital, upon which the police officers gave back their business cards and walked out.

For two hours I spoke to an intern. That was it. She didn't know anything about mental health. She was doing it as a "grade." She gave me places to go to. And I went to those places the next day.

I met a man that didn't like his job, I could tell. My sister took me to see him. I spoke to the man for an hour, and considering I didn't have health insurance, he wasn't prepared to work "for free." So he told me my anguish and mental health problems were fake, and that maybe I should consider college to alleviate my turmoil. And he sent me on my merry way.

That night, I was at the dinner table, not saying a word. My sister and her boyfriend were uneasy. They didn't know what to say. My sister asked me, "What's wrong, Carl?" And I told her this idea I had. I thought it was a *great* idea.

I said, "I want to write a book about my life."

My sister said, "Yeah right! Who in the *hell* would read a book about *your* life? *Ha!* You're nothing special."

"What do you mean?"

"You're not special! You are just a punk kid!"

"So . . . ?"

"You're wasting your time, Carl. Honestly."

"I will one day. I'll make it real, I'll make it about me and about my life as a skateboarder."

"Good luck. Nobody'll read it. Nobody."

My sister and her boyfriend continued to eat. After awhile, I finally said, "You'll see. One day you'll see. I'm going to be famous. I'm going to write a book that will knock the socks off everyone that reads it. And they will finally understand my madness—they will finally know about the *real* Carl Klitz. They will know why I want to kill myself, why I'm so fucking sad, why I hate myself—and they will also know the good, or 'un-good,' I've caused in the world. If nobody reads it, fine—I don't care. But if they *do* read it and like it, well, then I hope they would pass it around to friends . . . or some shit. I hate you guys, sitting there and eating. Stuffing your damn faces. I'm going to my *room!*"

And I left the table and went into my bedroom.

I opened up my Pages app on my 2010 Macbook Pro. I looked at the screen and thought about everything. I thought and thought . . . Then it came to me. I wrote those words down. I wrote them down and they felt good. They felt like pellets rushing down on the screen, it felt like blood was spilling out of me. It felt like freedom.

It took me two years to write a novel.

I didn't know what to name it. It was about a kid who went to my highschool and got involved with a drug that pretty much caused instant cancer. But you find out at the end he's depersonalized, and that the entire book is a single loop. That was my idea. I also wanted all my books to be interconnected, in some way. I wanted them to all have all the characters knowing each other and helping each other. I wanted everything to be my own little world that I controlled. Only me.

I didn't know what to name this first novel. So I thought of my middle school Myspace name. It was perfect. "Bi-" infers "two." The drug was Marijuana and Mushrooms—two drugs that couldn't possibly combine —and I combined them. "Flocka" means "nothing," quite literally, though a year later upon the book's publication, in South Florida, a real life drug named "Flakka" was released into the public and made people go insane, which sort of freaked me out. Nevertheless, the name was perfect, in my eyes.

I called the novel *Biflocka*. I sold it to friends and family. I found out later that Kevin Klix, Sally Fairfax's boyfriend, had the same idea. I was pissed at that. He released it before me. But I still sometimes wonder if I'll ever "make it" as an artist.

Oh well . . .

I'll keep trying while I'm at it.

Photo by Bree Fesh

kevin klix is a blogger, is an award-winning painter, and is a lover of film-making. He lives in South Florida.

THE NOVELS OF KEVIN KLIX

BIFLOCKA
A Novel

ISBN 978-0-9965410-0-8 (paperback)

From his debut novel that catapolted Kevin Klix into the best-seller's list comes Clyde Clark, a highschool senior that comes in contact with a highly-toxic drug that is both lucrative and addicting to not only himself but his entire suburb of South Florida.

ELEVATOR MUSIC
A Novel

ISBN 978-0-9965410-4-6 (paperback)

"Great, powerful piece. . . . The real question: 'What is normal?' Venture and decide for yourself."
—Duy Lam, CEO of *Country Club Company*

A LION IN YOUR NUMBER
A Novel

ISBN 978-0-9965410-2-2 (paperback)

"Klix explores the question of Autism. With consistant voice, ambitious in scope, Klix has developed a novel that is easy, consuming, and poetic."
—Jonathan Spradlin, author of *American Creamy*